JURASSIC FRONTIER
A LASSEN MALONE ADVENTURE

TRISTAN HOWARD

TRISTAN HOWARD
PRODUCTIONS
PUBLISHING

Jurassic Frontier: A Lassen Malone Adventure

Published by Tristan Howard Productions Publishing
Humboldt County, California

Cover art and maps by Tristan Howard

Library of Congress Control Number: 2022908992

Revised First Edition: May 2026

ISBN 979-8-9861228-0-9 (paperback)
ISBN 979-8-9861228-2-3 (hardcover)
ISBN 979-8-9861228-1-6 (e-book)

CONTENTS

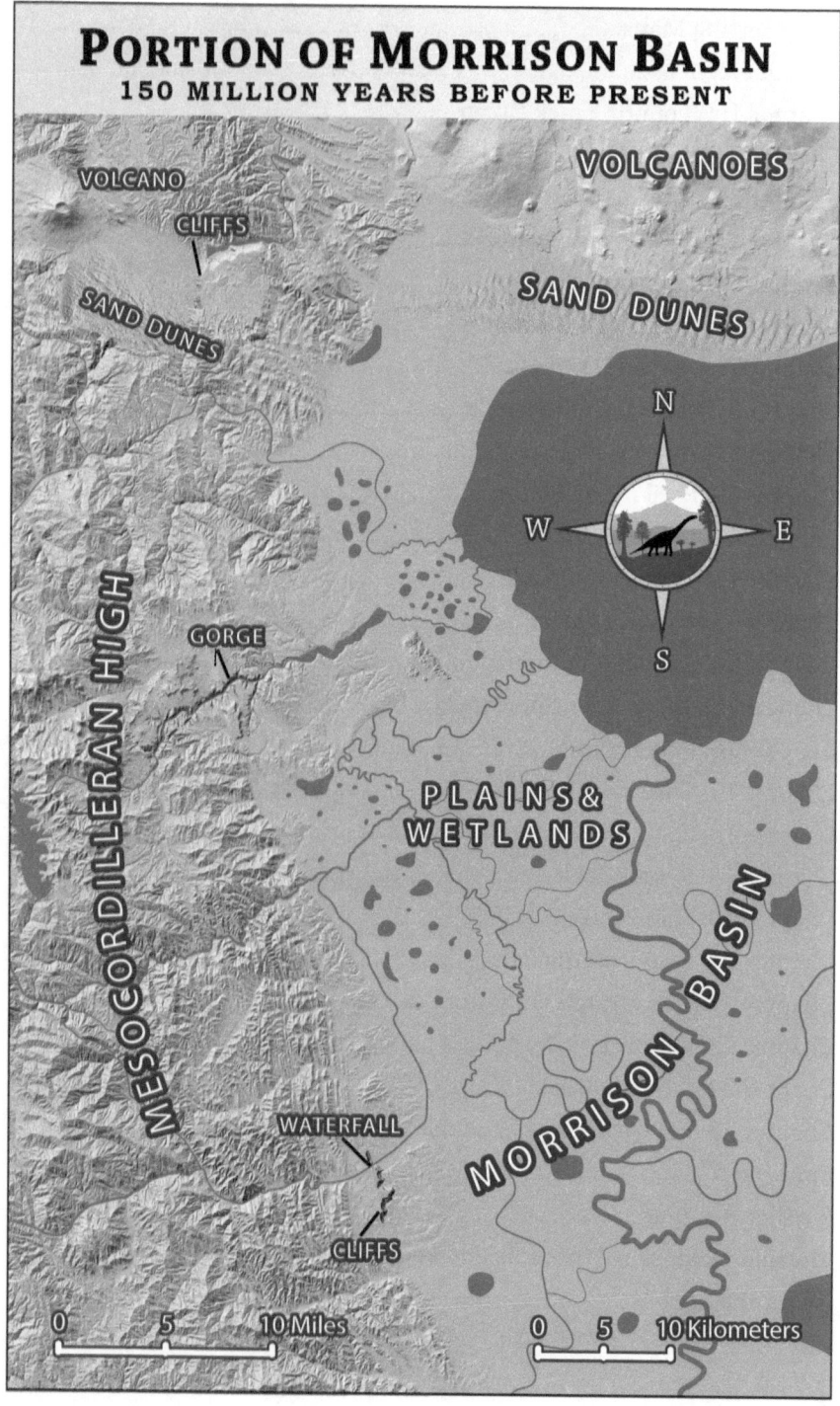

PORTION OF MORRISON BASIN
150 MILLION YEARS BEFORE PRESENT

VOLCANO

CLIFFS

SAND DUNES

VOLCANOES

SAND DUNES

N

W E

S

GORGE

MESOCORDILLERAN HIGH

PLAINS & WETLANDS

MORRISON BASIN

WATERFALL

CLIFFS

0 5 10 Miles

0 5 10 Kilometers

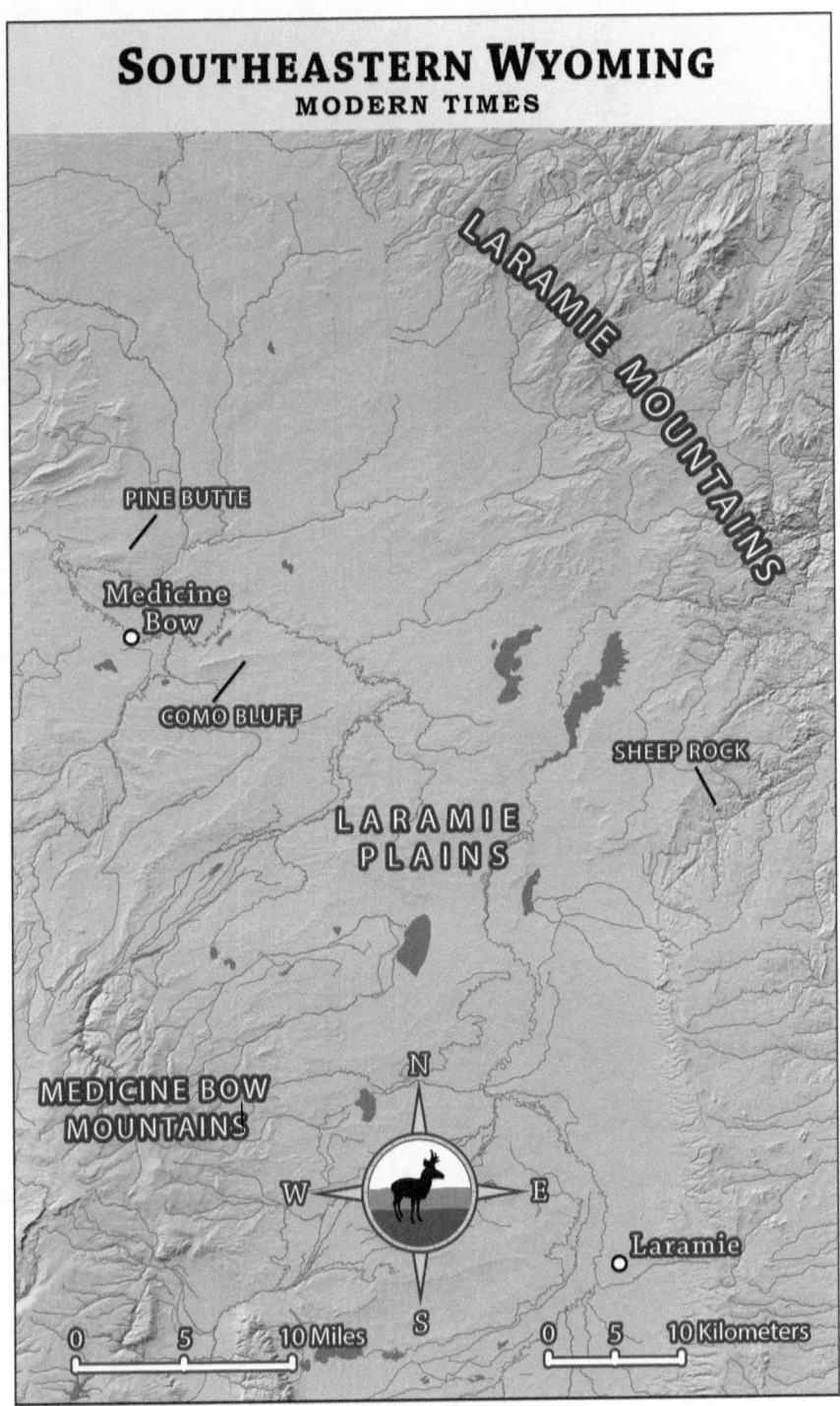

SOUTHEASTERN WYOMING
MODERN TIMES

LARAMIE MOUNTAINS

PINE BUTTE

Medicine
Bow

COMO BLUFF

SHEEP ROCK

LARAMIE
PLAINS

MEDICINE BOW
MOUNTAINS

N

W   E

S

Laramie

0   5   10 Miles

0   5   10 Kilometers

PROLOGUE

In a desolate and remote corner of the American West, a cloudless light blue sky hung over red and tan badland rock formations. Seams of juniper and sagebrush adorned nearby hills. A lone raven cawed as it flew over a dinosaur fossil dig site.

Under a gray tarp set up for shade at the base of a nearby low hill, several graduate students delicately chipped away at Jurassic sandstone with small geological picks. Metal clinked on rock as a gentle wind undulated through the area, kicking up dust. One graduate student was slathered in sunscreen and wore a straw fedora. The other students had weather-beaten faces and wore baseball caps.

In the shade of a nearby boulder, Doctor Kailani Nakai moved a hand through her glossy dark hair and sighed as she looked at a photo on her phone. In the image, she smiled with an old friend, but now, she was off on another adventure, and he was long gone.

This was Kailani's first time supervising a crew of graduate students in the field as an assistant professor. She had completed her PhD program a few months earlier. So far, she and her team had uncovered several *Allosaurus* teeth, some *Diplodocus* tail vertebrae, teeth from a crocodylomorph called *Amphicotylus*, and many unidentified dinosaur bone fragments. She hoped for more, and she knew there was much more to be found.

Under the shade tarp, the student with very obvious sunscreen, Martin Weatherby, gently tapped his hammer against rock, and to his surprise, a large chunk of sandstone split off, revealing an amazingly preserved fossilized cylinder-like structure with what appeared to be an elongated tube.

"What is this?" Martin muttered to himself. "Professor Nakai! You have to come look at this!"

Kailani slipped her phone in a vest pocket and strode toward the shade tarp. As Kailani approached, she saw the other students crowd around Martin, who was crouched on the ground, examining his strange discovery with a magnifying glass.

"Looks like a cowboy gun," said a male student looking over Martin's shoulder.

"Yeah," a female student added. "The wood handle rotted away, and the metal got fossilized, but that doesn't make sense. Old West frontier times were way too recent to have resulted in a fossilized six-shooter. We're talking like 150 years versus 150 million years."

"Maybe it's an intrusive vein of more recent rock," another student said. "Some sort of tectonic forces could have shoved it down into the Jurassic rock."

"No," Martin said as he closed one eye and intently squinted into his magnifying glass. "This is all solid Morrison Jurassic sandstone from a river deposit. The microstructure is uniform." Martin looked up as Kailani arrived. "Professor, what is this?"

"It appears to be a fossilized revolver pistol from the 1870s," Kailani said.

"How in the world did this get here?" Martin asked with distressed bewilderment. "*When* in the world did this get here?!"

Kailani smiled and said, "Well, Martin, I could tell you, but I don't think you'd believe me."

CHAPTER 1: WYOMING TRACK DOWN

JUNE 5, 1879 – DAWN

An orange sun rose over southeastern Wyoming Territory's rugged Laramie Mountains. Bright morning light shot past the alpine granite outcrops of Laramie Peak, illuminating sagebrush-studded plains to the west.

On the plains, a sage-grouse raised its head at the sound of hooves. Two horses with riders cantered east. A meadowlark's melodic warbling filled the air. Short green grass billowed in a slight breeze. A lone pronghorn buck watched the riders continue toward a distant cluster of wooden structures: the town of Medicine Bow.

Medicine Bow stood where the Central Pacific and Union Pacific railroads met at a bend of the Medicine River. The town featured a general store, hotel, and two saloons. A station house and water tank for train engines stood on its outskirts.

"Almost there, Durango," Lassen Malone said as he patted his tan buckskin horse on the neck.

"Good," Durango Mesquite said from atop his black horse. "I could use a real breakfast at the hotel. I'm tired of only chawin' on jerky and biscuits."

"I know what you mean, pal," Lassen said as he took off his tan hat and removed a folded pile of tattered beige papers from inside. Lassen unfolded reward posters for members of the infamous Traxton Gang. All posters featured sketches of outlaw faces. Some "Wanted" poster drawings were crude; others were not too bad. Lassen knew none of the illustrations belonged in an art museum, but he recognized good art when he saw it.

The first poster Lassen unfolded stated that Arvo Avarette was wanted dead or alive, and it provided more details on his crimes and last known whereabouts. According to the poster, Avarette was convicted of murder, card-cheating, and horse-thieving. In the poster illustration, Avarette had a distinctive mustache. His face also appeared well-groomed, and he wore a dress suit.

The next poster proclaimed that Jed Gantry was wanted for stagecoach robbery and rustling. Among other details, it said he used to work on the Chadwick Ranch near Cheyenne. Gantry was confused-looking with a disoriented expression and plain clothes. This contrasted with Avarette who seemed dapper and cheerful.

Lassen unfolded a third poster, which stated that Randall Blaze was wanted dead or alive for rustling, disorderly conduct, and illegal dueling. The poster showed a young smiling face with too much confidence. Blaze was last seen in Salt Lake City where he had provoked three brothers into a duel in which he mowed them down with execution-style precision.

*   *   *

Arvo Avarette and Jed Gantry stood on a balcony above the hardware store in Medicine Bow. The streets bustled with activity. Wagons rolled by. Hooves kicked up dust. Cattle mooed and paced in crowded pens. In corrals just outside town, sheep ravenously ate their morning feed. A train whistled as it stopped for water.

Avarette wore a white shirt, shiny blue vest, and red silk bandana. He tugged at the right side of his mustache.

"Calm down, Gantry," Avarette said with a smooth Southern accent as he readjusted his clean wide-brimmed black hat. "Keeping watch for Blaze up here isn't so bad." As Avarette spoke and peered at the eastern horizon, he absentmindedly shuffled a deck of poker cards.

"But Branigan and Holt get to sleep in," Gantry said. "We're stuck out here with cold biscuits." Gantry wore a long oilskin duster and tattered brown hat. His clothing smelled of cow manure and the open trail. Avarette's nose shuddered when Gantry turned to speak to him.

"We may have had an early awakening," Avarette said, "but the sunrise was gorgeous, and there will be reward enough when we pull off our next job."

"Yeah, the next job," Gantry said. "With my cut, I want to get my own spread in Mexico. I could get longhorns. They're easy to find, but they taste real stringy. But they're hearty beeves. Real durable. Corrientes might be cheaper though. You know what I mean?"

Avarette's reply was to merely cast a defeated sideways smirk at Gantry.

Gantry grunted and said, "When's Blaze gonna get here? I don't like bein' in town. I miss the open range back with my old boss's herd. That was fun. But you know, it doesn't pay well. Rustlin' paid better. Workin' for Traxton pays even better than rustlin.'"

Avarette sighed. Gantry was not going to stop talking about cattle, and he was saying too much.

"Hey, uh, heh, heh, you know," Avarette said, "if you don't mind me sayin'—you see that 'Wanted' poster over there?" Avarette pointed at a poster nailed to a telegraph pole on the street below.

"That is for you know who," Avarette continued. "You see *that* poster over there?" Avarette took off his hat and pointed it toward a poster nailed to the side of a store. "That is also for, uh, you know who. We work for a certain person. You might not want to say his name out loud in the middle of a public area."

Both posters advertised an enormous reward for Tardell Traxton.

"Oh, yeah," Gantry said. "You're right. You're right, Avaretto. What do you want to do with your share?"

"Not my name," Avarette said. "I'm not sure. I might go back to New Orleans and set up my own casino. If I can get enough to—hand me that scope, will you?"

"Uh, yeah," Gantry said as he pulled a brass military scope from a pocket of his duster and passed it to Avarette.

Avarette peered through the lens and directed it toward the west end of town. Randall Blaze had just arrived. He was a dark-haired, unshaven young man wearing a red shirt and black vest. He soon tied his horse to a hitching rail outside a saloon and stepped inside. As Blaze walked through the saloon's batwing doors, he flexed his fingers and rested them on the handles of his Colt forty-five pistols, which hung from an ornate engraved gunbelt.

"It's Blaze," Avarette said, "and it looks like he's thirsty this mornin'—and maybe thinkin' he'll need to fight for his drinks. That is a fancy two-gun rig."

"Now that he's here," Gantry said, "let's go tell Branigan and Holt. With the money Blaze brought, we can pay off the telegraph operator and be done with this town."

"Of course," Avarette said, "but wait a minute. There are two riders coming in from the west. They're far away, but they seem familiar. I'm gettin' an uneasy feeling."

Avarette adjusted his scope and saw a black horse and tan horse with riders in the middle of a conversation. One of them reviewed sheets of paper from inside his hat. The other did most of the talking.

"Gantry, I think we've got a problem," Avarette said.

"What?" Gantry asked.

"Two of the best bounty hunters in the territory are on their way into town," Avarette said.

"Wait a minute," Gantry said. "Is it . . . ?"

"It's them," Avarette said. "Lassen Malone and Durango Mesquite. They're going to be here in a few minutes. Go tell Branigan and Holt. I'm going to stay out here and get in position. Get the rifles. You know what we need to do."

"Traxton's not gonna like this," Gantry said. "He hates those righteous do-gooders. I reckon we're not gonna like it much either. Remember that last time we tangled with Malone and Mesquite?"

"Yes," Avarette said as he bit his lower lip with anxiety. "I remember. Do not remind me."

"They're more of a challenge than conning widows, churches, and orphanages," Gantry said. "That's for sure."

"Indeed, son," Avarette said. "Indeed."

*   *   *

Lassen Malone and Durango Mesquite rode into Medicine Bow and stopped at the hotel where they smoothly got off their mounts and tied them to a hitching post. Durango grabbed his coiled leather lariat off his saddle and slung it over his right shoulder.

"Why are you taking that?" Lassen asked.

"I need to buy more leather," Durango said, "and I want it just like what I have in this rope. I thought I could bring this into a store to help find a match."

"Not a bad idea," Lassen said. "Plus, we might need it."

"I hope we don't need to use it before breakfast," Durango said. "I'm so hungry, I could eat a buffalo."

"Bison," Lassen said.

"Same thing," Durango responded.

"Not exactly," Lassen said.

The bounty hunters stood and looked over the town while a red-tailed hawk called. Lassen and Durango were in Medicine Bow on business: bounty hunting business. Lassen rubbed his chin in thought as his eyes scanned the townsfolk. Things seemed normal, but he knew that could change in an instant. He was looking for a distinctive young and mean face: the face of Randall Blaze.

Young Blaze had recently joined the Traxton Gang. Lassen thought other members of the Traxton Gang may have also just arrived in Medicine Bow. Lassen and Durango had been in pursuit of Tardell Traxton and his gang for over two years.

As he stood, Lassen unfolded another "Wanted" poster. It stated that Hobart Holt was wanted for claim-jumping, assault, and high-grading. One of his last known whereabouts was Virginia City, Nevada. Holt's image showed him with a tired, dirty face and significant wrinkles under his eyes.

Lassen whistled slowly to himself as he unfolded the bottom poster on the stack. It advertised a higher reward than all the others. In bold font, it stridently announced that Shanahan Branigan was wanted dead. He had committed murder, assault, land fraud, tax fraud, and card-cheating. His known criminal associates were Tardell Traxton and Britt Thornby. The sketch showed a wide, bearded smiling face. Branigan looked charismatic. *Friendly enough to gain the trust of most anybody—before exploiting them,* Lassen thought. *You can never trust those who act too friendly.*

Led by the mysterious and intelligent Tardell Traxton, the Traxton Gang had unleashed disorder and violence across the American West for the last several years. The posters Lassen had read represented about half the gang. The Traxton Gang focused on robbery. They robbed banks, trains, and stagecoaches, and they took whatever supplies they needed. If bystanders got in the way, they were unfortunate. Traxton enjoyed traditional blunt force outlaw tactics, but he also had Shanahan Branigan and Britt Thornby run more sophisticated organized crime schemes that involved complex fraud, bribing politicians, and making the most out of loopholes in grazing, mining, and homesteading laws.

Campfire stories and unbelievable rumors attributed Traxton with remarkable foresight and special tools. Lassen only believed what he saw, but what he heard made him think Traxton belonged more in the pages of a Jules Verne novel than in 1870s Wyoming. Lassen did not carry a poster for Traxton. He had confronted the outlaw in-person and remembered more than enough about him.

"Durango," Lassen said as he felt empty bullet loops on his gunbelt, "we should probably head to the general store first. We're low on ammo."

"Oh, come on, Lassen," Durango said. "I really want to chaw restaurant grub."

"So do I," Lassen replied, "but we've been on the range a long time and need more supplies. My only bullets are the ones in my six-shooter. Looks like you're low, too, and don't forget: we ran out of rifle ammo a week ago. We could run into Blaze or other members of the Traxton Gang any second."

"We've been here, what, two and half minutes?" Durango said. "What are the odds we'd find anyone so soon?"

Blaze casually stepped out of a nearby saloon and walked down the street. The young face and mean expression immediately tipped off Lassen. Lassen sighed and looked at Durango with raised eyes. Durango subtly nodded to Lassen and winked. The bounty hunters separated and walked on opposite sides of the street toward Blaze.

Athena Pryce stepped out of the general store with a package wrapped in brown paper. She was familiar with the locals but kept an eye out for newcomers whenever she came to town. Athena wore a chocolate brown split riding skirt with a turquoise blouse and a brown felt hat with a cinch strap. After glancing down at her package, she looked up and briefly paused to view Lassen as he walked in her direction on the same side of the street.

For Athena, attention from men was easy to get. She was an attractive blonde in her early thirties in a region where women were scarce. Ignoring men had become customary for her, but Lassen caught her eye.

Lassen was dressed in a fairly ordinary outfit of brown pants, a beige button-up long-sleeve shirt, a brown leather vest with lapels, and a tan hat with a leather band. The hat had a wide brim. Its edges bent slightly upward on either side, and its crown had subtle impressions where Lassen regularly gripped it to put it on or take it off.

Lassen's outfit looked good on him, but Athena was struck by the bounty hunter's lean, youthful figure, his well-proportioned jawline, his remarkable emerald green eyes, and his neatly trimmed brown hair with slightly curled bangs that casually draped out from under one side of his hat. Lassen also walked with a notable quantity of confidence. He was comfortable being himself, and it showed.

As Lassen neared and started to make eye contact, Athena stopped staring and quickly turned around. As she did so, the edge of her package caught on a hitching post. The paper tore, and a book fell out onto the dusty street. Athena blushed with embarrassment.

"Morning, miss," Lassen said as he walked up to her.

"Hello, sir," Athena said in response, regaining her composure.

"Let me get that for you," Lassen said as he bent down to pick up the fallen book.

As he bent over, Athena subconsciously raised her eyebrows and affirmatively nodded her head. Lassen grabbed the book and patted dust off it.

"Encyclopedia Britannica," Lassen said as he read the book's leatherbound spine. "Ninth Edition: Volume Three: ATH to BOI. Nice."

"Yes," Athena said, "I've waited some time for this volume."

"It's a good one," Lassen said, smiling. "Especially the biology section. Still, at the rate these are being published, I don't think we'll have all the ninth edition volumes until 1889."

"Yes," Athena said. "That may be so."

"Nice meeting you," Lassen said as he walked away. "Take good care of that book."

"Of course," Athena said. "I'm Athena Pryce, by the way."

"Nice name," Lassen said, turning around to speak to Athena while also keeping an eye on Blaze. "I'm . . ." Lassen trailed off as he realized he should not be advertising his name. He continued, ". . . on a business trip. See you later."

As Durango sauntered down the street, he glanced over at Lassen's interaction with Athena and felt a mix of curiosity and jealousy. They had only been in town a few minutes, and a pretty girl was *already* talking to Lassen who was probably just being himself and not even trying to be smooth with the ladies.

Durango Mesquite dressed entirely in black with black leather boots, cotton pants, and a button-down long-sleeve shirt. A gunbelt with a few silver bullets adorned his waist and carried an 1873 Colt forty-five pistol with black wooden grips. The gun rested in a low-slung holster.

Lassen wore a more modest brown leather gunbelt that held an 1873 Colt forty-five and a leather sheath carrying an antler-handled knife. A little boy whittling in front of a hotel examined

Lassen with curiosity. Lassen's holster especially intrigued the boy. He had never seen one quite like it. It was tied down and slung low—well below the hip. The boy had only ever seen them worn at waist level. Lassen and Durango wore custom rigs that allowed them to make super-fast draws. Their holsters placed their guns at exactly the level of their hands.

As Blaze moved forward, he glanced over his shoulder when a dog somewhere behind him loudly barked. By chance, he happened to see Durango, who looked vaguely familiar. Blaze turned to the opposite side of the street and saw Lassen. His eyes narrowed with focus. He then saw a little girl reading a dime novel on the steps of the school. In ostentatious, ornate font, the title of the girl's beat-up paperback stated, *The Adventures of Lassen Malone: Quest for Outlaw Gold.*

Blaze's eyes widened as he realized who he was looking at. As far as young Blaze knew, Malone and Mesquite were legends in their own time. Though barely 30, they had pursued and captured desperadoes across the American West. From Monterey, California to Leavenworth, Kansas. From Tombstone, Arizona to Missoula, Montana. West to east. South to north. And everywhere in between. Over badlands, mountains, prairies, and deserts. These Westerners knew their stuff. At least according to the stories.

As Blaze's eyes widened, he thought of the name he could make for himself if he took down Malone and Mesquite. He would be more famous than both of them. He could start his own outlaw gang, women would love him even more than they already did, and he would be respected by everybody. Without hesitation, Blaze drew his guns with lightning speed. Lassen and Durango saw Blaze's hands move.

"Everybody get down!" Lassen shouted as he drew his gun. "Get down! Get down! Get down!"

CHAPTER 2: INCIDENT AT AREA 54

High desert plains stood barren and still just north of Como Bluff, Wyoming. Seventy-five feet (23 meters) below ground, 30-year-old Adalya Nell gritted her teeth in frustration. She was stuck on a difficult equation. How could she ensure improved temporal coordinate precision while accounting for rubidium atoms, an infinite mass neutralizer, a transversable wormhole, and Planck energy unleashed by an antimatter reaction? She knew she was close, but the equation would take time. On the opposite end of the room, Professor Kira Sedora worked on the same problem.

Adalya and Sedora sat in an underground chamber. They worked in a top-secret government research facility: Area 54. The United Territories of America and Canada (UTAC) had established Area 54 specifically for testing the mechanics of devices based on advanced quantum physics.

The world's leading scientists knew time travel was dangerous. However, the world's leading powers wanted insights on time travel technology because of their fear of each other. By 2756, the recent proliferation of time travel research resembled the nuclear arms race in which the old United States of America and Russia had participated 800 years earlier in the twentieth century. With recent technological breakthroughs, time travel was achievable. Adalya had assisted her supervisor, Professor Kira Sedora, with time travel research for the last two years.

Adalya adjusted her hair as she worked out calculations on a touch screen that controlled holographic projections of numbers and symbols. The holo image crackled in and out of focus.

"Professor," Adalya said with a British accent. "My projection is flickering again. Have you encountered the same issue?"

"No," Sedora said without looking up from her work. "Try technical assistance."

"Okay," Adalya said as she pressed a request button on her holo control panel. Both Adalya and Sedora wore standard two-piece shirt-and-pants uniforms with boots. Their clothing was made out of comfortable synthetic material and was primarily gray but broken up by purple and silver geometric patterns to denote their research science affiliations at the facility. They also wore utility belts, and their uniforms had a series of cargo pockets. Adalya's brown eyes glanced at a glowing clock on the wall. Tech support always seemed slow.

Sedora was focused and driven as her fingers rapidly slid across her holo control screen. She bit her lower lip in determination as she moved a hand through her silver-streaked bronze-colored hair and sat back in her chair. By her mid-forties, Sedora had become UTAC's top expert on time travel.

Adalya sat in a plain room that resembled the typical office of the twenty-eighth century. Lots of holo chips littered a plastic desk, a miniature food generator sat in a corner, and moving holo images of beautiful scenery glowed on the walls. The room was well-lit and pleasant-looking. When Adalya started work at Area 54, she was surprised by how warm and comfortable her laboratory felt. She had imagined metallic walls and dark blue lighting. That occurred in some of the facility's hallways, but most workspaces were more comfortable.

An underground paramilitary research base was not Adalya's favorite choice of scenery, but she was so distracted by her work that the setting was not too important. When she was younger, she did not expect to be at Area 54 by the time she was 30.

Adalya was of South Asian descent, but she grew up on the outskirts of Adelaide, Australia, and because of her early schooling abroad, she spoke with more of a British than Australian accent.

Adalya was consumed by her groundbreaking work and wanted to make the most of an extraordinary research opportunity. Just the process of getting security clearance to work at Area 54 had taken three years. Adalya was hand-picked out of dozens of potential candidates. She felt lucky, but her position was also well-earned because of her tremendous intellectual prowess. In the scientific community, even among critical peers, she was known as a genius among geniuses. Her work rivaled the scientific pioneering efforts made by Newton, Hawking, and Einstein centuries prior. However, Adalya and Sedora were far ahead of their predecessors.

Adalya narrowly focused her efforts on time travel research, quantum physics, and mathematics and was adept with quantum computers but not enough to readily fix all technical issues. A technician finally arrived to assist Adalya. He looked to be in his mid-thirties and wore a uniform similar to Adalya's, but it was white. His badge identified him as Brent Cordon. She had seen him around before, but they had never had a conversation.

"It keeps intermittently flickering in and out at intervals of exactly two minutes, 33 seconds," Adalya said as she gestured at her holo projector control pad.

"Let me take a look," Cordon said as he plugged a device into Adalya's holo pad.

"It is about time you showed up," Sedora said. "Records show these systems were serviced only 23 hours ago and *were* running smoothly. What did *your* people do wrong?"

I am not actually in charge of anybody, Cordon thought, *and I would not say I fit in with those other technical support losers who only know quantum computers. Pathetic nerds. No imagination. No ambition. But never mind that.*

Instead of speaking his thoughts, without betraying emotion, Cordon said, "I will try to get to the bottom of this as fast as I can, Professor."

"These things happen," Adalya said. "Thank you for getting here when you did."

"Sure, miss," Cordon said.

"Miss?" Sedora said. "It is *Doctor* Nell."

"It is," Adalya said, "but my computer is a much higher priority than my title."

Sedora was great at what she did, but she also embraced being an authority figure in a way Adalya did not. Adalya cared more about the research opportunities of her position than about the prestige it offered. In contrast, Sedora had impatient terseness and an emphasis on authority that was strengthened by years of military service.

"I am aware of *Doctor* Nell's credentials," Cordon said. "I apologize for my informality."

Cordon never liked Professor Sedora on a personal level, but he actually respected her and Adalya more than most employees on the base because he recognized their astounding intelligence. He thought Adalya was alright, and under different circumstances, he might have tried to get to know her better.

Cordon disconnected the device he had connected to Adalya's computer earlier. "That should fix it, Doctor Nell," he said.

"What was the problem?" Adalya asked.

"The light conductor circuit was loose," Cordon said. "I transmitted realigning coordinates to it. It should work fine now."

Adalya tapped a button on her control panel, and her equations shimmered back to life with crisp focus. "That seemed to resolve the problem," Adalya said. "Thank you."

"No problem, Doctor Nell," Cordon said with a smile. "Let me know if you have any other questions."

"Okay, thank you," Adalya said as she returned to her work. Her current physics problem had been giving her trouble for weeks, but she always felt like she was at the edge of solving it. When confronting major research problems, Adalya became obsessed with solving them and did not give up easily.

*   *   *

Cordon left the room and strode down a hallway. He seemed mostly ordinary. His appearance was average. However, Cordon was far more than a quantum computer technician at Area 54. Cordon had not only solved Adalya's holo projection problem—he had also caused it during the previous day, solely for the purpose of infiltrating Adalya's research records. He now had the technical readouts of the latest temporal transporter developed by Adalya and Sedora. In other words, he had the plans for the most sophisticated time machine ever developed: the prototype B2700X Temporal Transporter. At Area 54, the terms "temporal transporter" and "time machine" were used interchangeably among staff, though Cordon thought it would be simpler if everybody just called the vehicle a time machine.

Cordon entered the technicians' breakroom and glanced at his holo watch. He had time to review the technical specifications before he took action. Coworkers tried to engage Cordon in small talk, but he brushed them off and opened his holo reader. His last reader file was still open. It was a Western novel entitled *Ambushed by the Traxton Gang*. Cordon was intensely interested in the history of western North America during the late 1800s. He reveled in stories of outlaw gangs, bounty hunters, and stagecoach holdups.

Cordon believed that in the Wild West of the late 1800s, you could be what you want to be, do what you want to do, go where you want to go, and spend time with whomever you please—or nobody. It was a land with few obstacles. With a horse and a gun, you could change your life, see what is over the next horizon, find your fortune, or even find love. Modern historians may have argued that things were much more complicated with the genocide of indigenous people playing a major role that was decidedly less glamorous. Cordon chose his own narrative.

One thing of which Cordon was sure was that Wyoming in the 1800s would not have quantum computers that needed fixing. And, there would not be incompetents asking him for help with technical problems that were often not actually problems but merely due to user ignorance. Cordon sneered. He had little patience for the unintelligent, and he hated things holding him back. He was tired of holding back his true feelings for the sake of job security. He wanted to go somewhere where he could be real.

Cordon closed the file for *Ambushed by the Traxton Gang*. Then, as he pulled up time machine schematics and instructions, he thought back to his youth.

*   *   *

In the rich light of early evening, nine-year old Brent Cordon played in the plastic simul-grass of twenty-eighth century Toronto's suburbs. He rode a hover stick horse with his feet in metal stirrups that stuck out to the sides. He also wore a small plastic gunbelt. A little brown sausage-shaped dachshund dog trotted behind him, panting. Cordon drew an orange polycarbonate Colt forty-five toy gun and pulled its trigger. Little holographic blasts of flame and smoke emanated from its barrel.

"Take that, Clanton Gang!" Cordon said. "I'm Wyatt Earp, and me and my brothers will get you. Don't you stop by at the O.K. Corral no more!"

Cordon spoke to cartoonish Old West outlaw holograms in his yard. They raised their hands and quivered in fear.

"Let's get 'em, Toobler!" Cordon shouted as he leaned over to quickly pet his dog behind its ears. Then his stick horse reared and called out with a recorded neigh. Cordon rode his hover stick horse in circles around his small front yard. The ground was littered with accessories from his play, including a holographic campfire, a polycarbonate play rifle, and a real lasso. Cordon had been to a dude ranch near Calgary during the previous summer and had learned some real roping and riding skills, though he did not excel at either.

"Don't cross the law!" Cordon shouted. "Leave Tombstone for good! You're unjust, and there's no place for you here! After them, Deputy Toobler!" The dachshund barked and ran toward the holograms and then right through them. It stopped, turned around, and quickly blinked in confusion with its ears flopping about.

The hologram outlaws raised their hands and ran in place. Then a forced perspective illusion made it look like they were running away as they got smaller. The holograms faded out as Cordon heard a cruel cackle behind him.

Four teenage boys stopped hover scooters above a sidewalk. Next to them, a ceramic superconductor street stretched east to west.

"Look at the little dork!" one of them shouted. "He thinks he's in the *Old* West!"

"That's like, what, dude, a thousand years ago?!" another teenager shouted.

Cordon stared in surprise and embarrassment at his tormentors. People had given him strange looks before, but he was used to it. However, something was different about these older kids. He usually never saw teenagers around, and he had no siblings or teenage cousins.

Cordon was also surprised to see anybody else outside. Most people were inside watching a broadcast of a major annual athletic event. As a result, the streets were unusually empty and quiet.

Cordon noticed one of the boys swigged from an octagonal container. He knew it was alcohol and that teenagers should not be drinking it. His dad drank from octagonal containers a lot, and Cordon never liked that. Toobler trotted up to Cordon's feet and growled at the teenagers.

"Ooooohh," one of the boys said. "He's got himself a mean prairie wolf."

Toobler launched up and clamped his teeth into the teenager's leg.

"Get this mutt off me!" the boy cried in alarm. The boy kicked his leg hard. Toobler yelped, sailed away, and landed in a plastic hedge.

"Leave him alone!" Cordon yelled as he rushed toward Toobler. "You okay, boy?" Cordon asked as he picked up Toobler from the hedge and kissed the little dog on the head with his back turned to the teenagers.

Toobler whimpered and lowered his head. Cordon turned around to see a boy pick up his hover stick horse and snap it over his leg. The horse unleashed a distorted final mangled electronic neigh. Wires from within the stick tore and briefly spit sparks before oozing smoke. Suddenly, the landscape darkened as the sun began to set behind clouds to the west.

The boy laughed. "Try chasing after desperados now! We broke your horsey!"

Holding Toobler, Cordon watched, feeling helpless. His eyes reddened, and he felt tears welling up.

"Little cowboy is gonna cry!" one of the teenagers shouted with unrestrained mocking.

Cordon gently set down Toobler, and the dog limped away. With tears streaming down his face, something inside Cordon snapped. He felt helpless and intensely angry. He wanted power. He wanted control. He wanted revenge.

Cordon sniffled as tears dripped off his nose. He hugged Toobler. Then he repeatedly curled and uncurled his right hand into a tiny fist and began hyperventilating. Toobler whimpered nearby. The teenagers cruelly cackled at Cordon.

"Little sniffler is goin' crazy!" the oldest boy shouted as he and the other teenagers scornfully pointed.

"I," Cordon said. "I, I, I, I am gon—gon—gon—gonna guh—guh—guh go get my da—da—da—dad!" Cordon spoke with a debilitating stutter. Years of government-sponsored speech therapy had minimized it, but when he was upset, it returned full force.

"Oh, you're gonna get daddy?!" the oldest teenager said.

"Yuh—yuh—yuh—you bet I will, polecat!" Cordon sputtered.

"Did he just call me an old cat?" the teenager asked his friends while pointing two fingers at himself.

"I don't know," one of the other boys said, "but I see the sunshade going up on a window of this kid's house. I think maybe we should go."

"Okay, sure, whatever," the oldest teenager said. "Keep your octotainers out of sight."

The boys jetted away on their hover scooters, laughing scornfully. Cordon's father stood inside the house, looking out the window. He was overweight, informally dressed, and wore a blank expression. Cordon looked pleadingly at him and rushed inside. By the time Cordon stepped in the door, his father was slouched on the couch and swigging from an octotainer while watching an enormous holographic display of brutal competitive downhill somersault sword dueling.

"Dad!" Cordon said. "Dad! They broke my huh—huh—huh—"

"Just say it!" Cordon's father shouted in frustration without turning to look at his son. "You're interruptin' the big game."

"My HORSE!" Cordon continued. "And they were really mean! Help me get them! It's not fair. It's nuh—nuh—not fair!"

"Shut up, yapper!" Cordon's father snapped back. He took a swig from his octotainer. "I just wanted to see what the noise was."

"But dad, daddy!"

"*Daddy?*" Cordon's father said. "Do not talk like no baby, son. I'm trying to watch the game! Shut your mouth and stop cryin'!"

"But they took it!" Cordon shouted back through tears. "They took it and broke him! They took Thunderbolt! They broke him! I loved Thunderbolt. He was a good horse!"

"That's a toy!" Cordon's father said. "And an expensive one at that! Your mom shouldn't of wasted so much money on you before she left us for that asteroid mining supervisor. You need to look out for yourself and protect your things better! And don't rely on me or anybody else to get you things. Get your own!"

Cordon went back outside. His head hung low with dejection. He then sat with his back against a plastic hedge. Toobler trotted to him and hopped in his lap.

"Good doggy," Cordon said. "Good doggy. I luh—luh—love you, tuh—tuh—tuh—Toobler." Cordon squished his cheek against Toobler and petted the little dog as the sun set to the west behind a backdrop of brilliant orange-red clouds. Cordon looked to the west and saw brightness and hope. He saw himself on a horse, riding through sagebrush-filled plains, packing a six-gun, and not tolerating trouble from anybody.

*　　*　　*

Cordon sighed as he thought back to that pivotal day in his life. He had made it West, but he was stuck underground, and despite several requests to have his shifts changed, he was not permitted to visit the surface during the day. He felt claustrophobic and trapped and had become increasingly lonely and rageful. It would not last much longer.

Cordon began to review time machine operation guidelines. In his peripheral vision, he saw Adalya move through a hallway.

Adalya walked past a room where two technicians tested plasma beams of assorted colors. One scientist flipped a switch, and a golden plasma beam shot out of a brass transmitter. The scientist then saw her male assistant's eyebrows fall to the ground as a powder of black ash.

"Do not stand so close!" the scientist scolded.

"But it is so powerful, and there is so much *shine*," the assistant replied. His eyes abruptly widened when he said "shine."

He did it again, Adalya thought.

The technician with the burnt eyebrows pulled a small tube-like device from his pocket and rubbed it above each of his eyes. New eyebrows grew back in seconds.

"Looking good, Slaskeron," Adalya dryly said, standing in the doorway.

"Thanks, Doctor Nell," Slaskeron said as he quickly gave her a thumbs-up. In the process, the corner of his lab coat sleeve burnt off as he dangled it through a slicing pink plasma beam.

Area 54 has some of the best, Adalya thought, *but they are not the best at everything*. Soon, Adalya scanned a card to open Storage Room 4B. She pulled out a handful of high-capacity data chips, and the storage facility automatically altered its inventory record to account for the removed items. As Adalya left the storage room, she saw Sedora walk down the hall.

"Professor," Adalya said, "what brings you here?"

"I need a precise combination of crystals," Sedora said. "I think I am close to solving our temporal precision issues. We need to focus the amplified energy properly. Getting the right crystals in conjunction with an amplification beam generator should help us solve the 52 variables in our current equation."

"That is good to hear," Adalya said.

"Yes," Sedora matter-of-factly stated before abruptly walking away. Sedora did not mess around when it came to science or getting things done. She was at a point in her career where she did not need to pretend to be social when she did not want to be. She was the best at what she did. Any institution for which she worked was simply happy she gave them the time of day. At least that was what she thought.

Sedora looked lovely and had a very sharp wit. Adalya knew her mentor professor could easily get plenty of social attention if she wanted it, but Sedora focused on larger things in life. Concentrating on epic quantum physics mysteries and pushing the boundaries of knowledge and technology meant far more to her than laughing with friends or holding hands with a companion.

*   *   *

Hours later, Cordon continued staring at time machine instructions and technical specifications. There was more to read than he expected. He wanted to read everything before a certain time tonight, but he settled on skimming some of the more crucial operations sections.

Cordon tapped his ear as he heard a tiny beep from an implanted communication device. A mysterious voice with a difficult-to-identify European accent said, "Now." Cordon closed his holo projector image and stood up.

"Where are you going, Cordon?" a coworker asked.

"I am just going to go grab a snack," Cordon said. "Want anything?"

"No, thanks," the coworker replied.

Cordon left the room and moved down a hall. He soon entered a janitorial closet, pulled a backpack out of a cabinet, and filled it with supplies, including black clothing, a felt hat, a valuable device called a database orientation module, and an ancient-looking canteen filled with water. He was entering the crucial phase of a secret freelance assignment for a massive multinational corporation, Vandanite Tech. At least that was what his contacts at Vandanite Tech thought. Cordon had his own ideas and was happy to use the resources and expertise of Vandanite Tech.

Cordon slung his pack over his shoulder and reached into a pocket of his uniform to retrieve what appeared to be a tiny portable computer. He then keyed in the proper values to launch a software virus into Area 54's security system. Cordon had worked with Vandanite Tech to develop the virus. Security cameras blinked off throughout the installation. Adalya and Sedora glanced up in confusion as their holo projections flickered, and the lights in their research office dimmed and returned to normal.

Cordon had spent years working to compromise Area 54's security. However, he would have to work fast to accomplish his mission before systems recovered. Facing Captain Glenko also concerned him.

Cordon entered a hallway lit by lines of blue lights and followed signs that said: "EXPERIMENTAL LAUNCH BAY." As he neared the launch bay entrance door, he slowly peaked around a corner to see a lone guard with his back turned. The guard carried a plasma pistol in a holster on his waist. It was the 2756 equivalent of an 1873 Colt pistol, but instead of primitively propelling chunks of toxic lead, it blasted bright purple plasma beams of superhot ionized gas. The plasma beams were generated by nanotechnology encased in the pistol's handle. A miniature power generator in the pistol produced energy levels equivalent to a giant power plant from centuries earlier.

Cordon snuck up behind the guard at the launch bay entrance door and quickly pulled out a plasma knife. In an instant, a brilliant yellow plasma beam briefly seared the guard's throat. The guard fell to the ground with a muffled grunt. Cordon quickly glanced left and right. Then he pulled the guard's access card from his belt and slid it into a socket on the wall to open the launch bay door. As the door opened, the massive launch bay came into sight. It was well-lit and housed a bizarre array of impressive-looking vehicles.

Cordon smiled as he saw the launch bay. He grabbed the security guard's plasma pistol and sprinted into the large room.

*   *   *

Meanwhile, the head of base security, Captain Glenko, briskly strode into Area 54's security control room. He was dressed similarly to Adalya and Sedora, but his uniform had dark blue geometric patterns to denote his security affiliation, and he had a different assortment of devices on his belt, including a plasma pistol.

"What is going on here?" Glenko asked with concern. "Security systems have been failing all over the installation. Scan the activity archives. I want to know what is going on. NOW!"

A group of control panel operators frantically flipped through holographic records.

"Sir," a young woman said from a corner of the room. "A virus appears to have infiltrated our system. Our bio-detection database indicates it was triggered by Brent Cordon."

"Cordon?!" Glenko responded.

"Yes, sir," the woman replied. "He is a base employee. Quantum Computer Support Division. Before launching the virus, his last known system activity was fixing a holo projector malfunction on Level Twelve in Professor Kira Sedora's research laboratory."

"The Time Travel Division!" Glenko shouted. "I think this could get bad. Get me Professor Sedora."

A glowing green hologram of Sedora suddenly stood in front of Captain Glenko. "What do you want, Captain?" Sedora said with irritation. "I am busy."

"So am I," Glenko said. "We have a problem. It appears that one of our computer techs, Brent Cordon, has gone rogue and disabled our security systems."

"I told you they needed to be stronger," Sedora said. "He was in here today."

"That is why I contacted you," Glenko said. "Your office was the last place he worked. Did he give you any indication of what he was going to do afterward? Did he gain access to your system files?"

In the hologram, Sedora quickly flicked her fingers across a touch screen. "My computer is clean," Sedora said. "But my assistant's is not. The B2700X Temporal Transporter specifications have been hacked—and copied. And despite my five requests in the last year, we never got a remote override system in place to disable a temporal transporter in case it was stolen."

Glenko muttered a curse under his breath. "I think Cordon is trying to steal one of the newest time machines. He could be a spy for the Southern Hemisphere Alliance, the Asian Federation, or Antarcticstralia."

"Or a private corporation," Sedora said. "I always thought we had too many private contractors here."

"I am sending a detachment to the launch bay immediately," Glenko said.

Glenko shouted orders, rushed out of the control room, and ran down a hall to a teleportation chamber where six security guards had just arrived.

"Launch bay!" Glenko shouted. "NOW!"

A security guard on the opposite side of the chamber pressed a button, and all seven guards dematerialized in translucent flashes of light points.

Meanwhile, in their laboratory, Adalya and Sedora frantically packed supplies in backpacks and attached communication, monitoring, and utility tool devices to their belts. Sedora also holstered a plasma pistol.

"Cordon has to be stopped," Sedora said. "He should not be smart enough to actually operate the technology we developed, but if one of our temporal transporters falls into the wrong hands, terrible things could happen."

Adalya thought of the science-fiction stories with which she grew up. In them, time travel to the past resulted in damaging and unexpected consequences for the present and future. People ceased to exist, civilizations collapsed, and the very fabric of the universe was sometimes torn. Based on her research, some of those dire consequences seemed theoretically possible but uncertain. More research would be needed to test the possibilities of timeline splitting, parallel universe creation, and space-time rupturing.

Now with tools and gear, Adalya and Sedora rushed out of their laboratory and ran down a hall to a teleportation chamber where they quickly faded into rippling translucent particles.

Meanwhile, in the launch bay, Cordon ran toward a time machine. Two identical-looking time machines floated together above a metallic floor. This surprised him. Records he hacked indicated there would be only one B2700X Temporal Transporter. Cordon decided he needed to quickly sabotage one machine, so he would not be followed.

The time machines looked like metallic three-dimensional half ovals and were covered in a series of metal handholds to enable maintenance access in specific areas. Each vehicle also contained a cockpit space and a few small rooms.

Cordon smiled as he neared one of the time machines and pulled out his plasma knife, ready for sabotage. Suddenly, he turned around as he heard the distinctive chiming of teleportation. Captain Glenko and his security guards (three men and three women) materialized from glowing particles as they arrived in the launch bay. Forget sabotage. This would have to be his getaway vehicle.

Cordon thought of his Western stories, pulled out his plasma pistol, and fired purple plasma bursts at the security guards. He was an excellent shot and immediately killed two guards. In his spare time, he liked to beam onto the plains when there was a full moon and practice his marksmanship on prairie dogs, rattlesnakes, and burrowing owls.

Glenko gritted his teeth in anger as he and his guards took cover behind very expensive vehicles. Glenko recklessly revealed himself and fired. A purple plasma beam bored through Cordon's backpack and left a smoking hole in a nearby wall.

Serious concern crossed Cordon's face as he took cover behind a stack of shipping containers next to the nearest time machine. Cordon quickly blasted off a series of shots that kept the Area 54 security forces pinned down. He then heard a voice from the communication device in his ear.

The European-accented voice Cordon heard earlier spoke again. "Cordon, where are you? Are you ready? What is transpiring?!"

"I'm leaving Dodge, partner!" Cordon shouted as he tore the communication device from his ear and tossed it to the floor.

"What are you bloody talking about?!" the voice from the device shouted in confusion. Cordon smashed the communication device to pieces with a boot while dodging a plasma beam that barely missed his head. Being caught by Glenko was not part of his plan, but the disruption could help mask his true goals from the agents who had recruited him. At this point, they were ready to abandon him rather than get their hands dirty tangling with official UTAC forces. As far as Cordon was concerned, the less attention Vandanite Tech paid to him, the better.

Glenko and his guards moved closer, taking cover behind vehicles and cargo containers. By constantly firing a coordinated barrage of plasma beams, the security guards kept Cordon at bay as they moved forward. Cordon fired back and activated the entry door of the time machine closest to him. He jumped in with plasma beams barely missing his legs.

Cordon set aside his plasma pistol, plopped into the pilot's chair, and frantically oriented himself to a bewildering control panel. He did not know how to close the vehicle's door and heard the approaching footsteps of base security. Cordon took a deep breath and tried to recall what he had recently read. He managed to close the door, start up the time machine, and move a control stick. The transporter swiftly moved right. Security guards ducked and dove to the floor as a whoosh of blue flames sizzled from vents in the back of the time machine.

Cordon realigned the time machine. Then he flipped a switch that remotely triggered a set of launch bay doors to open, revealing an exit tunnel. He pulled back on the control stick. The time machine shot forward, blasting long blue flames from its exhaust vents.

Adalya and Sedora materialized in the launch bay and rushed toward Glenko and his guards. Just as they arrived at Glenko's location, Cordon's transporter disappeared through the exit tunnel.

"Sedora!" Glenko shouted as he pointed. "He stole a time machine! We have to stop him!"

"Adalya and I can handle this!" Sedora confidently declared as she swung her arm forward and gestured at the second B2700X Temporal Transporter.

"I'll stay behind and secure the rest of the base!" Glenko shouted at Sedora and Adalya as they rushed toward the second time machine. "Cordon may not have been acting alone!"

Sedora thumbed the entry door button on the second time machine. She and Adalya jumped in. Sedora quickly eased into the pilot's seat with the comfort and familiarity of an air combat veteran, which was not difficult because she *was* an air combat veteran.

Sedora flipped switches, pressed buttons, and pulled on a control stick. With a mighty flame-blasting flourish and precise maneuvering, the second time machine blasted into an exit tunnel.

As soon as Cordon entered the exit tunnel, a ground-level hatch opened outside. It was now night, and a bright moon lit the high desert above Area 54. The hatch was the tunnel's surface exit and was extremely well-camouflaged. As it opened, it looked like a circular piece of prairie lifting off the ground on hinges.

As Cordon's time machine shot out of the tunnel, a frightened burrowing owl retreated into an abandoned prairie dog hole. The vehicle then settled into hovering about three feet (one meter) above the ground as Cordon flew across the plains. Sedora's time machine popped out of the exit tunnel in hot pursuit.

Cordon was clumsy with his controls. His vehicle wildly zig-zagged as he struggled to maintain direction, increase acceleration, and read holographic instructions. At one point, he nearly collided with a small herd of pronghorn, which bounded away with astonishing speed. Cordon input temporal coordinate specifications and punched in "1876." He rubbed his head in confusion as he struggled with what to do next. In the meantime, Sedora had nearly caught up to him.

Adalya said, "Should we go back in time to before Cordon stole the temporal transporter and just prevent it from happening?" As Adalya spoke, moonlit high plains scenery and stars streaked by, visible through the time machine's windows.

"Too risky," Sedora said. "We could literally run into our past selves that way."

"Then we need to stop him in the present," Adalya said. "How?"

"We can hack into his system," Sedora said as she began to press buttons.

Of course, Adalya thought. *Both temporal transporters have the same operating system and can exchange information through beamed signals.*

"We locked onto his system!" Sedora proclaimed as various holographic numbers and words burst out of a control panel. "The transporters are tied together." Then words flashed red, and a loud beep sounded. Sedora bit her lower lip as she said, "His vehicle's rubidium atoms and antimatter are now at sufficient temperatures for enabling time travel. We could lose him at any time—literally."

Cordon blinked bleary eyes and intensely furrowed his brow. He felt pressured by beeping and alarm signals from all over the control panel in front of him. He had input the destination year he wanted and activated baseline systems but what next? He quickly veered right, attempting to avoid a lone juniper tree. Cordon's machine missed most of the tree but tore a branch from it. The force of the impact propelled him to the side, and he shielded himself by slamming his palms against the time machine's control panel. As a result, he accidentally activated various commands. More alarms sounded, and concerning holographic displays popped up.

"Uh-oh," Cordon muttered.

"We should now be able to control—" Sedora started to say. "No, I think Cordon's machine might be controlling ours! How did he figure out how to do that?"

"Yeehaw!" Cordon yelled as he suddenly saw the holographic command prompt he needed and swiped it right. Cordon's time machine disintegrated in a brilliant flash of iridescent particles.

"Oh no!" Sedora shouted as she saw the temporal readout on her control panel switch from 2756 to sporadically displaying different years. The readout glowed with 1876 before showing 1985, 1955, 2015, 1885, 1891, 2026, and 1879. Then Sedora's time machine shimmered into a radiant incandescence of multi-colored light points.

*   *   *

On October 21, 1876, Cordon's time machine materialized on the plains of southern Wyoming. It still zoomed forward, now in daytime. Cordon struggled to regain power over the machine's controls after a disorienting ride through nearly a thousand years.

Suddenly, metal smacked rock with a terrible straining screech. Cordon winced as he veered right and severely scraped the side of his time machine against a steep geologic formation that towered over 7,000 feet (2,134 meters) above sea level. He had just crashed into the base of Sheep Rock, about 30 miles (48 kilometers) north of Laramie, Wyoming.

Cordon grimaced as his time machine's hover mechanisms destabilized. The vehicle fell, crashing into rocks. Cordon's head slammed into the machine's control panel, and he briefly blacked out. As he regained his senses, he heard a buzzing alarm. He recognized it as an evacuation signal and pressed a button to open an exit door.

Cordon grabbed his backpack of supplies and jumped out of the time machine. He tumbled down a steep slope, scraping his arms and knees. Panting, he stood up and looked back. The time machine had caught fire, and dark smoke rapidly enveloped it.

Cordon quickly ran away from the time machine but soon felt the shockwaves of a tremendous explosion propel him into the air and downhill. Various components of the time machine were incinerated. The vehicle's antimatter containment coating had substantially minimized damage, but the explosion was still astounding. Assorted debris were flung high onto the craggy ledges of Sheep Rock, including a tungsten carbide-coated parameter settings core. Cordon landed hard on loose dirt and covered his head. As he got up, smoldering debris dropped around him. Cordon wiped time machine debris off his jumpsuit and stumbled downhill.

In the shade of a rocky outcrop, Cordon opened his pack and removed black clothing, a wide-brimmed felt hat, and a set of saddlebags. Glenko's plasma beam had missed almost everything in Cordon's backpack when it tore through, except it had totally destroyed his database orientation module. As Cordon examined the module's remains, he remembered he had left his plasma pistol in the time machine and realized it must have been destroyed with the rest of the vehicle.

A smoke plume billowed from the crash site behind Cordon as he changed out of his Area 54 uniform and put on his black clothes. A red-tailed hawk cried, and a slight breeze kicked up dust as Cordon finished changing by putting on a black hat and pulling it low over his eyes. His hat featured a black leather band decorated with synthetic recreations of dirty blood-stained wolf teeth. Cordon then buried his pack and twenty-eighth century clothing under a pile of rocks and kicked dirt over them.

Cordon kneeled, unsnapped the lid of a saddlebag, and removed a black leather gunbelt and holster. It was a low-slung rig—very similar to that worn by Lassen and Durango. Cordon retrieved a black case out of another saddlebag and unlatched it to reveal a gleaming Colt forty-five pistol nestled in a gray velvet base above rows of bullets. The gun had what looked like obsidian handle grips. However, what appeared to be gleaming volcanic glass was specially synthesized carbon fiber and not as heavy or fragile as real obsidian.

Cordon gently picked up the gun and reverently caressed it. He rolled its cylinder across the shirtsleeve of his left arm. Well-oiled metal lightly clicked as the cylinder smoothly spun. Cordon's eyes widened in delight. Smiling, he filled loops on the back of his gunbelt with bullets. With a satisfied sigh, Cordon placed his pistol in its holster.

A prairie falcon unleashed a squawking alarm call as Cordon stood up. Wind pushed scrappy pieces of dried sagebrush past

Cordon as he placed his gunbelt around his waist and buckled it. Squinting into the sun, Cordon held both hands on his belt buckle and surveyed the wide open high desert terrain that stretched before him. He inhaled deeply through his nose and exhaled with satisfaction. He savored the rich, wild scent of sagebrush.

Cordon's eyes suddenly cocked upward to see a red-tailed hawk swooping toward a fleeing prairie falcon. The hawk shrieked with aggressive fury. Much higher overhead, a small flock of turkey vultures circled, surfing thermal air currents.

In a shocking instant, Cordon drew his gun and blasted the red-tailed hawk. A puff of feathers burst out of the red-tail. Then its body tumbled to the ground. The prairie falcon was given relief from its pursuer, and it may have felt grateful, except . . . Cordon slightly shifted his body and pulled the trigger again. The prairie falcon exploded.

He then fanned the hammer of his pistol, launching off his remaining bullets. Feathers fluttered out of three turkey vultures before the birds hit the ground with crunching thuds. Cordon's target practice in the twenty-eighth century had paid off but not for the birds.

On the plains, a small Cheyenne Indian war party rode horses over a ridge. They had heard the explosion of Cordon's time machine, and they wanted to investigate the huge billowing black smoke plume that accompanied it. Their concerns increased upon hearing Cordon's gunshots and seeing birds fall from the sky.

The Cheyenne warriors lifted their weapons and galloped their horses toward the base of Sheep Rock. They saw Cordon's pistol glimmer with reflected sunlight as he smoothly spun it into his holster with a well-practiced flourish.

Cordon then unholstered his revolver and casually reloaded it. He smiled as he saw the Cheyenne Indians ride toward him. As Cordon moved forward, he positioned himself directly in front of the exploded time machine's smoke plume. Burning debris caught a nearby cluster of sagebrush on fire. It crackled into orange flames a few feet behind Cordon. With a hellish backdrop, the black-clad visitor from the distant future sauntered forward with cold, unnatural confidence.

"Well," Cordon said to himself with a practiced, deep somber affectation in his voice, "I reckon it's time for me to make my name." Cordon lifted his pistol.

When the gun smoke cleared, blood glistened on rocks, and several Cheyenne horses sprinted toward the horizon. Then . . . Tardell Traxton holstered his pistol for the first time.

Chapter 3: Medicine Bow Battle

June 5, 1879 – Early Morning

As the citizens of Medicine Bow scattered toward the sides of the street or dove for cover, Randall Blaze's hands moved in a flash as he reached for his guns. The young outlaw was trying to make a name for himself by gunning down two of the most famous bounty hunters in the West: Lassen Malone and Durango Mesquite. The bounty hunters were tracking Blaze and other members of Tardell Traxton's outlaw gang, which had become a formidable criminal organization by 1879.

Lassen dove toward the ground as he drew his gun. At the same time, a maniacal grin danced across Blaze's face as the outlaw pulled his guns up so fast that his hands looked like blurs. In mid-air, Lassen carefully aimed while Blaze fired two shots. Both bullets grazed Lassen's vest but missed.

While still in the air, Lassen fanned the hammer of his gun and fired two shots that knocked Blaze's guns from his hands and grazed the outlaw's right forearm. Blaze sneered and winced. Then Lassen hit the dirt with his right shoulder and smoothly rolled behind a wooden watering tough.

Blaze moved toward one of his guns, but just as he was about to grab it, it jumped backward with a bang and exploded. Then Blaze's other pistol sprang with a bang and shattered a nearby window.

"Don't try it, hombre!" Durango shouted. He nodded with a closed-mouth grin as he smoothly blew smoke away from his gun's barrel.

"It's Malone and Mesquite!" Blaze shouted as he gripped his bleeding forearm and looked up. "Get 'em!"

Lassen and Durango followed Blaze's glance and saw Jed Gantry and Arvo Avarette on balconies on opposite sides of the street. Gantry targeted a rifle at Lassen. Avarette aimed one at Durango.

Lassen lifted his pistol and fired at Gantry. Gantry fired milliseconds later, and his rifle barrel abruptly curled backward like a violently peeled banana as the bullet from Lassen's gun entered.

Gantry yelped, fell backward, and shattered a window while feeling the sting of gunpowder.

Avarette fired just as Durango leapt behind the trough where Lassen took cover. Avarette's bullet went through the trough, releasing a little geyser of water. Durango fired back but missed.

Lassen aimed at Avarette and fanned the hammer of his pistol with expert ease. Avarette yelled in pain and dropped his gun as a bullet ricocheted off the metal of his rifle and grazed his palm.

"They could be comin' down soon," Lassen said. "You okay, pal?"

"Never better," Durango replied.

Two men who had been watching the commotion from the edge of the hotel drew pistols and rushed toward Lassen and Durango.

"Bad news," Lassen said as he noticed the men. "Looks like Hobart Holt and Shanahan Branigan are in town. Durango, you take Holt. I'll handle Branigan."

Lassen fired at Branigan who wore a plaid shirt under a tattered suit jacket. Just as Lassen fired, the big outlaw abruptly jumped to the right to avoid a gray striped tabby cat that rushed out from under a porch. Lassen's shot missed as a result.

Durango rose and fanned off three shots, emptying his weapon. "Chaw lead, polecats!" Durango shouted while all his shots missed Holt who wore a heavy gray coat over suspenders.

Branigan and Holt took cover behind a stack of barrels in front of the general store. They quickly fired shots that further perforated and drained the trough in front of Lassen and Durango.

Blaze—who was still standing stunned in the street after having his arm grazed and his guns shot out of his hands—dove to the ground. Evidently, Branigan and Holt were not overly concerned about his safety as their bullets nearly hit him.

"Durango, you better reload and fast!" Lassen said. "I've only got one shot left!"

"Sure thing, pal!" Durango said as he pulled his last two silver bullets from black leather loops on his gunbelt and slipped them into his pistol's cylinder.

Lassen cocked his head with concern as things suddenly got quiet. Branigan and Holt stopped firing.

"Over here, boys!" Branigan shouted with an Irish accent. "Come get us, you blood money huntin' scum!"

The outlaws fired several more rounds. Durango instinctively fired back, launching off his last two shots. One of them grazed Holt's shoulder, and the outlaw impulsively sprinted into the open in rage while firing at Lassen and Durango. Branigan followed from behind but was more cautious.

As the two outlaws charged, Lassen cocked the hammer of his six-gun, stood up for an instant, and fired with hyper-alert precision. As he ducked back down, his last bullet zipped through beams of sunlight made visible by dust. The bullet hit the cylinder of Holt's pistol, kicking it into the air. The bullet then sharply ricocheted down to the right where it hit the spade of a shovel leaning against a hitching rail, and then it ricocheted diagonally up to the left where it grazed Branigan's arm and forcefully knocked his gun out of reach under a boardwalk.

Lassen smiled with a loud sigh of relief as he holstered his now empty pistol. In the meantime, Holt's gun sailed through the air. A panicked farmer riding past blinked in surprise as he reached out and smoothly caught Holt's revolver. "Whoa!" the farmer shouted. "I can sell this for 40 bits!" The farmer rode out of town toward the distant horizon.

"Good job, pal!" Durango said. "Not the best ricochet maneuver I've seen you do but pretty good. I'd put it in the top seven—and hey, that one guy just got a new gun."

"Thanks," Lassen dryly said. "What happened to Avarette and Gantry? Did they come down from the balconies?"

The little boy who was whittling when Lassen and Durango rode into town suddenly called out from the open window of a nearby building. "It's Sheriff Gratton and Deputy Caddock! They're lockin' up the outlaws!"

"Hey," Durango said. "They are. Good lawmen in this town."

Lassen quickly turned around and saw Avarette and Gantry being escorted into the middle of the street with their hands cuffed behind their backs. Sheriff Gratton and Deputy Caddock walked behind them with rifles drawn.

Blaze stood up and started to run. Caddock shot the ground near his feet and shouted, "Hold it right there, partner!"

Blaze froze and grimaced in frustration as Caddock soon cuffed him. Blaze had a chance to take down two of the best bounty hunters in the West, but instead, a fresh-faced deputy was handcuffing him. He was furious.

In the meantime, Branigan and Holt looked around in confusion and tried to gain their bearings. They had just been disarmed in a manner that made them feel like they were part of a circus trick. That would normally irk Branigan, but he was particularly incensed because this was not the first time Lassen had done that to him.

"Freeze right there," Lassen said as he cocked the hammer of his empty gun.

Holt sighed with resignation and raised his hands over his head. Branigan sprinted toward the side of the street where pitchforks leaned against the general store.

"I said stop!" Lassen shouted with confident authority.

"You're both outta bullets!" Branigan shouted. "I was countin.' You never reloaded again."

"You want to bet on that?" Durango said as he stood up and pointed his gun at Holt who continued to stand with his hands in the air.

"No need!" Branigan shouted as he picked up a pitchfork that leaned against the general store. "I also heard Malone say something along the lines of 'I've got one bullet left.' He said it real loud. Then he fired his pistol."

"Well, what if Lassen wasn't countin' right?" Durango said. "Did you count on that?"

Lassen put a palm on his forehead and sighed. Holt narrowed his eyes in confusion and looked back and forth between Lassen and Durango and Branigan.

"Oh, he's good at countin', alright," Branigan said as he now held a pitchfork. "Better than my defense attorney was in Sacramento. I'll tell you that, laddie!" Branigan then launched his pitchfork like a spear.

Lassen's eyes widened as sharp metal sailed toward him. He holstered his gun and rolled right. The pitchfork pierced ground where Lassen had been fractions of a second earlier. Branigan grunted in anger, ran, and retrieved the pitchfork. Lassen's roll brought him in contact with a shovel leaning against a hitching rail. Lassen grabbed the shovel handle just in time to block a violent pitchfork lancing.

Shiny metal pitchfork tines and shovel spade collided and made tiny sparks as Lassen and Branigan engaged in primal, clacking battle. Holt looked at Lassen and Branigan and then at Durango. When Durango turned to watch Lassen and Branigan's impromptu fencing match, Holt ran down the street to the east.

Durango saw Holt flee in his peripheral vision. In response, the bounty hunter holstered his empty gun, grabbed his lariat off his shoulder, and swung a wide loop over his head. Then he threw it. With the force of a biting cobra, Durango's lasso launched through the air, and a loop landed right in front of Blaze's feet. Durango pulled hard. Holt fell face-first into the dusty street as a rope cinched tight around his ankles.

"Don't bolt, Holt!" Durango shouted.

On the east side of town, a crowd gradually formed as people came to watch the action after the shooting stopped. The little boy who was whittling when Lassen and Durango entered town stared in wide-eyed wonder. So did the little girl who had just been reading a Lassen Malone dime novel. A scruffy dog appeared to be perpetually smiling as he panted and watched the most action Medicine Bow had seen in years. The little boy absentmindedly petted the dog as all his attention was on Lassen and Durango battling the Traxton Gang.

Lassen and Branigan moved down Main Street toward the west as they continued their pitchfork/shovel duel. They soon neared a flimsy wooden corral that was overfilled with longhorn steers destined for cattle cars on trains heading to the East. The cattle mooed in agitation. It was bad enough being in overcrowded, fetid conditions, but now they were riled up by the ruckus Lassen and Branigan caused.

As Lassen backed against the corral, he realized his shovel was momentarily stuck between the tines of Branigan's pitchfork. Both men grimaced and strained their arms as they struggled to free their manual labor tools-turned weapons. Then Lassen's shovel snapped back and hit the creaky boards of the cattle corral behind him. Several rough-hewn pieces of pine snapped in half. Cattle began to aggressively push against the damaged portion of the corral while the entire structure shook.

As Branigan fell backward from the force of the weapon separation, Lassen regained his composure and used his shovel to bat Branigan's pitchfork out of his hands. Branigan lunged at Lassen but repeatedly backed up as Lassen wildly swung his shovel. Branigan then recklessly got close, kicked Lassen's shovel out of his hands, and rushed at the bounty hunter with a furious tornado of flailing fists.

Lassen's eyes widened as he backed up with fear. Branigan was about a foot taller than Lassen and a *lot* wider. Lassen dodged various attacks and occasionally made some hits, but they were quick and light compared to Branigan's power.

Lassen groaned in agony as Branigan's fist slammed into his stomach. The bounty hunter fell to the ground, thoroughly deprived of breath. As he struggled to breathe, Lassen placed a hand out pleadingly. His body language begged Branigan to back off. Branigan responded with a mean smile as he formed another enormous fist.

Then a disoriented rancher who was visiting Medicine Bow for the first time rode into Main Street from a nearby alley. He was confused, lost, and looking for a cattle buyer who had written to him several weeks earlier. His horse whinnied and reared in alarm as he nearly ran over Branigan.

Branigan turned around and saw a horse with a saddle and a rifle in a scabbard. Transportation and a weapon. Convenient. As the nearby horse's front hooves settled back to the ground, Branigan impulsively grabbed the rancher off the horse and threw him to the side like he was a sack of potatoes.

"Agghhh!" the rancher called out as he was thrown into mud.

Branigan got on the horse and began to unfasten the rancher's rifle from its scabbard. As Lassen stood up and struggled to catch his breath, the sound of wood cracking and creaking emanated from the nearby corral full of worked-up longhorns. Lassen saw the inflamed red veins in the longhorns' eyes. Then he sprinted toward a boardwalk, unleashed a shrill whistle, and shouted, "Horizon, get over here! Now!"

Lassen jumped onto the boardwalk and ran east. He saw Sheriff Gratton and Deputy Caddock on the boardwalk ahead of him with their guns drawn on Avarette, Blaze, and Gantry.

In the meantime, Branigan abandoned his clumsy efforts to retrieve the rifle on his stolen horse and spurred his new mount east. As Branigan fled down Main Street, Durango finished tying up Holt and hauled him onto a nearby boardwalk.

"Whoa!" Durango exclaimed as Branigan zoomed past.

Holt chuckled as he saw his outlaw companion escaping. "Try to rope that," Holt said with a snicker.

Caddock fired several shots at Branigan, but the outlaw rode low and dodged the bullets. In the meantime, at a hitching rail at the hotel, Lassen's trusty buckskin horse, Horizon, had heard Lassen's whistle and surged into action. Horizon effortlessly untied himself with his teeth while Durango's black horse, Yonder, watched in amazement. Horizon ran up the street toward Lassen.

Suddenly, an entire panel from the longhorn corral popped off. Frightened cattle tore out of their pen and rushed toward bystanders who quickly scattered.

"Stampede!" somebody on the street yelled while Lassen reached Gratton, Caddock, and the apprehended Traxton Gang members. Horizon arrived seconds later.

"Horizon!" Lassen shouted. "Good horse!" Lassen turned to Gratton and Caddock and said, "I'm out of bullets. Can I borrow a gun?!"

"Sure thing, Mister Malone!" Caddock said as he unholstered his pistol and tossed it to Lassen who adeptly caught it.

"Thanks for the pistol, pal!" Lassen shouted as he leapt on Horizon and rode east.

The young deputy replied, "Any time, Mister Malone! Go get him!"

"How did you know who that was?" Gratton asked, raising his eyebrows.

"He's famous!" Caddock said.

Lassen rode through Medicine Bow's Main Street just ahead of the dangerous longhorn stampede. He saw that almost all bystanders had scattered to safety, but a little girl with a book had tripped in the middle of the street. The street was too wide. The cattle were too fast. Lassen knew she would not make it without help. He quickly shoved Caddock's pistol in a saddlebag to free his hands.

As the little girl dropped her Lassen Malone dime novel, she struggled to regain her footing and glanced over her shoulder in wide-eyed fear as dozens of mooing longhorn cattle stormed closer. Suddenly, a dashing hero rode into view. Lassen! It was Lassen Malone himself. She knew he would save her. She smiled as Lassen strained his feet in stirrups and leaned far to the left.

"Grab on!" Lassen shouted. The little girl grabbed Lassen's left arm as hard as she could, and he pulled her up onto Horizon. She briefly rode behind Lassen with her arms around his waist.

Lassen swung Horizon left into an alley as longhorns stampeded past. He then gently set the girl down. Her parents rushed toward her in relief. Lassen moved Horizon onto Main Street and yelled back, "Be good and keep readin'!" The little girl smiled and waved.

Lassen continued pursuing Branigan with a stampede of cattle between him and his target. Soon, Lassen and Branigan rode beyond Medicine Bow. The cattle slowed, began to separate, and nibbled grass on the plains. A frightened killdeer called and flailed in an effort to distract attention from her nest. Horizon rushed onward through the longhorns.

Branigan looked back, noticed Lassen, and kept riding hard. Lassen began uncoiling the lariat attached to his saddle as he made a clicking sound with his mouth. In response, Horizon abruptly accelerated. Soon, Lassen was only about 30 feet (nine meters) behind Branigan, who suddenly stopped, freed the rifle attached to his saddle scabbard, and began to take aim.

Lassen swung his lasso and threw a wide loop that overshot Branigan but landed over his rifle barrel. Branigan's shot went wild as rope cinched tight around his rifle's barrel. Lassen flicked his wrist, and the rifle swung back into Branigan's head, knocking him to the ground. Branigan's vision wavered between clarity and nearly blacking out as he rubbed his head.

Horizon stopped. Lassen quickly dismounted and tied up Branigan. Lassen then rode into Medicine Bow with Branigan walking in front of him. The outlaw's hands were bound behind his back and connected to a rope tied to Lassen's saddle. Branigan spoke, but only faint muffled words came through the bandana tied around his mouth. Lassen normally did not gag prisoners, but Branigan was particularly foul-mouthed.

As Lassen entered town with his prisoner in front of him, people came out to stare. Some citizens were impressed and praised Lassen and Durango. Others were upset that bounty hunters had contributed to so much dangerous trouble.

Lassen brought Branigan to the jail where he saw Sheriff Gratton, Deputy Caddock, and Durango saunter out the front door.

"Got another desperado ready to check into the Crowbar Hotel," Lassen said.

"I told you he'd make it—and get Branigan," Durango said while gently shaking his finger at Gratton with defiance and a smile.

"He did at that," Gratton said, carefully patting down his gray mustache with a thumb and forefinger. Gratton turned toward Lassen and said, "I'm Sheriff Gratton, and this is Deputy Caddock. Welcome to Medicine Bow. There's a lot of hogwash in the dime novels. Caddock here thinks you're some sort of legend."

"Well, I uh . . ." Lassen began to respond.

"Pleased to meet you, sir," young Caddock said, cutting off Lassen.

"Likewise," Lassen said. "People say a lot of things, but the stories are usually better." Lassen handed Caddock back his gun. "Thanks for the loan."

"Anytime," Caddock said, smiling.

"Come on, Caddock," Gratton said. "Let's get Branigan put away with the others."

Lassen and Durango followed Gratton and Caddock as they locked up Branigan with Avarette, Blaze, Gantry, and Holt. As the outlaws seethed in a cell, Lassen approached Gratton.

"Would you mind if we had a chat with these boys?" Lassen asked.

"Chat away," Gratton said, "but I want to be here to listen."

"Sure, no problem," Lassen said.

"You'll never get Traxton," Branigan said with cold boldness. "He's too smart for you. And I don't think we'll be here long."

"True," Gratton said. "In a few days, you'll be hauled away to a bigger jail in Rawlins." Branigan rolled his eyes.

"Well," Lassen said as he casually stretched his arms with confidence. "As glad as Durango and I were to get you boys locked up and get some reward money, we're most concerned with your leader: Tardell Traxton. Any ideas where we can find him? What about his right-hand man, Britt Thornby?"

The Traxton Gang members were silent.

"Think this over carefully," Gratton said. "Talking could make things go easier for you."

Silence.

"Alright, fine," Lassen said. "I don't think they're gonna talk, Gratton."

"Appears that way," Gratton replied as he turned toward the prisoners. "The doctor will be over in a few minutes to tend to your wounded."

Durango's nose twitched as he caught the scent of bacon drifting into the jail from the hotel restaurant.

"I smell it, too" Lassen said with a smile.

"Sarita Socorro's bacon," Caddock said. "It's breakfast time at the hotel. You boys have your mornin' grub yet?"

"No, but we could go for some," Durango said.

"Come on," Gratton said. "I'll take you over to the hotel while my deputy takes over here."

The bounty hunters and lawman stepped away from the jail bars. Gratton loaded the new prisoners' possessions into a burlap sack. "We can give these a look-see at breakfast," Gratton said.

"Good idea," Lassen replied. "Might be some clues there."

After Gratton and the bounty hunters left, Caddock settled into a chair and kept an eye on the outlaws. Soon, he and Branigan engaged in an awkward staring contest.

"Deputy laddie," Branigan said. "Now that your boss man, Mister Gratton, is gone, I think we should talk business." Branigan especially rolled his r's with his Irish accent. "I don't reckon you make much money here. I never heard of Albany County payin' well. I think perhaps we could arrange a jailbreak in which you are disarmed while one of us pretends to be sick—and you somehow find an unclaimed bag of money on the prairie tomorrow."

Caddock scowled in response. "I can't be bribed, Branigan," Caddock said. "You're wastin' your time. This is just like that Lassen Malone story, *Sacramento Shootout*. The politicians couldn't bribe him, and you're not gonna pay me off."

"Suit yourself, laddie," Branigan said. "Just something to consider."

Branigan knew that pushing his proposal would agitate Caddock and make him refuse harder out of spite. Years of manipulating others had taught him that people were most likely to do his bidding when they thought they were making their own decisions.

Before joining Traxton's gang, Branigan was a politician in Sacramento. His political career ended when he was convicted of bribery through credible witness testimony. Branigan was always corrupt, but nobody testified against him until Lassen Malone captured one of his accomplices. Somehow, only Lassen had convinced him to talk.

In 1876, Branigan masterminded a complicated bribery scheme involving land seizures and spur lines of the Union Pacific Railroad. Branigan was proud of his clever setup involving a circle of bribery money, but it all came to an end when Malone interfered. Branigan wondered if some version of that incident had made its way into Caddock's novel. Branigan had a grudge against Malone, but his anger did not burn as intensely as Traxton's.

CHAPTER 4: PRELUDE TO PREHISTORY

Just after locking up the Traxton Gang members, Lassen, Durango, and Sheriff Gratton sat at a table, waiting for breakfast. Delicious salty and greasy aromas hung in the air. All three men had their hats off. Gratton dug through a burlap sack, sifting through the Traxton Gang members' possessions.

"Tobacco, ammunition, jerky, more tobacco—ah—some papers," Gratton said as he pulled out wrinkled sheets. Gratton unfolded one piece. "Hmmm—this is interesting. Here's a note from Blaze's vest. Looks like he planned to send it to Traxton. It says here that somebody named Smith Emory recently got hired on as a digger at Como Bluff."

"Why would Traxton be concerned about Como Bluff?" Lassen asked.

"Como Bluff is about 10 miles east of here, and there's a railway station there," Gratton said. "Traxton may be planning a train robbery. The Emory fellah might be an inside man."

"Maybe he's just using his digging job for scouting," Durango guessed.

"Durango and I have heard of Emory," Lassen said. "He's been in trouble, but we didn't know he was riding with Traxton."

"What are diggers doing at Como Bluff, anyway?" Durango asked.

"Dinosaurs," Gratton said.

"Dinosaurs?" Durango asked. "Lassen, you've tried talking to me about those before. What are they again?"

"Extinct reptiles," Lassen said. "The anatomist Sir Richard Owen came up with the term 'dinosaur' in 1842. It means 'fearfully great lizard.' So, sheriff, dinosaur fossils have been found in this area?"

"Yep," Gratton said, "fellahs have been digging up their bones at Como Bluff for the last couple of years."

Lassen rubbed his chin as his eyes narrowed in concentration. The conversation had just connected bounty hunting with one of his favorite hobbies: paleontology. In 1879, it was a new science. Lassen had never taken the time to become expert at it, but it interested him very much. As Gratton and Durango spoke, Lassen's mind drifted through the mists of time. He imagined life millions of years ago with enormous reptilian monsters crawling through humid, foggy swamplands. Then his mind snapped back to the conversation. "Did the dinosaur digs start with a university expedition?" Lassen asked.

"Naw," Gratton said, "but there's university involvement now. It all started back in '77 when a railroad worker found some dinosaur bones at Como on his way back from hunting antelope."

"What was his name?" Lassen asked. "Is he still in the area?"

Gratton smoothed down his mustache as he looked up at a chandelier in thought. Then he snapped his fingers. "Reed. William Reed. He comes into town every once in a while to hire diggers."

"How's a university involved?" Lassen asked.

"Reed and his men are on the payroll of Professor Marsh of Yale University back East in New Haven, Connecticut," Gratton said. "Marsh doesn't come into the field much, but his men are shipping him railcars of bones every week."

"Oh, yeah," Lassen said, "Othniel Charles Marsh. I've seen him speak at Yale. He's a brilliant paleontologist. Too bad he never taught any courses. I always heard he was too busy with research and organizing exhibits at the Peabody Museum."

"Yeah—the Peabody," Gratton said. "I read an article about it in the *Laramie Sentinel* a few months ago. Has lots of bones of strange old critters that have been cold as a wagon wheel for quite a spell."

"True," Lassen said. "Some incredible specimens, though. You ought to check it out if you ever go East."

"Yeah—maybe," Gratton said. "You think you boys are close to finally catchin' Traxton?"

"Hopefully," Lassen said, "but we've thought that before, and he always managed to be one step ahead of us."

"People say he can tell the future," Gratton said. "Bunch of bosh if you ask me, but Traxton's a mysterious fellah. No one knows where he came from. He showed up in Wyomin' a few years ago. People said he wandered into Laramie from the range. Been on the dodge ever since."

"We'll ride out to Como Bluff and ask Smith Emory some questions," Lassen said. "We just locked up half of Traxton's Gang. Traxton could be nearby, and Emory may have some answers."

"I'd like to help," Gratton said, "but I think Caddock and me should stay close while Traxton's boys are locked up. Traxton and more of his gang are still out there, including Britt Thornby."

"Yeah," Lassen said. "Britt Thornby. The English outlaw. Traxton's right-hand man. You ever tangled with him?"

"Not directly," Gratton said, "but some of the other Wyoming sheriffs have. He's bad business. Last I heard, he and Traxton had temporarily split up the gang."

"We think he's somewhere in southern Wyoming," Durango said.

"Yeah," Lassen added, "but that's based on a lot of vague rumors. Our sources haven't been entirely reliable."

"Or sober," Durango said.

"I've heard the same thing about Thornby's whereabouts," Gratton said. Then he sighed deeply and furrowed his brow. "I thought the West was finally settlin' down, but Traxton and Thornby have been causin' trouble for the last few years, and folks here are as scared as I've ever seen them."

"If we get more info," Lassen said, "we'll let you know, sheriff."

An alluring aroma of bacon, gravy, biscuits, hash browns, and eggs soon filled Lassen's nostrils. Sarita Socorro arrived with breakfast. Lassen and Durango stood up while saying, "Thank you, ma'am."

Gratton also stood up and said, "Miss Socorro, you've done it again. You make the best vittles in town."

"Smells out and out delicious," Durango said.

"That's a fact," Lassen added.

Sarita was attractive with dark skin, glossy black hair, and golden brown eyes. She smiled as she spoke. "Gracias, you gentlemen are very kind." As Sarita spoke, she quickly scanned Lassen with an up-down glance. Lassen did not indicate he noticed the attention, but Durango scowled with disapproval. The sheriff smirked as he detected what was happening.

"Durango Mesquite, ma'am," Durango said as he extended a hand to assist Sarita with serving food off a tray. "Let me help you with that." Durango lifted a plate of biscuits off Sarita's tray and placed it on the table. "You may have heard of me."

Sarita quickly bit her lower lip and looked up. Then she decidedly stated, "No, can't say I have. Enjoy your food, gentlemen."

Sarita smiled at Lassen and turned around to return to the kitchen. Durango had his mouth open to start another sentence, and his right index finger was extended to emphasize a comment that never happened. Sarita soon disappeared from sight. Durango lowered his finger and sat back down.

Gratton lifted a fork from the table and said, "Grab your eatin' irons, boys. Chaw time."

As Lassen grabbed a fork, he lightly blushed and scratched the side of his head with his left hand. He knew exactly what had just happened but did not want to upset Durango.

The food was good. Lassen and Durango cleaned their plates. They then thanked the sheriff, went over the paperwork to get their reward money, and walked to the general store to resupply.

As they approached the store entrance, the gray striped tabby cat that had messed up one of Lassen's shots during the morning's gunfight launched onto the boardwalk in front of the store, meowed, and stood directly in front of Lassen. Lassen and Durango stopped as the cat called out to them and stared up with big emerald green eyes that looked like glossy marbles. The cat trilled and purred as it rubbed against Lassen's legs. Lassen raised his eyebrows, turned around to look at Durango, and shrugged.

The storekeeper stepped into the entrance doorway. He was an older gentleman wearing an apron.

The storekeeper said, "His name's Toby. Friendly little cat—well, no, I guess he's kind of chubby—who hangs around the store sometimes. Belongs to Shelby down the street. He likes you. Why, he thinks you're a regular tabby daddy."

Lassen looked down and shook his head in bemusement as he lightly laughed. "Maybe in another life. I've got supplies to get."

Toby looked up and meowed in response. Durango approached the cat with a hand out and said, "Here, kitty. Want a pet?"

The cat hissed at Durango and trotted off the boardwalk.

"I guess not," Durango said.

Soon, Lassen and Durango stepped out of the store with burlap sacks of goods in hand. As they loaded supplies into saddlebags, Toby lazily watched from the shade under a nearby boardwalk.

It was now mid-afternoon and time to head out of town. Various townsfolk stared at the two bounty hunters. They were curious, but they were also intimidated and respected the men's privacy. In the West, many people made a habit of not butting into others' business. However, children were not always so considerate.

As Lassen and Durango prepped their horses for the journey to Como Bluff, the little boy and girl who had watched the morning's action ran up to them. A mutt dog trailed behind the children.

"I'm Lilly," the little girl said. "And this is my friend, Blake." The kids looked to be about eight years old.

"Hi, Mister Malone," Blake said. "Gee, Mister Malone! You're hearty as a buck. That was some ace-high shootin'!"

"Thanks, son," Lassen said with a smile. "What's your dog's name?"

"Oh, him," Blake said. "We call him Yarfer."

"Because," Lilly said, "whenever he talks, he says, 'Yarf, yarf, yarf!'"

Yarfer released three barks that sounded like what Lilly had just said.

"I can see how he got his name," Lassen said, smiling.

"Who's your helper?" Lilly asked, gesturing at Durango, who was packing saddlebags on Yonder.

Durango froze. His eyebrows rose with irritation when he heard "helper."

"Oh him," Lassen said as he pointed toward Durango with a thumb over his shoulder. "He's—"

Lassen's sentence was cut off as Durango said, "Durango Mesquite. I'm a bounty hunter, too, kids. You may've heard of me."

Blake and Lilly scratched their chins, looked at each other, and turned toward Lassen and Durango. "No," they said.

"But gosh," Blake said. "How'd you rope that Traxton desperado so fast?"

"It's all in the wrist, son," Durango said. "Here, let me show you." Durango untied his leather lariat from his saddle.

"Thanks for saving my life, Mister Malone," Lilly said.

"No problem, miss," Lassen replied. "How far'd you get in your book?"

Lilly held her tattered Lassen Malone dime novel.

"The part where you and Diego go after Shrike Pierson, and you're in a big mess of stampeding buffaloes."

"Diego?" Durango said with a derisive scoff as he pulled his lariat off Yonder. "Diego made the story? There are books about you and *Diego*—and all I get are occasional headlines in newspaper articles. Durango Mesquite Gets His Man. Well-Dressed Bounty Hunter Chased Out of Town. Durango Fights Through—who's writin' those books about you, anyway?"

Lassen looked down at Lilly's book and said, "Trenton Howarth."

"He's full of it if you ask me," Durango replied.

"It's good to see youngsters reading," Lassen said to Lilly and Blake, "but don't believe everything you read. Just because it's written doesn't make it true."

"Does that mean you didn't *really* outrun a grizzly, survive an avalanche, and fight off 20 bandits in California single-handedly?" Blake asked.

"Well . . ." Lassen said.

"Look over here," Durango interrupted as he formed a lasso and swung his lariat over his head.

Lilly and Blake turned toward Durango, who lowered his lariat, swinging a huge loop entirely around his body before jumping in and out of it several times. He then threw his lariat's loop. The rope sailed toward stacks of shovels and pitchforks that were strewn on the ground at the site of Lassen's battle with Branigan and Holt. The loop of the lariat caught on a pitchfork tine. Durango flicked his wrist. His lariat tightened around the pitchfork, which caught on two shovel spades. Durango slightly turned his arm and pulled hard and upward. The pitchfork and both shovels launched off the ground and became neatly stacked against a hitching rail in front of the general store. With a slight arm movement, Durango freed his lariat from the tools and began coiling it. The rope action was fast and expertly performed.

"That's how it's done, kids," Durango said.

"Gee!" Lilly and Blake exclaimed.

"That's neat!" Lilly shouted.

"Sure is," Blake added. "I want to go home and practice that."

"Me, too!" Lilly said.

"Good idea," Durango said, "but would you do me a favor and start by just restacking the rest of those shovels and pitchforks by hand?"

"Okay," Lilly and Blake said as they ran toward the shovels and pitchforks.

"Wait a minute," Durango said. The children stopped and turned toward the bounty hunter. Durango dug into his saddlebag and pulled out two shiny silver dollars. "A good job deserves good pay." Durango used his thumb to quickly flick both silver dollars into the hands of Lilly and Blake. The kids nimbly caught the coins.

"Swell!" Lilly said. "Thanks, Mister Mesquite."

"Yeah, thanks!" Blake added.

"You tell your friends the famous bounty hunter, Durango Mesquite, gave you those," Durango said.

"Sure thing, Mister Mesquite," Blake replied. "You'll be news to them because none of them know about you."

Durango loudly cleared his throat.

"Will you two ever come back to Medicine Bow?" Lilly asked.

"I don't know," Lassen said as he and Durango climbed onto their horses. "Traxton needs to be caught, and Durango and I aim to do just that. We better get moving."

"So long, kids," Durango said as he and Lassen got on their horses.

"Goodbye, Lilly," Lassen said. "Bye, Blake."

The kids waved goodbye. Lassen and Durango waved back as they rode out of town. Lilly and Blake ran toward the general store. Yarfer barked and chased Lassen and Durango at a distance. The dog then stopped and stared at the bounty hunters as the mounted figures got smaller and smaller toward the horizon.

Soon, Lassen and Durango rode in the wide open spaces of southern Wyoming's shortgrass prairie. Vultures circled high overhead. A prairie dog darted out of its burrow and quickly sunk back in as Horizon's hooves tromped nearby dirt. Lassen and Durango rode east toward Como Bluff. Behind the bounty hunters, Medicine Bow was merely a distant cluster of buildings. Hills surrounding Como Bluff stood far to the east. The mighty Laramie Mountains jutted out of the plains in the distance.

"We'll get to Como Bluff by sometime tomorrow morning," Lassen said.

"You think we'll see some dinosaur skeletons?" Durango asked.

"Not likely," Lassen said. "At dig sites, the bones are often scattered. Articulated skeletons with all the bones together can be rare. Plus, dinosaur skeleton mounts are assembled out of the field. I've only seen an articulated put-together skeleton once. A few years ago, I saw a *Hadrosaurus* skeleton mounted at the Academy of Natural Sciences in Philadelphia, Pennsylvania. It was roughly the shape of a kangaroo but twice as tall as a man. In life, that dinosaur must have looked like a big two-legged lizard."

"Huh . . ." Durango said, "I wonder how soon we'll be back in Medicine Bow. I'd like to get to know Miss Socorro better."

"A lot of folks don't know what to make of dinosaurs," Lassen said. "Hold up a minute. Horizon's walking a little strange. I'm going to check his shoes."

Lassen and Durango stopped. Lassen dismounted and removed a small pebble from Horizon's back shoe. Lassen patted Horizon's neck and detected slight movement on a rock. Durango saw Lassen's expression change.

"Lassen, I know that look," Durango said. "You just *noticed* something."

"Just as I surmised," Lassen said as he pulled a pair of binoculars out of a saddlebag. "There's a lizard on a rock about 80 feet away. I want to take a closer look and figure out what species it is."

"Wha—wait," Durango said, mouth agape and eyebrows raised. "There's a rock out there with maybe some dried moss on it. That's *all* I can see. How do you notice these things before even getting binoculars out?"

Lassen focused optical glass on the lizard. "Looks like a prairie racerunner," Lassen said.

The lizard was about seven inches (18 centimeters) long. It had a white scaly belly and green, dark brown, and beige stripes running down its back. The little reptile contentedly soaked up sun. Then it cocked its left eye and blue-green head skyward.

Bright yellow, scaly sharp-clawed talons tore into the lizard and plucked it off the rock. Lassen's eyes widened. He swung his binoculars up to track the movements of a fierce-looking golden eagle. It shrieked bizarrely as it carried away the lizard. The massive bird's seven-foot (two-meter) wingspan impressed Lassen.

"Intriguing" Lassen said. "Now that looks like something out of the dinosaur times."

"I suppose so," Durango said. "Looks like that eagle just hit pay dirt. Speaking of which, I've been developin' a sparkin' plan for the next time we're in Medicine Bow. I'll get a handful of prairie flowers. Then I'll go into the restaurant where Miss Socorro works.

I know just the place to pick them. Remember that spring we rode by yesterday? Well, I thought I could—"

Lassen cut off Durango and said, "I wonder what might have flown in prehistoric times that was meaner than that eagle."

"So, as I was saying," Durango said, "I'll get this batch of flowers, see, and then—oh heck, I might as well be talkin' to Yonder."

Yonder snorted and pricked his ears. Durango formed a gentle closed-mouth smile and patted his friendly horse on the neck.

Lassen continued watching through binoculars as the golden eagle flew away. Then he lowered his optics.

"Remember a few months ago," Lassen said, "when I was telling you about that article I read describing *Pterodactylus*?"

"A *platypus*?" Durango asked. "I don't think Miss Socorro would want one of those."

"No, no," Lassen said. "*Pterodactylus*. That eagle reminded me of it."

"What?" Durango asked, starting to lose interest and get bored.

"Imagine a mix between a big bat and a lizard," Lassen said.

"Uh, okay," Durango said. "Seems kind of strange. So, as I was saying about Miss Socorro . . ." Durango trailed off as he realized Lassen would not give him an opening.

"It was named by Cuvier in 1809," Lassen said. "Had a wingspan of about five feet and a mean set of sharp teeth. Birds today don't even have teeth, but *Pterodactylus* wasn't a bird. It belonged to a group of animals called pterosaurs. They were flying reptiles."

"Uh, yeah," Durango said, "alright."

"You might be wondering," Lassen said, "if birds ever had teeth. If you look close, you'll notice that no birds you see today actually have teeth. Some might have serrated beaks, but none have teeth."

"Um . . ." Durango said.

"I remember in one of Professor Marsh's lectures," Lassen continued, "he talked about *Archaeopteryx*. It lived in dinosaur times and looked like a little flying chicken but with a longer tail and a lizard head full of teeth. It even had feathers."

"Wait," Durango said. "I thought we only found fossil bones of prehistoric animals. How do we know it had feathers?"

"Detailed fossil feather impressions were found in limestone" Lassen said. "Caused quite a ruckus when it was discovered in Europe in 1861. A fossil showing such a clear evolutionary transition from one form to another—reptile to bird—had never been found before. Some scientists staked their reputations on it. Others thought it was deviltry."

"A feathered flying lizard," Durango said. "That's, uh, something, but it's dead and gone. I'm more interested in what's in front of me right here, right now."

"That's just it, though," Lassen said as he pointed at a sage-grouse that flushed out of the brush to their right with a flutter of wingbeats. "The wildlife in front of us descended from incredible animals in the ancient past. Those mountains in the distance were pushed up by geologic forces acting a long, long time ago in *this* land—*not* far away. Heck, this ground could have been ocean floor. By learning about prehistory, we gain an enriched understanding of what *is* in front of us. Imagination and consideration of deep time can enhance any setting."

"Um, right," Durango said. "Still, I don't think a platyeracterus is going to keep me warm in my sleeping bag tonight."

"*Pterodactylus*," Lassen corrected as he raised his right index finger. "Also, for a reptile to fly, it probably had to have a fairly high metabolism. It may have actually been able to warm a sleeping bag."

"Uh, yeah," Durango said, "that. So, what did you think of that Socorro girl from the restaurant?"

"Well," Lassen said, "her cooking is as good as her looks, and those are both fine attributes, but I only talked to her for a few seconds. I don't know her, so I can't make a particularly informed assessment. For example, how good is her vocabulary? Is she bilingual? Trilingual? What do you think her science literacy is? If we were to go on a walk in the plains behind town, how many plants do you think she could identify? Does she buy into astrology? Would she be able to distinguish a sedimentary rock from an igneous one? How many bird species do you think she could recognize?"

Durango palmed his forehead in frustration.

"Lassen," Durango said, "Lassen, I told you, amigo, you want to be happy with women out here, you're gonna have to have different standards."

"Maybe you're right," Lassen said, "but I've had good conversations with women from the East at some of the train stations. Also, before the Traxton Gang tried to settle our hash back in town, I did meet an intriguing woman."

"Yeah," Durango slowly said, a bit awkwardly. "I saw you talking to her."

"Didn't have time to talk long," Lassen said, "but she was picking up a new encyclopedia. How many women do you know who collect encyclopedias?"

"Uh, some of the ones you've introduced me to," Durango said. "What's her name?"

"Athena Pryce," Lassen said.

"Nice name," Durango said. "And her name is *not* the only thing about her that was nice."

Lassen shrugged in a "Hey, what can I say?" kind of way.

A few hours later, Lassen and Durango rode in front of a dazzling sunset. Brilliant gradations of magenta, violet, and deep pink splattered across the western sky. A herd of mule deer browsing on sage-brush east of the bounty hunters looked up and saw the silhouettes of the two riders in the distance. Far to the north, a pack of coyotes howled and yipped as they gathered for twilight rodent hunting. Lassen and Durango stopped their horses at a lone rock outcrop and dismounted.

Soon, Lassen and Durango sat around a campfire at night. They fed their horses oats and lumps of sugar they had purchased in Medicine Bow. A pot of beans boiled. Bacon simmered. The powdery glowing brilliance of the Milky Way galaxy dappled the sky.

"Beautiful stars, aren't they?" Lassen said.

"I guess," Durango said, "but this bacon seems pretty beautiful to me right now."

As Durango tended sizzling bacon and stirred beans, Lassen stared up at the stars. The same amazing eyesight that allowed Lassen to shoot bullets directly into opponents' gun barrels also made him a fantastic stargazer. Lassen could identify numerous constellations with the naked eye. He noted the Big Dipper, Orion's

Belt, and a less commonly known constellation called Draco, which represented a dragon.

As Lassen lay with his head on his saddle, he pulled out his binoculars and examined Draco in more detail. Looking at Draco, Lassen recalled one of the Greek myths associated with the constellation: The 12 Labors of Hercules. In the myth, Draco was a dragon who guarded a golden apple tree that was given to the goddess Hera as a wedding gift when she married the god Zeus. The hero of the story, Hercules, had to battle Draco to the death and steal the golden apples he protected. After Draco died, Hera honored his memory by putting his image in the night sky.

Lassen thought one really had to squint to see a dragon. Still, he was intensely curious about seeing a dragon-like creature for real. Battling a dragon or something similar would be an exciting change from assorted human outlaws. Talk of dinosaurs, *Pterodactylus*, and bird evolution had primed Lassen's appetite for prehistoric wonders. He heard the howl of a lone wolf and smiled with a closed mouth and subtle sigh as he realized he was right where he belonged. However, he had taken a circuitous route to get there.

As Lassen pondered prehistory in front of a comforting, crackling campfire, he considered the circumstances that had enabled him to pursue scholarly subjects, like paleontology, despite being a bounty hunter in the West. He often surprised those who did not expect much from him when it came to encyclopedic knowledge or intellectual curiosity.

Lassen was an orphan of the California Gold Rush. Born in 1849, as an infant, he was brought to the eastern U.S. by ship around the bottom of South America. At the time, this was one of the safest and most boring ways to travel between California and the East. His parents had come West along the California Trail. Lassen suspected they may have named him after the frontier guide Peter Lassen or one of the landmarks that was labeled with his name, like Lassen Peak.

Lassen never knew his real parents and was told they died in California. In the East, Lassen moved from one orphanage to another until he was eight years old. As an orphan in New York City and New Haven, Connecticut, Lassen learned to be resourceful and use his wits and physical strength for survival. Ever since he was a little kid, he was called "durable" and recognized as intelligent.

One day, in New Haven, at age eight, Lassen saved nine-year-old Everett Fontane from teenaged street ruffians. When the fists flew, Lassen quickly devised an elaborate pulley system and managed to put several aggressors out of commission by cleverly manipulating shipping crates suspended by ropes. Lassen acted fast and did not know who he was saving, but he had a hostile history with the local street thug youths and knew an innocent needed help.

Everett's family witnessed Lassen's heroic acts and took him back to their estate for the afternoon. Lassen was in awe of the Fontanes' gardens, mansion, and magnificent library. Everett was the son of a biology professor who taught at Yale University and had married into a very wealthy family.

Though Lassen greedily ate a high quantity of gourmet cheeses without realizing or caring that he was breaking social norms, his first meeting with the Fontane family had gone well. Lassen visited the Fontanes more and more, and eventually, it was like he was part of the family. With the Fontanes, Lassen lived with well-educated children his own age, received high-quality schooling, and read and read and read. Lassen loved to read. Lassen had access to the Fontanes' expansive personal library and regularly patronized Yale University's library. He also had access to the latest scientific journals to which his adoptive father subscribed.

Starting at age eight, Lassen sat in on Professor Fontane's biology courses. While living with the Fontanes, Lassen cultivated a strong interest in nature and science in general. He also dabbled in history, law, and philosophy. Lassen's frequent reading and attention to detail made him an excellent writer. On the Fontane estate, Lassen learned how to ride horses, and he developed extraordinary marksmanship.

After his first day of shooting lessons, Professor Fontane had Lassen get his eyes tested, and the eye doctor proclaimed that Lassen possessed the most perfect vision he had ever seen. Lassen shrugged in response. After all, his vision was the only way of seeing the world he had known.

At age 16, Lassen officially enrolled at Yale. Not everything went well for Lassen at Yale. He got in trouble for fist-fighting in an effort to stop drunken hazing. He also faced trouble from peers and corrupt administrators after he exposed a widespread plagiarism and exam cheating scheme. Lassen's sense of justice and fairness could be both his greatest strength and most damaging vulnerability. Formally or not, Lassen always continued to educate himself.

Lassen first visited the West with the Fontanes in 1870 after the Transcontinental Railroad had been completed. At age 21, Lassen was so impressed with the scenery, plants, and wildlife that he never wanted to leave. He craved the wide open spaces, exposed geology, and opportunities for exploration over each horizon. The epic horizons impressed Lassen the most.

On his first trip to the West, while Professor Fontane collected plants, Lassen and Everett stumbled into serious trouble when they witnessed a U.S. cavalry troop massacre a small village of American Indians. Everett was shocked and traumatized. Lassen coolly acknowledged what happened and pursued justice. The incident led to Lassen's testimony removing a corrupt military officer. Lassen then became a freelance reporter focused on exposing corruption and getting to the truth of sensational stories.

While practicing journalism, Lassen based his activities in the West for several years and only intermittently visited the East afterward. As a reporter, Lassen was always on the move as he followed leads and pursued stories. He often lived out of saddlebags and slept under the stars. In some ways, his life as a journalist was not very different from his life as a bounty hunter.

By the early 1870s, Lassen was gaining a name as a muckraking reporter. However, being a reporter attracted serious trouble, and Lassen eventually became a sheriff's deputy, so he could more directly enforce justice. Why write about how certain people should be caught when he could go out and get them himself? Eventually, operating under the constraints of municipal law became too limiting, and Lassen opted to become a bounty hunter. Lassen continued to write newspaper articles under various pseudonyms. He knew the written word was often more effective than a gun, but he excelled with both instruments.

Throughout his travels in the West, Lassen regularly corresponded with his adoptive family in the East. Though he mostly operated in the American West, the Fontane family's wealthy connections helped Lassen get interesting jobs around the world. Lassen gained a reputation as a smart, fearless man who could solve a variety of problems and provide physical force when needed. Though he mostly worked as a bounty hunter, Lassen's jobs involved such varied tasks as escorting diplomats in India, combatting slavers in Argentina, stopping a sheep rustling ring in Australia, arbitrating diamond mining disputes in the South African Republic, and solving a murder mystery along San Francisco's Barbary Coast.

The gunfight, stampede, and other combat in Medicine Bow during the day were engaging for Lassen, but they were fairly tame compared to some of his other exploits. Lassen was actually a little disappointed by the mild levels of adrenaline he had felt, though the fistfight with Branigan was an exception.

Chapter 5: Digging into Danger

At 11:47 P.M., Medicine Bow was quiet and dark. Although Saturday nights were raucous with the arrival of cowboys from surrounding ranches, Thursday nights like this one were tame. At the jail, Deputy Caddock struggled to keep his eyes open in front of a cell filled with Traxton Gang members. He held a dime novel entitled: *Lassen Malone and the Battle at Black Butte.* He had just gotten to his favorite part of the story in which Lassen battles a group of lumberjacks on floating logs in a river in Central Oregon, but this was his third time reading the book. As such, it was comfort entertainment and did not keep him awake.

In the cell, most gang members slept. Hobart Holt was in a deep sleep, having a nightmare. *He coughed on dust and heard rocks tumble as pine timbers snapped, and a mine shaft collapsed. Darkness. Darkness everywhere. Fellow miners shouted in anguish, being crushed by rocks. Holt tried to move, but he was pinned by a massive chunk of silver ore. No matter how hard he tried to move, he could not. Everything was closed in. There was not enough space. There was never enough space.* Holt grimaced in his sleep as he relived a traumatic experience.

Being confined by a mine cave-in had inspired Holt to work for Traxton. Holt enjoyed the outlaw life much better than digging for silver ore in Virginia City, Nevada. Holt figured he was already working for robber-baron mine owners, so why not become a robber himself? More profit that way.

Outside, Tardell Traxton crept by the hitching rail near a saloon and quietly untied six horses while leading his own paint horse. Traxton stole a horse for each of his men in jail. He also stole an elegant chestnut Arabian horse that he thought he could sell for a lot of money to a buyer he knew in Cheyenne. He slowly led the horses down an alley.

"Hey, mister," a confused drunk cowboy said. "What you doesing? Whose cayuses is those?"

In a quiet instant, Traxton swung a rifle barrel into the drunk cowboy's head. A few horses lightly whinnied, but the assault happened so fast and quietly that some horses did not even notice. The cowboy dropped to the ground with blood oozing into his hair.

Traxton smoothly placed his rifle in its leather scabbard attached to his horse's saddle. The outlaw leader wore a black bandana around his face along with a gray vest, black shirt, black hat, and black pants and boots. He did not know if the cowboy was alive or dead; that did not concern him. The important thing was that a potential threat was quietly silenced. Traxton reveled in taking certain risks, but he did not want to risk being reported for horse-thieving at the moment.

Throughout his life, Traxton had recognized and eliminated obstacles, sometimes with harsh dismissal. Though not as daring and violent in his former career, Traxton had been just as cold and self-centered when he was known as Brent Cordon in the twenty-eighth century.

Cordon/Traxton had a history of only caring about those from whom he could benefit. If he could not benefit from somebody, he saw them as an obstacle. Some people had significantly helped him over the years and considered themselves his friends, but whenever they caused him trouble, and he no longer needed them, he immediately dismissed them. Cold focus and elimination of obstacles had enabled him to get his Area 54 job in which he did quantum computer technical support at one of the most prestigious government research facilities of the time.

In the twenty-eighth century, he had gotten very far for somebody in his position. However, he felt his Area 54 supervisors did not promote him fast enough or pay him enough for what he did, which he knew were tasks of which they would never be capable. Being bossed by intellectual inferiors irked him in his former life.

He had taken a corporate espionage job from Vandanite Tech and stolen a time machine after reaching his breaking point. He was frustrated and wanted to emulate the Old West outlaws in his favorite novels. They did what they wanted. They roamed wide open spaces. They were free. Now, in the 1870s, Traxton had become more legendary than many desperadoes in the fiction of the future.

As Traxton moved toward the jail, he seethed with anger. There would be no need for a jailbreak if Lassen Malone and Durango Mesquite had not intervened yet again. Traxton's history with Lassen and Durango was personal and bitter. The bounty hunters were obstacles Traxton planned to destroy once and for all.

In the jail, Branigan only pretended to sleep while he closely monitored Caddock's slumber situation. The big outlaw watched as Caddock closed his eyes and drifted to sleep. The deputy's dime novel slipped from his hands, falling to the ground. A few minutes later, Branigan sat up as he heard rustling and hoof clops. Caddock stirred but did not wake.

Traxton stood outside the prison wall and held a small cylindrical device with a transparent top. It lightly hummed and emitted faint light as Traxton used it to scan the walls of the prison. A blue holographic layout of the prison structure popped up from Traxton's scanner. In great detail, it featured the building's construction materials, architecture, and glowing images of all people inside. Traxton examined the imagery, searching for weaknesses.

He noted that Deputy Caddock was sleeping. The outlaw leader readjusted his black hat as he pulled out what looked to be an ordinary derringer pistol. He stepped forward, and a glowing yellow light beam launched from the derringer.

Branigan's eyes widened as he heard a low buzzing. A yellow plasma beam sliced into the jail wall and moved downward. Bits of brick dust emanated from the path of the cutting plasma beam. Branigan stared at the plasma beam as it carved a hole at the bottom of the prison wall. Avarette, Blaze, Gantry, and Holt slept, oblivious to the futuristic marvel. Branigan knew Traxton had special tools, but he very rarely saw them.

Branigan moved his right fingers together in anticipation as Traxton's plasma cutter finished carving an escape hole. As a section of wall fell toward ground on the outside, Traxton gently caught it with one hand and quietly lowered it into dirt.

Inside the prison, Caddock was sound asleep. With nudging from Branigan, the other imprisoned Traxton Gang members awoke and quickly stood.

"Traxton's here to bust us out, boys," Branigan whispered. "Get movin' quick-like."

Prisoners ducked through the low hole Traxton had cut. Outside, they found Traxton holding two heavy rolled blankets. He unrolled them, and a huge assortment of firearms, ammunition, and gunbelts fell out.

"Load up, boys," Traxton said.

Traxton's men quickly buckled on stolen gunbelts, holstered pistols, and loaded rifles with ammo before jumping on their new horses. Blaze was assigned to lead the stolen chestnut Arabian horse, and he tied it to his saddle.

At the sound of horse whinnying and a sudden commotion of hoof clops, Deputy Caddock opened his eyes and drew his gun. He glanced at the Traxton Gang members' cell and swore as he saw a hole in the wall and no prisoners. He rushed out the front door and ran toward the back of the prison while staying close to an exterior sidewall.

Traxton heard Caddock and intensely fanned his six-gun's hammer, launching off a fusillade of shots. One bullet lodged in the sole of Caddock's boot as the overwhelmed deputy ran back toward the front of the jail.

Traxton mounted his horse and led his men out of town in a hurry. As the sound of horse hooves pulsed into the distance, Caddock fired his gun into the air and shouted, "Lassen Malone's gonna get you! He's gonna get you, Traxton!"

As Traxton rode away, he faintly heard "Malone" in the distance. The outlaw leader's eyes narrowed in disdain. A yipping dog followed the outlaws and was soon near Traxton's horse. It was Yarfer. The dog was not quite in the way, but Traxton was annoyed by its barks and especially rageful after being reminded of Lassen Malone. As soon as Traxton noticed Yarfer was close, he abruptly moved his horse to the right. Horse hooves slammed into one of Yarfer's legs. The canine limped back toward town, howling in pain.

*　　　*　　　*

By mid-morning the next day, Lassen and Durango neared Como Bluff. The bluff looked like a tan, light red, and dirty white rock formation jutting out of the prairie. Large puffy white thunderheads hovered on the western horizon, complementing a gorgeous and sunny blue sky. A distant herd of pronghorn bounded away as Lassen and Durango approached.

As the bounty hunters got closer to Como Bluff, they heard the clinking of metal against rock. Ahead of them, several men dug in a square pit while others hauled piles of rocks with wheelbarrows. Some large fossil vertebrae were faintly visible in the middle of the dig site. One man stood above the pit, painting on a large piece of paper mounted on an easel.

A digger with calloused hands and a dusty face was not in a good mood as he dumped a pile of rocks outside the excavation perimeter. "How could I be so beef-headed as to be bamboozled into bone-hunting?" he said. "Marsh can afford a train ticket from the East, but he waits four months to pay us. Raises my bristles!"

"Excuse me," Lassen said as he rode up to the grumbling man.

"Eh, oh, hey, good morning," the digger said, embarrassed that a stranger may have heard his mumbling.

"Do you know where I can find William Reed?" Lassen asked.

"Why you lookin' for the boss?" the digger asked, suspicious. "I haven't seen you around here before. You working for Doctor Cope?"

As Lassen began to converse with the digger, the man painting put down his brush and listened.

"No," Lassen said. "Just want to talk to Reed about a job. My friend and I are looking for work."

What Lassen said was not entirely untrue. Finding Smith Emory was part of their work. Lassen did not want to say too much, for fear of tipping off Emory. For all Lassen knew, he could be talking to Emory right now.

"Hey, what have you boys been finding here?" Lassen asked. "Those look like neck vertebrae of an *Apatosaurus*. Or is it a *Camarasaurus*?"

"I don't know, mister," the digger said. "Haven't showed these to the boss yet. He can see them after we get paid."

"Hmm," Lassen said, scratching his chin. "Those bones look like they're from a sauropod."

"Actually," the digger said. "This *is* a sauropod."

"Soar of what?" Durango asked.

"Sauropod," the digger said. "Big long-necked dinosaurs. We've only been callin' these things sauropods for about a year, though. The big boss found one of these, an *Apatosaurus*, down in Colorado."

"The big boss?" Lassen asked.

"Professor Marsh," the digger replied. "You talk fancy smart like him. He might listen to you. Tell you what. I'll let you know where Reed is if you ask the big boss when we'll get paid. Don't tell him you talked to Fenton."

"Thanks, Fenton," Lassen said. "So, where's Reed?"

"He's having a picnic with the professor," Fenton said. "Reed and Marsh are over in the grove of cottonwoods at Robber's Roost." Fenton pointed.

"Thanks, pal," Lassen said.

"I was going to be heading over there soon," the man near the painting easel said as he walked over to Lassen. "I could go with you." The man had a mustache and bowler hat and wore suspenders over a white shirt.

Lassen and Durango rode up to him, and Lassen got a look at his painting. It was a watercolor and showed men with picks and shovels digging sauropod vertebrae out of the ground. It was crude, but Lassen liked that there was at least some sort of illustrated documentation of the excavation. In scientific fieldwork, context was key, and Lassen also recognized the historical significance of these early dinosaur digs.

"Howdy," Lassen said. "Not a bad painting. Nice blending of impressionism and realism, though I'm more of a romanticist when it comes to my art."

"Thanks," the painter said as he snapped both his suspenders with his thumbs. "It's not Alfred Bierstadt, but I try. Reed would say I spend too much time painting when I should be digging, but I want people to remember what we're doing here. Name's Arthur Lakes. Marsh and some of the boys here have been inspecting the quarries today. I was just going to meet them for lunch."

"You got a horse nearby?" Durango asked.

"Naw," Lakes said. "Robber's Roost isn't far. I can walk. Come on. I'll show you how to get there."

Lassen and Durango rode slowly while Lakes led them forward.

"How long you been working here?" Lassen asked.

"Only since last month," Lakes said, "but I've been digging dinosaurs for a couple of years."

"Not a common job," Durango said.

"No," Lakes said as he took off his hat and adjusted its brim. "It's not." Lakes then put his hat back on. "I used to work as a school teacher down in Colorado, but I always had an interest in geology.

In 1877, I was measuring some rocks near the town of Morrison when I found sauropod bones. Marsh is one of the only famous paleontologists in America, so I wrote to him about them, and he started paying me to get him dinosaur bones and ship them to Yale."

As Lassen, Durango, and Lakes moved past some tents, Lassen said, "You've got a nice little camp established here. Looks like you boys are settled in."

"It's alright some of the time," Lakes said, "but not when it's crawling with tiger salamanders or mice."

"Salamanders?" Durango asked. "Seems pretty dry for those."

"There's a lake nearby," Lakes said. "During afternoon thunderstorms, they'll move from the lake and crawl into the tents by the dozens. And mice have gotten into all our food and chewed up our cots."

"Sounds like a lot to cope with," Lassen said.

"Speaking of which," Durango said, "who's Doctor Cope? That digger seemed real concerned about him."

"Edward Drinker Cope," Lakes said. "He's a rival paleontologist in competition with Professor Marsh."

"I briefly met him in Helena, Montana three years ago," Lassen said. "Can't say I agree with all his theories, but he's a nice guy."

"Don't say that around Marsh," Lakes said.

"Him being nice?" Lassen asked.

"Yeah," Lakes said. "Marsh and Cope *hate* each other, though the rumor back East is that they used to be friends."

"How'd they end up hating each other?" Durango asked.

"Well," Lakes said. "I've heard a few things, though I don't know for sure how much is true. Word is that about 10 years ago, Marsh bribed some of Cope's fossil diggers in New Jersey to send bones to him at Yale instead of to Cope."

"That's pretty crooked," Durango said.

"Yeah," Lakes added, "but a few years ago, Marsh also recently exposed how the Bureau of Indian Affairs was corruptly ripping off the Sioux with inferior goods and spoiled food. He even managed to speak to President Grant about it and exposed it in the *New York Herald* newspaper."

"So, he's *part-time* noble?" Durango said.

Lakes shrugged. "Some of the Indians call him the Bone Medicine Man, but Cope doesn't have much respect for him. In 1868, in Kansas, Cope discovered a huge marine reptile called *Elasmosaurus*. He published his findings with a drawing of the skeleton showing the head attached to the tail instead of the neck. I heard that Marsh pointed this out to Cope in a very mean-spirited and humiliating way."

"So, Cope was angry and embarrassed as a result," Lassen said.

"I think so," Lakes replied. "Cope's reputation rests mainly on his work because he doesn't have university credentials. Marsh went to universities in Germany and was already Yale's Professor of Paleontology by 1866 when he was in his thirties."

"Impressive," Lassen said. "I just turned 30, and I'm no professor."

"I don't know, amigo," Durango said, "you sure sound like one sometimes."

Soon, Lassen, Durango, and Lakes approached Robber's Roost, which was a ravine under a railroad trestle at Como Bluff. A small party of men sat on the ground in the shade of cottonwood trees. Their horses were tied nearby.

One man in the group stood out. He was just under six feet (two meters) tall and had a rounded face and reddish beard. He also did a lot of talking. William Reed stood next to him.

"That's Marsh," Lakes said to Lassen and Durango as they approached the camp.

"The balding blue-eyed fellah with the beard?" Durango asked.

"Yeah," Lakes replied.

"Howdy, folks," Lassen said as he and Durango rode up to the group. "That smells good. Ham, crackers, and Swiss cheese, I reckon."

"Who are these men with you, Lakes?" Marsh asked with irritation. "Cowboys? Drifters?"

"Not exactly," Lassen said. "You know, one of your boys is making good progress uncovering what looked like an *Apatosaurus* neck a few miles back."

"What!" Marsh said. "What! An *Apatosaurus* specimen here? Reed, how come you never informed me of that?"

"First I heard of it," Reed said.

"You boys could be workin' for Cope," Reed said, narrowing his eyes with suspicion. "What are they doing here? Where'd you meet these men, Lakes?"

"Over at one of the quarries here," Lakes said. "Rode in off the range earlier today. Said they want work."

"That's right," Lassen said as he and Durango got off their horses. "I said we're looking for work, and we do *not* have it with Cope. Why would we want to work for him? He thinks evolution followed the Law of Acceleration and was powered by bathmism. Now *that's* Lamarckian predetermination nonsense."

Durango nodded and narrowed his eyes as if he knew exactly what Lassen was talking about and strongly agreed with him.

"Darwin and Huxley have it right," Lassen continued, pointing defiantly. "Natural selection *all the way*."

Nearby, Lakes and Reed raised their eyebrows, impressed by Lassen's knowledge of evolutionary biology and how adeptly he was handling Marsh's temperamental nature.

"My boy, you seem to know your stuff," Marsh said. "I'm Professor Marsh of Yale University. I'm head of the Peabody Museum. If you want work, you may have just found it."

"I'm honored, sir," Lassen said. "I saw you speak at Yale, and I read your descriptions of *Allosaurus* and *Stegosaurus* in the *Journal of American Science*."

"A young paleontologist?" Marsh asked.

Lassen shrugged with a lopsided grin. "It's a hobby."

"What about your friend?" Marsh asked, looking at Durango.

"Hi, sir," Durango said. "Uh, yes, sir, that stuff. Me too. I like things like arkeeoctoterrace and the various sauruses."

"What?" Marsh said, confused.

"He means *Archaeopteryx*," Lassen said. "We were just discussing that extraordinary evolutionary transition fossil yesterday. I wonder what else they'll find in the Solnhofen limestone."

"You don't say!" Marsh said. "The first bird with teeth. Fantastic! You boys should come over to this crate and examine the fossil mammal, crocodile, and *Ichthyosaurus* bones we found yesterday."

"Don't mind if we do," Lassen said with a grin. Marsh's initial coolness faded upon learning that Lassen was knowledgeable about prehistory.

"There were crocodiles in the Jurassic," Marsh said as he picked up a crocodylomorph vertebra bone. "There are fossil crocodile bones scattered across the Wyoming badlands."

"Intriguing," Lassen said. "Durango, if there were crocs here millions of years ago, this area may have resembled the African savanna or the swamps of Florida."

Durango nodded with an attentive expression, though he was genuinely confused and skeptical. What he saw looked like high desert plains, and he could not imagine how it would be a tropical environment, though he understood the similarities to Africa.

"Or perhaps something in-between," Marsh added, "with vast seasonal floodplains and dense forests."

"By the way," Marsh said to Reed. "When will Emory be here with the apples? No good picnic is complete without apples."

"Maybe no more than half an hour," Reed said. "Could be any minute now, though."

Emory's coming right to us, Lassen thought. *I can chat with Marsh until he shows up.*

"Find any miniature horses here?" Lassen asked. "Any *Eohippus* bones?"

"Not yet, son," Marsh said. "Most of the rock layers here seem much too old."

"I attended Huxley's lectures three years ago in New York," Lassen said. "Doctor Huxley did an excellent job describing the evolution of horses with sketches of your findings."

"He did at that," Marsh said.

"Hey," Durango said. "Who's this Huxley fellah you're talking about?"

"Renowned British scientist," Lassen said, "Thomas Henry Huxley. He's been called Darwin's bulldog for how strongly he supports Charles Darwin's theory of evolution by natural selection."

"Evolution," Durango said. "That's gradual critter change. Right?"

"Correct," Marsh said. "To doubt evolution today is to doubt science, and science is only another name for truth."

Lassen considered Marsh's words. Science often provided factual explanations for natural processes, especially geology.

However, Lassen was familiar with "science" being used to describe things like failed deadly primitive medical procedures, astrology, and spiritual mind reading. In the 1870s, the precise meaning of "science" was still being worked out. Many so-called scientists had no training or formal standards. However, Marsh was part of a new breed of scientists. Both Marsh and Cope were at the cutting edge of standardized rigorous science with peer review.

As Marsh launched into scholarly lecture mode, Lakes, Reed, and the rest of the party resigned themselves to silently eating while listening or at least pretending to listen.

"Come over here," Marsh said as Lassen and Durango moved to another crate. "I want to show you the small reptile fossils we found today. Look to be from some sort of ancient lizard but not a dinosaur."

"Wait a second," Durango said. "Aren't dinosaurs just big lizards?"

"No," Lassen said.

"He's right, son," Marsh added. "Dinosaurs have special hipbones that attach more like the legs of a bird than a lizard. They also possess characteristics of crocodiles and mammals that lizards lack."

"When I was a kid, nobody talked about dinosaurs," Durango said. "How come there's all this attention now?"

"The term "dinosaur" has only been around for about 40 years," Marsh said, "but we have recently been making discoveries at an unprecedented rate. Well, at least *I* have. Can't say the same for *Cope*! Am I right, boys?!"

Lakes, Reed, and Marsh's other employees unleashed contrived, agreeing laughter and slapped their legs.

"You said it, boss!" Reed shouted.

"Your rate of discovery *is* remarkable," Lassen said while authoritatively raising his eyebrows for emphasis.

Marsh smirked and nodded to himself in a self-affirming way.

"Lassen told me 'dinosaur' means 'terrible lizard' or 'fearfully great lizard' or something like that," Durango said. "How terrible were they?"

"That depends on the dinosaur, son," Marsh said. "*Allosaurus* was a 15 to 20-foot long carnivore that lived in Colorado. Imagine a 20-foot long reptile with knife-like teeth walking on two legs and dragging its tail. I would rather face a grizzly than an *Allosaurus*."

"Son of a catamount," Durango said under his breath. "Wait. These all look like old bones stuck in rock, but they're called fossils."

"That's because they're *fossilized* bones," Lassen said. "The bones have been replaced with rock over millions of years."

"Your friend's right," Marsh said. "Take this crocodile bone for instance." As he spoke, Marsh held up a brown crocodylomorph vertebra composed of ancient sandstone. "Back in the Jurassic, this bone belonged to a crocodile that probably stalked fish in the lakes and rivers of a warm floodplain. Enormous long-necked sauropods roamed the landscape along with peculiar-looking dinosaurs, like the plate-covered *Stegosaurus*. Sauropods and *Stegosaurus* fed on plants, and carnivores, like *Allosaurus*, hunted the plant eaters: the herbivores."

Durango scratched his chin as Marsh described a prehistoric lost world. The bounty hunter was losing focus and starting to get bored. Finding out about *Allosaurus* was notable because of its apparent ferocity, but it was long gone, so it mattered little to him. Instead of pondering the vastness of geologic time or the preservation of bone structure over eons, Durango was feeling anxious and wanted to focus more on how to handle Smith Emory. Plus, how could the desolate sagebrush and grass-covered plains of southern Wyoming be lush and full of exotic reptiles? Durango did not know, and at the moment, he did not care much. At times like this, Durango thought Lassen was losing focus on the task at hand, but he thought of a question and decided to make a contribution to the discussion.

"Professor," Durango said, "how can you tell what's plain rock and what's a fossil made of rock?"

"When it's not obvious, you can lick the specimens," Marsh said. He licked the vertebra bone he held and rolled his tongue around in his mouth. "That's certainly a fossil."

"Uh, okay," Durango said. "What does that tell you?"

"Fossilized bone, like regular bone, is porous," Marsh said. "It is full of tiny holes, and when you lick a fossil, your tongue will slightly stick to it because of the porosity."

"Hmmm," Durango said, scratching his head. "It's like your tongue gets traction."

"Precisely," Marsh said.

Durango stooped over, picked up a small rock, and licked it. "Pretty smooth," he said.

"Here," Marsh said as he handed Durango the crocodylomorph vertebra. "Try this."

Without hesitation, Durango licked the bone right where Marsh had licked it.

"Hey," Durango said. "It does stick. Nifty."

Durango passed the vertebra toward Lassen who subtly shook his head and dismissively gestured with his hand. Then Durango gave the bone back to Marsh.

"Millions of years ago," Marsh said, "the crocodile that had this bone died. Maybe from a drought or an attack from a fellow crocodile. Its body may have drifted down a river and settled to the bottom where sediments gradually covered it. Its flesh decomposed, but its bones were durable enough to survive as several hundred feet of sediment buried the crocodile skeleton over millions of years."

Marsh enthusiastically moved his hands with grandiose sweeping gestures as he talked. "Groundwater deposited minerals into the crocodile bones' pores, which turned the bones to rock and fossilized them. After millions of years, geologic uplift raised rocks containing the crocodile fossils to the Earth's surface, exposing them to the elements."

"Okay," Durango said. "When the rock with fossils was raised to the surface, rain and wind wore it down. And eventually some fossilized bones were exposed where people could find them?"

"Correct," Marsh affirmed. "Unfortunately, most prehistoric animal remains are scattered after death from scavenging and water movement. Finding a complete skeleton is rare and fortuitous. Furthermore, only so many remains happened to be fossilized."

"So," Lassen said, "how long did it take for a dead Jurassic dinosaur to become a fossilized skeleton you can excavate at Como Bluff? How long did it take for this area to transition from a tropical floodplain to high desert prairie?"

"Many millions of years," Marsh said, "but we do not know exactly how many. One million is one thousand thousands. Envision that." Marsh spread his hands far apart.

"Hard to imagine that much time," Durango said.

"Correct," Marsh said as he moved his right hand while he talked. "Our lifespans are miniscule, which makes it difficult to envision huge time scales. One minimum estimate for the age of the Earth places it at two billion years old. That's 2,000 millions."

"Son of a catamount," Durango said. "A fellow is lucky to live to be a hundred."

"The span of Earth's history makes a human lifespan seem like a pebble next to all the Rockies," Marsh said.

"True," Lassen added. "Our planet is *old*. I read about vast time scales—deep time—in Hutton's *Theory of the Earth* and all the volumes of Charles Lyell's *Principles of Geology*."

"Splendid references," Marsh said. "According to Hutton, after the Earth formed, it was reshaped through erosion, sediment deposition, volcanic eruptions, and mountain building. Lyell examined how these forces operated over enormous time spans."

"Whoa," Durango said. "What exactly does that mean?"

"Essentially," Marsh said, "wind, water, volcanic eruptions, and other forces repositioned dirt and rock over millions of years. Mountains rose and fell. Seas formed and dried up. The surface of the Earth changed, and it is always changing."

"He's right," Lassen added. "Remember when we saw seashell fossils when we rode through Kansas last year? That all used to be the bottom of an ocean. Changes like that don't happen overnight."

"And not all critters stayed the same," Durango said while observing a jackrabbit hop away at the edge of nearby cottonwoods.

"Precisely," Marsh said, "which is what makes very ancient history such a worthy field of study. Dinosaurs are now extinct, but there are lost worlds of fantastic species waiting to be uncovered in the rock."

"Extinct," Durango said. "Meaning no longer here?"

"Correct," Marsh said.

"When a species has undergone extinction," Lassen said, "all its members have died off. A French scientist, Georges Cuvier, noticed that the farther back in time animals lived, the less they looked like modern animals. Early in this century, he proposed the extinction concept when comparing prehistoric elephant fossils—mammoths and mastodons—to the remains of modern elephants."

"So," Durango said, "the Earth has been changing a lot, and different animals have been changing along with the Earth, and sometimes completely dying off."

"That's right," Marsh remarked. "Some species extinctions are mysterious, but natural disasters must have played a strong role. In Charles Darwin's *On the Origin of the Species*, he lays out how animals have been gradually evolving over time as a way to survive as their surrounding conditions changed. Darwin was influenced by Lyell's work about geologic time spans, so he envisioned time in a very big picture sense. In Darwin's proposed narrative for evolution, inherited traits beneficial for survival are passed on to future generations. Species without beneficial traits to pass on to their offspring eventually died off—went extinct. What was beneficial depended on changing environments. The animals most fit for current conditions survived. This natural selection via survival of the fittest resulted in the varieties of life we see now and all varieties that have lived and gone extinct in the past."

Durango blinked hard as he forced himself to return focus to Marsh. The professor's monologue on evolution had triggered him to zone out and start to daydream. Sure, Durango thought prehistory was *kind of* interesting, but it was all so distant, and he kept thinking about Sarita Socorro.

"Exactly," Lassen said, "animals change over time, and if they can't adapt to changing times, they die off forever. I wonder how long humans will last."

"Excuse me, professor," Reed said. "It looks like Emory's riding up with the apples." A blonde young man wearing a gun and riding a horse approached the picnic grounds. A mule carrying burlap sacks of apples was tied to Emory's horse.

Horse hooves crunched dry cottonwood leaves as Lassen turned around. Emory looked a little confused at the sight of Lassen and Durango.

"Who are these boys?" Emory asked as he got off his horse.

"Hmmm," Marsh said. "I never got your names."

"Lassen Malone," Lassen said.

"Mesquite," Durango said. "Durango Mesquite." Durango spoke with a confident edge in his voice as if identifying himself should be impressive to all.

Emory gulped with anxiety. He did not recognize the bounty hunters' faces, but he knew who they were. Traxton had warned him about Malone and Mesquite.

"We thought maybe these boys were working for Cope," Reed said.

"Uh-huh," Emory replied, nervously nodding. "I don't know. I've never seen them before. Okay, bye." Emory began to get back on this horse.

"Hold on, son," Marsh said, "you haven't unloaded the apples yet. I'm of a mind to chaw one of those right now."

"Of course, professor," Emory said as he unfastened sacks of apples from the mule.

"You alright?" Lakes asked Emory.

"Why are you in such a hurry?" Lassen asked.

"I'm fine," Emory said. "Everything's fine with me, fellahs." As Emory spoke and moved in a flustered, haphazard fashion, a letter fell from his pocket. Lassen quickly picked it up without Emory noticing.

"According to this," Lassen said to Marsh and Reed as he held the letter, "Doctor Cope was going to pay Emory for any fossils he could steal and for information on where your men are digging."

"What!" Marsh shouted, his eyes bulging with rage. "What! What's all this?!"

Marsh and Reed grabbed the letter out of Lassen's hands and tried to quickly read it with each of them holding one side of the paper. In the meantime, Emory sprinted away.

"Hold it, pal!" Durango shouted as he quickly grabbed his lariat from Yonder and swung a wide loop in front of Emory's feet. Durango pulled his lariat tight. Emory tumbled into leaves as supple woven leather bound his ankles together.

"Drop it," Lassen said as he smoothly drew his pistol and pointed it at Emory. The young outlaw gulped and slowly unholstered his gun and tossed it onto dry cottonwood leaves. Durango started tying Emory's hands behind his back.

"Malone—and Mesquite," Reed said. "I remember those names now. Of course. I heard you were around again."

"You know these boys?" Marsh asked Reed.

"Not personally," Reed said, "but I've heard of them. They're bounty hunters." Reed turned to Lassen. "Last I heard, you were after Tardell Traxton. Ever catch him?"

"No, but Traxton could be in this area," Lassen said while Durango put the finishing touches on an elaborate knot around Emory's wrists.

"Traxton the infamous outlaw!" Marsh exclaimed. "Knowing he's around adds a dash of excitement to this trip.

Reminds me of when I was charged by a buffalo bull in Kansas in 1870. The great beast was upon me, but I smote him before he could trample me under his thunderous hooves."

"Sounds like a close call," Lassen said.

"You bet it was, son," Marsh replied.

"We've heard that story before," Reed quietly muttered under his breath, just out of earshot of Marsh.

"Durango," Lassen said. "Emory might have clues about where to find Traxton. You better check for more letters."

"I've got nothing you'd care about," Emory grumbled as Durango approached.

"Sounds good, amigo," Durango said. "Then you've got nothing to worry about."

Durango sifted through Emory's vest pockets and found a bundle of letters and fossil teeth. Emory said nothing but breathed hard with anxiety. Lassen reviewed Emory's letters. Durango handed the fossil teeth to Marsh.

"*Allosaurus* teeth!" Marsh exclaimed. "Excellent condition, too. No doubt you would have handed these over to Cope. Turncoat! I ought to show you who your real boss is!" Marsh balled his right hand into a fist and sneered.

"Easy, professor," Lassen said. "There's a letter here from Traxton. Looks like Emory was supposed to 'dispose' of the Como Bluff railroad station agent next week. Seems it's all part of a plan for the Traxton Gang to rob the train."

"The station agent's David Chase," Reed said. "We actually get along with him. Emory, if you do anything to hurt Chase . . ."

Emory was silent, but his face conveyed new fear.

"Emory," Lassen said, "we've already got evidence here to convict you of theft and conspiracy to commit train robbery. Professor Marsh has plenty of men who can take you to the sheriff in Medicine Bow or Laramie."

"If you're gonna talk," Durango said, "now would be the time to do it. If you can help us get Traxton, that would go a long way for you."

"Sympathy from a jury," Lassen said. "Maybe some sort of pardon."

"Okay," Emory said. "Alright. Alright. Alright. It's true, but I didn't plan on killing the station agent. Thought I could just tie him up and stash him for a bit. My plan was to take Traxton's money and then go off to Mexico. I figured I'd lay low here while working as a bone digger and then take off after I got payment from Traxton."

"You don't know Traxton very well," Lassen said. "He never pays his men *before* they do a job for him. It's always *after* and only *sometimes*."

"Yeah, but he said—" Emory started to say.

"Trust me," Lassen said, cutting off Emory. "I've talked to a lot of outlaws to whom Traxton has broken promises. He's a slithery polecat, and you shouldn't trust him—especially where money is concerned."

"When were you going to get paid?" Durango asked.

"This evening," Emory said. "Just after sundown, I was supposed to meet Traxton about eight miles northwest of here in the badlands around Pine Butte. There's a map in the papers you took."

"He's right," Lassen said as he unfolded a map from the pile of letters.

"There's something else you ought to know," Emory added. "When I got those apples off the train, I heard that Traxton broke his boys out of jail in Medicine Bow last night. Branigan, Holt, Avarette, Gantry, and some kid will probably be at Pine Butte with him."

"Blaze?" Lassen asked. "Is that the kid?"

"Yeah, that's the kid," Emory replied. "He's a trigger finger, that one. *Loves* his guns. Crazy kid. Crazy and dangerous."

"That's a fact," Lassen said. "Was anybody hurt in the prison breakout?"

"No," Emory said, "but I heard Deputy Caddock got in big trouble for sleeping on the job, and there's also a hole in the prison wall."

"What about Britt Thornby?" Lassen asked. "You know where he and the rest of the Traxton Gang are?"

"Nothin' definite," Emory said, "but a couple weeks ago, I overheard Gantry say something about Thornby and Sheep Rock. Maybe he's there. Don't rightly know. Gantry talks a lot, but he's not very reliable."

Lassen smirked before saying, "Yeah, we've met Jed Gantry before. Reed, Lakes, I suggest you have Emory taken down to Laramie. Sheriff Gratton and Deputy Caddock are probably busy hunting the Traxton Gang now, and I doubt the prison's repaired, so Medicine Bow would be a no-go." Lassen turned toward Durango and said, "Come on, pal, we've got outlaws to snag."

Lassen and Durango untied their horses from nearby young cottonwoods. As Lassen got in his saddle, he waved at Professor Marsh.

"Thanks for the lecture, professor," Lassen said. "Once we get Traxton, we might try our hand at fossil hunting."

"Pleased to talk to you, boys," Marsh said.

"Oh, and one more thing," Lassen added. "When are you going to pay your men?"

Lakes, Reed, and the other men in Marsh's party raised their eyebrows at Lassen's question. They had all experienced issues with Marsh being stingy and paying late.

"Heck, I've been working here two weeks, and I still never got paid," Emory added.

"Shut up!" Marsh shouted at Emory.

"They seem to work hard," Lassen said, "and I doubt they're digging for their health."

"In due time," Marsh said. "I'll pay all the boys in due time."

Marsh seemed offended at Lassen's unexpected question. Lassen did not enjoy asking it, and he liked visiting with Marsh, but he had made a promise to a dig worker, and he kept it.

*   *   *

Lassen and Durango rode away from Como Bluff to the northwest. They crossed Rock Creek and spent the afternoon riding over shortgrass prairie toward the 7,000-foot (2,134-meter) plateau of Pine Butte. The butte loomed to the northwest and was surrounded by groves of pines at its base that faded into sagebrush flats. Following Traxton's map took the bounty hunters on a circuitous route designed to hide tracks. By evening, they detected fresh tracks from the outlaws' horses, but the tracks were faint.

The fluffy white cumulonimbus clouds that hovered over the plains in the morning had grown immensely. Their bottoms were now laden with water and splotched with stormy, menacing dark gray. Bright blue sky existed beyond the clouds. Portions of the plains were intermittently covered in shadow as an enormous storm grew. Thunder rocked the open range. Occasional beams of sunlight shot through gaps in the richly textured cloud layers to the west.

Horizon lightly whinnied. "Easy, boy," Lassen said. "Just a little thunder. That's nothing compared to the gunshots you're so used to."

"Looks like there could be a big storm tonight," Durango said.

"Yeah," Lassen responded. "It would effectively cover Traxton's trail."

"What's your plan?" Durango asked.

"Well," Lassen said, "we're going to be outnumbered, but based on where the gang plans to meet Emory, we should be able to sneak up behind them in the rocks. I'll do some shooting to distract and separate the gang members. We should focus on isolating Traxton from his compadres. Traxton is top priority."

Later, the sky darkened as the sun set. Thunder increased. Distant puffs of lightning lit the sky. The sunset was one of the most spectacular Lassen had ever seen and featured clouds that were black, gray, and white with growing shades of purple and red. Little holes of blue sky barely eked out an existence. Meadowlarks sang a goodbye to the day. Crickets started to chirp.

"We should be getting real close," Lassen whispered to Durango as their horses moved over eroded clay embankments.

The storm made the landscape prematurely dark. Little drops of rain began to fall, causing tiny emanations of dust on dry ground. Lassen soon smelled the rich aroma of fresh rain on dusty dirt. He took a deep breath and readjusted his hat as the rain began to pour. Lightning flashed, the landscape grew dark, thunder rumbled, and a coyote howled in the distance. Suddenly, a rifle sounded.

In the strangely glowing, lightning flash-dappled sunset twilight, Traxton Gang riders ominously appeared from behind a clay embankment about 75 yards (69 meters) ahead of Lassen and Durango. The Traxton Gang immediately fired at the bounty hunters.

Lassen and Durango pulled their rifles from their scabbards and returned fire. The outlaws rapidly retreated while firing back. To Lassen, it looked like Traxton was leading his men to cover just ahead of them. The outlaws rode closer and closer together as badland rocks in a "V" formation narrowed, enclosing a piece of flat land where Traxton's men traveled. Once the Traxton Gang reached the narrowed point, they could quickly go into the rocks and pick off Lassen and Durango.

A dazzling iridescent glowing explosion of light suddenly appeared in front of the Traxton Gang. Outlaws' horses stopped and reared. Traxton's men stopped firing, startled and confused. Lassen and Durango continued their pursuit, despite shock and confusion at the extraordinary occurrence.

A hovering metallic vehicle appeared out of the light. Inside the time machine, Adalya Nell and Professor Kira Sedora looked out windows at the darkening but still somewhat colorful sunset-glazed landscape.

"Doctor Nell," Sedora said as she read holo-projected words and flipped switches. "Cordon interfered with our temporal coordinates when we linked the machines. We landed in 1879, but we have bigger problems in that the seal on the antimatter compartment has been breached. This transporter has never had such an intense field test, and it is not ready for rigorous use outdoors."

With focused, narrowed eyes, Adalya asked, "How long will the automatic emergency sealant last?"

"Maybe five minutes," Sedora replied as she quickly got up and opened a wall compartment. She pulled out a tool and handed it to Adalya. "Go solder the seal back together while I fine-tune the seal settings from in here."

"I am on it," Adalya said as she grabbed the tool and rushed into the rain. Adalya knew she was given the more dangerous job. Rushing outside into a rainstorm in an ancient time was not a wise idea. However, Adalya was also well aware that only Sedora knew how to fine-tune an antimatter compartment seal with some of the most advanced software ever developed.

As Adalya exited the time machine, she smelled mud and sagebrush and felt cool flecks of rain on her face. While lightning flashed, Adalya briefly caught sight of several men on horses and little puffs of light exiting the weapons of two men in the distance.

Adalya was astounded that she and Sedora had stumbled into a Wild West gunfight. This was the sort of thing she had read about in a world history class as a child. This was dangerous—and somewhat intriguing—but she had a time machine to fix.

Adalya knew all too well that an antimatter compartment breach would destroy the time machine and possibly much of the surrounding terrain. Adalya used metal handholds to climb up on the roof of the time vehicle. She then quickly got to work with a sophisticated plasma welder that emitted blue bursts of energy.

Lassen and Durango continued firing at the Traxton Gang, pushing them toward the foreign hovering object that had terrified their horses. Avarette and Holt had been thrown to muddy ground by uncontrollable mounts. Avarette was not happy that his once neatly curled mustache was now misaligned, and his shiny vest was dirty. Holt was frustrated and confused, but, being a former miner, he was grateful that he was at least facing trouble aboveground.

Within 38 seconds, Adalya fixed the time machine's antimatter compartment seal. Inside the vehicle, a flashing red light turned green. Sedora sighed with relief. Adalya climbed down from the roof of the time machine and hopped onto the ground.

Suddenly, a sizzling purple bolt of lightning struck the time machine. The entire vessel briefly glowed. Faint smoke emanated from its surface.

At the same instant, jolts of electricity radiated through the metal of Lassen and Durango's rifles, and they instinctively tossed them to the side and shook their hands, which tingled from minor electrocution.

Adalya fell to the ground, mildly electrocuted from residual energy. Lassen and Durango paused as they neared the outlaws. Everybody was temporarily blinded from the lightning flash. Gunfire stopped.

Inside the time machine, Sedora frantically flipped switches and pressed buttons while monitoring holographic readouts.

"What?!" Sedora shouted as the time machine hummed, powering up for a time journey no one had specified. "No!"

Adalya regained her vision and stood up. She saw Lassen, Durango, and Traxton Gang outlaws trying to get oriented as they dealt with a chaotic series of events. Avarette and Holt tried to get their footing in mud while the other 1870s citizens were still on horses.

A brilliant translucent ripple of iridescent light blasted out of the time machine, covering a radius of about 50 yards (46 meters). Lassen, Durango, Adalya, the Traxton Gang, and horses suddenly dematerialized in sparkling flourishes of gleaming iridescent particles. A faint chime-like swirling sound drifted over the landscape.

Blaze's horse disappeared from under him, and the chestnut Arabian horse he was leading also faded away. Blaze fell toward mud, cursing and confused.

CHAPTER 6: FOSSIL STROLL DISRUPTION

Shortly after sunrise, PhD student Kailani Nakai wandered the base of Morrison Formation rock outcrops at Como Bluff in southeastern Wyoming. Kailani was 25 years old and attending a Systematics and Evolution graduate program at the University of Alberta with the goal of becoming a full-time dinosaur paleontologist.

Kailani was half Native Hawaiian and half Native American and was sometimes amused or annoyed by how often people incorrectly guessed or assumed her heritage. She wore khaki cargo pants, a button-up long-sleeve beige shirt, a well-worn brown oilskin canvas fedora, and a brown cotton safari vest. It had lots of pockets and resembled vests television journalists often wore when reporting from war zones. Kailani also wore leather lace-up hiking boots with sturdy treaded soles that enabled her to carefully negotiate steep rocky terrain. Her boots were scuffed and dusty with well-worn tread. Kailani's hair was tied back in a simple ponytail. She also carried binoculars in a leather case attached to her belt.

Kailani's outfit resembled what was often worn by paleontologists on documentaries. Kailani was not trying to fit in, but her clothing happened to be useful for fieldwork. Her vest pockets provided room for bone fragments, pens, a notebook, energy bars, and a smartphone. She also wore a canvas backpack containing notebooks, a first-aid kit, and a metal water bottle.

On this trip, Kailani used her phone to reference maps, electronic scientific papers, and paleontology e-books. She had plenty of paleontological reference materials on her phone's 512 gigabyte (GB) micro SD card.

Kailani peered closely at the ground to survey the terrain near what was known as Quarry 10 back when William Reed excavated the area in July 1879. She carefully scanned the ground, looking for bone fragments. After years of looking for dinosaur fossils, her eyes had become trained to distinguish fossil bone bits from rock. She knew bone had unique microstructure porosity that ordinary rocks lacked. If she found bone fragments, they could lead her to full bones or even skeletons, which could be eroding uphill of where she was searching.

After Reed and Marsh had met Lassen Malone and Durango Mesquite in the summer of 1879, Como Bluff quarry workers found *Brontosaurus* at Quarry 10. Marsh named *Brontosaurus*—which means "thunder lizard"—and its skeleton eventually went on display at the Yale Peabody Museum. Kailani had observed the skeleton at Yale and was impressed by its size and completeness. However, when the bones of *Brontosaurus* were originally found and displayed, an incorrect skull was associated with the dinosaur. This led to inaccurate museum displays, eventual correction of the skull issue, and reclassification of *Brontosaurus* to *Apatosaurus*.

Decades later, in 2015, further study showed *Brontosaurus* was a legitimate species, and the public and various paleontologists once again embraced the name *Brontosaurus*, but this did not mean *Apatosaurus* went away. Despite the revival of *Brontosaurus*, *Apatosaurus* was still a legitimate dinosaur based on other fossils. In fact, paleontologists believed that multiple species of both *Apatosaurus* and *Brontosaurus* lived in the Jurassic.

Kailani was hoping to find new *Brontosaurus* fossils, which may have eroded out of the rock since the last time the area was excavated. Her dissertation project focused on the ecology of diplodocid dinosaurs of the late Jurassic in North America. Diplodocids were a dinosaur group that contained famous species—like *Diplodocus*, *Apatosaurus*, and *Brontosaurus*—as well as other similar dinosaurs, like *Barosaurus* and *Supersaurus*. All diplodocids were sauropods, which were long-necked dinosaurs that were often immense. Diplodocids were known for their long whip-like tails, narrow skulls with pencil-like teeth, and their dominance of late Jurassic North America, which was home to a variety of diplodocids at the same time.

Kailani wanted to better determine how the huge long-necked diplodocid dinosaurs may have coexisted. She was researching niche partitioning and feeding habits as well as learning more about the overall Morrison ecosystem where these dinosaurs lived.

Fossilized evidence from the Morrison ecosystem was preserved in the Morrison Formation, a huge geologic rock layer spanning much of the American West from northern Arizona and New Mexico up through Colorado, Utah, Wyoming, eastern Montana, and portions of the Great Plains. The formation was named after the small town of Morrison, located at the base of the Rocky Mountains, just west of Denver.

In March 1877, about two years before meeting Lassen and Durango, Arthur Lakes found sauropod bones near Morrison before he worked for Marsh at Como Bluff. Based on isotopically dating clay minerals found in altered volcanic ash in mudstones, early twenty-first century paleontologists believed the Morrison Formation was deposited during the late Jurassic Period, approximately 157 to 150 million years ago.

Some of the most famous and popular dinosaurs of the Morrison Formation—*Stegosaurus, Apatosaurus,* and *Allosaurus,* for example—came from Colorado, Utah, and Wyoming. Internationally famous Dinosaur National Monument in northeastern Utah is in the Morrison Formation and includes a large exhibit building constructed on top of the partially excavated dinosaur fossils of the Carnegie Quarry. Much of the quarry was excavated from 1909 to 1924, and the removed fossils were sent to museums and universities throughout the United States. However, a large portion of the remaining quarry was left alone as a tourist attraction showcasing dinosaur fossils in place.

Jurassic National Monument in Utah—which includes the Cleveland-Lloyd Dinosaur Quarry—is also in the Morrison Formation and includes a disproportionately high number of *Allosaurus* fossils as well as a visitor center featuring a mounted *Allosaurus* skeleton.

Kailani had been to Dinosaur National Monument seven times but had only been to Jurassic National Monument twice. On a spring afternoon, one of her boyfriends (now an ex) was not a fan of the muddy unpaved 13 miles (21 kilometers) of road that needed to be traversed to reach the monument after leaving State Highway 10. Still, she knew his boyfriend status was limited after he struggled to keep up with her on a hike during the previous day. It was bad enough that he could not keep up, but he hardly seemed to appreciate the destination, which featured early Jurassic theropod tracks at Utah's Red Fleet State Park. While Kailani searched out and photographed tracks in the area (many were visible because the nearby lake was low), her boyfriend scrolled through his phone. Not only that, but later in the trip, he had wanted to leave the Utah Field House of Natural History State Park Museum in Vernal after only 45 minutes. He went back to their motel early, but Kailani stayed for six hours and was especially intrigued by the nearly complete *Haplocanthosaurus* specimen on display.

Kailani was in excellent physical condition, which was an essential trait necessary for standing in museums all day or undertaking successful paleontological fieldwork, which could include days of hiking through rugged terrain as well as arduous fossil excavation with hammers and picks. Kailani's looks attracted men, but her constant talk of biostratigraphy, paleoecology, and diplodocid phylogenies drove some away.

So far, Kailani had found only a few bone fragments, but she was hoping her fortunes would change. She had driven down to Wyoming from Calgary, Alberta and was hoping to find something significant before the end of her trip, though she knew finding unique large vertebrate fossil specimens from the time of the dinosaurs could sometimes be very difficult.

Kailani had secured private landowner permission for her searches at Como Bluff. She was taking some days off as part of a long weekend to do fieldwork and take a break from grading papers and being stuck inside.

The life of a science PhD student often involved being a teaching and/or research assistant who did much of the instructional or lab work of tenured professors while getting paid far less, but Kailani enjoyed teaching, and her teaching and research duties came with substantial financial aid for tuition, so she thought she had a pretty good deal.

The drive down to Wyoming was pleasant and scenic. Kailani enjoyed nice weather and listening to episodes of interesting paleontology podcasts during the 15-hour drive. Some of her favorites were *I Know Dino, Palaeocast, Terrible Lizards, Common Descent*, and *Paleo Nerds*.

Before going back to Calgary, Kailani planned to visit the University of Wyoming Geological Museum in Laramie. She had been there before and never grew tired of visiting. She loved that she could see the skeletons of *Brontosaurus, Stegosaurus, Allosaurus*, and the Eocene terror bird *Diatryma* all in one fairly small museum.

Kailani was determined to forge a career as a dinosaur paleontologist, but she also knew that paleontology was a competitive profession. Other paleontologists had encouraged her to focus on other fields of paleontology, such as climate studies, paleobotany, or the fossil fuel industry, but she wanted to study dinosaurs. That was her mission, and she knew she would succeed. Becoming a gainfully employed paleontologist of any sort was not easy, and positions focused on full-time dinosaur paleontology were quite limited. As Kailani thought back to dinosaur documentaries she had watched in her childhood, she remembered that the same paleontologists (a Canadian guy and two American men with beards) kept appearing in interviews.

Kailani had first dug up dinosaurs as a teenager while enrolled in a program that enabled members of the public to work as dig site volunteers. By 2026 and earlier, there were various volunteer dinosaur fossil fieldwork opportunities available from both academic institutions and commercial businesses. A full-time academic job in paleontology would be living the dream, but Kailani knew there were other ways she could engage in paleontology if that did not happen, including volunteer fieldwork and providing services to museums, which often relied on volunteers to help with outreach and fossil cleanup and preparation.

As Kailani picked up a bone fragment and gently set it down, she reflected on the path that led her to where she was now. In high school, she learned that in the U.S., there were no paleontology programs where one went to school and just took paleontology classes to become a paleontologist. Paleontology was a very interdisciplinary field that drew from various scientific disciplines.

Before getting into a graduate program at the University of Alberta, Kailani pursued the "Paleontology Option" at Montana State University as part of earning a Bachelor of Science in Earth Sciences. This degree required her to take a variety of classes focused on chemistry, math, physics, geology, and climatology. A few of them, like Field Paleontology, were actual paleontology classes, but most were not.

Kailani was an excellent student and excelled in all her courses, even when they did not involve paleontology. Some people thought Kailani's advanced knowledge and academic prowess had come to her easily. They were not entirely correct. Kailani was a fast learner and smart, but through the years, she had worked very hard and did not hesitate to ask for help from more qualified or knowledgeable individuals when she needed it. Just a bit of assistance from others or a slightly different way of viewing a problem sometimes gave her research a tremendous boost. Unlike some other scientists, she recognized the value of collaboration and cared more about unlocking the secrets of the dinosaurs than she did about her ego or publication record. Nonetheless, her publication record was formidable for a graduate student in her mid-twenties. As Kailani spotted another bone fragment, she wished she could just go back in time and witness diplodocid ecology for herself.

*   *   *

On the night of June 6, 1879, Sedora wiped sweat from her forehead with the back of her hand as she flicked through holographic displays and controls in the cockpit of her time machine. Then she pressed a button, shouting "Geo-temporal tracking activated. Locked on!"

The time machine sizzled and disappeared in a phosphorescence of iridescent light accompanied by chime-like sounds. The outlaw Randall Blaze fell into the mud after his horse and the horse he was leading disappeared. He looked up and squinted against bright lights as the time machine dematerialized.

*   *   *

In June 2026, Kailani continued her morning fossil search and covered her eyes to shield them from the sun as she glanced at a raven flying over. The raven ominously cawed and joined its companions feeding on the husk of a nearby old pronghorn carcass. Suddenly, all the ravens squawked in unison and flew away in a flutter of black wings. Seconds later, bright lights flashed to the right of Kailani, and she abruptly turned her head. Between Como Bluff outcrops and where she stood, Lassen, Durango, Adalya, Traxton Gang members, and associated horses materialized. The new arrivals turned their heads in confusion and squinted against the suddenly bright light.

"Where is we, boss?!" Gantry called out.

"We all get struck by lightning or something?!" Holt asked.

"No . . ." Traxton said as he frowned with dour concentration.

Then Sedora's time machine appeared right in front of Adalya and crashed into the side of a rock outcrop. It got dented, and the outside of the machine began to faintly glow blue. Inside, Sedora frantically looked out the windshield and glanced down at holo displays.

"What?!" she exclaimed as she looked at geography and chronology information on a holo display. "Why did my location change, and how did we all end up in 2026?"

As Sedora flipped switches and keyed in values, the time machine's blue glow increased. Sedora input the precise time and location in June 1879 from which she had just arrived. Suddenly, the blue glow surrounding the time machine expanded and made contact with floodplain claystones of the Morrison Formation as it radiated outward and transformed into sparkling iridescent beams of energy. The energy enveloped Adalya, the horses, and the citizens of the 1870s while it penetrated late Jurassic rock. It also swept through Kailani who stood staring in awe at what she could hardly believe she was seeing. She looked down at her disappearing hands as her vision became dappled with colored spots.

Inside the time machine, Sedora pulled back on a lever and shouted, "Activate!" Values in a holo display that included "1879" became scrambled. Suddenly, "Mesozoic Era" appeared in glowing blue letters in front of Sedora, and all references to 1879 were gone. "That's not right at all!" Sedora yelled. Then another display appeared which stated:

TEMPORAL COORDINATES MODIFIED BASED ON SURROUNDING ROCK STRATA
TEMPORAL DESTINATION: LATE JURASSIC PERIOD – 150.127856 MILLION YEARS AGO
EXTERNAL TRANSPORT BEAM INITIATED

LIFEFORMS TEMPORALLY TRANSLOCATED:
1 HUMAN (Homo sapiens) FROM 2756
1 HUMAN (Homo sapiens) FROM 2026
7 HUMANS (Homo sapiens) FROM 1879
9 HORSES (Equus caballus) FROM 1879

GEOGRAPHIC DESTINATION MISALIGNED
FINAL GEOGRAPHIC DESTINATION: WEST-CENTRAL UTAH

Sedora peered at precise decimal degree latitude/longitude coordinates that holographically appeared.

That lightning caused major problems, Sedora thought as she let out a deep breath. *Inputting temporal destinations based on surrounding geology was never part of the programming, but that could have resulted from a corruption of the geo-temporal tracking feature. And somehow another person got swept along— and why are they going to Utah instead of staying in this part of Wyoming? I have to go after them, but this vehicle needs repairs.*

The time machine hummed, and a new series of readouts stated:

TEMPORAL ERROR CORRECTED
ORIGINAL DESTINATION JOURNEY COMMENCING
FINAL VEHICLE DESTINATION: SOUTHEASTERN WYOMING, 1879

Sedora gritted her teeth and held on tight to the time machine's control console. She realized she would be lucky to even get back to 1879 as she heard strained mechanical noises and felt asymmetrical vibrations.

Chapter 7: Jurassic Dawn

Just after sunrise, a little furry rodent-like mammal with an elongated snout scurried out of a primeval forest filled with conifer trees and ferns. The creature, a *Priacodon*, scuttled across a sandy riverbank and inquisitively sniffed the air before licking up water from a calm sheltered pool connected to a river with whitewater rapids in its interior. Suddenly, the tiny mammal squeaked in alarm and retreated into the forest as iridescent bursts of light appeared above rushing water.

Lassen and Durango (still on their horses) and Adalya materialized above rapids. The Traxton Gang and their horses materialized above water farther downriver. People and horses fell into rapids with dramatic splashes. Just north of the river, Kailani fell from the air onto the edge of the riverbank. The surface of the ground was sandy and cushioned her fall. As she gained her bearings and stood up, she realized not everyone had it so easy.

Lassen and Durango managed to stay mounted as their horses frantically swam toward shore. Horizon and Yonder were good swimmers and pumped their legs hard, propelling themselves toward the shore where Kailani stood.

Without a horse to shield her impact, Adalya plunged beneath the surface of the river. In remarkably clear water, she opened her eyes and saw *Morrolepis* and *Hulettia* fish while small turtles swam away from her in fear. A lone crayfish picked its way over gravel.

Seconds later, Adalya's head popped out of the water. She was a fair swimmer, but the rapids overwhelmed her. Adalya struggled about 30 feet (nine meters) downriver from Lassen and Durango. She swiveled her head, trying to figure out what was happening and where she was. Then she noticed Lassen and Durango.

"Help!" Adalya shouted. "Over here!"

Lassen and Durango turned their heads toward Adalya. Both bounty hunters were shocked, confused, and disoriented, but few things grounded them better than rescuing beautiful women.

"Just stay above water!" Lassen shouted over the sound of noisy foaming rapids.

"One rescue coming up, miss!" Durango added.

Durango unfastened his lariat and threw a wide loop toward Adalya. The bounty hunter nearly fell off his horse as he leaned as far as he possibly could to ensure his lariat achieved maximum distance.

As remorseless, pulsating water tugged harder on her legs, Adalya reached out and barely caught the end of Durango's rope just in time. Adalya tightened her grip and pulled on the rope with both hands. With the expert skill of a veteran roper, Durango wrapped his lariat around his saddle horn, providing a firm anchor. Durango was no rodeo cowboy, but he had learned from some of the best in Cheyenne.

Though Horizon and Yonder angled toward shore, the river was strong. Rapids forced Adalya and the bounty hunters downriver. Adalya pulled herself farther up Durango's lariat. She blinked quickly and frequently as foamy water splashed into her eyes.

"Hey!" Durango shouted at Lassen. "I thought I saw Traxton and his men when we hit the water!"

"I see them right now!" Lassen said as he pointed downriver.

Traxton, other outlaws, and horses flailed in the river, which was especially turbid in their vicinity. Despite the rapids, two riderless horses made their way onto land: Blaze's gray horse and the stolen chestnut Arabian he was leading. The horses were no longer tethered together, and they trotted into nearby forest.

"Oh, yeah!" Durango yelled. "There they are!" Then the Traxton Gang seemingly disappeared in an instant. "Son of a catamount!" Durango proclaimed.

"Yeah . . ." Lassen apprehensively replied as he realized what had happened to the Traxton Gang. "Yah, Horizon! Yah! Keep it moving, boy!"

Durango also encouraged his horse. "Old Yonder, you'll get so many oats when we get out of this!" Yonder neighed with dismay. "Alright, alright," Durango said. "I guess you're only middle-aged— and I'll add molasses." Yonder nodded approvingly.

Adalya's eyes widened as she turned around to see the river disappear off a vertical cliff face. She was soon only feet from the rim of an 80-foot (24-meter) high waterfall.

Horizon finally made it to the sandy edge of the riverbank. Lassen breathed hard and smelled the piney odor of conifers and musty forest duff. He turned to the right and nodded at Kailani who stood nearby on the riverbank.

"Hello, miss!" Lassen called out over loud rapids.

Kailani tentatively waved a greeting as she stepped forward. In the meantime, Yonder made it to land where the strong black horse planted himself like a post. Durango dismounted and began to pull on his rope, hand over hand, bringing Adalya toward him—he hoped. At the moment, he could no longer see her.

Surrounded by rapids, Adalya gripped Durango's lariat as tightly as she possibly could as she felt her feet edge over the waterfall. She groaned with tough effort as she tried to summon the strength to pull herself forward, but the water was too strong. Adalya held her breath and went under.

Back on shore, Lassen smoothly slid off Horizon and helped Durango pull Adalya toward shore.

"We're not strong enough!" Lassen shouted. "We need more power!"

"No, I know I can do it!" Durango said.

"I'm not sure physics are on our side!" Lassen replied.

Suddenly, Lassen and Durango felt their efforts get easier as a new force pulled on the rope. They quickly turned around and saw Kailani pulling on the rope a few feet behind them. Arms honed by months of swinging rock hammers and carrying heavy dinosaur encyclopedias and plaster-jacketed sauropod fossil leg bones were an effective advantage in the struggle to beat the waterfall and rescue Adalya.

"Much obliged, ma'am," Lassen said as he turned his head back to the river. "All together now! I think we've got this!"

The bounty hunters and paleontologist pulled the rope hand over hand. Adalya felt the lariat she gripped move away from the waterfall. She held on tight as the other time travelers slowly pulled her out of the strongest currents and into calmer water.

As soon as the current subsided, Adalya launched to the surface, gasping for breath. She was flummoxed, exhausted, and an immense amount of adrenaline coursed through her. Nailing a difficult quantum physics calculation in the lab was exciting, but nothing like what Adalya had just experienced. By almost losing her life, she felt more alive than ever.

A few minutes later, Adalya slogged onto the river's north shore. She moved soaked and glossy dark brown hair out of her face to get a better look at her rescuers as she stepped onto wet, sandy ground. Anxious and confused, she wondered who these people were and what had gone wrong with the time machine. She also wondered where Sedora was and if she was okay.

"Thank you," Adalya said. "I am indebted to you."

"Happy to help, ma'am," Durango said as he took off his hat with a flourish.

"Glad we could be of service, miss," Lassen added.

Lassen tipped the brim of his hat up with his right hand. He took note of Adalya's British accent. Though he had visited five continents, he still found her accent charming. Durango took note of Adalya's striking golden brown eyes, symmetrical attractive face, and certain curved physical features. Kailani thought Adalya looked unnaturally elegant and pristine, almost like she was genetically engineered or at least always got the right amounts of sleep and had really good exercise and nutrition. Lassen and Durango thought she looked way better than anybody they had met in the 1870s, but Lassen thought she seemed oddly out of place somehow, like a slightly more evolved human.

"Who are you?" Kailani asked. "Who are these two dudes? Why did a bunch of cowboys just go over a waterfall? Where are we? What happened? Are my molecules still assembled properly? My hands were disappearing earlier."

Adalya gasped as she continued catching her breath. She considered how much information she should reveal. UTAC protocols prohibited sharing too much information with citizens of the past, but she had just almost died, she could be stranded wherever she was forever, and these people had saved her life. She thought it would be logical to be transparent and straightforward to enable full cooperation and trust to get through whatever was about to happen. If there was an opportunity for mind-wiping later, she would consider it, but survival was top priority.

"Based on your word choices," Adalya said. "I am guessing you are another scientist."

"Yeah, I am," Kailani said.

"What is your field of study, and what year did you come from?" Adalya asked.

"Paleontology," Kailani said. "And I was in 2026 when you all showed up."

"I am from 2756," Adalya said, "and these two men and the others who arrived here are from 1879. However, I am confident this is not 1879, 2026, or 2756. We all traveled through time."

"Whoa," Durango said, "hold the telegraph. We're in a different *time*? Exactly what time?"

"I am not sure," Adalya said as she looked up at sunlight through forest branches and heard strange shrieking in the distance. "If we are still Wyoming, this could be the distant future or the distant past relative to our temporal departure points."

"Time travel," Kailani said under her breath. "Time travel. Brilliant! I know the laws of physics say it's possible, but I never thought I'd experience it. This is heavy." Kailani had grown up on time travel stories—including a popular trilogy of movies—and she enjoyed science fiction. As a result, she readily understood and embraced the general concept of time travel. To Lassen, the concept was jarring and confusing.

"This doesn't make sense," Lassen said. "Just through existing, we're always traveling forward through time in the present, but how could one travel backward at all or far forward? Is there a version of me still living life in 1879 beyond the time I left?"

"Theoretically, there will be," Adalya said, "but only if you survive and return to a time beyond your departure point. The version of you that left is the version you are right here, right now, but if you were to go back to a time in which you were still alive, you could encounter your younger self. This would not be a copy of you but simply you existing before you went back in time."

"Okay . . ." Lassen said with hesitancy.

"Versions," Kailani said. "Are we even ourselves? When I was zapped here, my hands looked like they were disappearing."

"You should be over 99.972538 percent intact," Adalya said, "and essentially yourself."

"But not exactly myself?" Kailani asked, cocking her head with concern.

"Perhaps not," Adalya said.

"What?" Durango said with confusion while he held his right hand inches from his eyes.

"So, we got copied?" Lassen asked.

"In a manner of speaking," Adalya said.

"But if we got copied," Lassen said, "shouldn't I have an original somewhere?"

"No," Adalya said. "You were not duplicated. You were broken apart at your departure time and reassembled in whatever time this is."

"How?" Lassen asked. "How could somebody even live through that? That doesn't seem scientifically possible. How could the body completely break apart and then form again? I saw people and horses fading away around me. It was like we were being broken apart molecule-by-molecule and moved to some*where* or some*time* but how?"

Adalya sighed before saying, "I will try to explain the basics of how time travel technology works. I am assuming you all saw an unusual vehicle just before your time jumps."

"Yep," Durango said. "Big weird metal thing. What was it?"

"In the most basic terms," Adalya said, "it is a time machine."

"A *time machine*," Lassen said. "A vehicle that enables you to travel through time?"

"Precisely," Adalya said.

"I never heard of such a thing," Durango said.

"I suppose you would not have," Adalya said. "The novel *The Time Machine* by H.G. Wells gets published in 1895, so the term must not be widely known in your culture yet. The machine itself is simply a modified vehicle that hovers with levitation technology invented in the twenty-third century. It typically hovers about a meter above any surface, but it can fly higher as needed. The actual time travel function of the machine is powered by contact between matter and antimatter."

"Antimatter?" Lassen said with confusion. "What is that?"

"In a basic sense," Adalya said, "it is oppositely charged matter."

"Opposite to what?" Lassen asked.

"Standard matter," Adalya said. "Every particle has a twin antiparticle with an opposite charge. For example, electrons have antielectrons, which are called positrons."

"What's an electron?" Lassen said.

"Oh," Adalya said, "electrons had not yet been discovered by your time. They are tiny particles with negative electrical charges that compose matter at an atomic level. They are found in atoms along with protons and neutrons."

"Okay," Lassen said, "I know what an atom is."

"The particles I am talking about are all small pieces of matter or energy," Adalya said. "Contact between matter and antimatter is explosive. For antimatter-powered time travel, scientists in my time use a combination of antihydrogen and standard hydrogen to create a tremendous amount of temporalport energy that surrounds and envelopes a time machine, creates a transversable wormhole by ripping space-time itself, and transports the machine and its occupants particle-by-particle at a speed faster than light through the wormhole. The wormhole appears and disappears so quickly that it is virtually invisible to the naked eye, though light reflection artifacts are visible as transported objects dematerialize. We had a lot of problems with surpassing light speed until we developed an infinite mass neutralizer."

"Infinite mass neutralizer," Kailani said as she bit her lower lip and furrowed her brow. "Part of Einstein's theory of special relativity says that if something nears light speed, its mass will become infinite—infinite mass—and it will never be able to go any faster than light. But, I read once that based on equations, backward time travel is possible if light speed can be surpassed. So, did you use an infinite mass neutralizer to enable faster-than-light nonlinear time travel?"

"Yes," Adalya said, nodding her head in surprise. "Yes, we did."

"What's temporalport energy?" Lassen asked.

"That is a term we coined in the twenty-eighth century," Adalya said. "It describes the energy that makes time travel possible."

"Wormhole," Durango said. "You mentioned we traveled through a wormhole. What do worms' holes have to do with this?"

"'Wormhole' is a physics term," Adalya said. "I used it to describe a shortcut through time—a bridge in the form of an energy tunnel that connects one distorted portion of time to another. Imagine folding North America in on itself so the Pacific coast and Atlantic coast are right on top of each other. Are you following?"

"Kind of," Lassen said while Durango stared at nearby trees in confusion.

"The time travel we just experienced is like that," Adalya said. "A wormhole connected the time we just left to the time we are currently in. By the twenty-sixth century, we were able to generate wormholes and transport materials through them, but back then, wormholes were only used as shortcuts through space."

"Why did we have to break apart into our constituent particles?" Kailani asked.

"To survive the physics of being in a wormhole," Adalya said. "If you were not disassembled in a controlled manner, the wormhole would disassemble you in a very undesirable fashion. Before traveling through the wormhole, the time machine and its occupants are exposed to temporalport energy, which breaks the vehicle and time travelers into super cold rubidium atoms in a Bose Einstein condensate state. The particle conversion process occurs nearly instantaneously. When objects—including people—are broken into rubidium atoms, they release light that contains all the information needed to reconstruct the objects. For our time jumps, the reassembly light and the broken-down particles of our bodies traveled through a wormhole at a speed that is faster than light."

"Wait a second," Kailani said, "if everything is moving faster than light, how does the light with reassembly instructions move faster than . . . itself?"

"It is insulated in a force field capsule capable of faster-than-light travel," Adalya said.

"Uh, okay," Kailani replied.

"So," Lassen said. "Let me get this straight. We got broken into atoms, which passed through a wormhole along with light containing the directions necessary for our bodies to be reconstructed after arrival on the other side—and once we got to the other side, we arrived in a different time—and we got reassembled?"

"Yes," Adalya said, impressed with Lassen's comprehension.

Durango stopped staring at trees and turned toward Kailani and Adalya.

"Let's take a break from the science talk for a bit," Durango said. "Ladies, we haven't even been introduced yet. I'm Durango Mesquite. You may of heard of me."

Lassen shook his head. It appeared as if he and Durango had just become time travelers—and learned time travel was a thing. He was still trying to comprehend the concept of time travel and wanted more explanations and evidence. In contrast, after momentary surprise, Durango seemed nonchalant within minutes and was already distracted by women.

Durango paused to wait for recognition. "Well, anyway, I've got quite a reputation in Wyoming and the other territories out West. My partner here is . . ."

"Name's Lassen Malone," Lassen said with casual confidence as he subtly lifted an index finger in greeting. "In 1879, Durango and I were chasing down an outlaw gang at sunset in Wyoming when a flash of light took us to Como Bluff during the day and then to here seconds later."

"I'm Kailani Nakai," Kailani said. "In 2026, I was searching Como Bluff in Wyoming for dinosaur fossils when I saw you people, a bunch of cowboys, and a spaceship-looking thing show up. Then there were bursts of light, and we all ended up here."

"I am Doctor Adalya Nell," Adalya said, "and I am a quantum physicist who was working at a Wyoming research facility in 2756, which is 877 years beyond 1879 and 730 years beyond 2026."

"Physicist," Kailani said. "Of course. So, why were you traveling back in time in the first place, and what exactly happened in 1879 and 2026?"

Adalya summarized a convoluted series of events while Durango stared into the forest, and Lassen and Kailani asked follow-up questions. Adalya discussed her work with Professor Sedora, their pursuit of Brent Cordon, their arrival in 1879, and the lightning strike, which caused a malfunction in which temporalport energy radiated outward instead of inward and transported nearby objects through time. Adalya speculated that the lightning was responsible for the seemingly random time jump to 2026, and she explained that more damage to the time machine in 2026 brought them to their current time. Lassen and Durango explained their history with the Traxton Gang and confirmed that those outlaws were the time travelers swept away in the river.

"Why do you pursue them?" Adalya asked. "Are you law enforcers?"

"Yeah, you could say we are," Lassen said. "Not officially, though. We're bounty hunters. Justice drives us."

"And fortune and adventure," Durango added.

"Bounty hunters," Kailani said with unease. "So, you kill for money?"

"No, ma'am," Lassen said. "We bring them back alive when we can." He turned toward Adalya and asked, "How long do you think we'll be here?"

"Professor Sedora could arrive at any minute," Adalya said, "and return us to our respective times, but the damage to the time machine may be irreparable. We could be here a very long time."

"When are we?" Kailani whispered to herself with serious contemplation as she examined the nearby vegetation and thought over the possibilities. Based on the plant life, she knew it was possible that they were in the distant past—maybe even the Mesozoic. Then an intense hope sparked inside her. Could it be? Could she actually be in the late Jurassic? She had to find out.

"Let's move toward the edge of the cliff," Kailani said. "We should get a better idea for where and when we are."

"Good idea," Lassen said. "From a high vantage point, we can assess the terrain and maybe see if Traxton and any of his gang survived."

The time travelers walked toward the edge of the cliff with Lassen and Durango leading their horses by the reins.

CHAPTER 8: PROFILES IN DINOSAURIA

Lassen, Durango, Kailani, and Adalya pushed through dense vegetation as they walked toward the edge of a cliff where cascading water tumbled into a sparkling clear pool. A splash sprinkle-generated rainbow shimmered above the waterfall's impact zone.

Lassen shoved aside cycad fronds. He thought they looked like short palm trees with narrower fronds. They reminded him of sago palms he had seen in southern Japan when he and his friend Diego were hired to recover a stolen crown for a Belgian duke. Still, Lassen knew sago palms were actually more closely related to conifers than to true palms.

Tree ferns grew between clusters of cycads. To Lassen, they resembled ferns he had seen in the Pacific Northwest of North America, but they sprouted from wooden trunks with rough brown bark instead of straight from the ground. As he looked closer, he realized he had seen very similar plants in New Zealand.

Thick, tall bunches of *Equisetum* grew beneath the tree ferns and cycads. *Equisetum* was the genus name for a plant known by a variety of common names, including horsetail, scouring rush, and puzzle weed. The *Equisetum* had green tubular, segmented stems. Mature *Equisetum* resembled tall, dark green tubes, whereas younger plants sprouted short, bright green needles. Some mature *Equisetum* plants grew over seven feet (two meters) tall. Lassen had seen *Equisetum* at the edge of rivers in the 1870s.

Over the sound of the loud waterfall to his right, Lassen heard strange shrieking and low guttural booming. Then he and the other time travelers emerged from the vegetation and had a clear view of the landscape visible from the top of the cliff. Lassen and Kailani stood to the left of Durango and Adalya.

Lassen's eyes grew wide, and he dropped Horizon's reins. Kailani's eyes sparkled with instant tears, and she smiled as a wave of rapturous joy washed over her.

"Son ... of ... a ... catamount ..." Durango slowly said with wide, unbelieving eyes.

Adalya smugly smiled and nodded her head. Lassen flashed a dashing grin of white teeth and felt around Horizon's saddlebags for his binoculars without taking his eyes off the landscape. At the same time, Kailani pulled her binoculars out of their leather case on her belt.

Lassen saw plains, forests, and sparkling strings and splotches of water extending for hundreds of miles to the north and east. The air was crystal clear with a slight warm breeze blowing from west to east. Puffy gray-white clouds floated in the distance. Rain from the previous night had cleansed the sky of dust.

Lassen smiled as he viewed the epic floodplain of the prehistoric Morrison Basin. Millions of years later, this landscape would be preserved as the Morrison Formation rock layer and repeatedly buried before eventually becoming partially exposed in the American West of modern times.

Low mountains stood to the west of the basin and were fringed by forested foothills. Expanses of pinkish granite bedrock projected out of the higher portions of the mountains. Dense clusters of forest and undergrowth covered the foothills' lower expanses and followed the edges of rivers and streams onto the plains. Vast flat fern prairies dotted with termite mounds dominated most of the landscape. An enormous lake shimmered far to the north. Lassen could barely make out the shape of sand dunes just beyond the lake. Mountains—as well as distant conical volcanoes with gases billowing from their rims—marked the end of the visible horizon to the northwest. If he had any doubt that he traveled through time, this view completely erased it.

Cycads, araucarian conifers, tree ferns, sequoias, and gingko trees made up much of the forests. Lassen also saw cheirolepidiacean conifer trees and shrubs. Cheirolepidiacean plants would be extinct by modern times. They did not look familiar to Lassen. In contrast, some of the araucarian conifers reminded him of monkey puzzle trees he had seen when he was pursuing a notorious slaver in southwestern Argentina. The tallest of these trees were about 150 feet (46 meters) high. He also saw araucarian conifers that resembled Norfolk Island pines he had observed while treasure hunting in the South Pacific. The tallest sequoias visible were about 170 feet (52 meters) high and looked very similar to giant sequoias Lassen had seen in the Sierra Nevada Mountains of California. The gingkoes were in more open stands than some of the other trees. Ginkgoes would exist in the 1870s and be native to China, but Lassen remembered them from urban landscapes in the northeastern U.S. where they had been planted for decoration.

Most rivers and streams flowed east and north from the west and south. Many streams and rivers snaked across the floodplain in large, complicated branching systems. A few major rivers—500 to 1,500 feet (150 to 460 meters) wide—crossed the landscape, and some of these drained into the massive lake to the north. Streams and rivers were sandy and braided.

Seeing semi-tropical-looking verdant savanna scenery in the American West impressed Lassen, but he was especially awestruck because he saw *dinosaurs*. Not fossil skeletons. Not sculpture reconstructions, like those he had seen at the Crystal Palace in London. Lassen gazed at living, breathing dinosaurs with muscles rippling under their skin. He saw big dinosaurs, little dinosaurs, active dinosaurs, and resting dinosaurs and was struck by how colorful they were.

Lassen and Kailani peered through binoculars at the prehistoric wonderland that unfolded below them. For a few minutes, the bounty hunters and scientists silently took in their surroundings.

Small flocks of pterosaurs swooped over the plains. Lassen quickly tracked them with his binoculars. The pterosaurs were *Mesadactylus*, which were pterodactyloid pterosaurs with small stubby tails. They flapped leathery, fuzzy reptilian wings above a majestic primal kingdom. Lassen did not know what species the pterosaurs were, but they reminded him of artwork he had seen of *Pterodactylus*, which lived during the Jurassic in Germany. The *Mesadactylus* were bright green with beige underbellies and dark red mottling on their backs. They flew with six-foot (two-meter) wingspans and bared conical teeth when they loudly screeched. Despite the *Mesadactylus's* wide wingspans, they each weighed a mere one and a half pounds (one kilogram).

Through his binoculars, Lassen followed a flock of *Mesadactylus* as they swung low and started passing a dinosaur herd. Lassen refocused his binoculars to get a better look at some of the dinosaurs, which he recognized as sauropods. Then he lowered his binoculars and turned left, distracted by Kailani who was weeping and starting to hyperventilate.

"Ma'am," Lassen said. "You okay?"

"Yeah," Kailani said as she lowered her binoculars from her eyes. "Yeah, sorry. Yeah. I'm good. I'm very good. Sauropods, ornithopods, *Stegosaurus*—this is a spectacular Mesozoic menagerie."

"Bit emotional, isn't it?" Lassen said.

"Yes," Kailani said as she cleared her throat and loudly sniffled. Kailani smiled and sighed before saying, "I've studied things like this most of my life, but it was always with fossils and rock. I never thought I would see dinosaurs and their habitat alive. To live and breathe the experience of being in the Jurassic, it's—it's overwhelming. Too see dinosaurs alive—I'm a dinosaur paleontologist, so this is indescribably wonderful."

"Yes, it is," Lassen said with a smile as his eyes slightly watered. "Yes, it is."

Kailani put her binoculars back in their case, pulled her phone out of a vest pocket, and began taking numerous photos and videos.

"What's that?" Lassen asked as he arched his eyebrows in curiosity.

"It's a cell phone," Kailani said. "It's primarily a communication device, and I can explain more later, but right now, I'm using it as a camera. I can record photos and moving pictures with it."

"I actually know what a camera is," Lassen said. "It's so small. And moving pictures. Amazing. I've never heard of those."

Durango repeatedly muttered, "Wow . . . wow . . . wow."

To his right, Adalya gazed out onto the plains with one hand shielding her eyes from the sun. She then began adjusting instruments she detached from her utility belt.

Lassen scanned the sauropods with his binoculars. He guessed they made the low grunting and booming that echoed across the landscape. Sauropods were the most prominent animals on the floodplain. The adult sauropods were enormous with long snake-like necks and tails. They also walked on elephant-like legs. Most of the biggest sauropods Lassen saw ranged from roughly 40 to 90 feet (12 to 27 meters) long.

Juvenile sauropod herds of various species were especially numerous across the plains and outnumbered the adults. The smallest of the juveniles were striped and mottled in a variety of earth tones, whereas larger subadults had colors and patterns that appeared intermediate between those of the tiniest sauropods and the adults.

Lassen could tell there were different sauropod species, but he did not know any of their names. Fossils of some of them had not been discovered by 1879. Some also looked similar but slightly different from each other. Lassen had always imagined sauropods with wrinkly elephant-like skin. Though many had skin folds, overall, their skin was more pebbly than elephantine.

The adult sauropods came in a variety of colors and patterns that included bright striping and intricate mottling. Some of the colors reminded Lassen of parrots, exotic lizards, and snakes from the tropics. Some patterns also brought to mind colorful North American birds, like western tanagers, meadowlarks, and certain wild duck species.

"They're so colorful," Kailani said as she regained her composure. "I suppose that when you're that size, it doesn't matter if a predator can see you."

"Not all those sauropods are colorful, though," Lassen said. "Looks like the younger ones aren't."

"Camouflage for predator evasion," Kailani added.

"I bet it is," Lassen said. "I thought these big long-necks would be drab colors, like elephants and rhinos, but they're not."

"These sauropods must be able to see color very well, like birds," Kailani said. "That's not the case for large mammals in modern times."

Lassen noticed that all the sauropods walked on straight legs with their tails and necks held above the ground. They also seemed strong, active, and possibly warm-blooded as they fluidly moved their necks and tails. This differed from what Lassen had read about sauropods in the 1800s. Some scientists in Lassen's time claimed sauropods were lethargic dumb beasts that had to spend most of their time in water to support their weight. Some paleontologists also incorrectly believed that they dragged their tails and walked with a sprawling gait, like lizards.

The sauropods Lassen saw had somewhat supple necks generally held in S-shaped positions when not flexed in one position or another for feeding. A few sauropods flexed their necks to reach high-level conifer needles and gingko leaves. Other sauropods selectively picked at choice bits of ground-level vegetation as their straight horizontal necks rotated from side to side in wide arcs. Some particularly long-necked sauropods stretched their necks far out over muddy wetlands to nibble on nutritious low-growing aquatic plants while they comfortably stood on dry land.

"Those are some flexible necks," Lassen said.

"Yes, they are," Kailani added. "I met some sauropod researchers at a Society of Vertebrate Paleontology annual meeting who would not be happy to see this."

"Why not?" Lassen asked.

"It disproves their theories about neck flexibility," Kailani said. "They thought various sauropods had stiff straight necks with a very limited range of movement. Still, they never properly took into account the cartilage and musculature of live animals when they ran computer simulations with skeletal models, so I'm not surprised."

"Seems to me," Lassen said, "that those sauropods eat whatever they want and move their necks accordingly." Lassen then pointed at smaller dinosaurs built much differently and remarked, "Those dinosaurs about the size of big cows look like *Iguanodon*."

"Close," Kailani replied, "but I believe those are *Camptosaurus*. They're smaller than *Iguanodon*, but they're related, and both species are ornithopods with thumb spikes."

Herds of *Camptosaurus* fed in groups far from the sauropods. These dinosaurs were about eight feet (two meters) tall at the hip, roughly 25 feet (eight meters) long, and weighed about 1,500 to 2,000 pounds (680 to 907 kilograms). They had dark brown mottling on the tops of their bodies, and it faded into burnt orange, tan, and yellow shades as the color patterns extended onto their legs, tails, and underbellies.

Most *Camptosaurus* fed on four legs, but their front legs were much shorter than their back legs. Several *Camptosaurus* moved on two legs as they raised their bodies to reach higher plants or engage in social skirmishes. The *Camptosaurus* nipped off vegetation with beak-tipped snouts and ground tough cycad fronds and conifer shrubs with their teeth.

Small bipedal dinosaurs fed near and among the larger dinosaur herds. A few were also swimming across a large river.

"What are those little ones scurrying all around and swimming?" Lassen asked.

"*Nanosaurus*," Kailani said as she adjusted the focus on her binoculars, "though they were formerly known as *Othnielosaurus*—named after Professor Othniel Charles Marsh, who is famous for his role in the Bone Wars. My gosh. You probably lived while that was happening."

"Bone wars," Lassen muttered with a bit of confusion. "I met Professor Marsh only about seven hours ago. Durango and I talked to him near a dinosaur dig site at Como Bluff on the same day we zig-zagged through time."

"You met Marsh!" Kailani said. "What's he like?"

"Well," Lassen said, "the professor knows his stuff, but he came off as a bit abrasive. He'd be an interesting dinner party guest, but I wouldn't want him to be my boss."

"Fits with what I've read," Kailani said, still peering through binoculars at the *Nanosaurus*.

The *Nanosaurus* were small bipedal herbivores that weighed approximately 11 to 30 pounds (five to 14 kilograms) and were roughly two and a half feet (one meter) tall and six to seven feet (two meters) long. They were bright green with turquoise mottling on their backs. The male *Nanosaurus* had saggy bright red neck skin folds. Many scurried among sauropod herds, eating short young fern sprouts. They also sliced *Equisetum* with tough diamond-shaped teeth. *Nanosaurus* were the most common dinosaurs visible.

Lassen pointed down to the plains as a different species of bipedal dinosaur moved out of riverbank forest. They were between the size of the *Nanosaurus* and *Camptosaurus*. "What are those?" Lassen asked.

"I think they're *Dryosaurus*," Kailani said. "They're another ornithopod, like the *Nanosaurus* and *Camptosaurus*."

Dryosaurus were less common than the *Nanosaurus* and moved in small herds. They had the same general body configuration but were larger, weighing about 200 to 250 pounds (90 to 113 kilograms). They were also two to four feet (one half to one meter) tall at their hips and six to 10 feet (two to three meters) long. They had orange mottling on their backs and sides and light blue underbellies, but their heads and the tips of their tails were bright yellow. The *Dryosaurus* fed on tough plants close to the ground and tended to be farther away from sauropod herds than the *Nanosaurus*.

"What are those big green-brown sauropods with the boxy heads?" Lassen asked as he moved his binoculars.

"*Camarasaurus*," Kailani said. "They're the most common sauropod species down there and also the most common dinosaur in the fossil record for this time and place, but interestingly, in my time, they are not very well-known to the general public."

The *Camarasaurus* were bright green with white underbellies and diamond-like brown patterns—resembling those found on rattlesnakes—on the tops of their bodies. They had shorter necks and tails compared to other nearby sauropods. Their heads were also more compact and box-like, and each featured a slight crest on its top. The crest on males was bright blue, whereas the crest on females was light brown. Adult animals were about 50 feet (15 meters) long and 15 feet (five meters) high at the shoulder. Some *Camarasaurus* held their necks about 20 feet (six meters) high as they strode over the plains. Others fed on low, tough shrubs and small conifers. *Camarasaurus* herds roamed throughout the floodplain and tended to concentrate near forest edges and tougher woody vegetation.

Subadult *Camarasaurus* chewed the fronds of low ferns and swallowed them whole. In contrast, the adults used their robust spoon-shaped teeth to chew tough araucarian conifer sapling needles. Near the bend of a river, several young *Camarasaurus* fed alongside fully-grown *Diplodocus*.

"Niche partitioning," Kailani said as she focused binoculars on juvenile *Camarasaurus* feeding with adult *Diplodocus*. "Different species are feeding on different plants, and the young of the same species are even feeding on different plants than the adults."

"Interesting," Lassen said as he moved his binoculars to view the same area as Kailani.

"So," Lassen said. "*Camarasaurus* looks impressive and must be well-known because of a good fossil record. Why isn't it popular in your time?"

"I think because it's kind of in the middle compared to other Morrison sauropods," Kailani said. "It's the not the biggest, tallest, or longest in its habitat."

"Looks pretty big to me," Lassen said.

"Yes," Kailani replied. "Some of those adults probably weigh about 30,000 pounds, which is about twice as big as an African elephant, but other dinosaurs here are taller or longer. The *Camarasaurus* are macronarian sauropods, but there's a bigger macronarian sauropod species that may be in the area. *Camarasaurus* are also not as long as diplodocid sauropods."

"Like those really long ones?" Lassen said as he pointed down at a group of sauropods feeding on ferns beyond the *Camarasaurus*.

"Exactly," Kailani said as she moved her binoculars to focus on the other dinosaurs. "Those look like adult *Diplodocus*: quintessential diplodocids. Beautiful. They even have dermal spines on their backs and tails. It looks like the fossil skin impressions from Wyoming's Howe Quarry showing diplodocid spines are representative of diplodocids in general. Brilliant."

"The spines are those yellow spike-like structures on their backs?" Lassen asked.

"That's right," Kailani said.

The *Diplodocus* were the longest animals visible. Most of the adult *Diplodocus* were 80 to 90 feet (24 to 27 meters) long. They were primarily light turquoise with beige underbellies. Their tails were mottled with a mix of dark and light turquoise lateral patterns. Their tall backs were adorned with lateral yellow stripes and white speckling. The yellow stripes continued up the dinosaurs' necks and gradually turned to black striping closer to their heads. The male *Diplodocus* had bright reflective orange-yellow neck folds that hung down under their lower jaws. Lassen thought the *Diplodocus* color patterns were very similar to what he had observed on collared lizards in the American Southwest.

All the *Diplodocus* carried extremely long whip-like, finely-tapered tails that regularly swayed. The back legs of the *Diplodocus* were much larger than their front legs. They had very muscular pelvises, and their tails angled upward, well above land.

Though much longer than the *Camarasaurus*, the *Diplodocus* were more slender and weighed about 20,000 to 30,000 pounds (9,072 to 13,608 kilograms). The bright yellow dermal spines on the tops of the *Diplodocus* were tallest on the backs of the animals and tapered to lower heights along their tails and necks.

Kailani continued looking through binoculars as she spoke. "I bet those spines are made of keratin. It's the same material that comprises human fingernails, horn coverings, and animal hooves. Keratin often does not fossilize, which is why fossil evidence for spines comes from skin impressions instead of bones."

"Intriguing," Lassen said as he glanced down at his fingernails and quickly looked up as a shrieking pterosaur flew over. Lassen then focused his binoculars on a group of adult *Diplodocus* feeding at ground level.

Not counting dermal spines, the *Diplodocus* were approximately 15 feet (five meters) tall at the top of their back hips. A few *Diplodocus* lifted their heads to over 20 feet (six meters) high to grunt at each other. *Diplodocus* necks methodically swayed from side to side in wide arcs as some individuals stripped leaves from ferns and cycad fronds with small pencil-like teeth. The *Diplodocus* feeding on ground-level plants moved at a steady three miles (five kilometers) per hour.

"Compared to the *Camarasaurus*," Kailani said, "the *Diplodocus* have longer, narrower, and more delicate skulls. They also have thinner teeth and appear to be swallowing food whole instead of grinding it. Differences in skull construction and tooth configuration explain why the *Diplodocus* tend to focus on lower-growing softer plants, whereas *Camarasaurus* are eating tougher, higher vegetation."

Lassen moved his binoculars and saw a huge herd of *Diplodocus* far in the distance that were digging shallow holes with their back legs. "What's going on way out there?" Lassen asked, pointing.

"Let me see," Kailani said as she adjusted her binoculars. "Brilliant. I think they're digging nests. This reminds me of the Cretaceous sauropod nesting sites found at Auca Mahuevo in Argentina in South America."

Kailani shifted her binoculars to another sauropod species before saying, "Yesssssss. Apatosaurs! I think those are *Apatosaurus*, but it's hard to tell without seeing the skeletons. They could be *Brontosaurus*."

"I've heard of *Apatosaurus*," Lassen said, "but not *Brontosaurus*. They're both called apatosaurs, though?"

"Yes," Kailani said, "both *Apatosaurus* and *Brontosaurus* fall within the apatosaur sauropod group, and apatosaurs are diplodocids."

Kailani watched a few lone *Apatosaurus* feed on the plains. They resembled *Diplodocus* in terms of overall body shape and feeding habits, but they were bulkier than their smaller diplodocid relative and weighed approximately 40,000 pounds (18,144 kilograms)—roughly twice as much as *Diplodocus*. The adult *Apatosaurus* were 70 to 80 feet (21 to 24 meters) long and light sky blue with red lateral striping. They had whip tails, like *Diplodocus*, and were about the same height. The *Apatosaurus* had dermal spines resembling those of *Diplodocus*, but they were bright red. They also had thick, heavily muscled bulging necks with wide vertebrae. The necks of male *Apatosaurus* had saggy metallic dark blue skin, which reminded Lassen of the blue on the necks and underbellies of male western fence lizards during their breeding season.

"So, what's the difference between *Apatosaurus* and *Brontosaurus*?" Lassen asked.

"They're very similar," Kailani said. "They both look like bulked-out *Diplodocus*, but *Apatosaurus* is more bulked out. I'd probably have to see them side-by-side to know which is which. *Apatosaurus* has a higher, wider neck than *Brontosaurus*. *Apatosaurus* and *Brontosaurus* also have different neck-to-head attachment mechanics, and *Apatosaurus* has a lighter snout than *Brontosaurus* and thus may make higher-pitched vocalizations."

"Sounds pretty technical," Lassen said.

"You don't know the half of it," Kailani said as she put away her binoculars and retrieved her phone to shoot photos and videos.

Lassen focused his optics on a lone male *Apatosaurus* feeding near a grove of tall ginkgo trees.

"In the twentieth century," Kailani said, "*Brontosaurus* was famous and inaccurately depicted for many years. There has also been a lot of confusion about its true identity and how its classification has changed. The first discovery of an apatosaur skeleton was in Colorado in 1877. It was named *Apatosaurus ajax*, so its genus was *Apatosaurus*, and its species was *ajax*."

"Of course," Lassen said. "I sometimes forget that dinosaurs are named with the two-part genus/species scientific name convention, but we often only refer to them by their genus names. That must be why their names are always italicized in publications. Our common names for dinosaurs are usually the first half of a scientific name."

"Right," Kailani said. "Often, only one individual of any given dinosaur genus is found. It can also be difficult to determine different species of a dinosaur genus based on minimal or poor quality fossils. *Apatosaurus ajax* was discovered in 1877, but in

1879, another apatosaur skeleton—which was nearly complete—was discovered at Como Bluff by Marsh's workers and named *Brontosaurus excelsus*. However, its full whip-like tail wasn't recovered, and its skull wasn't found."

"That could be a problem," Lassen said. "I'm sure Marsh would want to show off a nearly complete skeleton, but he wouldn't like that the skull was missing."

"Exactly," Kailani said. "When Marsh first reconstructed the skeleton of *Brontosaurus* in a drawing, he based the skull on a partial *Camarasaurus* skull that was found four miles away from the site of the *Brontosaurus* skeleton. Though it's now obvious that a macronarian skull on a diplodocid sauropod doesn't make sense, it took the broader paleontological establishment a long time to realize and accept that. In the meantime, *Brontosaurus* became the most famous early depiction of a sauropod, and the public fell in love with it."

"Interesting," Lassen said. "Sauropods are not well-known by the public in my time."

"Marsh seemed to have based the first reconstructions of *Brontosaurus* on *Camarasaurus*," Kailani said. "In addition to a macronarian skull, it was also depicted with a shorter tail that didn't taper to a fine point as diplodocid tails do. For years, *Brontosaurus* skeletons were mounted in museums with *Camarasaurus* skulls. In the early 1900s, better apatosaur skeletons were discovered in Utah, and one was found with a skull only 13 feet away that fit onto the neck. The skull was a narrow diplodocid skull, like that of *Diplodocus*, and much different than the boxier skull of *Camarasaurus*."

"What about the inaccurately short tail?" Lassen asked. "How does that get fixed?"

"In the same area of Utah where the new skull was found," Kailani said, "fossils were also found that showed apatosaurs had long whip-like tails."

"Okay," Lassen said, "that seems to settle some of the problems with how *Brontosaurus* was reconstructed, but what was the issue with its identity?"

"In 1903," Kailani said, "based on new material, *Brontosaurus excelsus* was recognized as a species of *Apatosaurus*, so its genus name was changed, and it became *Apatosaurus excelsus*. This created the impression that *Brontosaurus* was never its own dinosaur and was always just a type of *Apatosaurus*."

"But it ended up being its own thing, right?" Lassen asked as he continued to peer through binoculars at a male *Apatosaurus* near a grove of gingkoes. The *Apatosaurus* stood near a wide, placid river and raised its head high above the ground.

"Yeah, I'll get to that," Kailani said, "but you would think its appearance would be settled by the early 1900s."

"Seems that way," Lassen said. "With the correct skull and better tail remains, *Brontosaurus* could be re-created to look like some of those long dinosaurs down there." Lassen pointed at a herd of *Diplodocus*.

Kailani sighed and said, "Despite science being all about logic and evidence, old ideas can die hard in paleontology, like any other scientific field. An accurate depiction of what is now known as *Brontosaurus* didn't become widely accepted until after a 1978 scientific paper made a compelling case for apatosaurs having diplodocid skulls. As a result, museum displays were eventually corrected, and the *Brontosaurus* name fell out of favor. The prevailing view became one in which *Brontosaurus* was never a valid genus—especially the depiction with a *Camarasaurus* skull. Many people thought *Brontosaurus* was simply a misclassified *Apatosaurus*. However, in 2015, a detailed study of diplodocids was published, and it demonstrated that *Brontosaurus excelsus* was different enough from *Apatosaurus* to validate *Brontosaurus* being its own genus."

"So, *Brontosaurus* is a legitimate genus name and dinosaur after all?" Lassen asked.

"Yes," Kailani said.

To the right of Kailani and Lassen, and just out of earshot, Durango occasionally glanced through his binoculars, and Adalya kept adjusting her instruments.

In a low voice, Durango said, "Should we tell them we're ready to move on? They've been talking a *really* long time."

"Not yet," Adalya said. "If you listen closely, you can learn a lot. The nuances of dinosaur classification will probably be useless for our survival, but knowing their feeding habits and ecology could prove valuable."

"What's ecology?" Durango muttered.

The male *Apatosaurus* Lassen viewed through binoculars looked around and reared up on its hind legs. Its huge pelvic muscles and tail supported an animal that had become much taller. With its front legs dangling in the air, the *Apatosaurus's* head was 35 feet (11 meters) above the ground. The dinosaur tore off a mouthful of sumptuous, fresh green ginkgo leaves and lowered its body. With tremendous force, its front feet hit the earth.

"Bipedal rearing to reach high canopy vegetation!" Kailani exclaimed as her eyes became watery again. "Of course they totally did that! With its tail, it's like a tripod."

Lassen gaped in astonishment. After hitting the ground, the *Apatosaurus* unleashed triumphant rumbling booming sounds from its mouth and neck. Lassen saw the shiny blue skin along its neck undulate with vibrating air as it vocalized. He wondered if the dinosaur was calling for mates.

Most *Apatosaurus* stripped away the soft leaves of young tree ferns and other ground-level plants as they boomed and grunted. In contrast, other *Apatosaurus*—and some *Diplodocus*—reared on their hind legs as they plucked leaves and needles from the tops of very tall trees. The diplodocid sauropods shifted into tripodal feeding positions with ease and leaned back on their tails.

Some diplodocids let their front legs dangle as they reared. Others used thumb claw spikes on their front legs to grip trees and steady themselves. Lassen heard a thunking sound as an *Apatosaurus* jabbed a thumb spike into the trunk of a sequoia tree. Some *Apatosaurus* got firm grips on trunks and rotated entirely around trees as they ate as much high canopy material as they wanted.

As Lassen looked closer at the *Camarasaurus* and *Diplodocus*, he noticed similarities in their feet and remarked, "Looks like all the sauropods out there have thumb spikes on their front feet."

"Yeah, that's right," Kailani said. "If you look closely, you'll see that they walk with their thumb spikes held off the ground. This helps keep them sharp. Their back toes are also raised above the ground because of large fatty pads on their feet."

Although the sauropods' thumb spikes were prominent, their other front foot toes were very reduced and essentially elephant toe-like nubs. In contrast, the sauropods' rear feet had a more typical dinosaurian appearance with prominent claws.

Most *Apatosaurus* were accompanied by one to three *Stegosaurus*, which was the one dinosaur Lassen could confidently identify. Lone individuals and small groups of brightly colored 20 to 30-foot (eight to nine-meter) long *Stegosaurus* fed throughout the plains and slowly plodded along at about four miles (six kilometers) per hour. These bizarre four-legged herbivores weighed about 11,000 pounds (5,000 kilograms) and were roughly 15 feet (five meters) tall overall with 10-foot (three-meter) back legs and shorter front legs.

They had tiny beaked heads and two pairs of deadly spikes projecting out laterally near the ends of their tails. About 17 plates—some pentagonal and some triangular—adorned the back of each *Stegosaurus*. These plates were arranged in two rows of alternating pairs and reached heights of roughly three feet (one meter). The plates were largest above their hips and tapered to lower heights toward their heads and tails.

"What do the *Stegosaurus* use their plates for?" Lassen asked as he pointed at a trio of the animals.

"I don't know for sure," Kailani said. "Possibly for regulating temperature or maybe for mating displays."

The *Stegosaurus* were dark green with yellow underbellies. The plates of males were red with starburst black patterns in their centers. The plates of females were a monotone light orange. The tail spikes of the *Stegosaurus* were bright blue and consisted of bone cores covered in horn-like keratin sheaths that tapered to sharp points. *Stegosaurus* plates were also covered in keratin, and the largest resembled sharp-pointed pentagons without the rounded corners visible in fossil skeletons. The plates were generally smooth but had fine low ridges running up and down them.

Stegosaurus fed in the same areas as *Apatosaurus*, but they focused on tough cycads the apatosaurs avoided. *Stegosaurus* chopped cycad fronds with their beaks, shredded them with leaf-shaped teeth, and used strong tongues to help swallow their food whole. Occasionally, a *Stegosaurus* reared on its hind legs to eat conifer tree needles. The largest *Stegosaurus* on the plains regularly ate at least 110 pounds (50 kilograms) of food per day just to stay alive.

Suddenly, Kailani and Lassen heard deep, low honking sounds reverberate through the air. They quickly looked left.

Several hundred feet northwest of the time travelers, trees at the edge of the plains shook as animals brushed against them. This was a fair distance but still closer than most of the dinosaurs scattered throughout the distant prairies. With an enormous snap, a huge araucarian conifer fell down. Then a small herd of sauropods slowly emerged from behind a stand of enormous sequoias. Kailani teared up again as she realized what they were.

"Oh, brilliant, brilliant, brilliant!" Kailani euphorically proclaimed.

"What are they?" Lassen asked, furrowing his brow.

"*Brachiosaurus!*" Kailani said. "More precisely, *Brachiosaurus alithorax*. Discovered by Elmer Riggs in Colorado in 1900. Gigantic macronarian sauropod. Iconic. Famous. Rare for the Morrison Formation. Probably the tallest and heaviest dinosaur in this area."

"I never knew they existed," Lassen said, "but I can see why people would remember *Brachiosaurus* over *Camarasaurus*."

Tears streamed down Kailani's face as she stared at the dinosaurs. She put away her binoculars and took more videos and photos with her phone.

At the edge of a wide, shallow pond at the base of the foothills, a herd of four *Brachiosaurus* moved gracefully as they fed on the needles of tall sequoias and on the light green leaves of tall ginkgo trees.

The *Brachiosaurus* held their heads 30 to 50 feet (nine to 15 meters) above the ground and were about 20 feet (six meters) tall at the tops of their front shoulders. The legs, chests, and undersides of the *Brachiosaurus* were bright sky blue, which faded into intricate striated patterns of light brown and tan on the tops of their backs. The herd contained three females and a male. The male had saggy light purple folded neck skin and a small bright metallic-looking purple dewlap under his lower jaw. As they fed, the *Brachiosaurus* softly honked at each other, using crests on top of their heads as resonating chambers.

Unlike *Apatosaurus* and *Diplodocus*, *Brachiosaurus* had front legs that were taller than their back legs. The *Brachiosaurus* were about 60 feet (18 meters) long. The big male weighed about 100,000 pounds (45,359 kilograms).

"They must have to keep a lot of blood pumping to support being so tall and massive," Lassen remarked.

"Yes, they do," Kailani said. "For adult *Brachiosaurus*, blood is pumped from a heart weighing more than 800 pounds, and it moves over 25 feet up to the brain. *Brachiosaurus* are estimated to eat 400 to 900 pounds of food per day."

"Impressive," Lassen said. "That's a lot of food to keep them going. I bet the landscape can only support so many. Helps explain why they're rare. They're relatively close compared to the other dinosaurs—and enormous. Every time they take a step, I feel like the ground should be shaking, but it's not."

"Interesting observation," Kailani said. "Some people in my time thought sauropods shook the earth when they walked. However, biomechanical studies indicate they have substantial soft tissue pads on the bottoms of their feet that cushion their steps. So, in a manner of speaking, they are basically tiptoeing on cushioned heels."

"So, they're quiet, despite their bulk," Lassen said. "Fascinating, but it makes sense. When I was around elephants in Africa a few years back, their footsteps were actually really quiet."

"Elephants have cushioned pads on their feet," Kailani added.

"Of course," Lassen said.

To the right of Kailani and Lassen, Durango stretched his arms over his head and heavily yawned. Adalya sighed and put her hands on her hips while her eyes drifted to the left with impatience.

CHAPTER 9: TRACKING TIME

"Alright," Adalya said as she and Durango moved left toward Lassen and Kailani. "The local wildlife is quite interesting, but we should probably figure out what to do next."

Durango said, "I reckon you two have been talkin' for nigh on two hours already."

"Twenty-three minutes, 38 seconds—actually," Adalya said.

"I didn't see any sign of Traxton or his men," Lassen said, "but I was a bit distracted by the dinosaurs."

"A bit?" Durango said. "Sure. Anyhow, I had plenty of time to look, and I looked hard with binoculars and didn't see any people or horses down there. They could all be takin' a long agua nap at the bottom of that waterfall."

"Possibly," Lassen said, "but I wouldn't count on it. Traxton's a survivor—and we've seen Jed Gantry get out of how many close scrapes?"

"About eight," Durango said.

"More like eight and half if you count what happened in El Paso," Lassen remarked.

"I reckon so," Durango said.

"Not relevant," Adalya added. "The vegetation is thick along the river, which bends toward the hills and out of sight a few kilometers to the north."

"Traxton's men could have floated out of view," Lassen said, "or they could be hiding in the trees."

"Miss Nakai," Adalya said, "when do you think we are?"

"Late Jurassic Period," Kailani said. "Based on the dinosaur species out there, I'd say we're in the upper Kimmeridgian Age or maybe somewhere in the Tithonian Age of the Jurassic."

"How many years ago is that relative to where we came from?" Adalya asked.

"Well," Kailani said, "geologically speaking, 1879, 2026, and 2756 are all essentially about the same time and basically the blink of an eye away from each other. We're in an area that will be preserved as the Morrison Formation rock layer, which gets laid down about 157 to 150 million years before our times. Based on the animals out there, I'd say we're in an area that will be preserved in rock as the upper part of the formation, so we're probably about 150 million years in the past."

"How threatening are those creatures?" Adalya asked.

"Hard to say," Kailani said. "They've never seen people before—assuming we're the first time travelers here—so they might be especially afraid of us or totally unconcerned. Could vary based on species or individual. My guess is that it's like being around wildlife in modern times."

"Makes sense," Lassen added. "As long as we don't threaten their young or interfere with mating activities or a carnivore's food stash, we should be fine. Durango and I have seen lots of wildlife on our travels. Animals usually don't pose much danger."

"Yeah," Durango said, "we've seen deer and coyotes and such, but these are dinosaurs, Lassen. Remember when Marsh was talking about *Allosaurus*?"

"Oh, yeah," Lassen said. "Well, relative to the amount of plant-eating herbivores, predator densities tend to be low in any given habitat, so we might not see any *Allosaurus* or other carnivores."

"I wouldn't be so sure," Kailani said.

"Umm—what, uh, how's that?" Durango asked as he abruptly jerked his head left, then right—suddenly on alert for a nearby meat-eating dinosaur.

"Well," Kailani said, "with such a tremendous amount of prey nearby, there are bound to be predators waiting and watching—and maybe at higher densities than modern times, but I suppose that could depend on their metabolism. There are also a lot more predator species than *Allosaurus* out there. In fact, the late Jurassic has the biggest variety of large carnivorous dinosaurs out of any time in the Mesozoic."

"How many?" Lassen asked. "Which ones?"

"A fair amount," Kailani said as she removed her phone from a vest pocket and turned it on.

"Whoa," Durango said as he pointed at Kailani's phone. "It's a thick glowing card! Wait, I saw you holding that earlier, but I didn't get a good look at it."

"Just a phone," Kailani said. "A portable communication device from my time, but it has other resources including electronic books—and it can function as a camera to record still pictures and motion pictures."

Kailani opened a downloaded paleontology e-book and scrolled to a page showing a painting of an *Allosaurus*. She held her phone up, so the other time travelers could see. Lassen raised his eyebrows. Adalya sighed with unease.

Durango slowly whistled and said, "Son of a catamount. I hope we don't run into him."

"*Allosaurus*," Kailani said, "is the most common large carnivore in the late Jurassic in this area. By modern times, *Allosaurus* fossils will be particularly abundant in the Morrison Formation—specifically *Allosaurus fragilis* fossils. There were several species of *Allosaurus* in the Morrison Formation. The *fragilis* species can be found higher in the formation, which means it's more recent. *Fragilis* fossils are the most commonly found *Allosaurus* remains in modern times, and based on the dinosaurs we saw on the plains, I think it's a safe bet that if we see any *Allosaurus*, they will be the *fragilis* species. *Allosaurus jimmadseni* lived earlier and is found lower in the formation's rock layers. Its head crests are shaped differently compared to those of the *fragilis* species."

"Intriguing," Lassen said. "I read about *Allosaurus* in the *American Journal of Science*, but in my time, few of its fossils had been collected. Nobody was sure exactly what it looked like."

"*Allosaurus fragilis* averaged about 30 feet long and nine feet tall at the hip," Kailani said. "Or, in terms of the metric system, 12 meters long and three meters tall at the hip."

"Metric what?" Durango said.

"Metric or customary works for me," Lassen said.

"I did not know people of the twenty-first century still used customary measurements," Adalya said. "Primitive. I remember my metric-to-customary conversions from history classes, but Americans stop using the U.S. customary system for measurement after they join with Canada in the twenty-third century."

"Whoa," Durango said, "the U.S. will join *Canada*? I always forget Canada's up there, eh."

"We were there just last year," Lassen said. "Remember when we had to deliver a prisoner to Fort Edmonton up in Alberta?"

"Oh, yeah," Durango said. "And he only spoke French. You could understand him, but I couldn't. Area looked an awful lot like northern Montana."

"I go to graduate school in Alberta," Kailani said.

"Oh, so you're not even a professor or museum official yet?" Adalya said.

"Not yet," Kailani replied. "Only a PhD student who's been in the same program for years. The dissertation process can last a long time."

"Dissertation . . ." Durango said. "That some kind of bake-off competition?"

"In other words," Adalya said, "you're a real paleontologist, but you get paid low wages to teach, and granting your credentials is dragged out as a result."

"Something like that," Kailani said, "but I like my program."

"Same thing happens in the 2750s," Adalya said. "I was smart enough to get around all of it and go straight to pure research when I was 11, but some of my friends got caught up in it. Mister Malone, did you go to college?"

"For a time," Lassen said.

"And?" Adalya asked.

"The learning was good, and the library was great," Lassen said. "The people—eh, not so much."

"Let's get back to talking about dinosaurs," Durango interjected.

"Fair enough," Kailani said. "Anyway, one pound is the same as about half of a kilogram, and one meter equals about 3.3 feet."

"Huh," Durango said.

"I'll just use customary measurements when I talk," Kailani added. "In addition to getting up to about 30 feet long, *Allosaurus fragilis* could weigh roughly 1,500 to 2,000 pounds. But there's another large carnivore that's a bit smaller and probably lives around here." Adalya brought up an image of *Ceratosaurus*.

"Not too bad," Lassen said as he read part of Kailani's phone screen. "Only about 20 feet long. Intriguing and distinctive horns on its snout."

"And some were even bigger than *Allosaurus fragilis*." Kailani brought up more dinosaur images. Lassen and Durango eagerly examined them while Adalya stepped onto a large rock and looked over their shoulders.

"*Torvosaurus*," Lassen said, looking at another picture. "Doesn't look too much bigger than *Allosaurus*."

"Oh, it's definitely bigger," Kailani said. "Its skull could be over five feet long, and it could weigh over 4,000 pounds. That's about twice as much as *Allosaurus fragilis*."

"*Allosaurus frag-alus* doesn't seem so bad right now," Durango said.

"*Fragilis*," Lassen said.

"There's one more big one you should probably know about," Kailani said.

"Which one's that?" Lassen seriously asked.

"*Allosaurus anax*," Kailani said. "The largest *Allosaurus* species ever discovered. Its scientific name means 'different lizard king,' and it could also be in this area."

"That's a weird name," Lassen remarked. "Different from what?"

"What it used to be called," Kailani said. "*Saurophaganax maximus*."

"Ooooo," Durango added. "Now *that's* a fancy name."

"Yeah," Kailani said, "it means 'king of the reptile eaters,' but a paper published in 2024 showed that what had been known as *Saurophaganax* was actually based on a mix of *Allosaurus* and sauropod bones, so the *Allosaurus* bones were re-described and given the name *Allosaurus anax*. Only minimal fragmentary fossils had been found by my time, but *Allosaurus anax* is estimated to be about 40 feet long and weigh 8,000 to 10,000 pounds."

"That's one big chompy boy," Durango said.

"What about *Tyrannosaurus rex*?" Adalya asked. "*T. rex* would be its abbreviated species name. Are there any *Tyrannosaurus* out here? That's one species that had been a prominent part of popular culture for centuries by my time."

"No, luckily," Kailani said. "*Tyrannosaurus* is even bigger than *Allosaurus anax*, and it could crush bone with teeth that were essentially steak knife bananas in terms of size and lethality, but it won't live until the very end of dinosaur times, about 84 million years in the future relative to when we are. *Tyrannosaurus* will be a resident of the late Cretaceous, about 66 million years before modern times. A pretty recent dinosaur when you think about it. With *Tyrannosaurus* and other advanced carnivores, the Cretaceous may have worse dinosaur hazards than the Jurassic."

"*Tyrannosaurus* sounds bad," Durango said.

"Encountering one would be," Kailani said, but my main concern in the Cretaceous would be the dromaeosaurs—some of the deadliest predators that ever walked the Earth. At least there shouldn't be any large dromaeosaur species here."

"Dromaeosaurs," Lassen said. "I never heard of them."

"Dromaeosaurs are a dinosaur group that are also called raptors," Kailani said.

"But raptors are birds of prey," Lassen said.

"True," Kailani replied, "which is one reason 'dromaeosaur' is a more fitting name for the group. Dromaeosaurs are infamous predatory dinosaurs that are prevalent in the Cretaceous Period and known for bird-like skeletons, speed and agility, and formidable sickle-shaped foot claws." Kailani held up her phone to show a picture of a *Deinonychus* skeleton. She zoomed in on a foot claw.

"Whoa," Lassen said. "It's disproportionately large and would be even larger and sharper with a keratin sheath over it, which it must have had if it's like modern-day animal claws. Those look like they could be used to slice open an herbivore's neck."

"Maybe," Kailani said, "but by 2026, some paleontologists thought they were more suited for piercing and gripping. Most dromaeosaurs discovered in the fossil record are also relatively small predators. For example, despite what is depicted in popular culture in the twenty-first century, *Velociraptor* from Mongolia is about the size of a turkey, and *Deinonychus from* Montana is only somewhat larger. However, large North American dromaeosaurs did evolve, including *Utahraptor*, which was about 20 feet long."

"Those are no cougars or bobcats," Durango said.

"Yeah," Lassen replied, "but some of the carnivores here in the Jurassic are huge. It probably takes many square miles just to support a big carnivorous dinosaur. If the Morrison Basin of the Jurassic was the African Serengeti, these dinosaurs would be the lions and leopards. Hmmm. Lions hunt in prides."

"Some of the Jurassic carnivorous dinosaurs may hunt in packs," Kailani said, "but paleontologists in my time don't really know. There's more evidence to suggest some dromaeosaur species hunted in packs."

"I recommend we make our way down to the plains," Adalya said. They should be safer as we can more easily spot predators and be located if help ever arrives."

Adalya pulled a small metallic hexagonal device off her belt and pressed a button on it. In response, a blue three-dimensional holographic terrain image burst out.

"Whoa," Lassen muttered as he saw the futuristic marvel of a hologram for the first time.

"Son of a catamount—that looks like magic," Durango said.

"Just like in a movie," Kailani muttered.

"Just a holographic display from my database orientation module," Adalya said. "In my time, this technology is centuries old. Unfortunately, this module has sustained major damage, likely due to proximity to the lightning strike in 1879. Most terrain and orientation features seem to operate fine, but all encyclopedia database files are damaged and inaccessible. If we need paleontological knowledge, we will have to rely on Miss Nakai's expertise and on the severely outdated information found in publications stored on her communication device."

"Thanks," Kailani dryly said, "but I'm not sure how long we'll be able to use reference materials on my phone. Based on remaining battery power, we might only get a few more hours out of it."

"No problem," Adalya said as she pressed a metal device on her belt, triggering a slight buzzing.

Kailani looked down at her phone as her battery charge level jumped from 62% to 100%.

"How'd you do that?" Kailani asked.

"Basic universal sonic energy charging" Adalya said. "As long as your phone battery's physical components remain intact, the charge should last you about 30 years—give or take two and a half months."

"Battery charging through sound," Kailani muttered. "Incredible."

"What did you call that glow-maker thing?" Durango asked. "And what exactly does it do?"

Adalya paused to think of terms nineteenth and twenty-first century citizens would understand. In response, she said, "It's a database orientation module. It's like having a compass, all forms of survey equipment, a tracking device, and the information from every encyclopedia ever published crammed onto one tiny electronic device that projects images made of light."

"Wait a second," Lassen said. "Electronic device—electricity has a lot of potential. Just last year—1878 from my perspective—an electricity-powered incandescent lightbulb was invented. If electricity can transfer light, maybe it can transfer information and lots of other things."

"You are on the correct track," Adalya said. "In the year 2756, we have enormous amounts of information readily available in portable electronic devices."

Adalya panned over different parts of terrain on her holographic map by brushing her fingers against it.

"So," Lassen said, "you can scan terrain and get full topographic images of the landscape?"

"Yes," Adalya said, "but the range is limited. We can also determine our exact position relative to the terrain. This device has a quantum accelerometer. No communication with mechanical celestial objects, like satellites, is needed for us to know where we are."

"Brilliant!" Kailani exclaimed. "Of course there are no satellites in prehistoric times, so traditional global positioning system GPS devices wouldn't work."

"Can you scan for people with that technology?" Lassen asked. "That could help us find Traxton and the other outlaws."

"The ability to scan bio signs is very limited without the right upgrades" Adalya said, "which I do not currently have." Adalya did not bother explaining that she was missing the bio signs software for her module because the budget of her division did not cover it. She thought this was absurd. How could her division fund time travel but not some basic scanning functions for a module?

Adalya pressed a button on her module, triggering an additional function. The holographic display changed to a series of text and numbers.

"I am trying to determine how trackable we are by my supervisor," Adalya said. "If Professor Sedora can repair the time machine that brought us here and figure out how to follow our quantum trail to this time, she might come back for us, but if she does, she will need to locate us geographically. We may need to move a lot to find suitable food, water, and shelter in the meantime."

The physicist scrolled through holographic module readouts with her fingers before groaning in frustration.

"What is it?" Kailani asked.

"My database orientation module's location chip is damaged," Adalya said. "Probably from the lightning strike or water. This device can receive location signals but not send them. Professor Sedora will not be able to find us solely based on my orientation module. We are not emitting any signals she can receive. That could be a problem if we get separated and need multiple locator devices, but I still have something that should work."

"What?" Lassen asked.

"A durable, specialized location signaler," Adalya said as she removed a small metal object from a utility pouch on her belt. It looked like a silver cube with a blinking green light. "My facility gave these to us for emergencies. This location signaler emits temporal and geographic coordinates. As long as we have this, Professor Sedora stands a decent chance of finding us in time *and* space—if she can repair the time machine."

"What shape is that gadget in?" Durango asked.

"Seems to be in good working order," Adalya said as she scanned it with her module and read the results. "It is platinum-coated and weather-proof. We just need to hang onto it. Unfortunately, we have been having problems with temporal coordinate precision. We do not have complete control over exactly *when* we can travel in time.

"That's the truth," Kailani said with a bit sarcasm.

"Professor Sedora might attempt to program our current time into her time machine and arrive weeks, months, or years later or earlier than she intended," Adalya said. "These things can be very difficult to calculate. We need to keep this location signaler with us at all times and ensure nothing happens to it."

"We'll need to hang onto that signaler," Lassen said, "but I also want to find the two horses that didn't go over the waterfall."

"They went into the forest to the north shortly after coming onshore," Kailani said as she pointed into nearby trees.

"If we can find those horses," Lassen said, "all of us will have transportation."

"I am not sure riding a horse is a wise or safe course of action," Adalya said.

"Don't worry about it, miss," Lassen said. "If we can find the extra horses, I'll ride one, and you can ride my horse, Horizon. He's a good, calm horse and very patient with beginning riders."

Horizon happily neighed and moved his head up and down. Adalya almost cracked a smile but remained serious.

"Can you ride, Miss Nakai?" Lassen asked.

"Sure," Kailani said. "I grew up riding."

The time travelers took in one more look at the scenery and biodiversity that lay before them, sprawled over vast fern prairies and wetlands. They then turned around and walked west along the river, exiting the thick vegetation at the rim of the cliff. Kailani lingered and stood staring alone at the dinosaurs for a moment before reluctantly following the bounty hunters and physicist.

Soon, the time travelers moved along the sandy edge of the river where they had first arrived. The horse tracks were easy to see in the sand at the edge of the river, and Durango followed them as he and Adalya took the lead.

Lassen slowed his walking slightly, so he could walk next to Kailani. He turned to her and said, "You okay?"

"Yeah," Kailani said. "This has been a lot to process all at once, but being in the Jurassic is a dream come true."

"When is the Jurassic relative to the rest of dinosaur times and geologic time in general?" Lassen asked as he and Kailani caught up to Durango and Adalya.

"The Jurassic is the middle period in the Mesozoic Era," Kailani said. "The Mesozoic is the time of the dinosaurs and divided into three periods: the Triassic, Jurassic, and Cretaceous. Dinosaurs first evolved during the Triassic Period, flourished during the Jurassic Period, and continued to thrive during the longer Cretaceous Period before going extinct at the very end of that period."

"That sounds generally correct," Adalya said, turning her head around. "Even in my time, that outline is about the same, but I was too busy studying infinite mass neutralization theories and other physics problems to learn much about anything else."

"The plains below must be the prehistoric Morrison Basin," Kailani said. "Over time, this landscape will be buried, turned to rock, have various biological remains fossilized, be warped by geologic forces, and then gradually brought back to the surface and re-exposed via erosion about 150 million years from now. By 1879, some Morrison rocks will be sticking out of the ground in southeastern Wyoming and other parts of the American West."

"One hundred and fifty million years is a long time," Durango said. "How do people in your time know the Jurassic was that far back?"

"Mostly from radiometric dating based on the decay rate of radioactive elements leftover from the formation of the solar system," Kailani said. "Particular radioactive elements decay at consistent rates for fixed periods of time that stay the same for each type of radioactive element. All rocks contain radioactive elements. By measuring the decay of rocks' radioactive elements, we can determine how old they are. Different levels of decay correspond to different amounts of time, and radiometric dating can be very reliable. Still, it has limitations. For sedimentary rocks, radiometric dating can only be done with carbon—through a process known as radiocarbon dating—but radiocarbon dating only works for rocks that are no more than about 50,000 years old."

"Why the age limit?" Lassen asked.

"Because carbon decays quicker than other elements," Kailani replied.

"Wait a second," Lassen said, "I read sedimentary rock is where most fossils are found. Dinosaurs and a bunch of other fossilized prehistoric wildlife lived way more than 50,000 years before our times. How can we date older sedimentary rocks?"

"Excellent question," Kailani said. "Scientists often use a dating technique called bracketing to determine older fossil ages. Radiometric dating can be done on rocks much older 50,000 years if they're igneous rocks, which are—"

"Volcanic rocks," Lassen said as he narrowed his eyes with realization.

"Yeah," Kailani said. "'Igneous' is just a fancy word for rocks formed from lava. These rocks contain much longer-lived radioactive elements than sedimentary rocks, and in the rock layers, they're sometimes laid down before and after sedimentary rocks that contain fossils."

"I get it," Lassen said. "Igneous rocks below a fossil are older than the fossil. Those above are newer. If you can date those igneous rocks, you can determine the time range that contains—or brackets—the fossil. So, for example, if a 63-million-year-old igneous rock layer is under a fossil in sedimentary rock, and a 60-

million-year-old igneous rock layer is above the fossil, then the fossil would be somewhere between 63 to 60 million years old."

"Exactly right," Kailani said, smiling. "Rocks from the late Jurassic Period happened to be where I was looking for fossils when I was swept back in time with the rest of you."

"I wonder," Adalya said, "if the rocks had anything to do with why we got sent back here. The temporalport energy was penetrating the nearby embankments shortly before it brought us back in time."

"Interesting theory," Kailani said.

"If we're 150 million years back," Durango said, "how old is the Earth? Where do we fit on the grand scale of things? Just how insignificant am I? A professor I talked to said the Earth might be two billion years old. Is it even older?"

Lassen was wondering the same things and was surprised by Durango's introspective, philosophical questions.

"Well," Kailani said, "we should probably stop for this." She bent over to pick up a stick. Upon seeing Kailani bend down with her vest raising up and the back of her pants getting tighter, Durango raised his eyebrows and subtly elbowed Lassen. Lassen flashed Durango an expression that roughly translated his thought of: *Calm down, pal. We've got more relevant issues to deal with.*

Kailani drew in riverbank sand with the stick as she continued talking. "Let me make you a timeline."

"If my database orientation module worked," Adalya said, "we could have so much more up-to-date information, but we will have to settle for this."

"You're welcome," Kailani said. She drew a line about 30 feet (nine meters) long and drew a mark at its far left. "Let's say this is when the Earth formed. The Earth and the rest of the planets in our solar system formed approximately four and a half billion years before modern times. Our galaxy and the rest of the universe are even older: approximately 13.8 billion years old."

Durango slowly whistled under his breath in awe. "That's old," he said.

"It is," Kailani replied. "Even to a paleontologist. There are one thousand millions in a billion. So that's over 13,000 millions. Most people are used to dealing with three and four-digit numbers, like hundreds and thousands, but to truly grasp Earth history, you need a comprehension of six-digit millions and nine-digit billions."

Kailani walked far down the timeline and said, "Keep in mind that this is an approximation and not precisely to scale."

"Don't worry about it," Lassen said. "It looks great."

"Should be about 11 meters longer," Adalya said.

Kailani added another mark to the timeline to the right of the first mark. "The first life evolved roughly three and a half billion years before our millennia during the Proterozoic Eon," Kailani said. "Early life forms included cyanobacteria, which generated energy through photosynthesis and created oxygen as a byproduct. In fact, the buildup of oxygen and other gases released by primitive early life created atmospheric conditions that allowed many life forms—eventually including humans—to evolve and survive."

"Wow," Lassen said. "That makes sense, but I never would have guessed it."

"Seems vaguely familiar," Adalya said. "I may have learned this when I was three."

Kailani was appreciative that Lassen was such an attentive audience. While working as a teaching assistant to large classes of undergraduates, many of her students were apathetic and poor listeners, but there was the rare student who not only paid attention but also actually cared. Such a student would ask questions and even draft coherent papers with proper punctuation. Kailani recognized and appreciated the spark of learning she could see in Lassen.

"The first fish evolved roughly 500 million years before modern times during the Ordovician Period," Kailani said as she added another mark far to the right on the timeline. "Very primitive lifeforms existed before fish—like bacteria, corals, and algae—but fish are one of the earlier forms of back bone-possessing life—also known as vertebrates—people can commonly recognize. Fish appeared after the Earth had existed for roughly 90 percent of its entire history. Life as we know it with a variety of multicellular vertebrates is a relatively recent phenomenon."

"Intriguing," Lassen said. "In the context of geologic time, fish have barely been here."

Kailani moved to the right on her timeline and scraped a new mark in the sand. "This is the beginning of the Triassic Period," Kailani said, "about 245 million years before modern times. Between the Ordovician and the Triassic, the first insects, land plants, reptiles, and stem mammals evolved. Stem mammals used to be known as mammal-like reptiles, though technically, they were neither reptiles nor mammals but were on their way to becoming mammals. This was between 500 to 245 million years before modern times. The first dinosaurs evolved during the Triassic about 230 million years before our times. Dinosaurs are the dominant life forms on Earth for about 160 million years. They lived in the Triassic, Jurassic, and Cretaceous Periods of the Mesozoic Era. Mammals evolved at the end of the Triassic and coexisted with the dinosaurs, though they were mainly small rodent-like animals in the Mesozoic."

"Why did, um, *will* the dinosaurs go extinct?" Durango asked.

"Dinosaurs will die out at the end of the Cretaceous, 66 million years before our times," Kailani said, "when an enormous piece of space debris approximately seven miles wide will strike what will be Mexico's Yucatán Peninsula in modern times. There's compelling evidence from my time that this debris was an asteroid."

"Asteroid?" Durango asked.

Kailani said, "An asteroid is a chunk of rock from outer space. Some have argued that a fragment of a comet instead of an asteroid caused the extinction of the dinosaurs, but there's more evidence supporting the extinction-causing impactor being an asteroid."

"What's the difference between an asteroid and a comet?" Durango asked.

"The material they're made from," Kailani said. "Asteroids are comprised mainly of rock and natural metals, but comets are made largely of ice and dust. They also come from different parts of the solar system. Most asteroids come from the asteroid belt between Mars and Jupiter, but many comets originate from places—like the Kuiper Belt and Oort Cloud—which are far out at the edge of the solar system and in much colder regions."

"Helps explain why they're made of ice," Lassen said. "So, every single dinosaur species will go extinct?"

"Not exactly," Kailani said. "Some of them will evolve into birds. In fact, in the late Jurassic where we are now, some of them may already be birds."

"Well, now that I did not know," Adalya said.

"Of course," Lassen said. "Like *Archaeopteryx*."

"Exactly," Kailani said. "*Archaeopteryx* is an important transition fossil linking reptiles and birds."

"So, Huxley was right," Lassen said.

"Who?" Adalya asked.

"Oh," Lassen said. "Just a scientist from my time."

"Thomas Henry Huxley," Kailani said. "Also known as Darwin's bulldog. I read about him. He was friends with Professor Marsh."

"Yeah," Lassen said. "I attended some of his lectures in New York."

Kailani brought her stick close to the very end of the timeline and said, "The first modern humans evolved roughly 100,000 to 200,000 years before our millennia, though our ape-like ancestors had been around for millions of years prior."

"Intriguing," Lassen said.

"Aren't you shocked to find out you evolved from apes?" Kailani asked.

"Yeah," Adalya said. "According to my history lessons as a toddler, there were high levels of denial when that fact finally became clear to the scientific community."

"Meh," Lassen said, shrugging. "Durango and I have seen how drunk cowboys act in towns like Medicine Bow on Saturday nights. An ape connection is pretty in line with that behavior."

"Lassen's right," Durango said.

"Plus," Lassen added, "by 1879, the idea had been around for a few years. We know about Darwin."

"That's remarkably straightforward acceptance," Kailani said.

"After reading up on natural selection-based evolution, it makes more sense than any other idea I've come across to explain the diversity of life and our origins," Lassen said.

"Lassen's usually right," Durango said with a shrug.

Kailani said, "Between the extinction of the dinosaurs and the appearance of modern humans, mammals took over the Earth and evolved into numerous forms. Some of these species were strange and large and lived shortly before modern times. For example—remarkable creatures, like the woolly mammoth, mastodon, saber-toothed cat, and giant ground sloth—roamed North America until they went extinct at the end of the Pleistocene Epoch, which was the last ice age and ended roughly 12,000 years before our times. In the Pleistocene, this continent was also home to camels, lions similar to those found in Africa, and cheetah-like cats."

"Incredible," Lassen said. "12,000 years ago wasn't all that far back. Those prehistoric mammals coexisted with modern humans."

"They were practically here yesterday," Durango added, "well, relative to the 1870s."

"True," Kailani said. "In fact, some woolly mammoths persisted as recently as 4,000 years before modern times on Wrangel Island north of Siberia and until about 5,600 years before our times on St. Paul Island in Alaska's Bering Sea."

"So, there were mammoths at the same time as the ancient Egyptians," Adalya said. "Nobody taught me that."

"Intriguing," Lassen said. "Modern humans have existed for maybe a couple hundred thousand years, but dinosaurs ruled for about 160 million years. If we measure success in terms of longevity, they win for sure."

"Dinosaurs were a remarkable evolutionary success," Kailani said. "If we were to compress all of the Earth's history into one day, humans have only been around since about 11:58 P.M. So, to answer your question, Mister Mesquite, you fit in near the very end of anything in the history of the planet, and you are extraordinarily insignificant. No offense meant, of course. I'm just speaking literally based on geologic time."

"No, uh, offense taken," Durango said as his mouth got small, and his face appeared downcast.

*   *   *

The bounty hunters and scientists followed the trail of the two Traxton Gang horses, which took them into forest to the northeast. Lassen and Durango led their horses by the reins. Kailani and Adalya walked alongside them. Lassen took the lead as the time travelers hiked among araucarian conifers, sequoias, tall cycads, and tree ferns. The forest had an understory of varied fern species, *Equisetum*, and ginkgo saplings.

The vegetative understory filled with ferns reminded Lassen of old growth coast redwood forests in northwestern California near the Eel River. These redwoods were farther inland than other groves and had a somewhat drier understory as a result. However, the Jurassic understory vegetation felt more primal and exotic with its mix of plants Lassen had never seen together. Occasionally, small *Schillerosaurus* lizards jumped under logs and scurried up trees. The little reptiles weighed only a few grams.

As the explorers walked, Kailani pulled a small notebook from a vest pocket and furiously scribbled notes about the local ecology. She also took numerous close-up photos of plants.

Lassen followed a trail of disturbed vegetation and infrequent tracks. As usual, with his tracking technique, Lassen constantly searched for things that were out of place, like rocks slightly knocked loose and small branches that were overturned with their darker, moister undersides facing up.

Mysterious bushy-tailed rodent-like mammals regularly darted away from the time travelers and scampered out of underbrush to dive into burrows or climb trees.

"There are a lot of squirrelly critters here," Durango said. "Are these squirrels?"

"No," Kailani said, "this is long before the time of squirrels, but mammals in this area are as diverse as the dinosaurs."

"A lot smaller, though," Lassen said.

"That's true," Kailani added. "Most mammals in the Morrison Basin of the Jurassic weigh less than three and a half ounces. The biggest may weigh about six ounces, which is the size of a large mouse."

"What species have we seen?" Lassen asked.

"I can't identify the species in this forest," Kailani replied, "but we may be seeing *Priacodon, Fruitafossor, Comodon,* or *Dryolestes* among others. Many known Jurassic mammal fossils for a given species are merely fragmentary jawbones, so we don't know for sure what many of them actually looked like."

As Lassen walked Horizon around a massive downed sequoia tree, he turned toward Adalya and said, "Miss Nell, I'm convinced we traveled through time, but are we in the same place? When Durango and I left 1879, we were not at Como Bluff, but we ended up there after the time jump to 2026."

"The time machine was malfunctioning," Adalya said, "so I expect we also changed location. I did want to verify our precise location. Seeing the terrain in detail on my module still does not tell us where we are relative to the rest of North America or the globe. I started running some queries shortly after we arrived, and it has taken my module some time to gather the necessary data based on landmarks and quantum accelerometer data."

Adalya's database orientation module beeped. "Sounds like it just finished processing the data," Adalya said. "I can now determine where we are."

Adalya flicked through a series of holographic screens displaying decimal degree coordinates and topographic images of the surrounding landscape. The images then morphed into a holographic outline map of North America. Adalya overlaid nineteenth century political boundaries on top of the map. Letters at the bottom of the map said, "HISTORICAL BASEMAP: 1875."

"We *did* change location," Adalya said. "There was a notable geographic displacement effect. This makes it even more important for us to safeguard the location signaler, so Professor Sedora can find us. In the context of this map, we moved about 563.27 kilometers to the southwest of Como Bluff, Wyoming."

"That's about 350 miles," Kailani said as she saw confusion spread across Durango's face.

On Adalya's map, a blinking red dot appeared in the middle of Utah. "We seem to be in what will become west-central Utah Territory by the 1870s," Adalya said.

"Interesting," Kailani said as she looked at the map. "I know Utah Territory used to be bigger and include Nevada, but it looks like it has the same boundaries in the 1870s that it will have in 2026."

"Well, that's not *too* far away from southeastern Wyoming," Lassen noted.

"We are at the base of a series of mountains and hills," Adalya said.

"Paleontologists call those the Mesocordilleran High," Kailani remarked. "Twenty-first century geography reconstructions show them stretching all the way to California. If we were still near Como Bluff in Wyoming, the surrounding terrain would be completely flat."

"So, we went back in time *and* moved several hundred miles to the southwest?" Lassen asked.

"Somewhat," Adalya said. "We have actually moved much farther south than the distance between the Como Bluff area and this part of Utah in your time."

"How?" Lassen asked.

"Yeah, I don't get it," Durango remarked.

"Continental drift," Kailani said. "That's it. Isn't it?"

"Clever," Adalya said, "and yes, that is the reason. I did not realize twenty-first century people knew about that, but a lot of backwards thinking was changing around the nineteenth to twenty-first centuries. Some of that old history blurs together. Miss Nakai would probably know more about continental drift and the broader plate tectonics processes than me."

"Continental drift explains why we're farther south," Kailani said, "and is one reason the climate here is so different than it is in modern times."

"Continental drift," Lassen said. "You mean the continents are drifting—they're moving?"

"Yes, they are," Kailani said.

"Unbelievable," Lassen replied.

"I believe it," Durango said. "The Earth's a patrillion years old, dinosaurs had the greatest kingdom ever, and I don't matter at all. Plus, time travel's a thing. So, yeah, why wouldn't the continents move?"

"Well," Lassen said, "there'd have to be a suitable driving force."

"There is," Kailani said. "The Earth contains a tremendous amount of heat and energy in its interior, leftover from the space debris collisions that formed the planet. About 100 miles below us is a partially molten layer of the Earth called the asthenosphere."

Kailani sketched in her notebook as she spoke and drew a circle with another circle inside of it. In the space between the outer perimeter of the smaller circle and the inner perimeter of the larger circle, she wrote "Asthenosphere."

Kailani said, "Hot lava underground—it's called magma— periodically erupts from the asthenosphere. Some of it erupts in volcanoes, like those we saw in the distance from the top of the cliff." Kailani drew a few little conical stratovolcanoes on her diagram and drew lines of magma coming up to them from the underlying asthenosphere. "However, most of the magma comes up in mid-oceanic ridges."

"In the middle of the ocean?" Lassen asked.

"That's right," Kailani said as she sketched a few ridges with internal ruptures. "Huge amounts of magma erupt from the Pacific and Atlantic oceans. This magma forms new land and pushes existing land."

"Oh—okay," Lassen said. "A few years back, near the Cascade Mountains of northern California, I saw barren lava fields of black rock where lava had cooled not much earlier, maybe the late Pleistocene. I can picture how magma forms new land."

"The continents and oceans are on an outer layer of the Earth called the crust," Kailani said as she added a new outer circle to her diagram. She then sketched a second drawing of the Earth and added continents to it. "The crust is divided into a series of plates. Mid-oceanic ridge magma eruptions have been gradually repositioning crustal plates for millions of years." Kailani drew arrows on her illustration and sketched some plate boundaries between continents.

"So," Lassen said, "the Earth's outer crust is sort of floating around on hot lava and broken into different segments that slowly move?"

"Essentially," Kailani said. "Crustal plates move on top of the asthenosphere, which is viscous."

"Huh?" Durango asked.

"Viscous," Kailani said, "means it's a fluid-like solid—sort of like thick, wet mud."

"Intriguing," Lassen said. "Now that I think of it, in my time, the eastern part of South America looks like it could lock into western Africa like a giant puzzle piece."

"Prior to your time, they were connected," Kailani said. "A driving force for continental drift is clearly present, and matching fossils and other geologic evidence also support that the continents move."

"Wow," Lassen replied, "but of course. It makes sense. What you're saying adds up and fits. The age of the Earth, the movement of the continents, the evolution of life: science provides logical explanations that work."

"Ehhhhhh," Durango said, more uncertain.

"Old information," Adalya said, "but its basis seems sound enough." She moved her fingers over blue data projections on her module. "According to this, North America is about 400 miles farther south in the late Jurassic than it will be during our times."

Kailani added, "The fact that North America is closer to the equator helps explain why the landscape is more tropical than it will be during modern times."

"I can understand how that would make things warmer," Lassen said, "but in 1879, northern New Mexico is about 400 miles south of Wyoming, and its climate is about the same."

"Being farther south is only part of the reason for a warmer and moister climate," Kailani said. "In the late Jurassic, ocean currents are different because of different continent positions, and sea level is higher because there are no major ice caps. In fact, the whole planet is warmer because of increased gas in the atmosphere from high amounts of volcanic activity. In this time, lots of volcanoes have been erupting gas that traps heat that might otherwise radiate back into outer space."

"That makes sense," Lassen said. "So, we're still on Earth, but we're on a different part of the planet from where we left, and we're about 150 million years before modern times. Is the Earth even in the same part of space this far back in time?"

"Well, actually," Adalya said as she moved her fingers through holo projections, "now that you mention it, I guess I will explain that we are in an entirely different part of the galaxy than we will be in modern times."

"Whaaaaaaat?" Durango asked. "You're saying we traveled through outer space, but we're still on the same planet in a different time?"

"In a manner of speaking," Adalya said, "yes."

"Uh, how?" Lassen asked.

"Geo-temporal anchoring," Adalya said, "it's something Professor Sedora and I built into our time travel technology. The Earth is constantly rotating about its axis."

"Yeah, sure," Lassen said, "a rotation completes every 24 hours. That's how we get night and day. The parts of Earth that face the Sun during rotation experience day, and the parts that don't get sunlight are in night. Even in the 1800s, we know that."

"Yeah . . ." Durango said, "we . . . do. We definitely do."

"Glad to hear it," Adalya said, "and I am guessing you are also aware that the Earth revolves around the Sun, completing a revolution around it every 365 days, five hours, 59 minutes, and 16 seconds."

"I would have just said 365 days," Lassen replied, "but yeah, that's how we measure a year in our time. Thinking of the Earth moving around the Sun makes me realize that even though we're on Earth, we're always traveling through outer space. So, with geo-temporal anchoring, you and the professor developed a way for time travel to anchor you to a specific spot on the Earth, regardless of how far it moves in its rotation around its axis or its revolution around the Sun?"

"Precisely," Adalya said, "but it is actually more complicated than that."

"How so?" Lassen asked.

Adalya said, "The Earth is rotating around its axis at approximately 1,000 miles per hour."

"Son of a catamount," Durango said, "that's fast, but I don't feel anything. Everything looks like it's in the same place. How does that work?"

"You, me, and everything on the planet is basically moving at the same fast speed," Adalya said. "And it consistently stays the same. Within our frame of reference, nothing seems to change."

"Huh," Durango said.

"Have you ever been in a railcar on a fast-moving train with all the shades down?" Kailani asked.

"A few times," Durango said.

"Could you tell you were moving forward," Kailani said, "if there was no sound from the train engine and no view of anything outside?"

"Um, maybe not," Durango replied.

"It's like that," Adalya said. "Good analogy, Miss Nakai."

"Thanks," Kailani replied.

"In addition to moving quickly about its axis," Adalya said, "the Earth is moving around the Sun at a speed of approximately 490,000 miles per hour. Professor Sedora and I factored these numbers into our geo-temporal anchoring calculations, but we also accounted for the fact that the entire solar system—the Sun, the Earth, and the nearby planets that revolve around the Sun—is also orbiting around the center of our galaxy: the Milky Way Galaxy. A galaxy is a group of stars that—"

"We know what a galaxy is," Durango said. "I get a good look at the Milky Way on most clear nights just by looking up from my bedroll."

"Of course," Adalya said, "you would camp a lot with your transient freelance lifestyle of hunting criminals in remote regions."

Durango narrowed his mouth and crinkled his eyebrows in confusion.

"Our solar system completes an orbit around the galaxy once every 250 million years," Adalya said. "Here in the Jurassic, we are essentially on the opposite side of the galaxy than we will be in modern times. The star constellations we see tonight will be different than those of the 1800s or 2700s. So, there is a lot of math to work out to get geo-temporal anchoring right. If the calculations Professor Sedora and I developed were perfect, we would be in Wyoming and not Utah because that was our original departure point and we never input commands to change our location relative to the rest of Earth. With more refinement, we planned to enable our time machines to appear in specific places and times. Some in our division hoped to depart from Wyoming to visit places like Alexandria in ancient Egypt, the Aztec capital of Teotihuacan in Mexico prior to the Spanish invasion, or China's Forbidden City during the Ming Dynasty."

"I'm just glad we're still on Earth," Durango said.

"Yeah," Lassen added.

"No place quite like it," Kailani said. "No matter what time you're in."

Suddenly, the time travelers heard the sound of rustling dried leaves and needles and rapid flapping wings. Lassen and Durango instinctively drew their guns with lightning reflexes. Kailani looked up and shielded her eyes from sunlight streaming down past tree fern fronds. Adalya pivoted her head in confusion, trying to pinpoint the source of the sound.

An *Archaeopteryx* sprinted and burst off forest duff like a pheasant erupting into flight. It then pounced on a half-foot (15-centimeter) long juvenile *Eilenodon* basking on a log. The *Eilenodon* was a sphenodontid reptile that looked like an iguana. It was bright green and had a series of small dermal spines protruding from its head and back. However, it most closely resembled a tuatara. In modern times, tuataras are the last surviving sphenodontid reptiles and only live in New Zealand. The *Eilenodon* was not a dinosaur and had L-shaped lizard-like legs that sprawled out from its body. Its big eyes bulged as sharp claws tore into its torso.

The *Archaeopteryx* had light-colored gray feathers with dark tips and was about one and a half feet (one half meter) long. Feathers covered nearly its entire body, except for its clawed feet and toothed beak. Soon, the little avian creature tore apart the *Eilenodon* on a nearby log. Lassen thought the *Archaeopteryx* was about the same size as magpie birds he had seen in the Rockies. The prehistoric bird/reptile-like creature's long fan-shaped tail bobbed as it gripped its prey with three claws on the front of each of its wings and shredded flesh with its teeth.

"Son of a catamount!" Durango proclaimed.

At the sound of Durango's voice, the little avian hunter launched into the air with chunks of *Eilenodon* in its talons. It perched on a high tree branch and continued to eat while glaring down at Durango, hissing.

Lassen and Durango smoothly twirled their pistols back into their holsters. Adalya and Kailani were struck by how quickly and expertly Lassen and Durango handled their firearms. They were clearly professionals and very dangerous.

"That's an archaeop . . . archaeoctoterrace?" Durango said. "No, that's not it."

"An *Archaeopteryx*," Kailani said. "Or a close relative." Kailani retrieved her phone and began taking pictures.

"Of course," Lassen said while removing his binoculars from Horizon's saddlebags. As Lassen peered through his optics, he said, "It's like a little carnivorous dinosaur with feathers. Intriguing."

"Hey, Lassen," Durango said, scratching his chin. "I thought you said *Archaeopteryx* fossils were found in Europe."

"Well, yeah," Lassen said, "but I guess they were in North America, too."

"It makes sense," Kailani said. "In the late Jurassic, Europe is a series of islands and much closer to North America than it will be during modern times. Greenland also connects North America and Europe, and we know some of the same dinosaurs are on both continents. For example, late Jurassic *Allosaurus* and *Torvosaurus* fossils have been discovered in both the western United States and Portugal. Also, *Brachiosaurus* fossils were discovered in Colorado, and a species very similar to *Brachiosaurus*—known as *Giraffatitan*—was discovered in East Africa. Remember that just because certain fossils will not be found during our time in certain places does not necessarily mean those species did not exist in those locations. Only a small fraction of what existed happened to be preserved via fossilization."

"And," Lassen said, "an even smaller portion of what was fossilized happened to be discovered by people."

"Exactly," Kailani replied as she put her phone back in a vest pocket and pulled up her binoculars.

"Then it seems lucky anybody finds any fossils at all," Durango said.

"In some ways, it is," Kailani said while looking at the *Archaeopteryx* through her magnifying optics. "However, keep in mind that throughout Earth's history, millions and billions of individual animals of a variety of species were living and dying for hundreds of millions of years. Some individuals only lived for a few years, but their species may have persisted for several million years. With so many animal remains, something is bound to be preserved."

"The math works out," Adalya added.

CHAPTER 10: PERIL IN THE PLAINS

The bounty hunters and scientists continued trekking through the forest into late morning. They generally moved northeast through low foothills as the overall terrain began to slope downward and level out. As the day warmed, Horizon and Yonder constantly sniffed the unfamiliar forest with curiosity. In the background, male cicada mating calls permeated the forest as the insects contracted their muscles to produce high-pitched humming.

"Shuh," Lassen said as he raised a hand, gesturing for the others to stop. "I see the horses that escaped the waterfall."

A dark gray horse and striking chestnut horse stood ahead in the forest. They attempted to chew araucarian sapling needles but did not enjoy them. A lasso was tied to the gray horse's saddle. Adalya, Durango, and Kailani stood quietly as Lassen pulled a lump of sugar out of his saddlebags.

"Easy," Lassen said as he approached the horses. "Easy." Lassen spoke gently as he slowly gained the horses' trust. He broke his sugar lump in two. Soon, the horses crunched sugar chunks out of Lassen's hands. Horizon pricked his ears and snorted in jealousy.

"Hey, Horizon, pal," Lassen said. "I'll make it up to you and get you applesauce after we make it back to 1879. Trust me."

Horizon skeptically neighed.

"Looks like they're not afraid of you," Durango said.

"Naw," Lassen said. "These horses look pretty tame. We've got a gray gelding and a chestnut Arabian mare. Beautiful. I bet she's fast."

Lassen opened one of the saddlebags on the gray horse and rummaged through its contents. He found a bit of food and something wrapped in brown paper, which he removed.

"Huh," Lassen said, "it's an apple, and it's in good shape, considering all this fellow has been through. There's a note. 'For Graphite: the best horse in the world. Give this to him right before you close up at night.'"

Durango sighed and said, "Guy likes his horse."

"Well, some guy does," Lassen said, "but I don't think it's a member of the Traxton Gang. This note is signed 'Jonas Janson.' Looks like he had plans to leave Graphite in a stable with an apple for dessert. Traxton probably stole this horse to help with the jail break."

"I think we might need that apple more than him," Durango said. "We could be here a while."

"True enough," Lassen said. "Hey."

While Lassen and Durango spoke, Graphite had swooped his snout over to Lassen's hand and snatched the apple. In a few crunching bites, it was gone.

Kailani chuckled as she said, "Well, it was *his* apple."

"Fair enough," Lassen said.

Lassen looked through the saddlebags of the chestnut horse and found dried fruit and lots of dried beans. Then he said, "This saddlebag is labeled 'Ember.' Could be this horse's name."

Lassen patted Graphite on the neck, tightened the horse's saddle, and got on it. He then steered Graphite around a fallen snag with slight movements of his feet.

"Easy to ride," Lassen said. "Miss Nell, this would be a good time for you to practice riding Horizon."

"I am not sure," Adalya said.

"I'll see if Ember will accept me," Kailani said as she approached the chestnut horse and patted it on the head. The horse tipped its head up and down with approval. "She's friendly," Kailani said. She adjusted Ember's saddle and smoothly hopped on. "I think this will work."

From atop Graphite, Lassen said, "The forest looks like it starts to thin out just downhill from here. We'll be on the plains soon, and horses will make it easier to cover greater distances."

"How does one go about getting on a horse?" Adalya asked.

"It's easy," Durango said. "I'll show you."

As Durango tied Yonder's reins to a tree fern trunk, Lassen intently surveyed the surrounding terrain from horseback. He could just barely make out the edge of the plains far downhill.

Durango and Adalya approached Horizon, and Durango explained the basics of getting on a horse and riding it. Adalya was initially apprehensive, but Horizon quickly accepted her, and she was soon comfortable riding.

Durango untied Yonder as Lassen's new gray horse sniffed to an especially high degree while its ears twitched. The time travelers rode downhill, and the terrain gradually leveled out. The tree density also decreased, and vegetation undergrowth became sparser. Some new plant species were visible, whereas some that were common at higher elevations were no longer present.

Suddenly, Lassen heard branches snap in the distance. The horses started to get twitchy and nervous.

"What's all that ruckus?" Durango asked.

"I don't know," Lassen said as he pulled his binoculars from a saddlebag. Lassen lifted them to his eyes and adjusted them to bring objects into focus between numerous tree trunks and branches. He saw branches tumble to the ground with dust coming up. He also saw the plains were just beyond the commotion.

"There's a sauropod," Lassen said as he bit his lower lip with concentration and continued focusing his binoculars. "It looks like it's knocking down branches with its neck." About 150 yards (137 meters) ahead of Lassen, a large male *Apatosaurus* snapped off branches with its thick sturdy neck. It used its long red-striped blue neck like a wrecking ball.

"Why is it doing that?" Durango asked.

"Well," Lassen said, "the branches coming off what looks like a tall sequoia have lots of bright green new sprouts. There are also branches on the ground that have been stripped of needles. Looks like the dinosaur's eating new growth. Probably likes the taste of those branches better than others and wants to eat them from the ground."

"That seems like a lot of energy to expend for food," Kailani said. "I would think it could just as easily eat the needles in place."

"I don't know," Lassen said. "Maybe. Wait a second. There's another sauropod approaching. I think the branch snapping might also be part of making a statement."

"A territory claim?" Kailani wondered out loud.

"Possibly," Lassen said. "It could be like how members of the deer family rub their antlers on trees to mark their territory during the mating season."

"Like that bull moose we saw in Jackson Hole last fall," Durango said.

At the edge of the forest, another male *Apatosaurus* charged the male who was knocking down tree branches. The bright metallic blue folds on his neck were especially thick and vibrant. He also had notable red dermal spines on his back as well as bright red lateral stripes running down his back and sides. Low booming sounds emanated from his neck and mouth. This dinosaur was fat, healthy, and in full display mode. The *Apatosaurus* at the edge of the trees grunted defiantly, which vibrated his neck folds. He quickly pivoted around to face the charging male. A pair of female *Apatosaurus* placidly grazed not far from the males.

The males tromped toward each other with bellicose vitriol. As a collision seemed imminent, they abruptly paused and reared on their hind legs. The heads of each dinosaur were now about 40 feet (12 meters) above the ground as they walked a few steps toward each other, now looking bizarrely tall and imposing on two legs. They snorted angrily, and saliva launched into the warm morning air and glistened in sunlight. Dust kicked up from the ground, and bits of dried ferns and cycad fronds whirled at the sauropods' feet.

A trio of bright green-turquoise *Nanosaurus* that had been feeding in a nearby stand of *Equisetum* darted away in fear. One looked up briefly and saw two *Apatosaurus* heads high above. The sun was directly behind them, and light rays beamed through newly generated dust. The sight was dramatic and terrifying. The *Apatosaurus* were well-lit, and their shiny folds of blue neck skin heavily reflected light. Lassen squinted as flashing light entered his binoculars' lenses.

The two mighty titans of the plains clashed with primeval fury. They battered their necks together and boomed and rumbled bizarre, deep sounds that vibrated up through their necks. Then they pulled their necks apart and slashed at each other with thumb spikes on their front feet. Blood dripped onto ferns. One droplet hit a dragonfly's wing. The insect tumbled to the ground. A small mammal quickly snatched it and immediately backed into its burrow. The defending *Apatosaurus* dropped back to four legs on the ground and moved into the trees. His attacker also returned to a quadrupedal gait and pushed forward. Branches snapped, and trees broke like matchsticks.

The disturbance was too much for the time travelers' horses. Lassen tucked his binoculars under his gunbelt and focused on controlling Graphite as the horse reared. Yonder also reared, and Durango struggled to control him. Horizon and Ember whinnied nervously but remained calm.

"Whoa!" Durango said. "Easy! Easy, boy!"

An especially large sequoia tree fell to the ground. The tumult and crashing triggered Graphite, Yonder, and Ember to bolt into the forest to the south. Horizon stayed in place and looked from left to right, wondering what he should do. Adalya stayed on Horizon and felt the same way.

Lassen, Kailani, and Durango kept their heads low to avoid being hit in the face by conifer branches and tree fern fronds. Suddenly, ferns rustled furiously behind the riders as a pair of carnivorous *Ornitholestes* launched out of the undergrowth, hissing. The *Ornitholestes* were bipedal, roughly six feet (two meters) long, and weighed about 30 pounds (14 kilograms). They stood about one and a half feet (one half meter) tall at the hip and held their heads about two feet (one meter) above the ground. Their bodies were largely covered in colorful orange downy feathers, and blue stripes adorned their mostly featherless heads. Longer red feathers lined the *Ornitholestes'* necks and parts of their arms, making them appear as if they had small ornamental wings.

The *Ornitholestes* bared serrated, blade-like teeth as they hissed. One of them swung a dexterous three-fingered hand toward Yonder. Long claws drew blood as they scraped one of the horse's back legs. Yonder neighed in pain. Durango quickly turned his head and saw that his horse had crushed most of the eggs in a nest. Yonder ran forward with yolk residue on his hooves. The surviving eggs were elongated, oval-shaped, and a little larger than chicken eggs.

Graphite, Yonder, and Ember reacted to the *Ornitholestes* ambush by changing direction. Yonder and Ember galloped east while Durango and Kailani struggled to control them. Graphite turned around, bringing Lassen north toward the battling *Apatosaurus*. As the horses separated, the *Ornitholestes* split up. One pursued Lassen while the other chased Durango and Kailani.

Lassen leaned left and right to avoid branches as Graphite tore through the forest. Up ahead, he saw a startled orange-blue *Dryosaurus* stop its feeding and turn its yellow head in bewilderment before running onto the plains in fear.

Lassen struggled to control Graphite, employing incredibly quick reflexes to try to steer the horse past and over forest obstacles. Several little *Priacodon* and *Dryolestes* mammals dove for cover as Graphite disturbed their habitat.

The *Ornitholestes* that chased the time travelers were agile, speedy, and highly maneuverable. They had no problem keeping up with the horses and expertly evaded low branches and tree trunks as they sprinted, hopped, and zig-zagged in intense pursuit. Following larger animals was unusual for this pair of *Ornitholestes*. They spent most of their time hunting small mammals at night with the help of large eyes and sharp vision. However, their territory had been invaded. Their eggs were threatened. They had to take action.

"Son—of a catamount," Durango muttered in frustration as he gripped his saddle horn with his left hand and smoothly drew his gun with his right.

"Don't shoot!" Kailani shouted as she rode Ember alongside Durango.

Durango fired several shots at the individual *Ornitholestes* behind him. Every shot missed, though one got very close and blasted dirt into the dinosaur's eyes. Shocked and confused, the *Ornitholestes* stopped and slunk back into the forest while rapidly blinking.

"Heh, heh!" Durango yelled as he lifted his gun in the air. "Yeah!"

Durango's moment of triumph was fleeting. He shouted in pain as his hand slammed into a tree fern trunk, knocking his gun into the underbrush. Yonder and Ember continued running.

"You didn't have to do that!" Kailani said.

"Relax," Durango said. "I was only trying to scare that critter, and it worked."

The male *Apatosaurus* continued to fight while Graphite brought Lassen directly to their location. As a whipping *Apatosaurus* tail whooshed through the air like a bullwhip and sliced through saplings, the *Ornitholestes* in pursuit of Lassen finally stopped, but Graphite kept running.

As a downed ginkgo tree crashed in front of Graphite, the horse reared, and Lassen used the opportunity to lithely slide off the saddle. Now at the *Apatosaurus* battle site, Lassen landed in soft ferns and somersaulted out of the way of a falling tree. Based on how uncontrollable Graphite was, Lassen decided that he would be safer on his feet than in the saddle. Graphite tore through the undergrowth and ran into the plains to the north.

Lassen stood up and jumped left to avoid being crushed by the back leg of an *Apatosaurus*. Then he jumped straight up with lightning reflexes to avoid having this legs snapped by the end of an *Apatosaurus* tail. As he landed back in the ferns, Lassen heard familiar neighing and saw Horizon and Adalya rush toward him.

"Hop on, Mister Malone," Adalya shouted from atop Horizon as she extended her right hand.

"Thanks!" Lassen said as he jumped onto the back of Horizon and briefly gripped Adalya's outstretched hand. Lassen smiled at her as he got on Horizon, who bolted into a sprint.

"Hang onto me or you will fall off!" Adalya yelled as Horizon torpedoed through the trees. Lassen wrapped his arms around Adalya's waist just before Horizon leapt high to avoid a log. Lassen and Adalya then dodged left to evade a falling araucarian conifer split in two by an *Apatosaurus* tail. Soon, Horizon broke through the forest and galloped onto the plains.

In the meantime, the two battling male *Apatosaurus* were exhausted. The attacker had the upper hand. After a final neck battering, his defending opponent unleashed a guttural boom of defeat and limped onto the plains. The loser of the battle had numerous bloody chest and neck lacerations. His attacker was not much better off. The two *Apatosaurus* females to the south briefly looked up as the battle ended and continued feeding. If the battle was for their benefit, they showed no indication of caring.

As Horizon moved beyond the *Apatosaurus*, he slowed and cantered onto immense floodplains mostly covered in ferns. The plains also featured clumps of trees, tree ferns, cycads, and *Equisetum*. A herd of turquoise-beige *Diplodocus* with yellow lateral stripes slowly fed about a half mile (one kilometer) to the northeast. Small red pterosaurs flitted overhead in the distance. Lassen took his arms off Adalya's waist.

"Thank you, ma'am," Lassen said through heavy breaths laced with adrenaline. "I owe you. Not bad for a first-time rider."

Adalya also breathed hard. "No problem, Mister Malone," she said. "This makes us even for the river rescue. Plus, you should really be thanking your horse. I mostly just hung onto the saddle."

"Horizon knows his way around," Lassen said. "We should try to find Durango and Miss Nakai." Lassen pulled his binoculars out from under his gunbelt and pointed them to the south. He mentioned to Adalya that the others were riding toward them. He waved. Durango and Kailani waved back. He then panned his binoculars across the terrain, looking for Graphite. As he spotted the horse drinking from a pond about a half mile (one kilometer) to the north, he said, "I found our missing horse. Let's wait for Durango and Kailani and then go get Graphite. You okay?"

"I did not break my neck, and I am neither trampled nor the victim of a carnivorous dinosaur attack, so I suppose I am adequate," Adalya said.

"Considering what we just went through, adequate is good," Lassen said.

Lassen slid off Horizon and scanned more of his surroundings with binoculars. He followed the movements of distant pterosaurs and got a good look at the *Diplodocus* herd to the northeast. They serenely fed while their whip-like tails sinuously arced behind them. He also saw a small herd of brown-orange *Camptosaurus* and a few lone green-yellow female *Stegosaurus* with light orange plates.

Several minutes later, Durango and Kailani rode up to Lassen and Adalya.

"I scared away the one that was chasing me," Durango said, "but I lost my gun. It ran back into the forest—whatever it was. Everybody okay?"

"We're fine," Lassen said, "but we still need to catch Graphite. That horse is skittish."

Horizon neighed and pointed his head at Yonder. "What is it, boy?" Lassen said. "Yonder? Is Yonder okay?"

Durango got off Yonder and checked his horse's back legs. He winced. "He's a little scraped up," Durango said. "He should be fine, but there's blood."

"Blood," Lassen said. "Not good."

"Certainly not good with all the predators that may be nearby," Kailani said.

"We're going to have to get this taken care of," Durango said.

"Yeah," Lassen replied. "There's a river just ahead with a cluster of rocks by it." Lassen pointed to a bending, wide river to the northeast. "Let's go over there. You can clean up Yonder at the river, and hopefully, we can catch Graphite afterward."

"Right," Durango said. "I can clean the wound and bandage it."

The time travelers rode toward the river and spoke as they rode.

"What were those things?" Durango asked.

"I didn't get a great look at them," Lassen said.

"I was trying not to fall off a horse," Adalya added. "I hardly saw them."

"They were covered in feathers," Durango said. "They looked like big *Archae . . . op . . . teryxes?*"

"Yes," Kailani said, "small theropods of this time may resemble *Archaeopteryx.*"

"But I don't think they could fly," Durango added, "and they were bigger than *Archaeopteryx.*"

"They may have been *Ornitholestes,*" Kailani said. "Or possibly *Coelurus* or another small carnivorous theropod."

"Wait," Durango said. "What's a theropod? The opposite of a sauropod?"

"In a way," Kailani said. "They're a dinosaur group with species that are almost all bipedal, meaning they walk on two legs, and they're predominately carnivorous, so most eat meat. However, some theropods are omnivorous or herbivorous. Sauropods walk on four legs and eat plants, but they're also unique in having an extremely large size with long necks and tails."

"Those little theropods had *lots* of feathers," Durango said. "In some ways, they seemed more like big birds than dinosaurs."

"That makes sense," Kailani said. "In 1879, relatively few dinosaur fossils had been uncovered, but by my time, many dinosaur fossils had been discovered with feathers because birds evolved from feathered, carnivorous bipedal dinosaurs. At least in the fossil record, feathered dinosaurs will be more common millions of years from now in the Cretaceous Period. Aside from *Archaeopteryx* and what we just saw, there should also be a smaller carnivorous bird-like dinosaur in this area called *Hesperornithoides.* It's about the size of a chicken."

"I bet it eats more than seeds and worms," Lassen said.

As the time travelers reached the river and the jumbles of boulders that lined its banks, Lassen said, "Durango, you might want to go to the water and clean up Yonder. You could also refill our canteens. I want to go up in the rocks to get a better view."

"I'll go with you," Kailani said. "I want a better look at the landscape beyond the river."

"I will accompany Mister Mesquite," Adalya said. "I can sterilize the water with an instrument I have."

"Be especially careful near the water," Kailani said, "*Amphicotylus* may be nearby."

"Amphi what?" Durango asked.

"*Amphicotylus*," Kailani said, "though there could also be *Eutretauranosuchus* or possibly other crocodylomorphs."

"Crocodiles," Lassen said. "That makes sense. Durango, remember that bone Marsh was showing us?"

"Yeah," Durango said. "That croc bone could have been from this time period."

"*Amphicotylus* used to be classified as *Goniopholis*," Kailani said, which is a genus from Europe, but most goniopholidid species were later considered to be *Amphicotylus*, which was named by Cope in 1878."

"I'm surprised crocodiles have been around for so long," Lassen said.

"Well, technically," Kailani said, "*Amphicotylus* and *Eutretauranosuchus* are not true crocodiles. They're crocodylomorphs, which is a group that includes modern crocodiles and alligators as well as various prehistoric relatives. Crocodylomorphs have existed since shortly after the dinosaurs appeared in the Triassic, and they have not changed much up into modern times. The crocodylomorphs here are more primitive than ancestors of modern crocodiles and alligators. Based on fossils, the Morrison Basin should have both semiaquatic crocodylomorphs, like *Amphicotylus*, as well as some that are primarily terrestrial, like *Hallopus* and *Fruitachampsa*."

"Very interesting," Lassen said. "Dry land crocs."

"Essentially, yes," Kailani said. "Crocodylomorphs are much more diverse in prehistoric times."

The time travelers tied their horses to tree fern trunks. The day was getting hot with the temperature approaching 85 degrees Fahrenheit (29 degrees Celsius). Lassen got out his binoculars and scanned the river. It was about 300 feet (90 meters) across and slowly coursed northwest before hitting another river that moved northeast. The river was brown and silty.

As he looked through his binoculars, Lassen said, "See what looks like the tops of rocks out in the water and along the riverbank far to the northwest?"

"Yeah, sure," Durango said. "Looks like rocks and maybe some logs and tree branches that got washed downstream."

"There are a few logs," Lassen said, "but look closer. Some of those logs and rocks are blinking."

"Son of a catamount," Durango said. "Almost all those things are crocodiles."

"Well, crocodylomorphs," Lassen said. "Some are in the water, but you can only see their eyes, heads, and some of their snouts. The ones on the bank seem to be soaking up sun and are easy to spot. Miss Nakai, what species are they?"

"There appear to be dozens of them," Kailani said. "There are at least two species. I'm not sure which is which. I'm guessing the larger ones are *Amphicotylus*, and the smaller ones could be *Eutretauranosuchus*, but it's hard to tell as the fossilized type specimen of *Eutretauranosuchus* was a juvenile."

Lassen picked up a rock and tossed it into the closest part of the river. It splashed. Nothing else happened. Lassen threw two more rocks into the water with the same result.

"This part of the water seems safe," Lassen said. "I'm going to check the terrain for signs of Traxton."

"I'll refill the canteens and tend to Yonder," Durango said.

"Would you refill this as well?" Kailani said as she handed Durango her metal water bottle.

"Sure, ma'am," Durango said.

Durango, Yonder, and Adalya moved toward the river while Lassen and Kailani walked toward boulders. As Lassen and Kailani approached the rocks, brightly-colored dragonflies—red, green, purple, and blue—flitted out of the way. Most had bodies only a few inches long. The largest had six-inch (15-centimeter) wingspans. To Lassen, they looked similar to dragonflies he had recently seen along the Medicine River in Wyoming, but they were more colorful, and some were larger.

"So, you mentioned that Cope named *Amphicotylus*," Lassen said. "That's Edward Drinker Cope from my time? Right?"

"That's right," Kailani said.

"Marsh really did not like that guy," Lassen said, "but I actually met Cope once."

"Get out!" Kailani said.

"From where?" Lassen said. "I'm standing right here."

"You met Marsh *and* Cope!" Kailani exclaimed.

"Yeah," Lassen said. "I met Cope in Montana."

"What was he like?" Kailani asked.

"Smart guy," Lassen said. "We actually talked paleontology for a bit. Pretty easygoing compared to Marsh. Kind of a dandy, too. Friendly, and the ladies seemed to like him."

"Hmmm," Kailani said, nodding her head.

"Whatever ended up happening with Cope and Marsh?" Lassen asked. "When I met Marsh, it seemed like they were destined to make each other miserable, but if they reconciled and joined forces, they could be an amazing paleontology team."

"If only," Kailani said.

"Wait a minute," Lassen said. "When we were looking at dinosaurs up on the cliff and Marsh came up, you mentioned the Bone Wars. What's that all about?"

Kailani said, "It's a label scholars and journalists in my time sometimes use to refer to the famous Marsh/Cope rivalry."

"Wow," Lassen said, "they hated each other so much that it made the history books."

"Basically, yeah," Kailani said. "They spied on each other and tried to sabotage each other's dig sites, and their feud spanned decades. It reached a boiling point in 1890 when Cope gave a bunch of disparaging information and stories about Marsh to a journalist for the *New York Herald* newspaper. In newspaper articles, Cope publicly accused Marsh of fraud, plagiarism, and incompetence."

"Ohhh boy," Lassen said. "I can only imagine how Marsh would react to that. What triggered Cope to get slanderous stories published?"

"After Marsh became the U.S. Geological Survey's Chief Paleontologist," Kailani said, "he tried to get the Smithsonian Museum to confiscate Cope's fossils because Cope had been involved with government surveys."

"How did that go over?" Lassen asked.

Kailani said, "Not well for Marsh, actually. Cope was able to prove that he had paid for most of his fossil collection with his own money. He had detailed records and receipts. Later, there were political attacks on the U.S. Geological Survey, Marsh lost his position with it, and then the federal government wanted Marsh's fossils that had been paid for with Geological Survey funds, and part of *his* collection was confiscated."

"His scheme backfired on him," Lassen said.

"Yep," Kailani replied. "In the end, both men died poor and bitter, but in Cope's final days, he spent time with an early paleoartist named Charles R. Knight and helped him reconstruct what dinosaurs might have actually looked like in life. Knight's paintings became famous and had a huge impact on how the world would perceive dinosaurs and other prehistoric life. Knight produced early paintings of dinosaurs, like *Allosaurus* and *Brontosaurus*."

"Sounds like Cope made major contributions to science," Lassen said, "in spite of and because of his hate for Marsh."

"Yeah," Kailani said. "Cope ended up contributing to over 1,300 publications, and Marsh produced 270 publications. They did things in a rush, and their specimens weren't always well-organized, but nine of the dinosaurs Cope discovered and 23 of the dinosaurs Marsh discovered are still considered valid species by my time. Marsh thought birds evolved from dinosaurs, and at one point, Charles Darwin said that Marsh's work provided the best support for evolution that had appeared within the previous 20 years."

"That's high praise for a paleontologist," Lassen said.

"Cope or Marsh actually named several of the dinosaurs we have seen so far," Kailani said, "including *Apatosaurus*, *Camarasaurus*, *Diplodocus*, and *Stegosaurus*."

As Lassen and Kailani ascended rocks above the river, *Glyptops* turtles jumped from their rocky sun-bathing perches and splashed into water. The turtles were about six to eight inches (15 to 20 centimeters) long and weighed one to two pounds (one half to one kilogram). Lassen thought they were the same size as western pond turtles he had seen in the wetlands of California's Sacramento Valley. The *Glyptops* were bright green with blaze orange mottling on their shells. There were also a few *Dinochelys* turtles, which looked similar to Glyptops, but they were red and yellow and had a smooth outer shell surface, which contrasted with the distinctive ridges visible on the *Glyptops* turtles.

Durango cautiously soaked a bandana and cleaned blood off one of Yonder's back legs. He then tore up a spare shirt and wrapped part of it around his horse's leg, so it would serve as a makeshift bandage. Afterward, he filled canteens and Kailani's water bottle, and Adalya pointed a light from a small pen-like instrument into each hydration container before it was capped.

Lassen and Kailani reached the top of a large boulder overlooking the river and plains. Lassen scanned the horizon with his binoculars and noted a *Diplodcus* herd feeding about a quarter mile (one half kilometer) to the northeast. He then examined the river in all directions, checking for signs of Traxton's men. He saw none, but he noticed dense forests along the water to the north and south. If the Traxton Gang survived, they could easily hide.

Soon, Adalya and Durango joined Lassen and Kailani up in the rocks. While standing next to Lassen, Adalya said, "I'm going to gauge how well the location signaler transmits at this elevation." She removed the location signaler from a utility pouch on her belt. The signaler looked like a small metallic cube with a blinking green light, and sunlight glinted off it. Adalya activated her orientation module with her other hand and displayed a holographic readout of specifications about the location signaler's performance.

"Seems to be transmitting sufficiently," Adalya said.

A *Harpactognathus* flying high overhead cocked its head down. The pterosaur's eyes bulged with childlike curiosity as it spotted the tiny shiny object in Adalya's hand. The *Harpactognathus* released a little squawk and flew with an eight-foot (two-meter) wingspan. It weighed about 13 pounds (six kilograms) and was dark red with brown mottling. Unlike the *Mesadactylus* Lassen had seen flying over dinosaur herds earlier in the day, the *Harpactognathus* had a thin low crest on top of its head and a blunter beak. It also carried a tail that was roughly one foot (30 centimeters) long and capped with a diamond-shaped piece of skin. In contrast, *Mesadactylus* had a stubby tail.

Adalya focused on interpreting signal transmission statistics, Kailani intently looked through binoculars at distant *Diplodocus*, and Lassen and Durango surveyed the northern horizon with their hands raised to shield their eyes from the sun. The *Harpactognathus* flying above swiftly swooped down.

Adalya looked up as she detected a shadow and heard a piercing shriek. The *Harpactognathus* zoomed past Adalya like a fighter plane strafing its ground target. In the process, its wings brushed against Adalya's hands and knocked the location signaler into the air. As it zipped past, the *Harpactognathus* nimbly caught the signaler in its beak with the aid of widely-spaced conical teeth.

Upon hearing pterosaur shrieking and feeling the rush of wing-beaten air, Kailani lowered her binoculars while Lassen instinctively drew his gun. Durango reached for his holster but realized it was now empty.

Another *Harpactognathus* chewed a fish in the shade of nearby boulders. Lassen pulled back the hammer of this pistol, and the *Harpactognathus* on the ground launched into the air upon hearing mechanical clicking. To Lassen, the second *Harpactognathus* seemed to materialize from nowhere. It honed in on the shiny gun in the bounty hunter's hand like a flake of iron jumping to a magnet. As the first *Harpactognathus* flew away with the location signaler in its teeth, the second knocked the gun from Lassen's hands at the same instant the bounty hunter realized the flying reptile was present. As the pterosaurs flew away over the river, they flapped stiff-fibered wing membranes, which were covered with fine red and black hairs.

Shocked and confused, the time travelers watched Lassen's gun as it fell toward the river. Lassen expected a small plopping splash, but instead, a 10-foot (three-meter) long, 300-pound (130-kilogram) *Amphicotylus* sprung from the water and swallowed the pistol before submerging back below the surface. It had typical modern crocodile earth tone colorations with a light underbelly. Lassen did not know why a prehistoric crocodylomorph would want to eat a gun, but he guessed maybe the animal thought it was a jumping fish and merely acted on instinct.

Despite some wildlife species in the Jurassic being fantastically large, the *Amphicotylus* were not nearly as big as some modern crocodylomorphs. In Lassen's time, the American crocodile would reach 15 feet (five meters) long and could weigh 2,000 pounds (900 kilograms). Lassen had encountered them in the swamps of southern Florida and the jungles of Mexico. However, there were still very large crocodylomorphs in prehistoric times. For example, *Sarcosuchus* lived during the Cretaceous Period in Africa and may have reached 40 feet (12 meters) in length and weighed up to 17,500 pounds (7,938 kilograms).

"What just happened?" Lassen asked.

Adalya breathed hard, and adrenaline coursed through her as she spoke. "One of those flying dinosaurs took the location signaler, and another disarmed you."

"That actually wasn't a dinosaur," Kailani said. "What we just saw was a pterosaur."

"Are you okay?" Lassen asked.

"Yes," Adalya said. "It just scratched my sleeves a bit."

"How come they're not dinosaurs?" Durango asked. "We saw a bunch of them flying over dinosaurs this morning."

"They're flying reptiles," Kailani said, "and have key morphological and ecological differences compared to dinosaurs. However, they're closely related to dinosaurs and live alongside them throughout the Mesozoic Era."

"What species was that?" Lassen asked.

"I'm not sure," Kailani said. "In my time, many people are familiar with the Cretaceous pterosaur *Pteranodon*, though they incorrectly call it 'pterodactyl.' *Pteranodon* is a pterodactyloid pterosaur with a small tail and a long beak; it looks somewhat similar to what we saw flying over the dinosaur herds this morning. Those could have been *Mesadactylus*. However, what we just encountered looked like a rhamphorynchoid pterosaur. They have longer tails and shorter snouts compared to pterodactyloid pterosaurs. It might have been *Harpactognathus*, but there could be a variety of pterosaurs here for which no fossils will ever be found in modern times."

"Why's that?" Lassen asked. "Seems like a bunch of the dinosaurs here will be found."

"In modern times," Kailani said, "pterosaur fossils are particularly rare because they have fragile, hollow thin bones that are often not durable enough to become fossilized. They also don't receive the same level of attention from paleontologists as dinosaurs and other more popular extinct animals."

"Interesting," Lassen said. "After causing me to lose my gun, they're not very popular with me right now."

"A bigger problem," Adalya said, "is that we have lost our location signaler."

"How bad is that?" Durango asked.

"It could be worse," Adalya said as she pressed buttons on her module, "but it is not optimal."

A holographic image appeared. It displayed a stationary blue dot and a blinking bright red dot moving over a topographic map.

"The blue dot is us, and the red dot is the location signaler," Adalya said. "Right now, it is moving and still in the beak of a pterosaur. We can track the location signaler with my module. The signaler is intact and operational. Unfortunately, if Professor Sedora ever makes it to our time, she will be tracking a pterosaur."

"Then we have to get it back," Lassen said. "What direction is that flying reptile headed?"

"It is moving north," Adalya said. "It looks like it is paralleling the base of the mountains to the west."

"And it's not flyin' hither and yon," Durango added. "Seems to be goin' pretty straight, like it has a destination in mind."

"Maybe it's migrating or heading for a nest," Kailani said.

"We should go catch Graphite," Lassen said. "Then let's move north along the edge of the western hills and follow that pterosaur."

The bounty hunters and scientists moved off the rocks and traveled north toward Graphite. It took some time and another lump of sugar, but Lassen eventually regained the gray horse's trust. The time travelers continued north and rode through a portion of open plains between forested foothills to the west and a river to the east.

The day grew steadily hotter as morning transitioned into early afternoon. The bounty hunters and scientists began to sweat heavily and quickly grew tired in the semi-arid but still humid environment.

Lassen and Kailani rode side-by-side behind Adalya and Durango. Kailani regularly wrote in her notebook and took photos and videos with her phone. As Lassen yawned, he said, "I think it's harder to breathe here."

"That would make sense," Kailani said. "Not only is the Morrison Basin of the Jurassic hotter than what we were used to in modern times, it also has about three times as much carbon dioxide. As a result, breathing is a little harder."

"The dinosaurs must be used to it since they evolved with it," Lassen said.

Lassen took off his hat and wiped sweat from his forehead with the back of his hand. He took a swig from his canteen. The water tasted like warm canteen metal, but it was still a refreshing reprieve. Pterosaurs circled ahead in the distance. Some also regularly landed on and took off from trees in the forested foothills to the west. Little frogs hopped out of the way as the horses tromped through puddles and *Equisetum*-clad water seeps. A gentle breeze flowing eastward out of the hills provided brief relief from the heat and brought the scent of forest duff and what smelled like pine needles. Lassen felt slight relief from the heat as air currents dried the sweat on his face and the back of his neck.

The time travelers gazed at a distant herd of green-brown *Camarasaurus* to the northeast. Then Kailani pointed out a lone male *Stegosaurus* to the east. It changed position in an attempt to intercept the breeze drifting out of the hills. Lassen and Kailani stopped their horses. Ahead of them, Durango and Adalya slowed and reluctantly stopped.

"Thermoregulation," Kailani said as she took photos of the nearby *Stegosaurus* with her phone. "Brilliant. So, the *Stegosaurus* does use its plates for that. The breeze must blow across its plates and cool the blood inside them, which then circulates throughout its body."

"Intriguing," Lassen said. "I would have guessed they would mainly be display structures."

"They're probably used for multiple purposes," Kailani said. "They look showy enough for display but can also help with cooling."

Lassen and Kailani got out their binoculars to get a better look at the *Stegosaurus*. As Kailani peered through binoculars, she said, "The *Stegosaurus* plates and thagomizers are covered in keratin sheaths. They're bigger and sharper than what fossil bones show."

"What are thagomizers?" Lassen asked.

"*Stegosaurus* tail spikes," Kailani said. "They got that name in 1982 based on a publication by Larson."

"Strange," Lassen muttered, "but yeah, those tail spikes are strong and sharp. Look like the horns of a Texas longhorn. Must be used for defense."

"Good theory," Kailani said. "In fact, fossils indicate that *Stegosaurus* used their tail spikes to defend against *Allosaurus*."

"How do fossils show that?" Lassen asked.

"There are fossils from each species," Kailani said, "that provide evidence of hostile interactions. For example, a fossilized *Stegosaurus* plate has been found that has bite marks arranged in a configuration that matches an *Allosaurus* jaw."

"Wait a minute," Lassen said. "How do you know that plate wasn't just from a *Stegosaurus* that was already dead and was being scavenged by an *Allosaurus*?"

"That has been considered," Kailani said. "Bite marks on their own are not enough to prove interactions between live animals. It would be difficult to prove the *Stegosaurus* was alive when its plate was bitten. However, solid evidence of live interactions has been found, including an *Allosaurus* tail bone with a partially healed injury that appeared to be caused by a *Stegosaurus* spike puncture."

"Of course," Lassen said, "partially healed wounds would be the best evidence for live interactions because an animal has to be alive to heal."

"Exactly," Kailani said. "There was also an *Allosaurus* skeleton discovered that had a pubic bone with evidence of a substantial infection and an associated wound with a shape matching a *Stegosaurus* tail spike. Interestingly, in that case, the position of the puncture wound indicated that *Stegosaurus* had a prehensile tail. Based on the location of the wound, the *Stegosaurus* tail would have had to twist and launch straight up to impact the *Allosaurus* where it did. Fossils of *Stegosaurus* thagomizers that were broken and partially healed have also been found. These don't necessarily prove *Allosaurus* interaction, but they indicate that *Stegosaurus* used its spikes forcefully, possibly in defense against predators. Stress estimation and force analysis studies also show that *Stegosaurus* was quite capable of penetrating bone with its thagomizers. The keratin sheaths make the spikes extra durable compared to what they would be like if they were just made of bone."

"Yeah, that makes sense," Lassen said. "Bone by itself can be pretty brittle. I've seen mule deer bucks with broken antlers lots of times, and antlers are solid bone. Interesting. You've taught me so much new information about dinosaurs that I'll need a second brain to store it all."

"Well, actually," Kailani said, "some paleontologists used to think *Stegosaurus* had a second brain located above its hips."

"Does it?" Lassen asked, raising his eyebrows.

"No," Kailani said. "As far as we know, no dinosaurs have second brains, but the spinal cord tube in the *Stegosaurus's* back bones above its hips is disproportionately enlarged, indicating those bones—the sacral vertebrae bones—held more than just a spinal cord in that part of the skeleton. Some theorized there could have been a second brain—a hindbrain—in that enlarged portion of the bones. However, one brain and a spinal cord are enough to coordinate movement in dinosaurs. The enlarged sacral spinal cord region in *Stegosaurus* most likely stored glycogen, which is a form of energy-rich glucose. Glucose is a sugar that results from metabolism. In fact, most modern birds have an enlarged sacral spinal cord region, and it stores glycogen."

"What do birds use that glycogen for?" Lassen asked.

"No one actually knows for sure," Kailani said, "but we know it's not a brain."

As the travelers got closer to a distant *Camarasaurus* group, Lassen heard splashing and saw the sauropods slosh into a pond in an effort to ease the heat. Suddenly, a disturbingly loud sound penetrated the hot afternoon air like a cannon blast.

"What was that?!" Durango exclaimed as Yonder and Graphite reared while Horizon and Ember stayed steady.

"I don't know," Lassen said. "It could have been a gunshot, but it didn't sound quite right."

"It sounded like it came from near the river to the east," Adalya said.

"Yeah," Lassen said. "You should all take cover behind those trees."

Lassen pointed at a cluster of young araucarian conifers just beyond Durango, Kailani, and Adalya. He took out his binoculars and got off Graphite before handing the reins to Durango.

"I'm going to check out that sound," Lassen said. "If the Traxton Gang survived, we need to know."

"Wait up, Lassen," Durango said. "I'm comin' with you."

"No," Lassen said. "Stay here. This is just a scouting hike. If there's only one of us, there's a smaller chance we'll be detected."

Durango nodded in agreement before saying, "But I don't like it."

Lassen stealthily moved low and fast toward the direction of the sound. As he got closer, his nose picked up a rotten odor. Still crouching, he stood up just high enough to view the nearby river with his binoculars held over ferns. Scanning the river for signs of humans, he spotted several *Eutretauranosuchus* crocodylomorphs sunning themselves on a sandbar. They moved toward a mangled *Camarasaurus* carcass floating against the riverbank. Its green belly skin was pale, torn, dirty, and crinkled. Loose ribs protruded from the ghastly mass. Lassen squinted with concentration as the

Eutretauranosuchus began tearing at dried leathery skin to access soft rotten flesh underneath. Lassen readjusted his binoculars as a new shape came into view.

Another *Camarasaurus* carcass floated near shore, bloated and enormous. Lassen guessed this *Camarasaurus* died in or near the water days earlier and was washed into the middle of the river by flooding where it was out of easy reach for most predators. As a result, it stayed intact long enough for decomposition gases in its guts to cause it to bloat. Lassen wondered if the huge dinosaur body could expand any larger.

BOOM! The bloated *Camarasaurus's* abdomen exploded as a blast of bloat gas shot out with tremendous force. The force was so strong that several ribs snapped off and popped out of the carcass. Lassen lowered his binoculars and placed a hand over his nose as he ducked left to avoid being hit by a blown-off chunk of dinosaur rib. The stench was terrible. Lassen wriggled his nose as he stood up and peered through binoculars again. More *Eutretauranosuchus* stirred from their riverbank lounging and slunk toward the newest carcass to wash ashore while a flock of rhamphorynchoid pterosaurs landed on it.

CHAPTER 11: FORCED ALLIANCE

Lightning flashed. Rain pounded hard. Randall Blaze tried to walk without getting stuck in mud. Nearby, water flowed off a metallic time machine covered in black scorch marks from a recent lightning strike. Sedora stood nearby and quickly unholstered her plasma pistol. Just after returning to 1879 after a brief visit to 2026, she had come outside to survey the terrain. The first thing she found was Randall Blaze, a Traxton Gang outlaw left behind.

"What happened?!" Blaze shouted.

"That is confidential!" Sedora shouted back.

"I say it's not!" Blaze replied as he reached for his six-shooters.

Without hesitation, Sedora pulled the trigger of her plasma pistol. Sizzling purple energy beams blasted out of her weapon and sliced off Blaze's holsters while radiating intense heat against his hands. His holsters and guns fell to the ground.

Blaze snarled in pain and plunged his singed hands into cool mud.

"What's goin' on?!" Blaze yelled, pulling his hands out of mud and frantically flexing his fingers. His burns were painful and shocking but not bad enough to cause blistering.

Sedora fired again. Blaze's guns and holsters melted into slag from intense beams of energy, which punctured the mud and resulted in smoking, steaming holes of burnt dirt. Nearby, a little prairie dog jumped out of its hole with a smoking tail. The rain quickly extinguished the critter's combusted hair, and the prairie dog disappeared into the darkness of an ending twilight, searching for a safer burrow.

"I cannot tell you!" Sedora said.

"Yes you can, filly!" Blaze said as he stood up and charged Sedora.

Sedora flicked a switch on her weapon and shot Blaze straight in the face with a neon blue energy beam. Blaze's face briefly lit up, and bolts of energy danced across his chattering teeth. Then he fell to the ground, unconscious.

Sedora positioned Blaze's hands behind his back, reached into a utility pouch on her belt, and retrieved two coiled metallic bands that were comprised of a series of interconnected small hexagons. Sedora tossed one band at Blaze's hands, and it automatically whipped around his wrists, bound them together, and locked over itself with a click. She threw the other band at Blaze's ankles, and they were soon bound in the same fashion. The restraints were like extremely sophisticated snap bracelets.

"What am I going to do with this primitive cowboy?" Sedora muttered to herself. She placed her hands on her hips and sighed heavily. "I suppose he needs shelter."

Sedora picked up Blaze and slung him over her shoulder. As lightning flashed, and rain continued to pound, Sedora hauled Blaze into the time machine and locked him in a side room.

Sedora moved to the vehicle's control panels and assessed the damage of the recent lightning strike and rock collision. The temporal coordinate settings were malfunctioning and seemed to have been temporarily programmed to be based on stratigraphy, which was why a burst of energy had sent objects to the Jurassic Period after penetrating Jurassic rock. Various basic internal control settings were also scrambled. The lightning appeared to damage the software and programming of the time machine more than its physical components, which were remarkably durable. They had been designed to withstand sudden jolts of energy as a standard defense against weapons of the 2700s.

Sedora thought back to the control panel readings in 2026 that showed Adalya and the 1879 citizens were going 150 million years into the past. *So, Doctor Nell is stranded in the time of the dinosaurs,* Sedora thought. *Extremely fascinating from a paleontological perspective but also extremely dangerous. If I can fix the settings, and she has her location signaler, I can go back and get her. I do not know how to fix the settings right now, but if I could track Cordon, I could just use his machine. He may have arrived in the same time as me, though I do not know where he ended up.*

Sedora flipped several switches to direct the time machine's sensors to scan the terrain within a 400-mile (644-kilometer) radius of her location. She was hoping she could detect Cordon's stolen time machine or traces of its residual quantum temporal signature.

The first thing Sedora noticed when running her geography scans was that she was not where she thought she would be. Terrain scans showed she was in the badlands near Pine Butte. However, based on the trajectory of her time machine during the chase with Cordon, she should have been near Sheep Rock, which was about 45 miles (72 kilometers) southeast of her current location. Something had gone wrong, and she had traveled to a different location from where she started. That made her wonder just where in the world Adalya may have materialized. Sedora was worried she could have appeared literally anywhere, which could mean the middle of a boulder, deep in an oceanic trench, or thousands of feet in the sky. Sedora very much hoped Adalya at least ended up on Earth.

Sedora's control panel pinged, and she flicked a holographic display into existence. The display showed that her scans had detected levels of rubidium and titanium that would only be present with another time machine. However, the elements occurred in finely dispersed fragments, and there was also a lot of carbon, which indicated burnt materials.

The holographic display data confirmed that Cordon's vehicle was destroyed by an explosion. This dashed Sedora's hopes of using the stolen time machine for a rescue mission. She flicked through several more holo readouts, attempting to determine if the stolen machine's tungsten carbide-coated parameter settings core was still intact. If it was, she could use it to reset the settings of her own machine. The control panel pinged twice.

"Yes . . . it is intact," Sedora said under her breath as she confirmed that the parameter settings core was detected by her machine's scanners and undamaged. She transferred its decimal degree latitude/longitude coordinates into her database orientation module. Sedora hoped the software on the other time machine's parameter settings core fared better in an explosion than hers did from a lightning strike. She continued flipping through holographic readouts and learned that the settings core and all time machine debris had been at Sheep Rock since October 21, 1876.

Sedora would apprehend Cordon if possible, but she knew he could now be anywhere. Her main goal was to retrieve the parameter settings core from Cordon's machine while blending in with the locals and following established UTAC protocols. That meant she should not drive the time machine wherever she wanted or openly use advanced technology. The time machine actually had a holographic cloaking feature, but it was too badly damaged to be effective.

Sedora sighed as she considered her best course of action. Her prisoner had already seen too much, but she could erase some of his memories later. She also knew that he could prove to be helpful—if he was not so uncooperative.

A short time later, Blaze—still bound—sat in a chair across from Sedora. A small metallic table separated them. Thunder rumbled, and rain pattered outside. Occasionally, flashes of lightning were visible through a small window behind Blaze.

"Are you from outer space?!" Blaze asked with anger. "What is this?! What did you shoot me with? The top of my mouth is numb."

The inside of the time machine was brightly lit. In the light, Blaze noticed that Sedora was an attractive woman, despite her plain outfit with a utility belt. She was 45 years old, but futuristic technology and time out of the sun made her look 15 years younger. Her bronze red and silver-streaked hair also had an unnaturally glamorous sheen. However, Blaze was angry enough that Sedora's looks did not matter. Pretty or not, she was his captor and an enemy.

"I will ensure you get out of here," Sedora said, "but you need to talk first. I merely hit you with a low impulse beam of energy from my plasma pistol. I put it on the sleep setting, but it can kill. I want you to answer some questions."

"No, *you* need to answer some questions for me," Blaze said with hostile impatience. "Who are you? What is this? Let me go! Let me go now! I don't want to be tied up by no woman!"

"Not exactly proper grammar," Sedora said under her breath, "but you are talking. I am Doctor Lenora Hadley. I am a scientist from Europe on a top-secret mission, but I need your help."

"A scientist doctor?" Blaze said. "I never met one of them. You patch people up and do alchemy?"

"Not really," Sedora said. She decided not to mention that in her time, rearranging molecules to create a variety of precious metals was an old but expensive technology. Also, by her time, asteroid mining had eliminated the precious status of most rare metals because it caused them to saturate the market and more than meet demand.

"Also, I am not a medical doctor," Sedora continued. "I have several advanced degrees from prestigious universities across the northern hemisphere, but they are in quantum physics, temporal theory, space-time fabric, and hyper mega-energy mechanics—not physiology or medicine." Despite knowing about the importance of holding back information about herself and the future, Sedora still felt compelled to describe her degrees.

"Well, good for you, missy," Blaze said. "I never thought I'd meet a woman doctor, though I heard there was one down in Colorado Springs. Doctor Guinn or something like that. What is this thing I'm in? A train car without a track? A fancy stagecoach without wheels?"

"In a manner of speaking, it is," Sedora said. "My hover train car is broken, and I have been separated from one of my coworkers. She is lost somewhere out on the range, and I need your help to get her back."

"That woman from the storm who was workin' on the train car?" Blaze asked.

"Yes, that is the individual," Sedora replied.

"I don't think she's still out on the range," Blaze said. "I saw her disappear into light along with my partners and our horses."

"She should still be intact somewhere," Sedora said, "but I need to fix my hover train car to find her."

"Where did she go, and where did my partners go?" Blaze said with impatient puzzlement. "They disappeared in flashes of light. They're gone. I saw it with my own eyes."

"They may have disappeared from the space-time that immediately surrounds us," Sedora said, "but they should have reappeared somewhere else."

"*Where?*" Blaze said with annoyance.

"Somewhere far away," Sedora said, "but I will not know for sure until I can fix my train car."

"What's in it for me if I help you?" Blaze said. "I was countin' on money from my boss, and your hover train car disappeared him. I don't do charity."

"I could kill you," Sedora said as she glanced down at the plasma pistol strapped to her hip, "but I have not. You help me, you live."

"If you need my help," Blaze said smugly, "you won't kill me."

"No," Sedora calmly said as she stared directly into Blaze's dirt-smudged mean face. "I would. Having your help now could enable me to accomplish my mission faster, but I can get by on my own if need be, and I am sure I could find someone else to help."

Sedora was not easily intimidated. She may have spent most of her time behind a desk in recent years, but she also had years of air combat experience. Blaze was a historic novelty of a problematic member of humanity, but he was a problem she was confident she could handle.

An especially loud rumble of thunder made Sedora instinctively turn her head over her shoulder. In that fleeting instant, despite his restraints, Blaze attempted to lunge toward Sedora's plasma pistol. As Blaze was in mid-lunge, Sedora detected his movement and pressed a small metallic device on her belt. A brief buzzing sound was heard, and Blaze fell onto the table in pain.

"Owwwwww!" Blaze shouted. "What was that?"

"An electric shock," Sedora said. "I have a device tuned to your biosignature. I can trigger that whenever I want if you are not being cooperative, and that was just the low setting."

Blaze angrily sighed before saying, "What do you want to know? Doesn't look like I have much of a choice—for now." Blaze defiantly squinted.

"I will need information on the local geography and natives," Sedora said, "but I also want to know about the men with whom you were riding. My research assistant may be with them as well as the men who were shooting at you and your group. Who are your partners, and why was there a gunfight?"

"I was riding with a group of fellers on a business trip," Blaze said.

"For what kind of business were you traveling?" Sedora asked.

"Ummm—financial, uh, business," Blaze said. Sedora looked at him with tight lips and narrowed eyes that expressed disbelief.

"We transport money from—*for* people," Blaze said.

"So, you were with an outlaw gang who robs banks and possibly other financial service entities," Sedora said. "That was easy to guess."

"Hey, I never said that," Blaze replied. "We help with stocks, bonds, futures, and such. Legitimate money dealings. Do you even know what futures are?"

"Oh, trust me," Sedora said, "I know futures. Who were those men shooting at you?"

"Bounty hunters," Blaze said with a sneer. "I guess they thought there was a price on some of my business associates. Makes me wish I didn't join up with them. I'm an innocent man. This will be bad for business."

"Right," Sedora said with a hint of sarcasm. "Do you know anything about those two particular bounty hunters?"

"They were Lassen Malone and Durango Mesquite," Blaze said. "Mean desperadoes. They'd kill anybody for their blood money. If your assistant's with them, she's not safe. If everybody ends up in the same place, there's going to be a mess of trouble and shooting." Blaze glowered at Sedora. "When will you let me go?"

"I shall address your liberation in due time, mister . . ." Sedora said before pausing. "What is your name, anyway, cowboy?"

"Oh, *now* you ask," Blaze rudely snapped back. "Name's John Sage. I'm vice president of Sage Enterprises. Our main office is in Philadelphia, but we've got dealings out West: Cheyenne, Denver, Salt Lake City, and such. I'm an influential man. When word of this gets out—well, my lawyer will want to talk with you."

"Right," Sedora said. "Influential businessman in dirty clothes far out on the range and being pursued by bounty hunters. You are also what? Nineteen? Twenty years old? That does not make sense. I think you are wanted—and if you are, that gives me more leverage over you. I could kill you *or* turn you in, but if you help me out, things will be better for everybody."

"If you say so," Blaze said as he angrily flexed his fingers. He was disappointed that various conman tactics Shanahan Branigan had taught him were not working.

"Here is the plan," Sedora said. "Tomorrow, we go to the nearest settlement, get horses and supplies, and go to Sheep Rock."

"Sheep Rock?" Blaze said with recognition as his demeanor suddenly changed.

"Yes, Sheep Rock," Sedora said. "I need something from there. You know the area?"

Blaze nodded. "I can take you there. I know the water holes along the way and that it's good to steer clear of Fred McBray's ranch. He shoots trespassers on sight."

"Good to know," Sedora said. "You can assist with economic transactions and serve as a guide."

"I guess I can do that," Blaze said.

"Good," Sedora said. She wondered why Blaze suddenly became cooperative. She was skeptical but hoped he would actually be helpful. She knew things could go much smoother with a local guide knowledgeable about the physical and cultural geography. She would use her database orientation module and its historical records. However, although technology was useful, Sedora had learned that there was no substitute for actual human knowledge based on first-hand observation.

Chapter 12: Outlaw Interlude

150.77 MILLION YEARS BEFORE 2026 – AFTERNOON

Tardell Traxton and his men rode in thick vegetation along a river. They were about four miles (six kilometers) south of Lassen, Durango, Kailani, and Adalya. However, whereas Lassen and his companions were on the west side of the river, Traxton and his gang rode east of the river. Horse hooves regularly smashed down *Equisetum* plants. The Traxton Gang had finally dried off after struggling in water for a considerable distance. Traxton rode in the lead and reflected on how he and his men had crawled onto a riverbank covered in shrubbery and trees. They were exhausted, panting, shocked, and soaked.

Traxton had spent about an hour trying to explain to his men how and why they went back in time. He vaguely touched on the fact that he was from the future. His men were very confused, and Traxton found explaining to be challenging. Branigan and Avarette had an easier time believing Traxton or at least acting like they did. Gantry and Holt were more argumentative and confused, but nobody denied that something strange and radical had happened.

Traxton did not know exactly when he was, but based on observations of a few startled *Dryosaurus* drinking along the river, he knew he was millions of years prior to his time. Unlike Adalya, Traxton did not have a database orientation module. He had tried to bring one to the 1870s, but it had been destroyed during the plasma pistol shootout with security forces when he fled 2756.

Traxton planned to hunt Lassen and Durango as they had once hunted him. After hearing the gunshots Durango fired at a pair of *Ornitholestes*, Traxton had used his military grade 1870s field scope to spot Lassen, Durango, Kailani, and Adalya on the plains just before they disappeared out of sight to the north. Traxton was in a hurry to pursue, but the twisted river channels and frequent wetlands made travel circuitous and slow-going. Semiaquatic crocodylomorphs were a constant threat, and various river crossings did not look safe. Though Traxton wanted to head straight north, he and his men were veering east.

While looking through his scope, Traxton had recognized Adalya and noticed that Lassen rode Blaze's horse. Traxton was not sure what had happened to Blaze. He also did not recognize Kailani and wondered where she came from.

"We'll kill the bounty hunters and keep the women alive," Traxton had said. Traxton knew that if he were to return to the Old West of the 1870s from the *really* Old West of the Jurassic, he would need the help of somebody from his time. Adalya was essential, and Kailani could have also been somebody from Area 54. He was not sure.

Embarking on a mission to kill Lassen and Durango was a welcome diversion for Traxton. The outlaw leader was in a gloomy and desperate situation. The thought of revenge helped distract him from the fact that he was stranded in a strange and savage land. As Traxton snarled in frustration, he thought about a turning point in his history with Lassen.

*　　*　　*

In April 1878, Traxton rode through the bustling muddy streets of Denver, Colorado. As part of an elaborate robbery scheme, he was in disguise as a legitimate businessman and used the alias Terrence Vandergilt. He wandered through secluded alleys and examined nearby windows, high vantage points, and possible escape routes. Traxton developed a plan as he continued scouting streets near the Denver Mint. For a change, Traxton was clean-shaven and wore a finely-tailored suit. His horse was buckskin tan and recently stolen from a livery stable in Boulder.

As Traxton rode into a shadowy alley, he caught a glimpse of the sun setting over the Colorado Front Range to the west. The Rockies near Denver were high, ragged, majestic, and bold. Traxton knew they would form a gorgeous silhouette at sunset as dusk cloaked the western edge of the Great Plains. Sunsets were one of Traxton's favorite parts of his new life. He loved being in wide open spaces instead of a dark underground facility. He also preferred the glow of the sun and campfire coals to that of control panels and holographic projections.

A killdeer called from puddles at the edge of town. Suddenly, Traxton heard a woman shouting and the sounds of a scuffle from behind a nearby building.

"Yah!" Traxton exclaimed as he spurred his horse toward the sounds. As Traxton turned a corner, he saw a strikingly beautiful

Latina woman in a ruffled dress standing defiantly as three street ruffians closed in, knives in hand.

"Quiet down, pretty yowler," one of the criminals growled. "And give me your money!"

Traxton suddenly flashed back to role-playing ancient Wild West scenes on his stick horse as a child. Now, in a different persona, without his gang with him, he could actually be a hero. He also thought Terrence Vandergilt would rescue those in need. If he helped this woman, he was just maintaining his disguise—like any good master criminal would. Traxton's first instinct was to swiftly gun down each man with well-placed execution shots between their eyes, but that would attract too much attention. Traxton instead charged his horse forward, which knocked one man to the ground. He then leapt off his mount and tackled another man, who fell into Traxton's third adversary.

The woman being accosted watched Traxton rapidly kick and punch her would-be attackers into unconscious submission. Traxton dusted off his hands, smoothly took off his hat, and said, "All taken care of, miss. I reckon these ornery polecats won't be bothering you anymore."

"Thank you so much, sir," the woman said. "May I ask who performed such a gallant and noble gesture?"

"Vandergilt, ma'am," Traxton said. "I'm Terrence Vandergilt: businessman."

"I'm Solana Herdez," the woman said as she smiled with a symmetrical set of impressive white teeth.

As Solana smiled, Traxton became mesmerized. Solana was so beautiful and cute *and* talking to him directly, *and* her eyes sparkled. She was aware of him, and they were having a conversation. This thrilled Traxton, and old character traits he had attempted to suppress suddenly revived. Traxton wanted to know everything about Solana. The weakness of instant infatuation with a woman had emotionally debilitated Traxton in his former life as Brent Cordon. It had always proven to be one-sided and never ended well, reinforcing layers of loneliness and selfishness. Brent Cordon's sincere—though premature and unreciprocated—fondness had always transformed into bitterness and mistrust. He had come to see attractive women primarily as sources of pain to be avoided.

For now, Traxton did not even think of his past. His mind suddenly envisioned a future where he and Solana were together, watching sunsets, smelling sagebrush, riding horses, having picnics on the plains, and shooting down a variety of birds for target practice. Traxton also envisioned Solana sharing his worldview, never arguing with him, and being continually impressed with his accomplishments and personality. They did not know each other yet. Traxton did not have evidence to warrant disappointment. Theoretically, Solana *could* be everything for which he hoped. He did not know any differently yet, and his adult mind ran wild with the imagination of a naive foolish youth possessing meager social skills and potent impressionability.

Traxton paid a newspaper boy to alert law enforcement to the unconscious thieves in the alley. He then took Solana to dinner, and they watched a glorious sunset out the window of the restaurant. Traxton learned that Solana was a widow and in Denver awaiting the arrival of prize mustangs she was to purchase for her ranch in Santa Fe. Late that night, Traxton sent a message to his gang saying their job was going to be delayed by a day.

The following morning, Traxton stepped into a store to buy a new set of clothes for an afternoon ride with Solana. He left the store with brown pants, a tan hat, a beige button-up shirt, and a brown leather vest. Traxton thought his ride with Solana went great, and he and Solana made plans to have dinner again that night.

As rich pre-sunset reddish evening light permeated Denver and the surrounding plains, Traxton sat in a restaurant, waiting. He thought of leaving the outlaw life and settling down with Solana. Thinking of seeing Solana again filled him with excited anticipation. When Solana was absent 10 minutes after her scheduled arrival time, Traxton bit his lower lip and glanced at his gold pocket watch with anxiety. As time progressed, his anticipation turned to hope, which then morphed into solemn, ominous fear. Initially, Traxton thought something may have delayed Solana, but she would still appear. Then dark demons from his past returned, and Traxton thought of being rejected. The hard, mean outlaw confidence he had worked hard to build wavered. The evening light darkened with Traxton's mood.

After waiting for an agonizing 45 minutes, Traxton left the restaurant and stepped outside. During his anxious brooding, he had missed the sunset. Cool dusk darkness settled onto the land.

Then his eyes and mouth widened with impressionable recognition as he saw Solana walk toward him from across the street. Immediately, he sensed trouble.

"Hello, Miss Herdez," Traxton said. "Anything wrong?"

"Hello," Solana calmly and coolly said. "Are you really Tardell Traxton?"

"What?!" Traxton said with feigned disbelief. "I'm Terrence Vandergilt. I'm a businessman from New York. You know that. Where did you hear this?"

Solana slowly, quietly looked down. "I heard what happened, and I saw the 'Wanted' posters. But I had to see you again to know for sure."

"No," Traxton said. "That's nonsense!" Traxton's Solana-based fantasies began to quickly evaporate and billow away like steam blown from a hot spring in winter. She seemed unconvinced of his denials. And her accusations were based on what? Words from a stranger (he guessed) and some "Wanted" posters sketched by a two-bit frontier artist? Did she really care about him or trust him? Sure, they had only known each other for two days, but he thought they were developing something special. Intellectually, he knew she should not trust him, but emotionally, he desperately wanted her to, even if it was based on a false persona.

"Who told you that?" Traxton asked with a mean edge slipping into his voice.

Solana held her head down and began to walk away.

"WHO tuh—tuh—told you that?!" Traxton forcefully asked as his eyes began to glisten and redden.

"I'll tell you who!" a confident voice called out from behind a nearby building. "Miss Herdez, I suggest you make yourself scarce."

Just after Solana walked behind a brick building, Traxton heard a Colt forty-five pistol hammer click. Then he noticed a tan buckskin horse and black horse tied at a nearby hitching rail.

"MALONE!" Traxton shouted with vitriolic denunciation as he drew a pair of well-concealed pistols from shoulder holsters. A fierce gunfight ensued. Pistol shots flashed in the dusk. Solana fled to a safer part of town as Traxton battled Lassen Malone, Durango Mesquite, and local law officers. After the smoke cleared, the outlaw rode hard into the night on a stolen racehorse. Feeling a tumultuous mix of disappointment, rage, jealousy, resolve, and self-hate, he dismissed his recent notions about being a hero and leaving the outlaw life. More than ever, he now wanted to embrace the freedom and power of being an outlaw gang leader. His desire to exact vengeance on Malone and Mesquite was also greatly reinforced. Traxton wanted the bounty hunters and the foolish past chapters of his life shot to holes, dead, buried, and forgotten.

Traxton would kill the past, but now, in the Jurassic, he was literally trapped in it and needed to ensure it did not kill him first.

*　　*　　*

Traxton shook his head as his mind returned to the present. He ground his teeth with dissatisfaction at the thought of seeing Lassen with Adalya. *He will die*, Traxton thought.

Traxton and his men had not seen nearly as many Jurassic wildlife species as the bounty hunters and scientists. Aside from *Dryosaurus*, they had spooked up some mammals and saw a few *Mesadactylus* and *Archaeopteryx*. They had also caught glimpses of *Amphicotylus* and *Eutretauranosuchus*. However, they did not yet realize just how mighty the rulers of the Jurassic Morrison Basin were.

"Avarette," Traxton said in an impatient voice. "Go check on Gantry. He's riding ahead and supposed to be keeping an eye out for the bounty hunters, but I think he's talking to himself. Quiet him down." Faint talking could be heard in the distance.

"Sure thing, boss," Avarette said as he spurred his horse east.

As Avarette rode out of the trees to the edge of the plains, Gantry's voice got louder. Avarette wondered why he always ended up dealing with Gantry. He liked other members of the gang better. Traxton got a job done with cold, calculating efficiency. Branigan was a challenging poker player who actually taught Avarette new tricks. Holt was quiet, which enabled Avarette to concentrate on practicing card shuffling and sleight of hand when he and Holt spent long periods waiting together during ambush jobs. Gantry was not calculating, not quiet, and the only things he taught Avarette were things Avarette did not wish to know. For instance, Avarette now knew the weight of a Brahma bull. He wrote off Gantry as a blatherskite who could talk a donkey's hind leg off.

As Avarette rode, he thought he could hear Gantry muttering about a "ham dog." The gambler was simultaneously irked and fascinated by Gantry's tendency to sing bizarre songs that seemed to be made up on the spot. Gantry claimed they were cowboy songs other real people sang on the trail. Avarette was not convinced. He noticed that Gantry sang more when he was nervous. As Avarette approached Gantry, the fact that he was singing became unmistakable. Gantry was oblivious to Avarette's approach.

"Old Ham Dog!" Gantry sang from atop his horse. "Old Haaaaaam Dog. He was howling in the night. Old Ham Dooog. He was having quite a fright. Old Ham Dooooog. Ham Dog. Goin' yooowwwwooooo! Yoowwwoo! He was an old Ham Dog. Ham Dog livin' on the prairie. Ham Dog bein' real hairy. Ham Dog feelin' real scary. He was an old Ham Dog! Yooowwwwoooo! Chawed some ham. Yoowwoooo! Chawed some—"

Suddenly, Gantry and Avarette turned their heads to the left at the sound of branch snapping and leaf rustling. Two massive male *Stegosaurus* lumbered out of riverside forest and moved down a slight slope. Dust and leaves whirled as 10,000-pound (4,500-kilogram) behemoths engaged in lethal combat. They moved straight toward Gantry whose horse vigorously reared in fear. Gantry tumbled off his mount.

"Yowwwch!" Gantry shouted as he fell on his right shoulder into dark floodplain dirt. Avarette's horse reared and neighed. Gantry looked up to see what appeared to be exotic, colorful lizard monsters. He had a close look at the dark green skin of the *Stegosaurus* males and their yellow underbellies. He also observed their bright red pentagonal plates that were adorned with mottled black starburst patterns.

The aggressive *Stegosaurus* emitted low guttural grunts and angry raspy hisses. Red veins intensified in the whites of their eyes. They quickly and sporadically went from two-legged to four-legged stances as they pounded at each other with their font legs and intermittently swung sharp, spiked tails. Soon, they were right on top of Gantry's position. With lithe movements, the skinny outlaw clumsily but successfully managed to barely avoid trampling. As he tumbled about, he rolled out of his duster, which was immediately trampled and jumbled.

One *Stegosaurus* in the area would mate today. Two wanted the privilege. A primal battle for genetic legacy raged. The claws of the *Stegosaurus* were not as damaging as those of local theropod carnivores, like *Allosaurus*, but they were still dangerous. The male *Stegosaurus* slashed at each other's throats and chests with flailing feet. Blood fell, but damage was minimal because small internal bone plates—called dermal ossicles—provided the *Stegosaurus* with armor beneath their neck and belly skin.

As Gantry rolled out of the way, the *Stegosaurus* moved back into the forest, continuing their battle. Branches broke, and *Stegosaurus* sounds soon faded as cicada insects, pterosaur calls, a slight breeze, and the snappy wingbeats of flitting dragonflies once more dominated the afternoon soundscape.

"Well, how's that for rip-roarin' flusteration?" Avarette said as he rode his horse toward Gantry before dismounting.

Gantry slowly stood up and dusted himself off. He picked up his duster jacket and un-jumbled it before putting it back on. "Those critters almost gave me a whompin!" Gantry proclaimed. "Good thing I had practice steer-wrastlin' in 'Rado. Back in the arena, you have to get out of the way or get tromped."

"I could see that," Avarette said. "*Rado?*"

"Colorado—the rodeo in Denver," Gantry said. "Them musta been more of those dinosaur varmints Traxton was talkin' about. Didn't know they got that big. They must've been 50 feet long."

"Closer to 30," Avarette said. The gambler looked down and noticed his boot was pressed into the dust of an enormous *Apatosaurus* footprint. "Gantry," Avarette said, "I think they get even bigger."

"Well, I'll be whillakered o' jillakered!" Gantry said. "That's a thunderin' print. Hey, Avarette, we could capture one of these things. I could train it and sell it to a circus. Make a bundle."

"Whoa, Gantry," Avarette said. "Let me get this straight. So, this prehistoric fauna—the spikeyplatosaurus—whatever they're called—nearly annihilated you, but now you want to train one—for a circus? *You* want to be their circus trainer?"

"Well, yeah," Gantry said. "Somebody's got to show them who's boss. What better way to do it than be their circus trainer?"

"*Well*, that is one idea," Avarette said. "But keep in mind that you would need to have a circus. You see any circuses around here?"

Gantry turned his head from side to side. He looked like he was genuinely searching for a circus. Avarette guessed the cowboy-turned-outlaw had hit his head too hard for about the eighth time.

"Oh," Gantry finally said. "Hey, that makes sense."

"You might not find a circus," Avarette said, "but you should probably find your horse. If you don't, Traxton will not be pleased."

"Yep," Gantry said with a fear-filled gulp as he pushed out some dents in his tattered felt hat. "Might not be any circuses around, but outside the forest, there's lots of good open range. I always feel better bein' out in the open. Could run lots of head here, too."

"Those cattle better enjoy ferns," Avarette replied.

Gantry and Avarette heard plants rustling and startled horse neighing to the south.

"What's goin' on?" Gantry asked.

"I do not know," Avarette said as he mounted his horse, "but we should find out." With a sigh of regret, Avarette said, "Hop on, Gantry. It'll be faster if we ride double instead of finding your cayuse first."

Avarette and Gantry rode back to the rest of the Traxton Gang and found them on foot and in a surly mood. They had all been thrown from their horses.

"What happened here, gentlemen?" Avarette asked.

"We're not quite sure," Traxton said in a low, angry voice.

"We were ridin' along slowly," Branigan added, "mindin' our own business when this giant lizard with horns on its nose shows up. It was way off ahead in the trees. I was the only one who saw it—and that was just for a wee moment. The horses spooked. They spooked somethin' fierce."

"Just the scent was enough to set them off," Holt said. "I've never seen horses so afraid."

"I know why they were so full of fear," Branigan added. "I saw the lizard bare its teeth. They were like rows of steak knives. It was more dangerous than a tiger. More dangerous than a grizzly. No horse in his right mind would want to tangle with that beast."

"Where's this primordial monster now?" Avarette asked.

"When the horses ran, the big lizard spooked, too," Branigan said. "I saw him disappear into the trees to the north. He might not come back, but if we want to keep up with the bounty hunters, we've got to find our horses."

Gantry examined tracks in the dirt while his companions talked. "I reckon they lit a shuck for the southeast," Gantry said while crouched near a smattering of hoof prints. "And they're movin' fast. They want to be on the plains. It will take quite a spell to round them up."

"Aye," Branigan replied.

"We'll find the horses," Traxton said, "and maybe tonight, we'll camp by that lake to the northeast. The horses might spook less in the open where there are fewer surprises. We'll take care of Malone and Mesquite tomorrow."

"Sounds like a good idea, boss," Gantry said.

After much effort, Traxton and his gang recovered their horses and rode northeast through the afternoon. Soon, they reached a high river channel levee that blocked the flat eastern horizon. On the other side of the river channel, just out of sight, a subadult bloated male *Brachiosaurus* carcass drifted toward shore. Its dried brown-blue skin was pebbly and mud-caked. The faint purple hues on its neck were pale. Suddenly, the abdomen of the dead sauropod exploded with a bang. The horses of the Traxton Gang reared in alarm.

"What was that, boss?" Branigan asked in a whisper. "Do you think it's Malone and Mesquite shootin' at something?"

"I don't know," Traxton quietly said, "but we need to find out. Let's tie up the horses and take a look over that rise just ahead." Traxton pointed at the channel.

"Whooooeeeeeeee," Gantry loudly said as his nose twitched. "Something smells bad. Holt, you been eatin' too many beans again?"

"Shut up, Gantry," Holt said.

"You both need to shut up," Avarette quietly muttered. "Malone and Mesquite could be just on the other side of that rise."

Traxton and Branigan turned around and meanly narrowed their eyes at Avarette, Gantry, and Holt. The three outlaws instantly stopped talking. After tying their horses, Traxton and his men removed their rifles from saddle scabbards and crawled up the nearby river channel embankment. As the outlaws crept up a fern-covered slope, they heard the slight sloshing of river water as well as grunts, bellows, and foliage snapping. They soon peered over the top of the channel levee.

The outlaws saw the *Brachiosaurus* carcass floating toward shore. They also saw a herd of *Camarasaurus* feeding along the other side of the river. The sauropods chewed on araucarian conifers that lined the riverbank. The outlaws stared with wide disbelieving eyes for a few moments. While tracking their horses, they had seen some sauropods way off in the distance and lots of sauropod tracks, but this was the first opportunity they had to see sauropods up close.

"Those lizards are huge," Gantry said, "and it looks like a big dead lizard—different kind it looks to be—done gonned and bloated up and popped open. Like dead steers can after a while."

"Aye," Branigan said. "The odor does seem to be coming from that direction, and that could be the source of what sounded like a gunshot."

"I'll take a closer look," Traxton said as he removed his scope. He looked at the dead carcass. It was partially decayed, and little bits of tattered dry skin clung to ribs and slightly trembled in a slight breeze. Seven *Amphicotylus* swam toward the carcass. V-shaped disruptions of water began to converge toward the dead *Brachiosaurus*, and only the crocodylomorphs' eyes and snouts were visible as they swam.

"Oh, gee," Gantry said. "Gators. Gosh."

"They look a lot like the ones in Georgia," Avarette added.

"I wouldn't see this underground," Holt said.

Traxton scanned the horizon beyond the river with his scope. He saw a small open stand of gingko trees to the north that were bordered by clusters of tree ferns, cycads, and cheirolepidiacean shrubs. He also took a close look at the *Camarasaurus*. He was struck by how colorful they were. They were bright green with light brown patterns on the tops of their bodies that looked like viper snake mottling. The herd was comprised of 10 animals. The three males in the herd were a bit larger than the females, and their slight head crests were bright blue. The females' crests were brown. Different-aged *Camarasaurus* in the herd ranged from 15,000 pounds (6,800 kilograms) to 60,000 pounds (217,216 kilograms). The biggest members of the herd were about 50 feet (15 meters) long.

Unlike *Apatosaurus* and *Diplodocus* (which were diplodocid sauropods), *Camarasaurus* were macronarian sauropods. *Brachiosaurus* was also a macronarian. Compared to diplodocids, macronarians had blunter snouts, larger nostrils, and a different overall body shape that included longer front legs (relative to their back legs) and a shorter tail. As the outlaws stared at the *Camarasaurus* herd, the *Amphicotylus* below them tore into the *Brachiosaurus* carcass.

"No sign of Malone or Mesquite," Traxton said, still looking through his scope. "Wait, I see something."

"Aye," Branigan said. "There are critters coming out of the trees to the left of the herd. Similar to the horn-nosed beast I saw but bigger and different colors."

"Oh, yeah," Gantry said. "Yeah, yeah, yeah. I see them. I see them."

"Those are some sharp chompers," Avarette smoothly said as he saw three *Allosaurus fragilis* slink toward the *Camarasaurus*. The predatory toothy dinosaurs emerged from the shrubs at the edge of a gingko stand and moved slow and low with open mouths.

Allosaurus was the most common carnivorous theropod of the Morrison Basin. All the *Allosaurus* stalking the sauropod herd were 40 feet (12 meters) long. They also weighed about 2,000 pounds (900 kilograms) and stood about eight feet (two and a half meters) tall at their hips. The *Allosaurus's* skulls were about three feet (one meter) long.

They had three claws on each hand and three main toes on each foot, but they also had a fourth visible toe—a hallux (also known as a dewclaw)—that hung down on the inner side of each foot. In some modern birds—including birds of prey—the hallux is prominent, but for *Allosaurus* and other large Jurassic carnivores, the hallux is small and vestigial.

The *Allosaurus* moved with springy nimbleness as they slunk toward the *Camarasaurus*. The theropods had aquamarine blue skin with shiny ragged emerald green lateral stripes running down from their backs toward white underbellies. Their tails were tipped with red. There were two females and one male. The *Allosaurus* had a pair of pointy backward-facing crests that protruded from the tops of their heads, just in front of their eyes. The male had ruby red crests, and the females had duller pale blue crests.

As a *Camarasaurus* in the rear of the herd lifted its head from eating, it barely spotted an *Allosaurus* sneaking from behind. The *Camarasaurus* unleashed an alarm bellow. The other herd members broke into a run to the south as the *Allosaurus* sprinted in pursuit. The big sauropods kicked up dried ferns and cycad fronds as they rushed away.

The *Allosaurus* soon infiltrated the herd. Events turned chaotic. Some *Camarasaurus* continued to run. Others stood their ground and stamped their feet as the *Allosaurus* approached. The *Allosaurus* weaved between the stronger, faster members of the herd and focused on identifying an ideal victim.

A few *Camarasaurus* plunged into the river in an effort to escape danger. They were so tall that their front legs touched the ground in the middle of the river. The sauropods then moved forward with their front legs walking on the river bottom while their back legs and the back halves of their bodies partially floated and bobbed about.

The *Allosaurus* isolated a medium-sized female *Camarasaurus* that was slower than the rest. She was old and weak, and the *Allosaurus* knew she was vulnerable. An *Allosaurus* charged the old sauropod, opened its jaws, slashed with powerful six-inch (15-centimeter) claws, and raked almost all of its teeth against its prey's belly. The *Camarasaurus* grunted in agony. The other two *Allosaurus* closed in on opposite sides of the sauropod and similarly slashed at its belly. Blood dripped onto *Equisetum*, ferns, and low cycads.

Allosaurus teeth were shorter than those of other theropods in the Morrison Basin, like *Torvosaurus* and *Ceratosaurus*. With its shorter teeth, *Allosaurus* could more easily close its jaws around prey, which better enabled raking jaw attacks. *Allosaurus* also had flexible jaw joints that enabled them to open their mouths extremely wide, like some snake species do when they swallow prey larger than their heads.

The *Allosaurus* repeatedly slashed at the *Camarasaurus* but regularly paused their attacks as the sauropod ran beyond them or stopped to kick her back legs in defense. The *Allosaurus* had quick reflexes and deftly dodged being punctured by the *Camarasaurus's* foot claws.

The *Allosaurus* pushed the lone *Camarasaurus* back toward the gingko stand from which they had emerged. The *Camarasaurus* was now isolated, and the rest of its herd moved far away to the south. Its bleeding greatly increased. Intestines began to fall out of its body and drag behind it. It staggered and fell to the ground near a cluster of tree ferns at the edge of the gingko stand. The *Camarasaurus* collapsed onto its side with its legs splayed out and its dusty white underbelly exposed.

Two *Allosaurus* began to tear away at the sauropod's abdomen with their jaws. A third *Allosaurus* ran up to the sauropod's neck, stepped on it with one foot, and swiftly swooped its head down and crunched its teeth around the dinosaur's windpipe. The *Camarasaurus* gurgled its final vocalization. It would now serve as *Allosaurus* food for a week.

Traxton watched through his scope and smiled. Branigan sneered with satisfaction and grinned. Avarette lifted his eyebrows in admiration. Holt shook his fist in encouragement. Gantry broke into a cold sweat as he stared in wide-eyed horror with an open mouth.

While two *Allosaurus* focused on eating organs, another ripped open the muscles of the *Camarasaurus's* hindquarters. It steadied itself with one foot on the carcass and another on the ground as it tore off huge chunks of meat and swallowed them whole. The *Allosaurus* were messy and ate fast and greedily. The carnivores did not know when they would be able to eat again, so they tried to make the most of the opportunity. Although the *Allosaurus fragilis* would continue to eat the *Camarasaurus* for days if given the opportunity, they could also be driven away by *Torvosaurus* or even other *Allosaurus,* including the larger *anax* species. Each *Allosaurus* ripping away at the *Camarasaurus* would eat about 200 pounds (91 kilograms) of meat during their first feeding.

Little *Ornitholestes* and *Hesperornithoides* began to tentatively emerge from the nearby stand of ginkgoes. They would rush in for scraps as soon as they got the chance. *Mesadactylus* also circled overhead.

The *Hesperornithoides* were about two feet (61 centimeters) long and about one and a half feet (45 centimeters) tall. They were covered in strikingly colorful feathers, and they had small wings coming off their arms.

"See that, boys," Traxton said. "You could learn a thing or two from those reptiles. Focus on your target, don't back down, and get what you want."

"Aye," Branigan said. "You're right about that, boss."

The two *Allosaurus* at the back of the *Camarasaurus* slashed away and began eating choice internal organs. The *Allosaurus* by the sauropod's neck bobbed its head and gently cooed. Four baby *Allosaurus* trotted out of the trees toward the adults. They had brown and black mottling with light green spots. Their legs were also disproportionately long relative to the rest of their bodies—as if they had not yet grown into them.

One of the *Allosaurus* adults feeding on organs pulled its head out of the still-warm *Camarasaurus* carcass and dropped a slab of heart at the feet of the babies. They meekly snarled and nibbled on it with little mouths. Gantry smiled as he saw the babies eat. Then the baby dinosaurs jumped back in alarm as a rifle bullet zipped past them and exploded into nearby dirt.

Holt cocked the bolt of his rifle and ejected a spent shell. Avarette then instinctively fired his rifle, and dirt exploded behind the fleeing baby *Allosaurus*.

"What the hell are you doing?!" Traxton forcefully and contemptuously uttered under his breath. "You want Malone and Mesquite to know we're here? You want those carnivores to know we're here?"

"I just wanted some target practice, boss," Holt said.

"I did, too . . . I guess," Avarette added.

The *Allosaurus* looked up toward the outlaws' location after hearing the shots. The carnivores sniffed, but the wind was blowing away from the dinosaurs, and they did not smell the strange mammals.

"We're going to back away slowly," Traxton said.

The outlaws were soon out of sight as they crawled back behind the top of the river levee. Soon, they untied their horses and got back in their saddles.

As they rode away, Traxton said, "Holt and Avarette, that was stupid. We can't target-practice on the wildlife here. You two won't be shooting at these dinosaurs like you killed wolves and coyotes. We have limited ammunition. It should only be spent on Malone and Mesquite or on a dinosaur in self-defense."

"I apologize, boss," Avarette said.

"Sorry, Mister Traxton," Holt said.

"Just help me kill Malone," Traxton said.

"And Mesquite," Branigan added.

"Yeah, him, too," Traxton said.

Holt and Avarette were quiet and somber. In the 1800s, they often took great joy in shooting certain wild animals when they could. They especially liked to kill birds of prey and coyotes. No provocation was necessary, and they did not particularly care about protecting livestock. If Holt or Avarette saw a predator they wanted to shoot, they would try to kill it for fun. Traxton often joined them in the killing, so they were somewhat puzzled at how strong his reaction was to their attempts to kill a few baby dinosaurs. Still, they recognized that it would not be good to get the attention of the adult *Allosaurus*.

CHAPTER 13: SURVIVAL QUEST

In the afternoon, Lassen, Kailani, Durango, and Adalya continued to ride north through the open plains. To the north and east of the riders, rivers sparkled as they meandered toward a massive lake. Most of the fluffy clouds from the morning had faded. The sky was largely cloudless, clear, and bright.

Throughout the ride, Kailani and Lassen barraged Adalya with questions about the future, but, despite being transparent about the technical aspects of time travel, she revealed little and insisted on "protecting the timeline."

As the explorers passed slow-flowing water, Lassen turned his head as he noticed a furry little *Docodon* swimming with vegetation in its mouth. "What kind of mammal is that?" Lassen asked as he pointed.

"I'm not sure," Kailani said. "It may be a *Docodon*. I read they might have been semiaquatic, like the muskrats of modern times. It's actually fairly large for a Morrison mammal as it looks like it's about the size of a small squirrel."

"Definitely smaller than a beaver," Durango added.

"True," Kailani said. "In fact, if it is a *Docodon*, its jaw is only about one and a half inches long, and it would weigh only about five ounces."

Soon, the time travelers approached a junction where the river east of them met another river flowing from the west out of the foothills of the Mesocordilleran High. Where the rivers met, the water was shallow and clear with a firm gravel bottom. It was also easy to spot and avoid *Amphicotylus* and *Eutretauranosuchus*. Here, the bounty hunters and scientists crossed the river flowing from the west and rode northeast to stay in the open. Lush forest stood to the west and north.

Hours later, Lassen squinted in the late afternoon sunlight and noted a massive jumble of boulders several miles to the west. A huge lake sparkled miles away to the east. Eventually, the time travelers rode over fern prairies dotted with ponds.

Lassen looked down as he heard faint crunching under Graphite's hooves. He saw piles of small dried-up aquatic snail shells, which indicated he was crossing dry plains that had water only a few months earlier.

Adalya turned on her orientation module and checked the status of the location signaler. She determined that it had moved about 40 miles (64 kilometers) northwest from where it was taken. It had now been stationary for hours and was about 25 miles (40 kilometers) northwest of the time travelers' current position.

Not far ahead, several orange-brown *Dryosaurus* sniffed the air as they detected strange, large mammals moving toward them. Upon smelling the humans and horses, the 200-pound (90-kilogram) bipedal herbivores scurried into marshland shrubs to the northwest. Kailani shot photos of them with her phone while they fled. As the *Dryosaurus* scurried, they squawked in alarm. Their calls reminded Lassen of the sounds made by disturbed great blue herons.

Four blue-brown *Brachiosaurus* ate high leaves about a mile (two kilometers) to the north. The herd included an enormous male with shades of purple on the undersides of his neck.

Distant pterosaurs circled overhead. Occasionally, *Archaeopteryx* erupted out of ferns and cycads in pursuit of dragonflies and lizards. Some were gray with dark wingtips, and others were jet black.

Often, during the trek, little green-turquoise *Nanosaurus* jumped out of the ferns, startled by the horses. They scared up dragonflies and other insects. Small mammals also lived on the plains, but they were not as visible as they were in the forest.

"Lassen," Durango said, "it's getting late. We might want to think about setting up camp."

"Yeah," Lassen said. "It's not like we slept last night either—jumping from sunset to morning."

"I, um," Durango said as an involuntary yawn overtook him, "could use some rest. And some more food. I reckon we're gonna be runnin' low on vittles soon. My jerky and biscuits aren't gonna last much longer."

"Yeah," Lassen said. "We should preserve our saddlebag grub and gather up some wild foods."

"Where are all the pineapples?" Durango asked. "What about coconuts and bananas? This place looks tropical with the palm trees and all."

"Sorry to disappoint you, Mister Mesquite," Kailani said, "but fruit grows on flowering plants, and flowering plants may not be present at all in this place and time. Some of the plants here that look like palms are actually cycads and bear no fruit. They're more closely related to conifers than they are to palms."

"What?" Durango asked.

"Wait a second," Lassen said, "yeah. That makes sense. Grass is a flowering plant, and we haven't seen any the whole time we've been here. Where there would be grass in the future, here there mainly seem to be ferns."

Kailani said, "Though genetic studies indicate they evolved earlier than the late Jurassic, flowering plants do not become prominent in the fossil record until the early Cretaceous Period, approximately 125 million years before modern times. That means flowering plants may not become common in North America until millions of years after the late Jurassic."

"Well, then what can we eat?" Durango asked.

"We could try boiling tree leaves and finding some seeds from the trees," Lassen said. "We also might be able to catch fish and crawdads."

"Crawdads?" Adalya asked. "Why would we specifically pursue male craws with offspring?"

"Oh," Lassen said with a chuckle. "That's just another word for crayfish. They're basically little freshwater lobsters."

"I see," Adalya said. "I believe I saw some during my involuntary swim this morning."

"There's a pond up ahead," Lassen said, pointing. "Let's camp there and see if we can find some food."

Soon, the bounty hunters and scientist set up a camp in the shade of short conifers and tall tree ferns at the edge of a shallow pond. While unpacking items, they inventoried the remaining 1879 food.

"If we stretch this," Lassen said, "it could last us maybe four or five days, but we'd probably be hungry and weak most of the time—especially in this heat." Lassen wiped sweat from his forehead.

"We need supplemental nourishment," Adalya said. "In my time, we have food synthesizers, and anything we need to eat is available with the press of a button. All we have to do is enter the appropriate molecules into a machine, and we get meat, fruit, vegetables, just about anything."

"Unbelievable," Durango said.

"No killing," Lassen said. "I like it, but you don't happen to have a food synthesizer on you? Do you?"

"I do not," Adalya replied.

"I suggest we try fishing," Kailani said. "Fish are a high-quality source of fat and protein."

"Yeah," Lassen said. "And they should be relatively abundant. We've seen lots of them jump up to feed on insects."

With no line or lures, the time travelers used Lassen's antler-handled knife to carve spears out of conifer saplings. Based on Adalya's calculations, they split the end of each spear and inserted wood wedges to create double-pronged spears with enhanced skewering capabilities.

Spears in hand, the bounty hunters and scientists staked out their fishing spots at a nearby shallow pond. *Morrolepis* fish swam in waist-deep water, and *Docodons* swam at the edge of the pond. Occasionally, silvery blue flashes of fish leapt out of the water and chomped dragonflies before landing with little splashes. The *Morrolepis* were about six to 10 inches (15 to 25 centimeters) long.

Durango quickly lost his spear by throwing it at a fish, but Lassen, Kailani, and Adalya eventually impaled several fish and laid them on a large clean cycad frond. Lassen and the scientists were roughly equal in ability and had unfair advantages over Durango. Lassen had nearly perfect vision, being blessed with pristine and durable cone and rod cells in his eyes. Kailani was extremely detail-oriented and methodical. Adalya was astoundingly good at mathematics and geometry and rapidly solved equations in her head to anticipate fish positions and optimal skewering angles. She also benefited from future medical technology that ensured everybody had excellent vision.

Lassen loaned Durango his spear, and Durango finally managed to stab a fish, but it immediately flopped off the spear, and he lost it. While he frantically grabbed for it in the water, he suddenly lifted a hand in pain and shouted, "Ow!" An orange-brown crayfish dangled from his right pinky. It wriggled its five-inch (13-centimeter) body and snapped one of its three-inch (eight-centimeter) pincer claws. Durango shook his hand, and the crayfish fell to the ground. The bounty hunter winced as he grabbed his finger in pain.

"That little crab varmint's got a tight grip," Durango proclaimed.

"I noticed," Lassen said. "Also, technically, that's not a crab, though both crayfish and crabs are crustaceans."

"Call them what you want," Durango said. "What I know is that they taste good after they're boiled. Too bad we don't have butter and garlic."

Lassen, Kailani, and Adalya speared several more fish while Durango spent most of his time gathering crayfish with a net he wove out of fern stems. Durango was great at weaving and knots. In fact, he had braided the lariats that both he and Lassen used. Before he pursued bounty hunting, Durango made a living creating ropes, belts, whips, and other items from leather.

*   *   *

As afternoon faded into evening, rich orange and yellow hues coated the landscape. This was one of Lassen's favorite times of the day. A small herd of *Brachiosaurus* made low honking sounds about three quarters of a mile (one kilometer) to the north. Lassen also heard what he had finally determined were the soft cooing sounds of *Nanosaurus* and *Dryosaurus* scattered across the plains. Earlier in the afternoon, he thought he heard two more bloated sauropod carcasses explode, but the sounds were very distant, and he was not sure.

After cleaning their fish, the time travelers laid out their bedrolls. Luckily for Kailani and Adalya, bedrolls happened to be bundled with the rest of the gear attached to the saddles on Graphite and Ember. The temperature was about 90 degrees Fahrenheit (32 degrees Celsius). They would not need bedrolls to stay warm, but they would serve as barriers to shield against hard ground and strange insects.

After bedroll preparation, Lassen started prepping for a campfire while Durango gathered firewood, Adalya reviewed holographic map readouts, and Kailani prolifically wrote in a notebook. Lassen scraped a small piece of magnesium rock from his saddlebag against his knife to create sparks that ignited a fire. Soon, a respectable campfire crackled in the Jurassic evening.

Lassen left to gather additional firewood while Durango took over tending the fire. As Lassen walked to the peripheries of the camp, he noticed the moon had risen. It was beautiful and bright. The sun was just starting to set, so the moon was not glowing brightly, but it still stood out. Lassen thought the moon looked slightly bigger in the Jurassic than it did during 1879, but he could not tell for sure.

While the sun dipped below the mountains to the west, the sky began to glow with grapefruit pink hues behind inky black hill and tree silhouettes. With clear air, few clouds, and a small amount of particles in the sky to reflect light, the sunset was not dramatic, but it was still beautiful in its own way. Over the years, Lassen had developed an appreciation for all sunsets.

As he gathered firewood, Lassen paused to view the northern horizon. Distant softly-honking *Brachiosaurus* slowly moved among ginkgo stands while silhouetted black against a pink sky. Shrieking pterosaurs flitted above them. Lassen knew he may never escape the Jurassic, but for now, he was happy to be in the Morrison Basin 150 million years before his time.

While Lassen gathered branches, he heard a frog chorus begin. He remembered seeing a few little frogs hopping around in marshy areas earlier in the day. The sounds Lassen heard reminded him of the nocturnal Pacific tree frog calls he had heard so many times when camping near wetlands in the western United States. The tree frog sounds were familiar, but the *Brachiosaurus* honking, pterosaur calls, and strange dinosaur cooing were strange. Lassen was fascinated by the unique mix of familiar and exotic.

He soon returned to camp to find his companions each holding fish—on the ends of sharpened sticks—over the fire. They occasionally rotated the fish for optimal cooking. A pot full of water and crawling crayfish sat on the ground near Durango.

"These little fellers will be dessert," Durango said as he patted the pot.

The bounty hunters and scientists cooked fish and crawdads as pink dusk light faded into velvety blueish black darkness, and stars appeared. A male *Brachiosaurus* made an especially pronounced honking sound, and the time travelers felt the call's vibrations.

"Amazing," Lassen said. "In our times, there's no animal alive that's quite like a sauropod."

"True," Kailani said. "For millions of years in the Mesozoic Era, sauropods dominate most terrestrial ecosystems. They'll live through the very end of the Cretaceous Period and abruptly go extinct at the same time as the rest of the dinosaurs."

"What's an ecosystem?" Durango asked.

"Oh," Kailani said, "the word may not have existed in your time. An ecosystem is a group of lifeforms living in a certain environment. What we see is the Morrison ecosystem, named after the rock layer that will preserve its fossils. The dinosaurs, the plants, and everything alive here comprise an ecosystem."

"So, an ecosystem is just a bunch of alive stuff that lives in the same place?" Durango said.

"You could put it that way," Kailani replied. "In the 66 million years after the dinosaur extinction, no other land animal like the sauropods would evolve. *Paraceratherium* was one of the largest known prehistoric mammals, and it lived during the Paleogene Period about 30 million years before modern times, but it would only reach heights of about 16 feet at the shoulder and weigh about 30,000 to 40,000 pounds. In contrast, *Patagotitan* of the Cretaceous Period of South America was one of the largest sauropods to be discovered. It was approximately 120 feet long and weighed about 140,000 pounds."

"Now, that's a heckin' chonker," Durango said.

"How do they manage being so big when various other animals aren't?" Lassen asked.

"For one thing," Kailani said, "they could have a special efficient mode of breathing. Sauropods likely employ unidirectional breathing, which involves getting oxygen while inhaling *and* exhaling thanks to a system of air sacs. Birds and theropod dinosaurs also breathe this way."

"More oxygen for each breath," Lassen said.

"Advantageous math," Adalya added.

"Exactly," Kailani replied. "In contrast, mammals—including humans—breathe less efficiently via bidirectional breathing. When we breathe, air simply dead-ends at our lungs since we have no air sacs—and the lungs have to convert the air to carbon dioxide and expel it. We only get oxygen when we breathe in."

"Huh," Lassen said, "so unidirectional breathers, like birds and some dinosaurs—including maybe those sauropods out there—might be less likely to run out of breath from activity because they literally get more oxygen per breath than other animals."

"Yeah," Kailani said. "Unidirectional breathers can sustain aerobic activity levels not achievable by mammals. This could contribute to sauropods being enormous while still breathing and functioning effectively. It also helps explain why some birds can survive flights at extremely high altitudes, like 29,000 feet, or fly for days on end."

"How far can migrating birds actually go?" Lassen asked. "I always figured some moved quite a stretch, but I never knew exactly how far."

"Well," Kailani said, "one extreme example is the alpine swift, which migrates between northern Europe and sub-Saharan Africa. This bird can stay in flight for 10 months without a break."

"Whoa," Lassen said. "That's high endurance, and not sleeping must save a lot of time."

"Actually," Kailani said, "some migrating birds can shut down half of their brain and basically have different parts of their body take turns being asleep on extended flights."

"Most efficient," Adalya said. "Functioning while sleeping. Substantial time saver."

"Yeah," Kailani said. "In addition to probably using an air sac system for breathing, most sauropods probably also have an additional elaborate system of air sacs stretching from their necks to their tails and into their abdomens. These additional air sacs would fill spaces between bones and could help prevent overheating. Sauropods also have hollow spaces in some bones, including their vertebrae. Partially hollow bones and air sacs can help sauropod tails and necks be lighter and more flexible."

"With all those air sacs and some hollow bones," Lassen said, "there's not as much animal that needs to be fed, but how much sauropods need to eat depends on their energy levels. What was the metabolism of sauropods like?"

"What would you guess?" Kailani asked with curiosity.

"Being that big," Lassen said, "I would think they would have a slow, cold-blooded metabolism like turtles or lizards. That way, they wouldn't have to eat as much, and they could stay warm from the sun liked other cold-blooded animals instead of having to make all their own heat. Still, they seemed pretty active, which indicates they were warm-blooded."

"Good guesses," Kailani said. "Studies of oxygen consumption based on molecular biomarkers in fossilized bone show that sauropods and various other dinosaurs were endothermic."

"Endothermic?" Durango asked, raising his eyebrows.

"'Endothermic' is just a fancy word for 'warm-blooded,'" Kailani said. "Endothermic animals have a relatively high metabolism and generate their own body heat. Humans, other mammals, and birds are all endothermic."

"Oh, okay," Durango said. "So the opposite of cold-blooded."

"Wow, so they are warm-blooded," Lassen said. "With high metabolisms, they must have to eat all the time just to power their bodies. How do biomarkers of oxygen use enable estimates of metabolism?"

"Because the amount of oxygen consumed by an animal as part of breathing is an indicator of whether it is endothermic or ectothermic," Kailani said. "'Ectothermic' is basically a fancy word for 'cold-blooded.' More oxygen consumption indicates endothermy or warm-bloodedness."

"Oh, that makes sense," Lassen said. "Were all dinosaurs warm-blooded?"

"Many were," Kailani replied, "including theropods, like *Allosaurus* and other two-legged carnivores living in this ecosystem, but some ornithischian dinosaurs, like *Stegosaurus* and *Triceratops*, were ectothermic and may bask in the sun like modern cold-blooded turtles or lizards."

"We saw *Stegosaurus* today," Lassen said, "and now that I think about it, some did seem to be enjoying the sun."

"The spike-tailed platey critters?" Durango asked.

"Yeah, those were *Stegosaurus*," Lassen said, "but what's *Triceratops*?"

"Big herbivore with three horns and a head shield," Kailani said. "It won't be around until about 84 million years in the future in the late Cretaceous Period—and it won't be discovered until 1887, which is 8 years after your time."

"Wow," Lassen said. "So many dinosaurs I don't even know about. How old do sauropods get? Seems like it would take about a hundred years to get as tall as that big *Brachiosaurus*." Lassen pointed at the distant silhouette of an enormous male.

"Paleontologists have thought along those lines as well," Kailani said, "but studies of dinosaur bone structure have indicated that sauropods reached adult size within roughly 20 to 30 years. There is also a record of a 40-year old *Camarasaurus*."

"Well, that's not super old," Lassen said.

"But," Kailani added, "after reaching adult size, sauropods could have lived much longer. Some paleontologist friends of mine have been working on a study of sauropod ages, and they told me that based on retrocalculation of growth lines in bone, a *Diplodocus* they studied died with an upper estimated age of 60 years."

"Considering Galápagos tortoises can live for over 100 years," Lassen said, "that makes sense. Fascinating. We even saw *Diplodocus* today."

"But get this," Kailani added, "my friends also worked on estimating the age of an even bigger diplodocid sauropod called *Supersaurus*, and they determined its speculative estimated maximum age at death was 225 years."

"Whoa," Durango said. "That's one old long-neck."

"Seriously?" Lassen asked. "That seems unbelievably old."

"My friends would actually agree with you on that," Kailani said. "They're not convinced it was actually 225 years old because of limitations of their methodology, but they are convinced it was really old."

"Did we see any *Supersaurus* today?" Lassen asked. "I remember you said we were looking at diplodocids."

"No," Kailani said, "We didn't see *Supersaurus*, but they are a Morrison sauropod, so we might see them later."

"Well," Durango said as he pulled his fish away from flames. "If I want to keep my adult size and live to be 225, I'm going to have to keep eating. Chaw time, amigos."

During the dusk-to-night transition, the bounty hunters and scientists ate a large fish dinner. A dinner of fresh meat was greatly appreciated after the tiredness caused by traveling 150 million years in the past, nearly drowning, hiking through a forest, fleeing from carnivorous dinosaurs, getting in the middle of an *Apatosaurus* battle, being robbed by pterosaurs, and riding in intense heat.

"Mmmmm," Durango said as he licked his lips and threw a fish skeleton into the fire, "that's the best fish I ever chawed." The fish skeleton landed on coals at the base of a pot full of boiling water and crayfish. The crustaceans turned bright orange-red as they cooked.

"It's good," Lassen said. "Miss Nell, I've been wondering something. Is it just me, or is the Moon bigger in the Jurassic?"

Sensing the conversation was about to turn particularly scientific—again, Durango grabbed another cooked fish off a stick and chewed slower to make it last longer. Durango was finally learning to appreciate science, especially evolutionary biology, though that was not what he called it. However, he was very tired and could not always follow the conversations Lassen, Adalya, and Kailani had. Whenever he did not have much to contribute to a conversation, and food was available, Durango liked to eat. As long as he was eating, people did not expect him to say anything, which worked out fine.

Adalya glanced up at what was now a glowing, nearly full moon. She thought it was strange to see it so barren with no space exploration infrastructure. In 2756, there would be several permanent bases and mineral processing facilities on the Moon.

"Is the Moon bigger in the distant past?" Adalya said. "I would say yes and no."

"How do you mean?" Lassen asked.

"The Moon should be about the same size," Adalya said, "but we are closer to it in the Jurassic, so it looks slightly bigger."

"Why are we closer?" Lassen asked.

"Because the Moon's orbit is increasing," Adalya said. "The Moon is spinning farther and farther away from the Earth at a rate of approximately 3.76 centimeters or about one and a half inches per year."

"That doesn't seem very fast," Lassen said.

"Over geologic time, it would add up," Kailani remarked.

"It's about the same rate at which human fingernails grow," Adalya said. "So . . ." Adalya moved the fingers on her right hand as she rapidly did mental calculations. "Let's see, 3.76 times 150 million. That's 564 million centimeters. There are 160,934 centimeters in a mile. 564 million divided by 160,934 comes out to roughly 3,504.54."

"*Roughly?*" Durango said, raising his eyebrows.

"We are about 3,500 miles closer to the Moon now in the late Jurassic than we will be during our times," Adalya stated. "Around the time of the 1870s and 2700s, the Moon is, on average, approximately 238,900 miles from the Earth, though its distance varies based on where it is in its orbit. So we are closer, but not much closer relative to the total distance from the Earth to the Moon."

"So," Lassen said, "why does the Moon's orbit keep moving it a little farther and farther from the Earth?"

"Primarily because of ocean tide forces," Adalya said. "The Earth keeps the Moon in place by exerting gravitational force on it. However, the Moon also applies gravitational force to the Earth, which causes the oceans to bulge out on opposite sides of the planet. These tidal bulges provide the Moon with energy that gradually pushes it into higher and higher orbits."

"I kind of understand," Lassen said.

"I need to review my astronomy textbooks," Kailani added.

"You know," Durango said as he stirred the nearly done crayfish with a clean stick that had been stripped of bark, "if we're gonna survive, we might want to focus less on the sky and more on what we have to deal with right here on the ground."

"Fair enough," Lassen replied. "We should discuss the geography and local wildlife. Miss Nell, did you get more topographic scan data for the terrain that's ahead?"

"Yes," Adalya replied as she flicked her module on, displaying a glowing blue terrain map. "We are here." Adalya pointed at part of the map that was on flat plains and west of the western lobe of an enormous lake. "And since early this afternoon, the location signaler has been in one position." Adalya moved her fingers so the map would display more terrain. "The object we seek is located about 25 miles northwest of us. Oh, this is interesting. A scan must have picked this up while we were fishing this afternoon."

"What is it?" Lassen asked.

"We now know the terrain that surrounds the location signaler. It is located on the rim of a volcano at the western end of a very low valley."

"Is the volcano active?" Lassen asked.

"I do not know," Adalya said, "but it projects about 4,000 feet above the surrounding terrain, and it is steep and conical."

"A stratovolcano," Kailani said as she glanced at a glowing holo projection of the volcano.

"I reckon we've got some climbing to do, then," Durango said.

"Quite a lot, it appears," Adalya added as she zoomed in on part of her holographic projection of the terrain. "Not only is there a steep volcano, but the valley at the base of the volcano is hundreds of feet below a series of cliffs."

"Whoa," Lassen said as he examined the holographic imagery. "Is there even a way to climb down those, or will we have to go far out of our way around to another side?"

"Let me check," Adalya said as she input a query that took into account human capabilities, terrain, traction levels, the length of their ropes, and other factors. "There's a way down, but just barely—and it will not be feasible for the horses."

Lassen winced. In the background, Horizon whinnied with concern.

"We can make it down by foot," Adalya said, "though we will occasionally need to use rope for some of the steeper descents."

"Okay," Durango said as he removed the pot of crayfish from the fire. "So, we've got that fun trip to look forward to. The crawdads should be cool enough to eat in a few minutes."

"Sounds good," Lassen said. "There seems to be a lot to eat down here, and we haven't tangled with any carnivores since the *Ornitholestes* or whatever they were. We should probably keep moving north in the plains and then veer northwest through the hills to get to the valley with the volcano and location signaler."

"Sounds like a reasonable strategy," Adalya said.

"Good," Lassen said, yawning. "I'm tired. I hate to say this, but somebody should be awake at any given time to keep watch. There could be dangerous sharp-toothed critters moving through here at night. Might even be some that never made it into the fossil record."

"The Traxton Gang could also still be out there," Durango said.

"I'll take the first shift," Lassen said.

"I'll take the next shift," Kailani added.

"I will assume responsibility for the subsequent shift," Adalya said.

Lassen, Adalya, and Kailani all looked at Durango. Durango looked behind his shoulder as if he was wondering what they were looking at.

"Alright, hey, I'll take the morning shift," Durango remarked.

"We'll keep watch for two and a half-hour shifts," Lassen said.

Soon, the time travelers cracked open Jurassic crayfish. To Lassen, Durango, and Kailani, they tasted the same as modern crayfish. To Adalya, their flavor and texture were like chewy synthesized shrimp. As they cracked open pincer shells and scooped meat from crayfish tails, Kailani skimmed through dinosaur e-books and showed her time-traveling companions various pictures while enthusiastically unleashing a torrent of technical paleontological knowledge.

Lassen was attentive and fascinated. Durango mainly paid attention when big predatory dinosaurs were discussed. Adalya quietly listened and occasionally checked her instruments. Lassen was thrilled to finally learn more about the dinosaurs he had seen earlier in the day, but he was surprised by how little was known about specific dinosaur species by 2026.

Lassen thought several depictions of dinosaurs he had seen were kind of close but not quite accurate when it came to what some species actually looked like. He was also intrigued by the fact that some sauropods he had not seen were supposed to be present in the Morrison Basin of the late Jurassic, including *Barosaurus*, *Haplocanthosaurus*, *Suuwassea*, and *Supersaurus*. *Barosaurus* with its extremely long neck and *Supersaurus* with its old age and length of over 130 feet (40 meters) especially intrigued Lassen, and he wondered if he would see any.

Two armored dinosaur species, *Mymoorapelta* and *Gargoyleosaurus*, were also likely in the area based on fossil finds. Kailani said they were similar to the Cretaceous dinosaur *Ankylosaurus*, which Lassen had never heard of. It would not be discovered until 1908.

At Durango's urging, Kailani skipped forward in time in her reference materials and skimmed through some Cretaceous species. Lassen was intrigued by the variety of head ornamentations found on the crests of hadrosaurs, like *Parasaurolophus* and *Corythosaurus*. He and Durango were also amazed by the variety and ornamentation of the frills and horns of ceratopsians, like *Triceratops* and *Styracosaurus*.

Both bounty hunters were struck by the size and ferocity of *Tyrannosaurus rex* and learned that it was one of the very last dinosaurs to exist. It would go extinct with numerous other species during the end-Cretaceous mass extinction event 66 million years before modern times.

As Kailani scrolled through pictures of *Tyrannosaurus*, a discrepancy in the imagery caught Lassen's eye.

"Wait a minute," Lassen said. "Go back to that last picture."

Kailani tapped her phone and held up its screen to Lassen as she asked, "This one?"

"Yeah, that's the one," Lassen said. "That *Tyrannosaurus* skeleton has ventral ribs directly underneath the main rib cage. There are the main ribs that attach to the back bones and radiate down, but there are also belly ribs. A bunch of the other theropod skeleton pictures you were showing us don't show those ventral ribs, which make the *Tyrannosaurus* look a lot fatter."

"Excellent observation," Kailani said. "Yes, those bottom ribs do a better job of showing how big some dinosaurs were. Dinosaur belly ribs are called gastralia. They're not always well-preserved or easy to reconstruct. As a result, they're often simply excluded from various museum skeleton mounts without any mention of them in museum labels or interpretive materials."

"Intriguing," Lassen said.

"I see that as a disservice to the public," Kailani said, "as it can create a misleading picture of what some dinosaurs actually looked like. This picture shows the Sue specimen of *Tyrannosaurus rex* at Chicago's Field Museum after it was redone in 2018. The updated skeleton has gastralia, but it was on display without them for the previous 18 years. Sauropods also have gastralia, but their skeletons are rarely mounted with them in museums."

"Well, that was good," Durango said as he threw the last of the crayfish exoskeletons into the fire, "but I'm all-in tuckered out, and I think my belly ribs can't hold any more food. It's the bedroll for me."

"I also must get some sleep," Adalya said.

Kailani heavily yawned. "I know what you mean," she said.

"Okay," Lassen said. "I'm going to let the fire die down, and I'll keep watch."

The night was hot. As the other time travelers drifted to sleep, Lassen intently listened to the landscape and looked up at unfamiliar star constellations in a part of the galaxy that was totally new to him. He heard strange animal calls he had not heard earlier in the day. The frog chorus loudly continued, crickets joined the background noise of the frogs, and a *Brachiosaurus* gently honked. Lassen thought the herd to the north was gradually moving closer to camp as they fed through the moonlit night.

Lassen saw a few little mammals scurry by at the edge of camp. He noticed one pounce on a large beetle and heard its teeth crunch through the insect's exoskeleton. He was absorbed in his observations and feeling particularly contemplative. Here he was in a time when little scroungy mammals (his ancestors or at least relatives of them) were living in the shadows of the mighty avian and reptilian rulers of the Earth: the dinosaurs. Mammals hid in the forest and in the underbrush. They came out to hunt insects and lizards at night. They seemed so insignificant and small: literally and figuratively. Yet, Lassen knew they would evolve into what some scientists considered the most influential and important species on the face of the Earth: *Homo sapiens.*

By Lassen's time, humans had harnessed the power of the Earth by using coal to fuel the Industrial Revolution. They had also tied together the coasts of a continent with the building of the Transcontinental Railroad across the U.S. And, in the twentieth and twenty-first centuries, people would undertake many planet-altering accomplishments and tragedies beyond Lassen's imagination.

Notably, humans would have the power to cause species extinctions. Human-caused extinction was already well underway by the 1800s. Lassen recalled the tragic case of the flightless dodo bird, which once inhabited the Indian Ocean island of Mauritius before being driven to extinction because of European exploration and colonization that began in the 1500s. Lassen also thought of the Steller's sea cow, which was basically a giant manatee that inhabited the North Pacific Ocean in the Bering Sea between Alaska and Siberia. Steller's sea cows weighed roughly 9,000 to 24,000 pounds (4,000 to 11,000 kilograms). They provided meat to Russian sailors who, in the 1700s, hunted them to extinction within a period of roughly 30 years.

Lassen heard rustling in nearby ferns. In the moonlight, he saw a dinosaur called *Coelurus* spring out of the ferns and pounce on a little *Dryolestes* mammal. Lassen stared in wide-eyed, open-mouthed astonishment. The *Coelurus* was covered in feathers and resembled the *Ornitholestes* that had startled the horses earlier in the day. However, its feather patterns were different, and it was a little longer and heavier. *Coelurus* was about seven and a half feet (two meters) long and weighed about 44 pounds (20 kilograms). Compared to *Ornitholestes*, it had a slenderer neck and body, shorter arms, and longer legs. Its head was also shaped a bit differently.

Lassen stayed silent as he watched the *Coelurus* snatch up the furry *Dryolestes* with its teeth and fling it in the air. The mammal flew up just above an open mouth, and the *Coelurus* swallowed it whole. Lassen noticed the dinosaur had particularly wide eyes. He suspected it was well-adapted to seeing in the dark and was primarily nocturnal. After consuming its midnight snack, the *Coelurus* disappeared into tall ferns to the west.

Gulped down by the dinosaurs, Lassen thought. *No wonder it will take the impact of a giant asteroid to help mammals inherit the Earth and rule it for not nearly as long as the dinosaurs. Hard to beat 160 million years.*

Later, Lassen gently tapped Kailani's shoulder. She slept soundly on her bedroll.

"Miss Nakai," Lassen whispered. "Your turn to keep watch."

"Mister Malone, yeah, okay . . ." Kailani whispered. She blearily blinked her brilliant brown eyes and asked, "Anything to report?"

"The *Brachiosaurus* to the north seem to be moving closer," Lassen whispered, "and there are a lot of little mammals. I saw a small carnivorous dinosaur eat one before moving away to the west. Might have been *Ornitholestes* or *Coelurus*. I don't think it will cause us any harm. It looked to be only about 40 pounds."

"Nocturnal predation," Kailani quietly said. "I hope I see something like that."

"Otherwise," Lassen said. "Things are pretty quiet. I'm gonna hit the bedroll. Shout if you see something."

"Okay," Kailani said. "Goodnight, Mister Malone."

"Hey, Miss Nakai" Lassen said as he turned around on his walk to his bedroll. "You can call me Lassen."

"Okay, Lassen," Kailani replied.

Lassen laid on his bedroll, stared up at the stars, and heard a *Brachiosaurus* honk. Then he quickly drifted to sleep. Kailani and Adalya had uneventful experiences keeping watch.

Very early in the morning, Durango felt an irritating poking sensation in his right shoulder. "Ow," he muttered while still half asleep. Adalya lightly pressed his shoulder with the end of a stick. "Mammers, I don't want to go to school," Durango said. "I know more than the teacher. It's a waste of time. Get away."

"Mister Mesquite," Adalya said, "your turn to take watch."

"Huh, wha, yeah, sure," Durango said as he blinked in confusion. "Miss Nell, you're not my mammers." Durango sat up, rubbing his eyes.

"No," Adalya matter-of-factly whispered. "I am not your *mammers*. However, I did confirm we were out of harm's way for the last two and a half hours."

"Okay," Durango said with a yawn. "I guess I'll get up and keep watch. Let me know when the eggs are frying for breakfast."

"Sure," Adalya said sarcastically, "and while I am at it, I will fry up some beef steaks with fluffy biscuits and gravy."

"Yeah," Durango said. "That's some of the best woman's work there is, but hey, we'll have some of your fish for breakfast. Get some sleep, Miss Nell. I'll protect you."

"I am sure you will, Mister Mesquite," Adalya said before walking back to her bedroll. Adalya was still exhausted from an epic journey, and she quickly drifted to sleep.

CHAPTER 14: JURASSIC ROUNDUP

Lassen woke at dawn to the sound of gentle honking. A *Brachiosaurus* herd fed just east of camp. The huge sauropods stripped off sequoia needles from tall trees at the edge of a nearby pond and regularly resonated sounds through their head crests. The big male's honks were especially loud, and the bright purple dewlap under his mouth vibrated as he called. Saggy purple skin on the male *Brachiosaurus's* neck was bathed in soft dawn light as the sun rose over completely flat plains to the east. Little *Nanosaurus* hopped around at the feet of the sauropods, snapping at recently disturbed insects.

Lassen yawned and stretched his arms as he emerged shirtless from his bedroll. As he dug into his saddlebags and searched for a light blue shirt to replace his dirty beige shirt from the previous day, he glanced around camp. He saw Durango sitting on a log, smiling as he watched the *Brachiosaurus* herd.

The male *Brachiosaurus* let out an especially loud booming noise and snorted air through his nostrils. The *Brachiosaurus* was much closer to Lassen than any of the sauropods he had seen the day before. Lassen noticed its nostrils were near the tip of its snout, but the night before, he saw pictures where the nostrils of *Brachiosaurus* were above its eyes and on its head crest. This was partly because openings in the skull made the crest seem like a logical place for nostril openings. However, early paleontologists also reasoned that this nostril position could help the giant dinosaurs breathe underwater. Later, examination of muscle attachment scars on fossil bones revealed a more accurate location for *Brachiosaurus* nostrils.

The loud *Brachiosaurus* boom woke Kailani and Adalya. Kailani opened her eyes, raised them, and tipped her head back to see the herd of sauropods behind her. She rolled her head to the right and saw Lassen. *Affirmative*, she thought as she caught a glimpse of Lassen without his shirt and saw how muscular he was.

As Lassen buttoned up his fresh cotton shirt, he turned to the east and saw beautiful swirls and dapples of pink and red in the sky. He then slipped on his scuffed brown leather vest. In the meantime, Kailani used her phone to shoot photos and record videos of the nearby *Brachiosaurus*.

A flock of *Kepodactylus* pterodactyloid pterosaurs flew past the colorful sunrise canvass as black silhouettes. They had wingspans of approximately eight feet (two and a half meters). Two distant herds of *Camarasaurus* moved as silhouettes to the east.

Lassen sighed and shook his head with wonder and satisfaction. He knew he was in danger, and he needed to focus, but he felt like he was visiting a fairytale land. However, it was not a fairytale land. This land was full of incredible tales (and tails for that matter), but they belonged to *real* animals in a *real* world that was actually his own world—just older.

Lassen greeted Kailani and Adalya who debriefed him on what they observed during the night, which was mostly mammals scurrying past. Lassen and the scientists walked toward Durango.

"About time you woke up," Durango said.

"Good morning to you, too, pal," Lassen replied. "Anything to report from your time on watch?"

"These *Brachiosauruses* eat a lot, and the full moon here is really bright," Durango said. "No apparent danger, but I heard some strange sounds."

"I think we all did," Lassen said.

"Son of a catamount," Durango said, yawning. "I could use some breakfast."

"I know what you mean," Lassen said, "but we should probably get moving before it gets too hot."

"He is correct," Adalya said. "Furthermore, we consumed quite a lot of nourishment last night. We can go some time without food."

"Yeah," Durango said, "but I was—whoa, wait a second— shhhhhuuusssshhh." Durango held his finger to his lips and pointed to the left where ferns rustled.

A housecat-sized reptile emerged from the undergrowth and walked into the clearing containing the time travelers' camp. It strode east with purpose, sniffing the ground as it moved its head back and forth. It was about three feet (one meter) long with rusty brown mottling on its back and a yellowish-brown underbelly.

"What is it?" Lassen asked. "Looks more like a little dry land crocodile than a dinosaur."

"Yeah," Durango said, "but like a skinny little croc with long legs and fangs."

Kailani squinted to get a better look at the creature. It had little bits of egg shell stuck on the edges of its mouth.

"I think it's *Fruitachampsa*," Kailani said as she quietly lifted her phone and took a photo of it. "Its remains have been found among dinosaur egg fossils. It's unusual because it's a crocodylomorph but is believed to be primarily terrestrial instead of semiaquatic."

As the bounty hunters and scientists observed the *Fruitachampsa*, the sun rose farther over the flat eastern horizon and broke through some clouds, further illuminating the landscape and its wildlife in rich morning light. The *Brachiosaurus* looked particularly picturesque with the sun revealing the intricate details of their pebbly blue-brown skin.

"If bones of this critter have been found with dinosaur eggs," Durango said, raising an eyebrow, "then this could be our ticket to an egg breakfast. Let's follow that little feller."

"Crocodylomorphs have an excellent sense of smell," Kailani said, "because their brains contain large olfactory lobes. This creature could be sniffing out a meal."

The little *Fruitachampsa* ignored the time travelers. Soon, not far north of camp, it climbed up the side of a small dirt mound. Other dirt mounds were nearby, and the surrounding vegetation looked recently disturbed with crushed ferns and *Equisetum*. The bounty hunters and scientists watched as the *Fruitachampsa* crunched onto an egg. Yolk spilled out, and the reptile raised its head to swallow the remainder of the egg—shell and all.

"He's got one!" Durango said.

"Quiet," Lassen said, just barely maintaining a whisper.

At the sound of Durango's voice, the little *Fruitachampsa* turned around in alarm. It made eye contact with Durango. Then it scurried away into ferns.

"Let's go check out what he found," Durango said.

The time travelers discovered a round shallow nest dug in soft dirt surrounded by ferns and *Equisetum*. The nest contained about 20 beige eggs with light brown speckles. Each egg was about the size of an ostrich egg at six inches (15 centimeters) in diameter. Kailani took a photo of the nest.

"Jackpot," Durango said. "Wait a minute. I think those *Ornitholestes*, or whatever they were, chased after me earlier because Yonder had stepped on their eggs. We could be asking for trouble here."

"Perhaps," Kailani said. "How do these eggs compare in size to what you saw in the forest?"

"A lot bigger," Durango said.

"Hmmm," Kailani said as she examined the nest. "Based on the size of the eggs and how they're deposited, they appear to be from a sauropod."

"Those guys are *huge*," Durango said as he gestured with his left thumb to the nearby *Brachiosaurus*. "I don't want to make *them* mad."

"We may not need to worry about that," Kailani said. "Fossil evidence indicates that some sauropods may have laid their eggs and then abandoned them."

"Pretty slipshod parenting," Durango said.

"Apparently, the young were expected to fend for themselves," Kailani said, "before growing and eventually joining herds of older animals."

"Sounds odd," Lassen said, "but that's the way sea turtles do it."

"How's that?" Durango asked.

"Female sea turtles lay eggs on a beach at night," Lassen said, "and then go back to the ocean. After hatching, the baby turtles have to make it to the ocean and take care of themselves. Many don't make it and get eaten by predators, but there are a lot of them, so as long as some always survive, that egg-laying strategy is an evolutionary success."

"Seems risky," Durango said, biting his lower lip.

"Sea turtles nest in large colonies, so eggs from many individuals hatch at once," Kailani said. "Based on the other mounds in this area and excavation activity I saw in the distance yesterday, I think sauropods do the same thing. Considering how recently disturbed the plants and dirt in this area look, I would say these eggs were deposited recently. There's a good chance they don't have well-developed embryos yet."

"Well, come on," Durango said. "Let's have omelets for breakfast."

Lassen placed two dinosaur eggs in his vest. Kailani picked up one and carefully studied it. Durango filled his hat. Soon, the time travelers cracked a single enormous egg into a modest cast iron frying pan. Kailani held her breath, worrying that a partially-developed sauropod hatchling might fall out. Instead, the contents looked like those from a giant chicken egg. The yolk was huge and dark yellow.

"This one's mine," Durango said, "though I'm not sure it's big enough."

Lassen and Kailani looked at each other and simultaneously raised their eyebrows. Adalya shook her head as she looked away.

As Durango tended to frying his egg, Lassen said, "That *Fruitachampsa* looked like what a crocodile might look like if it were better adapted for land. Makes me think of the evolutionary transition of some species from water to land. How exactly did that happen?"

"Originally," Kailani said, "all vertebrate animals lived in the ocean. Sometime between roughly 300 to 400 million years ago, the first amphibians evolved, which represented a transitionary state between land and water. Reptiles also evolved from amphibious ancestors within this time range and were adapted for land."

"Frogs and salamanders are amphibians," Lassen said to Durango who looked confused.

"Oh, yeah . . . okay," Durango said. "Frogs can walk around on land, but they spend a lot of time in water, and they're slimy and stuff."

"Exactly," Kailani said. "In fact, frogs and other amphibians have to lay their eggs in water. Reptiles arose after amphibians, and they lay eggs with hard or leathery shells that contain amniotic membranes that protect their developing embryos. The development of amniotic eggs was a key feature that enabled vertebrates to live on land."

"So," Lassen said, "in a sense, by enclosing their eggs in shells, the reptiles developed a way to carry water with them to enable reproduction."

"Yes," Kailani said. "Vertebrates are still very water-dependent, including humans. In fact, with our moist, constantly blinking eyes, we're ensuring we have physical conditions enabling sight."

"We may have left the swamps and oceans behind," Lassen said, "but I guess we still have to carry them with us in our eyes."

"True," Kailani said. "Eyes in vertebrates originally evolved to see underwater and first evolved from light-sensitive proteins in aquatic bacteria. Eventually, fish developed excellent eyesight and could see fine details in very low-light environments. However, we'll never be able to see as well as some of our aquatic ancestors because light bends and causes distortions when it moves from one substance to another. With watery eyes in water, this distortion does not occur, but we see light that moves from dry air into our wet eyes. Moving from dry to wet bends light and distorts what we see."

"I did not know that," Adalya said with a bit of modesty.

"Wait a minute," Durango said as he stirred his sauropod egg with a battered old metal fork. "How come vertebrates didn't just adapt and come up with dry eyes that were great for seeing in dry air? Couldn't they just evolve something better when there's a need?"

Lassen was surprised at the depth of Durango's question. Durango's interest in science was evolving.

"Because that's not how evolution by natural selection operates," Kailani said. "Evolution retains what enables survival and reproduction. If suboptimal vision was good enough for certain species, it persisted. It changed here and there when enabling selective survival, but eye evolution didn't just start over. Animals had to evolve with what they already had."

"I see," Durango said.

Lassen smiled to himself as he recognized Durango's unintentional pun.

"Generally," Kailani said, "evolution happens when species gradually evolve advantageous characteristics and pass on and improve those characteristics over time, but it's not always that simple. As we just discussed, things that are simply good enough—like human eyes—may get passed on. Species have to work with what they already have and can't just design what's best. Ultimately, evolution isn't just about survival of the fittest. It's about survival of anything that enables a species to survive *and* reproduce. For example, some evolution is driven by sexual selection, which can result in things that can help an animal be more attractive to mates but might not provide an overall survival advantage."

"Like the super colorful and cumbersome feathers of male peacocks," Lassen said.

"Exactly," Kailani added. "Those feathers can make it more difficult to avoid predators, but they enhance the ability to reproduce, so they're always passed on. Some species may also retain features that are basically useless in their time but leftover from the past."

"Like the tailbone on humans—the coccyx," Lassen said.

"That's right," Kailani said. "It's the remnant of a tail that our monkey-like ancestors had before evolving into more ape-like forms. Plus, genes that provide a species with an advantage may also be associated with a less advantageous characteristic, but those genes keep getting passed on because of the advantage."

"What are genes in this context?" Lassen asked while Durango muttered a comment about denim jeans.

Kailani described genes as biological units of heredity that are made of molecules and contain DNA sequences with information on how living things are made. She described genetics as a branch of biology that focuses on heredity and the architecture of living things. When Lassen asked more about DNA, she said it stood for deoxyribonucleic acid but also said they should discuss it further at another time and admitted that she did not know as much about genetics as she knew about paleontology and geology. Kailani also explained that genetic mutations are gene changes that result in new characteristics in animals.

"Fascinating," Lassen said as he smiled. "Earlier, you indicated that the same genes may give species both advantageous characteristics and less useful traits. What's an example of that?"

"The big toes and enlarged opposable thumbs of humans," Kailani said. "There is a pleiotropic linkage between them, which means that one gene influences multiple traits. We can't have our useful and dexterous opposable thumbs without having big toes because they're influenced by the same genetics. Big toes in modern humans are much less useful than thumbs and may cause mobility problems. Still, the opposable thumb is such a substantial advantage that the DNA controlling both thumbs and big toes is consistently passed on, and people have both."

"Interesting," Lassen said. "I wonder if some sort of pleiotropic linkage explains why *Tyrannosaurus* has such tiny arms. Maybe a gene for a giant head or long legs is associated with small arms."

"Good theory," Kailani said, "but we have no way of verifying that from the fossil record."

"Evolution into practical survivable animals seems like it would take a very long time with a lot of unlikely chance events that might not always build up as needed," Lassen said. "How likely is it that species will simultaneously evolve the various things they need for survival? For example, how could seals evolve flippers, oily fur, and other things needed for living in the water from a chance genetic mutation?"

"Things don't have to happen all at once," Kailani said. "Through inherited genetics, species are constantly inheriting mutations that could be neutral or beneficial, and these are kept. The chance of suddenly getting all the mutations for novel adaptation can be small, but evolution doesn't have to work that way because it can happen with generations of accumulated beneficial mutations."

"Huh," Durango said.

"Think of poker," Kailani said.

"That I know," Durango replied. "I should tell you about the time I got a full house in Tucson."

"With a game of chance, like poker, you play one hand, and you move onto another," Kailani said. "You might get a winning set of cards like a full house on your first hand, but you can't keep it for the next one."

"Sure," Durango said. "That's how poker works. So?"

"Well," Kailani said, "in various cases, in evolution, through inherited accumulated mutations, species are keeping the full houses from various hands of poker and passing these onto subsequent generations who have their own hands of poker to play in various environments. So, for something like seal evolution, one remarkable full house that enables simultaneous multiple traits, like flippers and oily fur, isn't necessary because at any given time, a seal ancestor could have many genetic full houses in its DNA that—given the right conditions and genetic combinations—could enable it to evolve beneficial traits that would incrementally help turn it into a seal as we know it."

"That . . . might make sense," Durango said.

"Good analogy," Lassen said. "I get it."

"Most intriguing," Adalya said. "And the math works. Getting a full house from one hand of cards would be very unlikely, but if you played hundreds of thousands of hands over geologic time, full houses would stack up."

"Exactly," Kailani said. "Evolution is not always gradual and slow, though. Sometimes, it can happen very quickly. For example, bacteria can evolve in a matter of days, and by my time, they were quickly evolving resistance to certain drugs intended to counter them. Moreover, by the early twenty-first century, there will even be bacteria that evolve to digest synthetic plastics, which will not be widespread until the mid-twentieth century."

"Most intriguing," Lassen said, furrowing his brow, "but with tiny organisms that reproduce quickly and don't live long, like bacteria, rapid evolution makes sense. What about bigger animals?"

"Evolution can happen quickly with bigger animals, too," Kailani said. "For example, the evolution of thicker beaks in Galápagos finches was observed over the course of two years in the 1970s as an adaptation to drought. Thicker beaks made it easier for the finches to eat available seeds. Evolution of body changes within relatively short time periods has also been observed in a variety of vertebrates as a response to occupying new habitats. This has happened with male sockeye salmon developing deeper bodies at a beach in the Pacific Northwest, stickleback fish changing body armor in a lake in Alaska, anole lizards developing shorter back legs on islands in the Bahamas, and wild rabbits in the Australian outback changing weight and ear size after being introduced by Europeans. Plus, think of the huge variety of domestic animals that exist and look totally different from the wild counterparts from which they were bred."

"Oh, yeah," Lassen said, "like a gray wolf and a poodle. If humans can develop a bunch of odd-looking domestic dog breeds over the course of hundreds or thousands of years through artificial selection, then why couldn't nature do something similar over a similarly short time period?"

"Exactly," Kailani said. "Evolution can be slow, fast, gradual, abrupt, logical, and sometimes counterintuitive and surprising. Like many things in science, it doesn't always fit into one simple narrative."

*   *   *

About seven miles (11 kilometers) to the southeast, the Traxton Gang slept in. The night was uneventful, which was a stark contrast from the day before, which was their first day in the Jurassic.

The gang camped near the shore of a huge lake. Their bedrolls laid on sand just below where a lakeshore beach transitioned to fern prairie. Just after sunrise, Holt woke up first. Still in his bedroll, he stared down at the lake. Small waves lapped onshore. To Holt, the huge lake seemed like an inland sea. Holt saw something move at the edge of the water about 50 feet (15 meters) away. He did not know what it was and rubbed sleep bleariness from his eyes, trying to get a better look.

On the light brown sands of the beach, a six-foot (two-meter) long lungfish slithered toward the water. It breathed with primitive lungs and weighed approximately 80 pounds (36 kilograms). Holt was confused and silently muttered to himself. To Holt, the lungfish looked like an enormous, flopping catfish. Then the outlaw saw a parting of the water beyond the lungfish. Something big swam toward it.

A 17-foot (five-meter) long *Ceratosaurus* swam toward shore. The carnivorous theropod dinosaur weighed approximately 1,500 pounds (680 kilograms). An excellent swimmer, the *Ceratosaurus* sculled through the water with gentle back-and-forth motions of a flexible tail. It quietly emerged from the water and stood up. Water dripped from its four-fingered hands and glistened in the morning light. Holt gasped.

The *Ceratosaurus* stood about six feet (two meters) above the ground at its hips. It opened its mouth, baring approximately 60 teeth. The top of its body was light orange with black speckles, and its underbelly was off-white with lighter speckling. The color was reminiscent of a leopard or cheetah, but the orange faded into shades of blue on the dinosaur's neck and head, and its tail was tipped in faint blue. The top of its snout sported a blade-like bright green horn just behind and above its nostrils. The theropod also had prominent shiny blue brow ridges with smaller bright green blade-like horns above each eye. The horns gave *Ceratosaurus* a particularly menacing, devilish appearance. A ridge of knobby armor made of osteoderms ran down the dinosaur's back.

Compared to other carnivorous dinosaurs in the Morrison Basin, *Ceratosaurus* had slender arms with a relatively weak grip.

So, the dinosaur relied on its jaws as it snapped them around a huge lungfish and snagged it off the beach. The lungfish flopped and gasped as the *Ceratosaurus* dragged it into water. Except for slight splashing, the conflict was quiet. Holt was still the only outlaw who was awake. The *Ceratosaurus* quietly slunk back into the water and swam north near the lakeshore. It moved out of sight around a distant peninsula of land, leaving a rippling "V" of water in its wake.

The rest of the gang soon woke up. Holt talked about his *Ceratosaurus* sighting. Then there was a discussion about running low on food. Avarette suggested they try fishing. Gantry happened to have fishing line, hooks, and some metal lures. He often fished during cattle drives. Though he never tired of *talking* cattle, he sometimes grew weary of eating beef for weeks at a time. Fish provided an interesting change.

Somehow, despite his protests, Avarette was assigned to help Gantry fish for breakfast. While Avarette and Gantry strolled down to the lake, Holt prepared a pot of coffee, Branigan worked on starting a fire, and Traxton used his scope to scan distant terrain, looking for signs of Lassen and Durango.

Soon, Avarette and Gantry stood near the lakeshore, holding sticks with fishing lines attached. They threw lines with attached lures far out in the water. Then they slowly moved their stick rods back and forth, causing submerged shiny lures to spin. To Avarette's surprise, they did pretty well—and pretty quickly. They soon piled fish beside them.

"I'll be whillakered o' jillakered," Gantry said. "This is kinda fun."

"Indeed," Avarette replied.

In the background, Branigan's campfire efforts began to yield smoke and little flames. Gantry was in a good mood, which inspired him to sing. Avarette cringed as he heard the words.

"Bacon Caaaaat!" Gantry sang. "Oh, Bacon Cat knows where it's at. Bacon Cat just saw a rat. Bacon Caaaat. Bacon Cat sniffs some bacon." Gantry vigorously sniffed. "Sniffs some bacon." Gantry sniffed again. "Sizzle. Sizzle. Started shakin'. Bacon Cat sniffs some bacon. Doesn't care about the rat. That's not where it's at. When he got—started shakin'. Sniffs some bacon. Oh Bacon Cat gone meeeeooowww meeeeoowoooww meeooww. Meooow meeeooow meeooowww. Sizzle. Sizzle. Oh Bacon Caaaatttt!"

"Gantry buddy," Avarette said.

"What is it?" Gantry asked.

"Could you keep it down?" Avarette said. "You're gonna subject the poor prehistoric critters of this time to a premature extinction."

"Ah, come on, Avarette," Gantry said. "I haven't got to the best part yet, and this here singin' is based on a true-to-life story. Happened to me personally when I was drivin' beeves from Santa Fe to Cheyenne. I met Blaze on that trip."

"You don't say," Avarette remarked. "Look, your fishing, uh, implements are doing a fine job, and you're helping catch our breakfast. I appreciate that, but please make this the last song of the morning."

"Oh—okay," Gantry said, "but only because you asked politely. You're not mean like Branigan."

"Much obliged," Avarette said.

Gantry continued his song. "The old cowboy—he was fryin' up some grub. He was gonna have some morning bacon in the makin', but old Bacon Cat started shakin' when he smelled the bacon! He saw a rat, but that wasn't where it's at because he was a *Bacon Cat*! Sizzle. Sizzle. Bacon Cat. Meeeooww meeeooow meeeooow meeeoowoww. He was a baaaaacccooooonnnnnn cccaaaaaaaatttttt. He knew where it's aaaatttttt! Old cowboy was gonna chaw at dawn, but when he stopped to yawn, he found his bacon was gone. Old Bacon Cat got his bacon and moved along. Baaaacccccoonn Caaaaaatttt! Sizzle! Sizzle!"

Subconsciously, Avarette had started to move his right boot to the beat of Gantry's song. Gantry was not particularly talented, but sometimes his melodies stumbled into catchiness.

Suddenly, half a dozen shadows fell on Avarette and Gantry as a flock of sharp-toothed, hungry *Harpactognathus* swooped down to the fish piled next to the two outlaws. The flying reptiles screeched and bared yellowish teeth. The pterosaurs' fuzzy, leathery red-brown wing skin was translucent in the morning sun, and various veins were clearly visible in their wings. Gantry panicked, unholstered his pistol, and started blasting away. Avarette pulled his gun but paused as he took a moment to absorb what was happening.

"You addle-headed, cowpoke!" Traxton shouted as he rushed toward the fray of gunfire and pterosaurs snatching at fish. "I told you not to fire your guns until we tangle with Malone and

Mesquite!" As Traxton spoke, he swiftly sliced air with fists and boots. The outlaw gang leader punched and kicked *Harpactognathus* individuals out of the sky with expert, rapid skill. "These varmints are light, and they don't fire back. Conserve your ammo!"

With Traxton's furious assault, the *Harpactognathus* quickly retreated, dropping partially chewed fish in their wake. Traxton mightily jumped high, grabbed the lowest *Harpactognathus* by the tail and violently slammed it into the sand—snout-first. Then he backhanded Gantry in the face. "You chucklehead! The bounty hunters will know where we are now!"

Gantry winced, dropped his gun, and fell into the sand, his face stinging from the pain of Traxton's assault. Gantry sullenly stared into the nearby lake's lapping waves. Clear water sparkled in the morning light. It was gorgeous, but Gantry was not feeling so great as his eyes glistened. He was trying not to cry and kept thinking of his memories with Bacon Cat in an effort to get a glimmer of positivity from a happier, more stable time in his life.

*   *   *

Shortly before Gantry sulked in depression, Lassen moved a forkful of yellow-white fried sauropod egg toward his mouth. He and his fellow time travelers were just finishing breakfast. He paused as he heard gunshots to the south.

"I hear them, too, pal," Durango said. "Somebody's shootin' a Colt forty-five."

"We're not alone," Lassen said.

"At least some of Traxton's men must of made it," Durango added.

The nearby *Brachiosaurus* herd briefly stopped eating at the sound of gunfire. Then the dinosaurs continued eating sequoia needles, unconcerned.

"Yeah . . ." Lassen apprehensively said.

"You believe they are in pursuit?" Adalya asked.

"They have to be," Lassen said. "Traxton would follow us to Neptune for revenge if that's what it took. Still, they may be having trouble with the local wildlife. I'm not sure why else they would fire their guns while they're still so far away."

"Why does he despise you so much?" Kailani asked.

"There are some long stories," Lassen said.

"Lassen," Durango said. "We lost our guns. We've never gone up against the Traxton Gang without our guns. That's not good. This changes things. We might be able to outrun the dinosaurs on our horses—"

"But we can't outrun bullets," Lassen said. "Guns are tools. Convenient tools, but tools, nonetheless. We're just going to have to work a little harder. There are materials around here we can fashion into weapons. We just need to be creative."

"We'll need more than a knife and some wooden spears if we're gonna go up against the Traxton Gang again," Durango said.

"We can make bolas," Lassen said. "I used them when I spent time with gauchos in South America."

"What's a bola?" Durango asked.

"A weapon made of rocks tied to ropes," Lassen said. "Bolas usually have three heavy rocks tied together with some sort of cord. They were developed by South American natives for hunting. They're used for taking down animals, like guanacos and large flightless rhea birds. After being spun and thrown, bolas can entangle animals' legs. South American cowboys—gauchos— sometimes use bolas to stop cattle. They can work pretty well." Lassen removed his lariat from his horse. "We're going to have to cut up my lasso."

Lassen did not even consider cutting apart Durango's lariat for making bolas. He knew how much it meant to his friend. Lassen was competent with lassoing and other ropecraft, but Durango was an expert and very fond of his lariat.

Lassen spoke as he uncoiled his rope. "The Traxton Gang is here and still causin' trouble. Let's make some weapons. Then it's time for an outlaw roundup."

"Hmmm," Durango said, "so instead of a spring cattle roundup, we'll have a Jurassic roundup."

"I am not sure actively pursuing human adversaries will make us any safer," Adalya said, "especially when they are armed primitives from the nineteenth century."

"What are we supposed to do when we find them?" Kailani asked. "Just take them along as prisoners?"

"We're bounty hunters," Durango said, "that's what we do."

"But would they even find us if we just continue on our way?" Kailani said. "This is a vast landscape."

"Traxton will find us," Lassen said. "Maybe not today. Maybe not tomorrow. But he'll find us. In fact, there's a good chance he's already seen us. He was shooting at Durango and me the last time we saw him. We'd be better off finding him first. Trust me."

"So, if we do, then what?" Adalya asked. "Dragging along five prisoners for an indefinite period of time is hardly practical."

"Depends on how soon your professor can rescue us," Lassen said.

"If she can rescue us," Kailani added.

"She can," Adalya said.

"They might not be our responsibility long if we get rescued," Lassen said, "and if we're all going to be stuck here for a while, we may need to learn to live together."

"Traxton and Branigan are going to try to kill us first chance they get," Durango said.

"Maybe," Lassen said, "but I think we can reason with the other gang members. Avarette is an opportunist, Holt's just greedy, and Gantry will go along with whoever's in charge."

Lassen cut sections of rope while the others gathered rocks that weighed about a half pound (0.2 kilograms) each. Finding suitable rocks was easy as the landscape and nearby water channel edges were full of small rocks polished by flowing water.

With rope sections cut, Lassen tied together the ends of three of them with a knot. The result was three dangling rope strands with a knot at one end. Eventually, Lassen had three sets of bola lashings. He then tied a section of rope to each lashing set, so the lashings would have a handle for swinging.

With rocks acquired, the time travelers each worked on tying rocks to their own bola lashings. As they worked, the nearby *Brachiosaurus* herd moved farther and farther south, slowly eating. Durango was great with knots, Lassen and Kailani were meticulous and detail-oriented, and Adalya was precise and deliberate. Soon, the bounty hunters and scientists each had an effective-looking bola.

"Let's test these weapons," Lassen said as he stood up from a crouch, bola in hand.

"Okay," Durango said, "see that dead branch sticking out from that tree about 60 feet away?" Durango pointed, and the others nodded. "Let's try to hit that. I'll go first."

Durango held his bola by its rope handle and swung it over his head. As it gathered circular momentum, it resembled a blurry brown disc. Then Durango leaned forward and released his grip. The bola shot forward and ripped through a cluster of *Equisetum* near the target tree. Durango groaned in frustration.

"Hey, it was your first time using one of these things," Lassen said. "Kailani, you want to give it a shot?"

"Alright," Kailani said as she swung her bola over her head before quickly throwing it. Her aim was true, and the bola lashed itself tightly around the target branch.

"Son of a catamount," Durango said. "Looks like it tied its own knot."

"Excellent," Lassen said. "Miss Nell, show us what you can do."

"Very well, then," Adalya said. "Let us see if I can get triple efficacy."

"Huh," Durango said.

Adalya swung the bola over her head, narrowed her eyes in concentration, mentally did a series of quick geometry calculations, and released her grip. Her bola shot through the air. One of its rocks broke off the target branch, and the other rocks broke off two adjacent branches.

"Did you mean to do that?" Durango said, mouth agape.

"Yes, I did," Adalya said.

"Triple efficacy," Lassen said, raising his eyebrows. "Very fancy." Then he swung his bola over his head in wide circular arcs, bit his lower lip, and released it. The weapon sailed forward with straight, precise momentum and hit the portion of tree trunk where the target branch had broken off.

The bounty hunters and scientists made more bolas. Then they packed dinosaur eggs (for future meals) into their saddlebags with care, padding them with fern fronds. Lassen cinched Horizon's saddle tight and discussed his plan for the rest of the day. "We need to get out of the open. Here, we're easy targets for Traxton."

"Then I suppose we should move into the forest," Adalya said.

"Yeah," Lassen replied. "The risk of predators might be greater, but we can double-back and sneak up on the Traxton Gang."

*   *   *

An hour later, Lassen, Adalya, and Durango rode west to the edge of a dense forest. They were still in the open, but there was now a short understory of brush, shrubs, and *Equisetum* instead of mostly just ferns. Durango wriggled his nose.

"You smell that?" Durango asked.

"Yeah," Lassen said. "Smells like something faintly rotten."

"I smell it, too," Kailani added.

Adalya waved her hand in front of her nose. Then the time travelers heard crunching sounds from the ground.

"Whoa," Lassen said. "Hold up. What are the horses stepping on?"

"Eggs," Kailani said, looking down. "Well, eggshells, anyway. Something hatched here recently. These shells must be from dinosaur eggs."

"Yep," Durango said as he looked closer at the ground.

The time travelers' horses were stepping on eggshells in shallow crescent-shaped nests. The shell fragments and nearby intact eggs in other nests were initially hard to see because they were loosely covered with soft soil and decomposed plants. Lassen scanned the vicinity with his binoculars and realized there were hundreds of nests. Occasionally, he saw the edges of eggshells poking up from underneath dried ferns and dirt. The vegetation around the eggs looked like it had largely recovered from being trampled by the adult sauropods that had laid the eggs. Therefore, this nesting site was older than the one the time travelers had encountered in the morning. The eggshells on the ground indicated some eggs had already hatched.

"This is a huge nesting ground," Lassen said.

Suddenly, eggs cracked nearby.

"What's goin' on?" Durango asked.

"They appear to be hatching," Kailani replied. Kailani raised her binoculars and scanned the southern horizon. "Most of them seem to be hatching at once. I can understand the efficiencies of not offering parental care, but this must be very dangerous for the hatchlings."

Lassen looked down and saw dried leaves and dirt tumble off a nearby egg as it cracked open. The egg was spherical and about nine inches (23 centimeters) in diameter. A little sauropod baby's snout popped up through an eggshell. Lassen noticed a tiny triangular keratin bump on its snout that was used to break the shell. This was a feature known as an egg tooth. Crocodiles and birds in modern times would also use them for hatching. More and more cracking reverberated across the landscape as little sauropods began to push out of their eggs.

"We're in the middle of a hatch," Durango said, "and it kind of stinks."

"I believe," Kailani said, "that the odor is the result of metabolic gases and other wastes being released from the eggs."

For a few moments, the time travelers sat still on their horses and watched as hundreds of little sauropods wriggled out of their eggs. Freeing themselves seemed to take tremendous effort, and Lassen thought they looked exhausted. Each nest contained roughly 20 to 30 eggs. Lassen could not tell exactly what species they were but guessed they were *Apatosaurus* or *Diplodocus*. The baby dinosaurs' heads and eyes were disproportionately large compared to those of their adult counterparts. Kailani shot photos and recorded videos with her phone.

The hatchlings were green-brown with dappled and streaked patterns that helped them blend in with surrounding vegetation. The babies' color patterns reminded Lassen of the striping on baby emus, and he guessed their colors greatly changed as they got older. The adult sauropods were bright and showy and did not seem concerned about standing out.

Lassen watched wet, tired baby sauropods emerge from eggshells and struggle through dried plants and dirt. These babies would receive no parental care and were ready to move about in the world upon hatching. In this sense, they were somewhat like precocial birds of modern times, like waterfowl, which can move around and feed shortly after hatching. In contrast, altricial birds—swallows for example—hatch blind and helpless and require parental care just to eat.

As soon as they left their nests, the baby sauropods made their way toward the densest vegetation they could find. Many headed toward the forest. Others stumbled into particularly concentrated clusters of ferns and *Equisetum*. Then Lassen saw why.

A patchwork of small shadows suddenly fell on the nesting ground. Both red-brown rhamphorynchoid *Harpactognathus* and blue pterodactyloid *Kepodactylus* pterosaurs flew over and descended on the hatchlings. Tiny sauropods were skewered by *Kepodactylus* beaks and pierced by *Harpactognathus* teeth. Squeaking, shrieking, and hissing filled the air. Graphite and Yonder reared, but Horizon and Ember stayed calm.

Suddenly, theropod carnivores entered the scene. Four *Marshosaurus* dashed out of the forest and snatched up baby sauropods. The *Marshosaurus* were about six to seven feet (two meters) tall, roughly 20 feet (6 meters) long, and weighed about 550 pounds (250 kilograms). They had gray sides, beige underbellies with brown speckling, light brown backs, and chestnut brown heads. The *Marshosaurus* pack was comprised of two males and two females. Each male *Marshosaurus* had a shiny dark green band on each side of its head. The shape and color of the bands reminded Lassen of coloration he had seen on modern waterfowl, like green-winged teal and American wigeon. *Marshosaurus* was named after Professor Othniel Charles Marsh.

Graphite and Yonder galloped to the south, bringing Lassen and Durango straight into the nesting ground. Horizon and Ember followed to keep pace with Adalya and Kailani at the reins. Events abruptly turned chaotic as the horses sped past *Marshosaurus* running in the opposite direction with baby sauropods in their jaws. Lassen ducked to avoid being smacked in the face by a swooping *Kepodactylus*. To the left and right, Lassen saw several fuzzy *Coelurus* pouncing on hatching sauropods. Their bronze and white feathers sparkled in the sun. He also briefly caught a glimpse of a lone *Ceratosaurus* pulling two hatchlings out of a nest with its jaws. The sudden appearance of another new carnivore startled Lassen, who was immediately struck by its leopard-like coloring and the bright green horns on its snout.

Several chicken-sized feathered *Hesperornithoides* emerged from the undergrowth and pounced on sauropod hatchlings. Their red, blue, and yellow color patterns reminded Lassen of golden pheasants. As the small carnivores nimbly hopped onto hatchlings, Lassen wondered if they could fly, but he never saw any take to the air, like *Archaeopteryx* had. The *Hesperornithoides* used disproportionately large sickle-shaped claws on each of their feet to grip baby sauropods and keep them in place. This reminded Lassen of the pictures of dromaeosaurs Kailani had shown him.

A low-flying *Kepodactylus* knocked off Lassen's hat in its rush for breakfast, and the bounty hunter swung low to the left to catch his hat just before it hit the ground. What had started out as a tranquil scene of sauropods hatching into a new bright, green world had turned into a savage, frantic feeding frenzy.

Marshosaurus, *Coelurus*, *Hesperornithoides*, and a *Ceratosaurus* pounced on sauropods while pterosaurs attacked. Little sauropods shuffled along as their peers became snacks. The babies were tired and wet, and their eyes were bloodshot with fear, fatigue, and adrenaline. Lassen's expression turned pensive as he made eye contact with a baby and clearly saw red veins in its big eyes. It was then snatched up by a *Marshosaurus*.

About 60 to 80 percent of the hatchling sauropods would end up being eaten before the hatch was finished, but this was a normal part of sauropod nesting in the area. Sauropods evolved a "quantity over quality" reproductive strategy in which having a huge amount of offspring ensured enough survived to enable species perpetuation, despite lack of nurturing.

The horses eventually slowed, and the time travelers entered the forest. The primordial sounds of the bloody hatching event faded as the time travelers moved deeper into the trees. Everybody breathed hard as they got off their horses.

"That was terrible," Kailani said.

"Nature," Lassen said, "red in tooth and claw."

"Son of a catamount," Durango added. "Never saw anything quite like that."

"I hope Professor Sedora finds us soon," Adalya remarked.

For the next hour, the time travelers walked their horses through the forest as the vegetation had become too thick for riding to be practical. They soon walked along a river. Plants grew particularly densely near the water, and *Equisetum* was prominent. As they moved farther along, Lassen occasionally noticed little sauropods chewing *Equisetum* before scurrying into streamside vegetation. He saw other baby sauropods nibble mushrooms before disappearing into thick clusters of ferns. Lassen guessed these had hatched a week or two earlier. This part of the forest looked like an excellent refuge for hatchling sauropods because of the water, nutritious plants, and abundance of hiding places.

Chapter 15: Sheep Rock Showdown

In the pre-dawn chill of Wyoming's open range, a bucking horse threw Sedora to the ground. She got up and tried riding it again. Sedora practiced riding horses under a variety of scenarios involving numerous horse breeds with varied temperaments. Finally, she turned off her holographic simulation program and decided she was as ready as she could be for horse riding.

Randall Blaze awoke in a sour mood as he gradually realized where he was and what had happened. His hands and ankles were chafed from struggling against his restraints. With a whoosh of air and beeping, the door to his small room opened. Sedora stood in the doorway. However, Blaze only knew her as Doctor Lenora Hadley, a scientist. As he saw her, he remembered that he had introduced himself as John Sage, a businessman.

"Good morning, cowboy," Sedora said. She stood with a window behind her. The sun had just risen, and the morning light made the back of her bronze-silver hair sparkle.

"I'm not a cowboy," Blaze rudely responded. "I can make more in a week than a cowboy makes in a year."

"Right, right," Sedora said. She wore a simple white button-up blouse with a long brown pleated split riding skirt and boots. She also had a set of saddlebags draped over both shoulders, and she wore a time period-appropriate utility belt and pouches that still housed her original equipment. Sedora had synthesized the new clothing and accessories the night before with the time machine's molecular sculptor. In the 2700s, molecular sculptors would be common appliances widely used in homes.

In addition to a new belt and clothes, Sedora had synthesized a sidearm that had all the inner workings of a plasma pistol but the external appearance of a Colt forty-five pistol. Her new Old West-looking plasma pistol hung holstered at her side.

"You'll fit in more with that getup," Blaze dryly stated.

"Thanks," Sedora deadpanly replied. "We have a bit of a walk today, and I have prepared supplies. The nearest settlement is Medicine Bow, which is approximately 10 kilometers southwest of us. Or, as you would think of it: 6.21371 miles."

"Huh," Blaze said. "We're about five miles from Medicine Bow. What supplies do we have? I lost mine when my horse got disappeared."

"I acquired food and water for you," Sedora said as she gestured toward the saddlebag draped on her left shoulder. "In here, you'll find beans, biscuits, jerky, and a full canteen."

"Great," Blaze said, "the basics to allow me to not die. Like feedin' a dog."

"Life is a precious thing," Sedora said. "Be grateful." As she spoke, she felt concern for Adalya as well as determination to fix the time machine and rescue her.

"When we go to Medicine Bow," Blaze said, "maybe I should just wait outside town in the trees by the river, and you should go in and get the horses."

"Why?" Sedora asked.

Blaze faltered momentarily and then sputtered, "I had a business deal go bad there recently. Some of the locals might not like having me around again."

"Would any of these locals be law enforcement officials?" Sedora asked. In reply, Blaze just cleared his throat.

"Okay then," Sedora said. "Sounds like you will need a disguise to avoid trouble. I will be back."

Sedora closed the door and returned several minutes later with a clean suit, a bowler hat, and a mysterious strip of hair in her arms.

"Hoity-toity," Blaze said. "That just might do the trick."

Sedora set the clothing on a shelf and removed a metallic device from her belt that had a bulb in the front and a handle in the back.

"Whoa!" Blaze said as he shoved his chair back quickly, nearly falling down. "Wait! Wait! I said I'd help you. I'll take you to Sheep Rock."

"This is just a hygiene flash zapper," Sedora said. "Relax, Mister Sage."

Sedora clicked a switch on the handle of the hygiene zapper, and a green light shot out and arced into separate beams that alternated back and forth as they swept across Blaze's head and face. Blaze closed his eyes and seethed in frustration as the light hit his face.

His scraggly hair was suddenly trimmed into a neat haircut with squared-off sideburns. Green light rays instantly dissolved bits of hair into constituent atoms and teleported them into a waste bin in another room. The light rays also gave Blaze a clean shave. Blaze opened his eyes and rapidly blinked. He wriggled his nose and licked his upper lip.

"It's smooth," Blaze said as he felt clean-shaven skin on his face without a five o' clock shadow. "What'd you do?"

"Instant haircut and shave," Sedora said.

"How'd that thing do that?" Blaze asked.

"It is just some physics," Sedora said. She tossed a strip of hair to Blaze.

"What's this?" Blaze asked.

"Mustache," Sedora said. "Part of the disguise."

Sedora tapped a device encased in leather on her belt, and Blaze's hand restraints fell off. Blaze held his hands in place and looked down at them with disbelief and suspicion.

"My hands ain't tied no more," Blaze said.

"You will need them free to change and put on that mustache," Sedora said. "Peel off the clear strip on the back, and put it on your upper lip."

"I don't think I want no stick-on 'stache," Blaze said disdainfully.

Sedora tapped her belt, and Blaze grunted and ground his teeth as a mild electric shock jolted through his skeleton.

"Do it," Sedora said. "The mustache will make the difference and keep you from being recognized. I have done the calculations. Trust me."

Blaze reluctantly peeled off the strip on the back of the mustache and stuck it on his upper lip.

"It itches," Blaze said.

"Too bad," Sedora replied. "We need a cover story to explain who we are, and why we are in town together."

"How about you're my mail order bride," Blaze said, "and I'm taking you into town to put you on a train because you're too much trouble."

"Yeah, no," Sedora said. "We could pass for siblings. I will use the name Mora Lamay, and you will go by Louis Lamay. We are visitors from Massachusetts who came to see the West. We will pretend we came by train."

225

"Eh, I guess people would believe that," Blaze said. "We'll need some money to rent the horses. All my money got disappeared."

"Oh, we have money," Sedora said as she patted her saddlebags. Her molecular sculptor had printed a variety of time period-appropriate 1860s and 1870s paper bills as well as some 20-dollar double eagle gold coins. The money had simulated wear and looked authentic.

Sedora and Blaze soon stood outside the metallic time machine and squinted their eyes at a rising sun. Light shot past the jagged Laramie Mountains to the east, filling the nearby plains and badlands with soft yellowish hues. Killdeer squealed, and meadowlarks sang. A circling red-tailed hawk cried. A distant pack of coyotes howled and yipped.

Blaze took a deep breath of fresh morning hair. He smelled sagebrush and newly sprouted green grass. His wrists and ankles were sore from his restraints, which were recently completely removed. Blaze enjoyed his new mobility, but he knew he would get an electrocution from Sedora if he stepped out of line.

Both Sedora and Blaze carried a set of saddlebags with supplies as they walked toward Medicine Bow. Sedora's technology had put high levels of detail into the synthesis of their wardrobe and accessories. For instance, the leather of the saddlebags looked, felt, and smelled real. It was even cracked, distressed, and hosted a re-created coating of local dust.

Later in the morning, Sedora and Blaze spotted Medicine Bow to the south. They stood among tall clusters of cottonwood trees near the Medicine River. Sedora was amazed at how little evidence of humanity existed on the landscape. The main living things she saw on their journey to town were cattle, pronghorn, and circling turkey vultures. In 2756, solar energy collection and water extraction infrastructure would cover enormous expanses of arid wildlands.

After crossing a bridge, Sedora and Blaze soon strode down the boardwalks of Medicine Bow's Main Street. A few people stared at them, but the outlaw and the time traveler fit in fairly well. Sedora heard a loud train whistle and saw a train chugging past the south end of town.

"Such primitive transportation technology," Sedora muttered.

Sedora and Blaze stepped up to a livery stable where the stable keeper nailed a new set of horseshoes onto a strawberry roan horse. The stable keeper looked up as he saw Blaze and Sedora approach. He was a large man and wore an apron.

"I don't remember seeing you pilgrims in these parts," the stable keeper said. "I'm Fenton Farnsworth. I run this here livery stable. First time in Medicine Bow?"

"Uh, yeah, it is," Blaze said.

Sedora nodded in agreement.

"Coming to settle or just passin' through?" Farnsworth asked.

"We're passin' through," Blaze coolly said. "Me and my sister wanted to stop off here and take a break from the train. This is our first time in the West, and we thought we'd rent horses and go for a ride."

"Oh boy," Farnsworth said. "Customers. That's great, son. I'll rent you horses. I've got one real good one, a former racehorse that's good with those who haven't ridden much. You folks know how to ride?"

"I am not particularly experienced," Sedora said.

"I can ride," Blaze deadpanly added.

"Okay then," Farnsworth said. "Ma'am, I'll get you the best horse I got. This horse is fast. Really fast. But only when you want her to be. You shouldn't have trouble ridin' her, but you'll need to be careful out there. Dangerous time to be travelin', especially with the Traxton Gang operatin' hereabouts. Just a couple days ago, there was a lot of excitement in town. Two bounty hunters, the famous Lassen Malone and his sidekick Daniel Chaparral, were in town facing off against the notorious Traxton Gang. There was a gunfight, cattle stampede, and fisticuffs. You shoulda seened it!"

"You don't say," Blaze said as he avoided Farnsworth's eyes and stared at a row of horseshoes on a nearby outdoor shelf.

"Sounds quite exciting," Sedora added.

"All the outlaws from the fight got locked up," Farnsworth said. "Some people were riled about the property damage and noise, but I for one was glad to see somebody finally help the sheriff deal with Traxton's men. No doubt the Traxton Gang was here trying to pull some form of shecoonery. Unfortunately, on Thursday night, Tardell Traxton himself sprung his boys. Five men in all got sprunged, and they're practically a who's who of Wyoming's most wanted."

"Who were they?" Sedora asked.

"Shanahan Branigan, Arvo Avarette," Farnsworth started to say as he counted on his fingers, "Jed Gantry, Hobart Holt, and a young feller, Randy, Blake—no, Randall Blaze. He's about the same age as your brother."

"Interesting," Sedora said. "Five men escaped." *With Traxton, that would be six total people,* Sedora thought. *The bounty hunters last night were pursuing six men. Traxton and his gang may be Blaze's "business partners" who are in the Jurassic with Doctor Nell.*

"It was a peculiar prison break," Farnsworth said. "A hole was cut in the prison wall, and nobody knows how Traxton did it. The cutting is real clean, and the brick looks like it was melted."

Like from a plasma knife, Sedora thought as she furrowed her brow.

"Mister Farnsworth," Sedora said, "where is the prison? I would like to see that."

"Oh, it's just down the street," Farnsworth said as he patted the neck of the horse he was shoeing and set down his tools. "I can take you over there real quick if you'd like. Don't listen to no one who says the West ain't wild no more. It's still plenty wild out here."

"Yes," Sedora said, "if you could show us, that would be great. How exciting."

Blaze cleared his throat and said, "I guess we'll go have a look."

Farnsworth continued to speak as he walked down the street with Sedora and Blaze. "Sheriff Gratton and Deputy Caddock have been looking for Traxton, Branigan, and the rest since they broke out, but I bet that rainstorm last night will make things harder. Word is that Traxton was going to meet up with that dangerous polecat Britt Thornby and the rest of the gang. I hear tell that Thornby and the other half of the Traxton Gang is hidin' somewhere out in the hills south of here. We could use the help of Lassen Malone and Dave Manzanita again, but nobody knows where they are."

"They might never turn up again," Blaze said with a smirk as he turned his face away from Farnsworth.

"I hope they do, son," Farnsworth said. "The frontier needs more men like them."

"I heard they were dangerous bounty hunters only out for money," Sedora said.

"Oh, they're dangerous," Farnsworth said, "but only to desperadoes with prices on their heads. I hear they're good men. I heard that Malone gives his reward money to orphanages. I think Dallas keeps his. I once met a man who rode with Traxton. He said Traxton always complained about the do-goodery of Malone. Said it was a bad influence on his business."

"Interesting," Sedora said with a tilt of her chin as she glanced at Blaze. "How did you meet this former Traxton Gang member?"

"He bought a horse from me after making a deal with the sheriff up in Casper. He said he was done with the outlaw life and would help the law get Traxton."

"Sounds a little too talkative for his own good," Blaze remarked.

"You could say that," Farnsworth said. "Heard Traxton shot him dead two days after he got a horse from me."

"Strong leadership," Blaze said. "Guess he was settin' an example to prevent betrayal."

"He's just a villain," Farnsworth said. "We're almost there. The hole's on the backside of this building."

Soon, Farnsworth, Sedora, and Blaze stared at a hole in the back of the prison. Sedora closely examined the edges of the hole with her hands on her hips.

"That is precision work," Sedora said.

"Sure is," Farnsworth added. "It's like Traxton had an iron hot razor or somethin.'"

"Or something," Sedora said as she felt the smooth edges of the prison wall. "Most interesting. We should get back to the livery and rent those horses."

"Right, ma'am," Farnsworth said. "Right. Follow me."

As they walked, Sedora thought about the puzzle of the prison wall hole. It seemed very likely that plasma cutting technology from her time had made its way to 2756, but how did Traxton get it? Did he take it from Brent Cordon? Who else had the plasma cutting technology?

*   *   *

By early afternoon, Blaze and Sedora rode horses far out on the plains. Sedora rode a lithe blonde quarter horse. Blaze rode a surly tan mustang with black legs. They rode east toward the southern end of the Laramie Mountains. Both riders saw Sheep Rock jutting up over 7,000 feet (2,130 meters) above sea level in the distance. Their horses soon forded the Laramie River. Blaze's and Sedora's legs got a bit wet, but the day was hot, and the water quickly dried. Blaze's knowledge of the terrain proved to be valuable, but Sedora was suspicious of the outlaw's helpfulness and suspected he would escape at any moment.

By late afternoon, the riders reached the base of Sheep Rock, which was a massive light brown rock outcrop that towered above surrounding terrain. An apron of slopes formed the base of the outcrop. Blaze and Sedora rode up a draw until they were between steep rocky slopes. They stopped in the shade of a small grove of junipers.

Sedora was ahead of Blaze and retrieved her database orientation module. She held it at an angle that did not allow Blaze to see it.

"We are close to my intended destination," Sedora said as she examined readouts.

"Good," Blaze said. "What are you after? Why are we here?"

"That is classified," Sedora said as she tucked her database orientation module into a saddlebag. The horses of the time traveler and outlaw nervously whinnied.

"These cayuses are pickin' up somethin,'" Blaze said. "They're scared." Then Blaze saw what initially looked like fuzzy branches sticking out of the dirt at the base of a juniper. Blaze readjusted his bowler. "We should probably move soon."

"Why?" Sedora asked.

"Because we're near a fresh catamount kill," Blaze said. "Look over there." Blaze pointed to the right. "Looks like a four-point mule deer buck was just killed, dragged under this juniper, and half-buried. You can see his velvet antlers sticking up."

"Catamount?" Sedora asked.

"Mountain lion, cougar, painter," Blaze said. "It's a wild lion in these parts."

Suddenly, a mountain lion jumped down from a nearby juniper. The horses vigorously whinnied and galloped uphill. Sedora and Blaze struggled to hold their reins and stay mounted.

The scent of humans made the mountain lion extremely anxious. With people too close for comfort, it had finally made the decision to bolt out of a tree in fear instead of waiting to be discovered. While panting heavily, the mountain lion quietly disappeared into nearby boulders like a ghost. It had relatively small lungs, which enabled short sprints but were not good for endurance running.

In the meantime, the horses of Sedora and Blaze abruptly stopped at the dead end of a rocky slope. The momentum flung Sedora off her horse. She closed her eyes as she hit dirt.

Sedora froze as she heard distinctive rattling. She opened her eyes and stared into the menacing eyes and glossy black forked tongue of a western diamondback rattlesnake. Six inches (15 centimeters) separated Sedora's face from the rattler. In that moment, she felt the intensity of primal survival.

"Move away fast!" Blaze shouted. "That's your only chance!"

Sedora stayed frozen. She did not trust Blaze. The snake had scaly skin with brown, black, and light tan mottling. It shook a formidable rattle at the end of its tail. The snake was six feet (two meters) long, but in its coiled state, length was difficult to judge. It sniffed Sedora with its tongue, which it repeatedly flicked in and out. Sedora knew she was in danger and that rattlers could release fatal venom with their bite. Many animal species from the 1800s had gone extinct by the twenty-eighth century—including an especially high number of amphibians and migratory birds—but rattlers had remained. Typically, they rarely posed a threat to humans, and they served as effective rodent controllers. In Sedora's time, rattlers were generally left alone.

Like other snakes in the pit viper family, the rattler Sedora encountered could detect warm-blooded prey by using heat-sensitive pits located on the sides of its head. It was an ambush hunter and had been waiting for three days for a mouse to move within striking distance on a rodent trail. Sedora was an unwelcome intruder, and the rattler shook its tail, warning her to leave.

Sedora slowed her breathing and stared into brown snake eyes with black slit pupils. She heard slight hoof steps. An antler-handled knife plunked into the dirt just behind the rattler. With lightning reflexes, the poisonous snake swiveled its body around and struck the knife with its piercing fangs. Sedora stood and quickly backed up while the rattler was distracted. She stopped as she backed into an unfamiliar horse and its rider's leg.

"You okay, miss?" the rider asked.

"I think so," Sedora said, breathing hard. "Just startled." Sedora noticed the rider was a young man with a brass star pinned to his vest. She wondered where he came from and guessed he had been concealed behind a nearby large boulder.

"Well, that old rattler shouldn't be causin' you any trouble," the rider said as the rattlesnake slithered away into the brush. "Looks like he broke a tooth on my knife. I'm Deputy Caddock, ma'am."

"Mora Lamay," Sedora said, "and that is my brother, Louis." Sedora gestured toward Blaze. "Why did you not shoot it? Seems like that is what most people around here would do."

"Too risky," Caddock said. "That snake was too close to you, and there was no need to kill it. When you were thrown, you surprised that rattler. He was just defendin' his territory. I read in a story that the knife distraction would work."

"What story was that?" Sedora asked.

"A Lassen Malone novel," Caddock said. "I think it was *Volume 38: Showdown at Salsa Meadows*."

Another rider appeared from behind a cluster of junipers.

"I'm Sheriff Gratton from Medicine Bow," the other rider said. "We're after some of the Traxton Gang. A slather of them broke out of jail in Medicine Bow the other night, but we also got word a separate Traxton group was hiding out here on Sheep Rock. What are you folks doing out here?"

Blaze narrowed his eyes with apprehension and anger. Sheriff Gratton was going to be trouble.

"It is a complicated story," Sedora said.

Just then, seven gun hammers clicked as a passel of Traxton outlaws emerged from surrounding high rock outcrops. They were all mounted, and their horses moved carefully on the steep slopes. Sedora and the lawmen stared up at the barrels of over half a dozen guns. Though the outlaws were a fair distance away, they were close enough to hit their targets.

"You can tell the story later!" a man with a deep voice and British accent called from atop a white horse high in the rocks. "Sheriff Gratton and Deputy Caddock, prepare to die!"

"Britt Thornby," Gratton said, recognizing one of Traxton's top men. Gratton's right hand hovered above his holstered pistol as he dryly added, "I guessed you'd be hiding up here."

"Hold off on the shootin', Britt!" Blaze called out. "It's me, Randall Blaze. I pulled that job with you in Cheyenne. Used to ride with Jed Gantry. You remember me!"

"Oh, yes, of course," Britt Thornby said. "Good chap, Blaze!"

"Blaze?!" Caddock said as he looked at Blaze in disbelief. "But you're so cleaned up—and the mustache."

"It's a fake, deputy," Blaze said as he peeled off his mustache. "Never been a 'stache man."

Caddock raised his eyebrows in response.

"Who's the girl, and what are you doing with the law?" Thornby asked.

"She's some scientist doctor holding me prisoner," Blaze said "She brought me here, and she's after somethin.' I don't know what."

"There are certainly some interesting things here," Thornby said. "Strange wreckage from an armored wagon. And something else."

"What?" Blaze asked.

Thornby reached into a pocket of his vest and pulled out the tungsten carbide-coated parameter settings core that had been flung from Cordon's time machine when it exploded.

The metallic object Thornby held glinted in the sun, and Sedora immediately knew what it was. How many other outlaws had been to the crash site? Was Cordon even alive? How much 2756 technology had been dispersed through the 1870s? Sedora wanted answers.

"She has a special train car and other things we could use," Blaze said. "Fancy European technology. We'll need her alive, but she's armed, knows how to shoot, and has a shocker she can use on me."

"What?!" Thornby asked in confusion. "A shocker, you say?"

"That's right!" Blaze shouted back, "and it hurts. As for these Medicine Bow lawmen, I didn't know they'd be here."

"Drop your guns, all of you!" Thornby called out. "Blaze's going to ride on over to us nice and easy, and you all shall stay put!"

"Sheriff," Caddock whispered. "They're gonna kill us once Blaze's clear."

"Stay calm, son," Gratton said.

Gratton took a deep breath, glanced at Caddock, and nodded. Gratton and Caddock dropped their gunbelts and slowly raised their arms in the air. Sedora did not move.

"Miss, dispose of your sidearm!" Thornby said. "And kindly join us without electrocuting Mister Blaze."

Sedora stood next to Caddock's horse. Blaze was not far ahead of her.

"Once it starts," Sedora whispered to Gratton and Caddock, "you stay low and get out of here."

"Once what starts?" Caddock said under his breath.

"You will know, deputy," Sedora said as her eyes set into an intense expression.

Sedora innocently batted her eyelashes and said, "I am dropping my gun, Mister Thornby! Just please do not shoot."

Suddenly, she pointed up into the rocks and shouted, "Look! The posse from Medicine Bow! They have found us!"

No posse was in sight, but all Sedora needed was a brief distraction. Thornby's men looked over their shoulders. Thornby was too smart to fall for Sedora's ruse, but many of his men were not. Sedora drew her plasma pistol in an instant and jumped to the left as she squeezed off an array of shots. Purple beams of plasma sizzled through hot afternoon air. Chaos erupted.

"What in tarnation?!" one of the outlaws cried out.

"Like one of Traxton's gadgetries," Thornby muttered as he ducked behind a rock.

Rocks high above Thornby and his men began to break apart and fall as intense bursts of plasma energy exploded their bases. Horses ran in all directions in the chaos, and the men started shooting at Sedora, Gratton, and Caddock while also struggling to control their mounts. Blaze dove off his horse and sought cover behind rocks.

Sedora concluded her jump by landing behind a thick clump of sagebrush. She switched a setting on her plasma pistol, kneeled, and fired a swarm of blue plasma beams at the outlaws. Men fell off their horses, and some were dragged with their feet in their stirrups.

The horses of Gratton and Caddock were somewhat accustomed to gunfire, and they milled in place. Caddock dove off his mount as rifle bullets zipped past. He grabbed Gratton's gunbelt and tossed it up to the sheriff who caught it with ease and fired from his horse. Caddock then found his own gunbelt in the dust, drew his pistol, and fired wildly at Thornby's men. He somersaulted behind a rock and breathed hard as he strapped on his gunbelt and reloaded his weapon.

Rocks above Thornby and his men continued to tumble and break apart. As they fell, they loosened more rocks and dirt. Soon, a massive rockslide barreled down the slopes of Sheep Rock.

"Sheriff!" Sedora shouted over the sound of gunfire and tumbling rocks. "You and your deputy need to leave! We all need to leave! Based on my calculations, we have approximately 22.3 seconds to exit the trajectory of that rockslide!"

"Looks like the mountain's comin' down!" Caddock yelled.

"Go downhill!" Sedora exclaimed as she continued shooting blue plasma beams from what appeared to be an ordinary Colt forty-five. "Get up on the eastern slope!"

Sedora ran from her cover of sagebrush. As she ran, she turned her head and wildly fired plasma beams behind her. One of her shots hit an enormous outlaw who immediately fell off his horse and landed in a grove of juniper saplings.

Sedora holstered her plasma pistol and broke into a primal sprint. Intense adrenaline had kicked in, and she was in full combat mode. She saw Gratton riding ahead of her, spurring his horse on. She also saw Caddock run not far behind. The horses of Blaze, Sedora, and Caddock were far downhill and ahead of everybody. Sedora saw them gallop up an eastern slope and realized they were now out of the path of the rockslide. Then she turned around and saw Caddock trip.

"Ow!" Caddock shouted as he fell to the ground and skinned his knee on a rock.

"Hurry up!" Sedora yelled as she ran back to Caddock, lowered her left hand, and pulled the young man up from the ground while hardly slowing down.

Caddock flailed as he struggled to keep up with Sedora. As she ran, Sedora looked back and saw a lone figure on a white horse disappear over the top of Sheep Rock: Thornby. Somehow, he had escaped the rockslide and gotten above it. Most of his men were sprawled on the ground. Riderless outlaw horses ran downhill behind Sedora.

Gratton made it up a slope to the east, Sedora soon joined him, and Caddock arrived just in time to avoid being pulverized by a tumult of tumbling boulders, small rocks, uprooted junipers, sagebrush, dust, and dirt chunks. Sedora saw Blaze run upslope above them. He was clearly visible against blue sky and was just about to disappear from sight. Suddenly, he stopped, yelped, and contorted with pain as Sedora tapped a device on her belt that sent jolts of electricity through him.

"Who are you, miss?" Gratton asked. "How can you do all this? What kind of gun is that?"

Sedora spoke with urgency, claimed she was a scientist from Europe, and provided vague, evasive explanations as she, Gratton, and Caddock moved uphill toward Blaze. She mentioned seeing Thornby escape over the top of Sheep Rock, said she needed something from him, and revealed that the men she shot were only unconscious. Caddock was overly trusting and listened intently, but Gratton was more suspicious and skeptical.

Soon, Sedora, Gratton, and Caddock reached Blaze, who stared up as he lay sprawled on the ground. Blaze tried to catch his breath and let electricity jolts fade from his teeth as Gratton cuffed him.

"Hey," Caddock said as he pointed down at a plume of dust way out on the distant plains. "Looks like a posse heard the commotion and is coming to check things out."

"Good," Gratton said.

Sedora and the law officers recovered their horses as well as Blaze's horse. They then rounded up as many of the other horses as they could and bound the hands and feet of the sleeping outlaws with lassos retrieved from various saddles.

"That was a lot of work," Caddock said.

"Not for me, it wasn't," Blaze said from the shade of a nearby juniper, hands cuffed behind his back. "I'd help, but my hands were tied." Blaze spat bitterly.

"Don't worry," Gratton said. "You'll have plenty more time to relax in the Crowbar Hotel. The rest of the posse will be here soon. We'll take these boys to Laramie."

"Good idea," Sedora said. "Their jail does not have a hole in it."

"And it's closer," Caddock said before nervously clearing his throat. Gratton was not pleased about the Traxton jailbreak. The sheriff partially blamed Caddock who was asleep on the job. Gratton's reaction to learning of the prisoner escape made a permanent impression on Caddock and expanded his vocabulary with colorful profanity that would make a rainbow seem dull.

"I guess you should be on your way if you'd like, miss," Gratton said. "Good luck with your mission."

"Thank you," Sedora said. "If I can, I will apprehend Britt Thornby and turn him over to you."

"Me and Caddock would be much obliged," Gratton said, "but are you sure you don't want to stay here longer? We could use your help, and we could get some boys to go with you once the posse shows up. They should be here soon."

"No," Sedora said. "Thornby is getting away as we speak. I want to pick up his trail while it is still fresh."

"I could go with you," Caddock said. "The posse can help the sheriff, and I could guide you. We can leave right now if you want."

"Well," Sedora said with a sigh as she contemplated the value of local knowledge, "I would appreciate your assistance. Thank you."

"And I promise," Caddock said. "I promise I won't ask too many questions. We're on the same side, ma'am. What do you say, sheriff?"

"I guess you can go with her," Gratton said, "but be careful. Thornby's a dangerous hombre. Watch yourself."

Soon, Sedora and Caddock rode their horses toward the top of Sheep Rock. They traveled to where Sedora had seen Thornby disappear over the top of the formation. They both dismounted. Caddock crouched down and examined Thornby's horse's tracks. In the meantime, Sedora pulled a small metal device from a pouch on her belt and tapped it. An invisible beam of energy swept down over Gratton, Blaze, and the unconscious outlaws. It selectively wiped their memories in specific timecode increments based on recordings from Sedora's database orientation module. All memories of her shooting her plasma pistol were erased. The discussion about wreckage, special technology, and the metallic device Thornby had held up were also wiped away. The outlaws would remember Sedora drawing a Colt forty-five and would remember most of the overall gunfight, but any sightings of plasma beams were deleted.

Sedora tapped her mind-wiping device again. A second layer of memory erasure swept over Blaze. This mind wipe was much deeper and wiped out most of their interactions together. Blaze would remember going places with Sedora, but he would not know exactly how or why they traveled together. After only a few seconds, Sedora put her mind-wiping device back in a belt pouch. She planned to use it on Caddock later.

"The tracks go north," Caddock said, "through a low draw on the other side of Sheep Rock."

"Thank you, Deputy Caddock," Sedora said as she got back on her horse. "Let's go."

CHAPTER 16: FOREST CLASH

Two hours after being caught in the middle of a violent feeding frenzy focused on sauropod hatchlings, Lassen, Durango, Kailani, and Adalya moved south through a dense Jurassic forest. They planned to circle around behind the Traxton Gang and surprise them. The time travelers were far enough into the forest to blend with the surroundings, but they were close enough to the plains to still keep an eye on the fern prairies.

"Whoa," Durango said, "why's there a huge red dirt mound up there? Doesn't seem like it fits in."

"That's no dirt mound," Kailani said as she narrowed her eyes in concentration.

"She's right," Lassen added.

"It's a sauropod carcass," Kailani said as they rode closer.

Soon, the time travelers stopped near a dead dinosaur. Lassen dismounted Graphite, and Kailani got off Ember. The bounty hunter and paleontologist stepped around the carcass. It lay in a forest clearing fringed by mighty sequoias and tall tree ferns. Lassen glanced to the east and saw that the clearing was actually the western end of a large finger of meadow that extended westward from the plains. That explained how a full-sized sauropod could get this far into the forest. There were low ferns to the east and charcoal-clad logs and tree stumps. Lassen guessed a bit of the forest had experienced a fire a few years prior, which created the meadow.

Mixed shadows covered the enormous dinosaur body. Sunlight lanced through shadows in distinct rays, illuminating the dead dinosaur's face. Kailani used her phone to shoot numerous close-up photos that captured fine details of the dinosaur's skin texture.

"Looks to be a diplodocid," Kailani said. "Brilliant. I never thought I'd see one so close. It's beautiful."

"What species is it?" Lassen asked.

"Since we got here, we've never seen this species," Kailani said. "If the diplodocids we saw from the cliff were *Diplodocus* and *Apatosaurus* or *Brontosaurus*, I think this is a *Barosaurus* because of the especially long neck. This dinosaur could weigh about 20,000 to 30,000 pounds and be about 85 feet long."

"Eighty-five feet," Lassen said as he looked from left to right. "I'd believe that."

"Their neck vertebrae—the individual neck bones—are almost 50 percent longer than those of *Diplodocus*," Kailani said, "which is a pretty long dinosaur in itself."

The dead dinosaur was a *Barosaurus*. It had the same general build as *Diplodocus* and *Apatosaurus*, including a long whip tail, but its neck was longer relative to the rest of its body compared to similar species. The *Barosaurus* also had rusty red skin with black lateral stripes, a light green underbelly, and black dermal spines on top of its tail, back, and neck.

The dead dinosaur's skin was bumpy and granular and did not resemble the skin of an elephant, rhinoceros, or hippopotamus. Instead, it reminded Lassen of the skin of a venomous Gila monster lizard. He had encountered Gila monsters during his travels in the American Southwest. Like the scales of other dinosaurs, the scales of the *Barosaurus* were small and densely distributed in honeycomb-like patterns.

Lassen got a good look at the *Barosaurus's* spines. They were black, shiny, made of keratin, and slightly grooved. Lassen and Kailani clambered over partially charcoalized sequoia logs as they further examined the dinosaur. Adalya and Durango remained mounted.

"Mister Malone," Adalya said, "we should get moving. It is not safe here."

"Yeah, sure," Lassen said, "I know, but this specimen is outstanding."

"It looks like it just died," Kailani added. Kailani bent down over the *Barosaurus's* head and touched its neck. Tiny bugs crawled on its face. "Its body's still warm, and its eyes are glassy. Looks like it was drooling. Maybe it was sick. I bet this dinosaur died in the last few hours." The *Barosaurus* had dirty, yellowed pencil-like teeth. Little fern fragments adorned the edges of its teeth and lips.

"Lassen, buddy—" Durango started to say.

"It is time to go!" Adalya cut in.

Kailani looked up from the sauropod's face, startled. Lassen stood up—arms outstretched with alert preparedness—and quickly pivoted his torso from side to side to survey his surroundings. As he swiftly moved, his vest dramatically billowed, and he steadied his hat with his right hand.

"What is it?" Kailani asked.

"Ohhhhhhh . . ." Lassen said while flashing a smile laced with irony and doom as he pointed into the forest to the west. "*That's* what."

Kailani bit her lower lip with anxiety. The horses whinnied. Yonder reared. Graphite and Ember immediately ran into the meadow to the east. Horizon held steady as Adalya tensed. Then Horizon and Yonder slowly backed into the forest. From atop their horses, Adalya and Durango could see what was happening in the clearing but were not clearly visible to the animal emerging from the forest.

An enormous old, scrappy carnivorous *Torvosaurus* male emerged from the shadows of the western forest and lumbered toward the dead *Barosaurus*. His head gently brushed against sequoia needles on tall branches. Lassen and Kailani slowly backed up as the 4,000-pound (1,814-kilogram) predator approached.

"What do we do?" Kailani whispered.

"Stay calm," Lassen whispered back. "You can sometimes scare away predators, but with big ones like this, I think it's best to just not draw attention. Let's just slowly, slowly back away, nice and easy."

Lassen and Kailani backed away as the *Torvosaurus* entered the clearing. Then Lassen fell backward as his pants caught on a sharp dead conifer snag. He knocked into Kailani, and they both fell to the ground only about 40 feet (12 meters) from the thighs of the *Barosaurus* carcass. Kailani grunted as she and Lassen fell into tall soft ferns at the base of a large log.

"Sorry," Lassen said, wincing.

"It's okay," Kailani whispered back.

However, Kailani got bruised in the fall, and one of her legs ached. She felt a strange mix of adrenaline, fear, pain, and excitement as she found herself unexpectedly close to Lassen. For a moment, they both laid against each other at the base of a large log that concealed them from the immediate view of the *Torvosaurus*. Then they separated. Lassen picked up a small handful of dried fern bits and dirt and dropped them. A slight breeze made them drift as they fell.

"The wind's blowing toward us," Lassen whispered. "That thing shouldn't be able to smell us right now, so let's stay low. Hopefully, it will eat and leave without caring we're here. What do you think it is?"

"Not sure," Kailani whispered. "It looked too big to be an *Allosaurus*. It could be a *Torvosaurus*, but I wasn't able to look at it very long."

"Oh man . . ." Lassen quietly muttered as he remembered the *Torvosaurus* illustrations Kailani had shown him in her e-books.

The *Torvosaurus* lowly and quietly growled as he approached the *Barosaurus*. *Torvosaurus* was one of the biggest theropod dinosaurs of the Morrison Basin. The carnivore sniffed the air with nostrils located 11 feet (three meters) above the ground. The 35-foot (11-meter) long dinosaur had a beige underbelly that gradated into a chestnut brown chest with white speckling. Its sides, back, and tail were turquoise with mottled lateral white striping, and the skin on its head was green with hints of faint red and purple. The dinosaur scanned its surroundings with red eyes that had round black pupils.

The *Torvosaurus* cautiously, slowly moved his four-foot (one-meter) long head back and forth. His body, especially his snout, was covered in scars incurred from a lifetime of survival in the prehistoric Morrison Basin. The *Torvosaurus* did not appear to notice or care about Lassen and Kailani as it raked huge steak knife-like serrated teeth into the *Barosaurus*.

On the ground, Lassen and Kailani heard low breathing and flesh tearing but could not see what was happening. They also smelled the coppery scent of fresh blood.

The *Torvosaurus* first tore out choice organs and swallowed them whole. His teeth then pierced the pelvic flesh near the base of the *Barosaurus's* tail. Like many theropods in the Jurassic, the *Torvosaurus* preferred to eat the huge contiguous masses of muscle that covered sauropods' back legs and hips.

The *Torvosaurus* used a battery of approximately 60 teeth as he tore flesh from bone. His biggest teeth were approximately six inches (15 centimeters) long. *Torvosaurus* teeth were especially robust and disproportionately large compared to those of other Morrison theropods. The dinosaur had three toes on each foot and three clawed fingers on each hand, which he used to grip the *Barosaurus*, steadying himself as he harvested lunch.

The *Torvosaurus* held its hands sideways as it gripped flesh because it could not pronate, which meant it could not turn the bottoms of its hands downward. The wrists of all theropods were not structured in a way that enabled them to pronate their hands. Pronated downward-facing theropod hands would be common in twentieth and twenty-first century reconstructions of dinosaurs (even appearing in museum skeleton mounts) but were inaccurate and not anatomically possible. To clarify this error, some twenty-first century paleontologists would say that theropods were clappers, *not* slappers.

The *Torvosaurus* shifted his weight back on his counterbalancing tail as he lifted his head and sniffed. As the *Torvosaurus's* nostrils quivered, and blood dripped from his teeth, he made a low deep raspy whooshing noise that sounded faintly like a gurgle.

Hearing the sound immediately reminded Lassen of a cassowary, which is a six-foot (two-meter) tall flightless bird that lives in the rainforests of northern Australia, New Guinea, and nearby islands in modern times. Though Lassen had only observed them from a distance, he had heard stories about cassowaries cutting people open by kicking at them with sharp foot claws.

Three shapes suddenly emerged from the forest beyond the *Barosaurus* carcass's tail. Lassen and Kailani heard vegetation rustle.

"Something else is out there," Kailani whispered.

"Yeah," Lassen said.

The *Torvosaurus* swung his head as three male *Allosaurus* boldly trotted out of the trees, crushing a stand of *Equisetum* plants. Each *Allosaurus* somewhat resembled the *Torvosaurus*, but they were smaller, colored differently, and had differently-shaped heads. Compared to the *Allosaurus*, the *Torvosaurus* had a more streamlined, elongated head. In contrast, the *Allosaurus* heads were shorter and had ruby red crests extending off the tops of their heads, just in front of their eyes. The *Torvosaurus* also seemed more bulked out and sturdy compared to the *Allosaurus*, which appeared more slender by comparison but were still large and deadly. The *Allosaurus* were a striking blue with shiny green stripes, white underbellies, and red-tipped tails.

The *Allosaurus* moved with springy nimbleness and ranged in length from 30 to 40 feet (nine to 12 meters). They also weighed from 1,500 to 2,000 pounds (680 to 900 kilograms), stood about eight feet (two and a half meters) tall at their hips, and had skulls about three feet (one meter) long.

Each *Allosaurus* bared teeth, harshly hissed, and flexed hand claws as they approached the old *Torvosaurus*. Muscles and tendons rippled underneath their arms. One after the other, they unleashed deep booming noises as their throats swelled with air. Lassen thought they sounded like ostriches he had heard while quietly sneaking up on outlaws in the long grass savannas of the South African Republic. Lassen had been surprised by the strange sounds and remembered the ostriches' necks notably swelled as they boomed.

The *Torvosaurus* replied by rumbling air out of his closed mouth. The air passed through sharp, dirty teeth, some of which were broken. The *Torvosaurus* vocalizations were raspy and mixed with chuffing, hisses, and inflections of irritation. Stringy pieces of flesh and reddish spittle vibrated between bloodied teeth. The *Torvosaurus's* neck swelled as he vocalized.

Lassen and Kailani felt vibrations from the vocalizations reverberate through the log they laid against. The *Torvosaurus* jumped and anchored his foot claws into the *Barosaurus's* back. He spun left and defiantly stomped a foot down from atop his perch.

"Sounds like some sort of confrontation is happening," Kailani whispered. "Maybe we should take a look."

"Okay," Lassen said, "but stay very low."

Lassen and Kailani knew it would be safer to stay as much out of sight as they could, but they were intensely curious. They took off their hats and slowly moved their heads up to where they could barely see over the log behind which they were hiding.

"Brilliant," Kailani whispered. "It's a confrontation over food. That big one is definitely a *Torvosaurus*. Its snout is distinctive, and it's heavily built. The others are *Allosaurus fragilis*. They're beautiful. Three together. Pack behavior. Incredible."

The *Allosaurus* trio moved toward the *Torvosaurus*, energetically bobbing and weaving like chickens running after worms in a garden. Suddenly, the leader of the *Allosaurus* trio jumped onto the *Torvosaurus* and tore into it with seven-inch (18-

centimeter) hand claws. Kailani gasped while Lassen narrowed his eyes in serious concentration.

As it made contact with the *Torvosaurus*, the attacking *Allosaurus* slashed away with strong arms. Compared to other theropods, an *Allosaurus's* bite was not particularly strong, but its claws and arms were. Bits of blood oozed out of the new gash marks, and some of it flew sideways as the *Torvosaurus* abruptly turned his head. Lassen and Kailani instinctively ducked to avoid the blood, but a few droplets landed on Lassen's shirt sleeve.

Bizarre behavior on the part of the Allosaurus, Kailani thought. *Such a move is practically suicidal. There must be compelling social dynamics in play.*

The *Torvosaurus* raked his teeth across the attacking *Allosaurus's* neck. The *Allosaurus* jumped off the *Torvosaurus* and backed away, hissing in pain as blood oozed from fresh scars on its neck. The wounded *Allosaurus* hopped backward directly toward Lassen and Kailani. The time travelers ducked back down. Soon, while pressed to the ground, they smelled fresh blood and looked up through tall ferns to see bits of bark and soil fly over before a blue red-tipped tail whipped into view. The tail arced and trembled as the wounded *Allosaurus* watched his companions face a dangerous opponent.

The other two *Allosaurus* cautiously approached their adversary. One circled toward the back of the *Torvosaurus* and snapped at its tail. The other tried to distract the *Torvosaurus* in the front. The *Torvosaurus* snapped his jaws at the *Allosaurus* in the front and swiftly swung his tail at the challenger in the back, knocking the *Allosaurus* down. However, the opportunistic theropod quickly jumped up, ready for more action. *Allosaurus* had a rough life. Many of their fossils would show evidence of bone breakage and infections.

As the commotion intensified, the wounded *Allosaurus* near Lassen and Kailani turned around, hopped onto the log in front of them, and launched off it, moving directly over the time travelers. As 2,000 pounds (900 kilograms) of carnivorous dinosaur blocked the sun above them, Kailani closed her eyes and buried her face in Lassen's shoulder. Lassen closed his eyes and held his hat tightly over his head. The feet of the jumping *Allosaurus* landed inches away from Lassen and Kailani and kicked up little bits of dried moss and sequoia needles into their faces. Lassen instinctively snorted dust out of his nose as the *Allosaurus* that leapt over moved out of sight into the forest.

Lassen and Kailani opened their eyes, breathed heavily, and looked at each other in relief, smiling. They then rose into crouching positions and surveyed their surroundings. Lassen rapidly moved his head, trying to monitor the forest behind him and the dinosaur fight. Kailani rose just high enough to look over their concealment log and intently watch the theropod combat.

The *Allosaurus* in front of the *Torvosaurus* jumped forward and hissed at the larger dinosaur's face. The *Allosaurus* in the back continued snapping at the *Torvosaurus's* tail and occasionally raked it with sharp teeth. Vegetation rustled, branches broke, and dust and forest duff drifted into the air as the dinosaurs battled. The displacement of air from the movement of huge fast-moving animals also created the equivalent of small breezes, and Lassen felt cool air on his face while his hair slightly moved.

The *Torvosaurus* was strong enough and mad enough to keep the *Allosaurus* at bay, but it also grew tired of the battle. Suddenly, the *Torvosaurus* charged the *Allosaurus* in front, scratched the *Allosaurus's* thigh with sharp claws, and ran into the forest to the west, disappearing from view.

The two *Allosaurus* who drove the bigger carnivore away triumphantly boomed, hissed, and jumped onto the *Barosaurus* where they quickly began eating. The neck-slashed *Allosaurus* that jumped over Lassen and Kailani emerged from the forest and started feeding on *Barosaurus* entrails loosened by its companions. However, all three *Allosaurus* nervously swiveled their heads between bites.

Lassen suddenly felt wind on the back of his neck, which meant his and Kailani's scent was now drifting toward the *Allosaurus*. An *Allosaurus* perched on the *Barosaurus* carcass abruptly stopped eating and sniffed the air. It swallowed a huge mass of flesh and trotted toward Lassen and Kailani while scratching its neck. As the *Allosaurus* sauntered toward Lassen and Kailani, Durango suddenly charged out of the trees on Yonder while swinging a lasso.

"I'll save you!" Durango shouted.

Adalya watched Durango's actions while sitting on Horizon behind a nearby cluster of tree ferns. The physicist palmed her forehead and winced.

The two *Allosaurus* that were still feeding lifted their heads in confusion as they saw Durango approach. They ran into the forest in fear as they had no idea what they were seeing. However, the *Allosaurus* approaching Lassen and Kailani abruptly turned toward Durango and charged him.

"What is Durango doing?" Lassen tensely whispered.

As the *Allosaurus* charged Durango, the bounty hunter threw his lasso loop. Then he sailed through the air as Yonder bucked him off. The frightened horse galloped toward the plains to the east. Durango smoothly landed on his feet while his lasso loop landed in front of one of the *Allosaurus's* feet. The dinosaur stepped right into the lasso. Durango instinctively pulled hard on his lariat, and the loop closed around the *Allosaurus's* leg. The *Allosaurus* stopped in confusion, changed direction, and ran.

Durango hung onto the rope and was pulled to the ground. The *Allosaurus* rushed toward the forest with the rope still on its foot. Durango hung onto his rope and awkwardly stood up while being dragged and trying to run.

Lassen sprang to his feet and shouted, "Durango, let go!"

"This is my best lariat!" Durango called back.

Soon, the *Allosaurus* jumped over jagged basalt lava rocks, which cut the rope. The *Allosaurus* was now free, though it had a loop of rope around its leg. Durango tripped on a log and fell to the ground, face-first. He spit dirt and bits of dried ferns and conifer needles off his lips as he stood and coiled his rope.

The roped *Allosaurus* paused and sniffed the air. Then it sniffed the loop of rope around its leg and turned to see Durango getting up and Lassen standing farther away. With the rope no longer dragging behind it, the dinosaur was less afraid and became curious again. From atop Horizon, Adalya nervously bit her lower lip as she seriously considered the possibility of having to continue her mission alone.

Durango slowly backed up. Kailani stood up next to Lassen, and they all tensely watched the *Allosaurus*. The *Allosaurus* continued sniffing the air. It turned to look at the time travelers. Then it turned to look at the *Barosaurus* carcass. Then it turned to look at the bounty hunters and paleontologist again. While the *Allosaurus* was distracted by the time travelers, the *Torvosaurus* that had originally claimed the carcass bolted out of a nearby stand of young sequoias and bit the *Allosaurus* in the neck. The smaller carnivore hissed in pain and fell to the ground as its neck bled out.

Lassen, Kailani, and Adalya looked on with open-mouthed shock. Lassen raised his eyebrows, Kailani audibly gasped, and Durango muttered, "Son of catamount—ow."

The old *Torvosaurus* stepped on the head of the now dead *Allosaurus* as it strode toward the *Barosaurus* carcass. The big theropod then climbed on top of the dead sauropod and gurgle-growled with deep guttural defiance while a pterosaur shrieked in the distance. The *Torvosaurus* tore a huge chunk of flesh off the *Barosaurus* and swallowed it whole as he resumed feeding.

In the meantime, Lassen, Kailani, and Durango slowly backed away toward the plains. Adalya and Horizon soon intercepted them at the edge of the forest, and the time travelers began searching for the horses that had fled.

Chapter 17: Time Off the Rails

Caddock and Sedora rode westward through a series of low sagebrush-clad hills. They were on the trail of Britt Thornby. The Traxton Gang outlaw was riding fast, having prioritized speed over stealth. Caddock did not find it difficult to find the hoofprints, loose rocks, and snapped bits of brush that marked Thornby's trail.

The sun was starting to dip lower in the western sky, but it was still hot and sunny. A red-tailed hawk cried as it flapped over the western horizon. A herd of pronghorn bounded away to the north as they saw the riders approach. The white fur on their rump patches flared as they ran. Turkey vultures circled overhead, and small lizards darted about on warm rocks as the riders passed by.

"Trail keeps goin' straight west, ma'am," Caddock said to Sedora. "Still a few more hours of daylight. I reckon we'll follow the trail until it gets too dark to see."

"Sounds like a sufficient plan," Sedora said.

"Um, yeah," Caddock said. "I wish Lassen Malone was here to help out."

"What do you know about him?" Sedora asked. "And what about his partner? Or sidekick maybe? Somebody named Durango, I think."

"Oh, yeah, there's Durango, too," Caddock said.

Sedora said, "Randall Blaze told me Lassen and Durango would kill anybody for money and indicated they were ethically compromised and depraved members of humanity."

"No, ma'am," Caddock said. "Not true at all. Those boys are true-life heroes. You should of saw what they did in Medicine Bow two days ago. I only saw some of it, but I talked to some of my friends who were unloading a freight wagon that morning. They saw all of it. There were five members of the Traxton Gang, including that Blaze sidewinder you already know. They started shootin' at Malone and Mesquite. They were on Main Street in broad daylight. Can you believe that? Lassen and Durango shot back and captured all five of them and didn't kill any. I heard Lassen was such a good shot that he shot the guns right out of the hands of those Traxton desperadoes. Lassen knows that killing isn't the only way to stop an enemy. Then Lassen rescued a kid, Lilly—she's a good girl who lives in town—from a longhorn stampede. I wish I could be half the man Lassen is. Meeting Lassen Malone that morning was one of the greatest moments of my life."

"Sounds like an impressive individual," Sedora said as she pondered what this meant for Adalya in the Jurassic. "But if you only first met him yesterday, how do you know so much about him?"

"Dime novels," Caddock said as he pulled a tattered book from a saddlebag and held it out for Sedora to see. "There's this fancy writer from California—Trenton Howarth—he's written slathers of stories about Lassen Malone, and he claims they're all true. And they only cost 10 cents. That's why they're dime novels."

"Intriguing," Sedora said as she raised her eyebrows. *The Adventures of Lassen Malone: Quest for Outlaw Gold*," Sedora said while reading out the name of the book Caddock held up. The cover of the novel showed a tall muscular man with a vest and well-defined jawline shooting a beer glass out of the hands of a mean-looking saloon patron. "What is that one about? Temperance advocacy?"

"Ohhhhh, man, um, I mean ma'am," Caddock said as his eyes got wide, and he twisted his mouth into an odd expression infused with fanboy enthusiasm. "This is one of the *best* ones." Caddock spread his hands out as he began to set the scene for his narrative.

"Picture this. May 1876. High in the Rocky Mountains of Montana. Lassen Malone has found Red Duvarney—he's a member of the Shrike Pierson Gang and wanted in two states and three territories. They get in a shootout, and Lassen wins and gets a letter off of Duvarney. Then Lassen gets chased by a grizzly bear, and an avalanche starts. He outruns the grizzly and the avalanche by using his vest like a sled as he shoots down the mountain in the snow. Then he rides away, meets his friend Diego in Cisco, Utah, uses the letter from Duvarney to find a stash of stolen gold bars, battles the Pierson Gang in a lightning storm, and chases down Shrike Pierson in the middle of a buffalo stampede before Pierson gets swept away in a flash flood. In the end, Lassen and Diego relax and have enchiladas at Diego's hacienda while beautiful women play Spanish guitar music."

"That," Sedora said, "was a very detailed synopsis. Sounds like the story is heavy on action without much character development, though."

"You shouldn't judge without reading it first," Caddock said. "It's good stuff."

Caddock and Sedora rode primarily in silence for the next several hours as they moved onto flat plains after exiting the Laramie Mountains' southern foothills, which surrounded Sheep Rock. The sun soon set behind distant mountains. As the sun lowered, dazzling neon pink striations of illuminated cloud strands filled the western horizon. Crickets began to sound, and a killdeer called in the distance. Scrappy pines and junipers stood as sky-lined black silhouettes in front of the glorious sunset.

At dusk, Sedora and Caddock set up camp against a large boulder. They did not start a fire because they wanted to hide their presence from Thornby, who was presumably somewhere west of them.

*   *   *

The quantum physicist and county deputy continued their pursuit of Thornby at dawn as soon as it was light enough to see tracks. They soon found Thornby's abandoned campsite from the previous night, which was marked by coffee grounds and an area where grass had been flattened by a bedroll. They continued following tracks west from the campsite as coyotes howled in the distance.

"Well, now, that's somethin'," Caddock said as he crouched over horse tracks on the ground while the sun rose, and meadowlarks loudly called.

"What?" Sedora asked.

"Looks like Thornby's horse is slowin' down because of a pebble in its shoe. Not sure how soon Thornby will notice, but we might be able to catch up."

Sedora and Caddock rode across a creek as the morning sun eased the dawn chill and bathed the shortgrass prairie in light.

"Now that we've crossed Rock Creek," Caddock said, "the railroad shouldn't be too far ahead. We're gettin' close to Medicine Bow, but Thornby's on the dodge, and he won't be visitin' town—"

Suddenly, Caddock's hat sailed off his head as if pulled by a string. A rifle shot rang out, and his horse and Sedora's reared in alarm. Caddock breathed hard in sudden surprise and squinted toward the western horizon. He saw the distant glint of a rifle barrel and a plume of dust near a lone pine tree.

"Thornby," Sedora coolly said as she spurred her horse forward.

"I don't get it," Caddock said as his horse caught up to Sedora's. Why would Thornby take a shot at us and then leave? Why not stay to finish the job?"

"He could be running away from something else," Sedora said. She then pointed to the southwest. "Or toward something!"

"I see it!" Caddock yelled over the sound of horse hooves.

A train chugged along the Union Pacific Railroad. Black smoke billowed out of its engine, and a series of cars trailed behind it. The train engine mostly pulled passenger cars, but it also hauled some freight cars that held cattle, pine logs, and a variety of wooden crates. The train moved past a series of telegraph poles and wires that followed the railroad. The telegraph poles looked like big Ts because each one had a horizontal wooden attachment near its top that held a set of wires. Soon, Sedora and Caddock clearly heard the train.

"We'll never catch up with him if he hops on that train!" Caddock proclaimed.

"I will get him!" Sedora replied as her horse quickly outpaced Caddock's.

As Sedora left Caddock in the dust, she rapidly caught up with Thornby. His horse was tired and slowing. As soon as Sedora was in range, Thornby drew his pistol and fired. Sedora ducked to avoid bullets and drew her plasma pistol. She fired several blue beams at Thornby. She did not take the time to carefully aim and was hoping her firing would distract the outlaw and slow him down. Instead, her shots motivated Thornby to move faster toward the train. Prairie dogs and lizards scurried for cover as Thornby pushed his horse hard.

Soon, Thornby caught up with the train, rode alongside it, and boldly reached out and grabbed a metal ladder rung on the back of a railcar. He was abruptly pulled off his horse as he flung himself onto the back of the railcar. Thornby's white horse galloped onto the plains to the east while the outlaw flailed about.

As Thornby held tightly onto a metal ladder, he quickly looked around, trying to figure out how to get into one of the cars. He pulled at a door, but it was locked. He wanted to stow away and avoid being tracked by the mystery woman with the light ray gun. He could handle Caddock, but Sedora concerned him. In fact, he had been aiming for Sedora when Caddock's hat flew off, but his rifle scope was misaligned from hard riding, and he did not know that until he fired the shot.

Thornby decided he would need to get on top of the train car to find his way to another car that was not locked. Then he saw that Sedora was surprisingly close. He was amazed at how fast her horse was. He quickly drew his pistol and squeezed off a shot. He barely missed, and Sedora kept coming. Then Sedora was out of range as the train sped forward.

Sedora did the math and calculated when and where she would have the most success with boarding the train. She rode her horse close beside the train, moved her feet out of her saddle's stirrups, and reached out and grabbed the train caboose's back railing just as it sped past. She smoothly slid off her horse and was soon standing on a small platform on the back of the train. Based on her observations, the fastest way to reach Thornby was to move on top of the railcars.

Sedora climbed up the caboose and stood on top of it. She held her arms out far to her sides as she got a feel for the train's acceleration and established a sustained balance. The train chugged along at roughly 25 miles (40 kilometers) per hour. Sedora's shining auburn-silver hair whipped behind her in the wind as the train moved past telegraph poles and miles of flat open plains. She spotted Thornby climbing onto the top of a train car far ahead of her. Taking a deep breath, she broke into a sprint and jumped from train car to train car in pursuit.

Thornby ran on top of a series of passenger cars. He guessed Sedora could not catch up with the train, and he was finally safe, but just in case, he quickly glanced over his shoulder to check. He saw Sedora running at him from the back of the train with determined athleticism and excellent balance. Thornby swore, drew his gun, and wildly fired at Sedora.

Sedora ducked, and the shots missed her, but one of them knocked a leather pouch from her utility belt. The pouch contained her mind wiper, and it fell onto the train tracks below. An abrupt crunch signaled the beginning of many train wheels pulverizing the mind wiper. Sedora briefly looked down as her mind wiper was destroyed.

In the meantime, various passengers inside the train stood up in alarm and curiosity as they heard gunshots and the sound of running feet on the roofs of their cars. Some people opened windows and twisted their heads upward to try to determine the source of the commotion. Passengers' hair billowed in the wind of the rushing train, and one woman lost her ornate Victorian hat.

Sedora drew her plasma pistol and blasted an array of blue energy beams at Thornby. Most missed, but one of them grazed his left hand. Thornby instinctively flexed his left hand's fingers as they tingled and began to feel numb. He fired one more shot behind him without looking and jumped onto the next railcar.

Sedora's plasma pistol was flung out of her hand as Thornby's last wild shot hit it. The plasma pistol flew off to the side and tumbled into grass. However, Thornby had returned his focus to what was in front of him and did not see this happen. As far as he knew, Sedora was still armed and very dangerous.

Thornby jumped on a car that had an open top and was loaded with wooden crates. He teetered on top of a tall crate and nearly fell over while distracted by the tingling of his left hand. Then he jumped down from the crate and stayed hunkered at its base. He would wait for Sedora to come to him. Why run in plain sight waiting to get blasted by a ray gun? As he waited, he read the crates' labels, which said:

COMO BLUFF PALEONTOGICAL SPECIMENS
PROPERTY OF O.C. MARSH
CURATOR, YALE PEABODY MUSUEM –
NEW HAVEN, CONNECTICUT

Thornby actually had some idea of what this meant and thought of newspaper articles he had read about *Iguanodon*, *Megalosaurus*, and the Crystal Palace dinosaur sculptures back in England.

Sedora continued running from car to car. She jumped from a stack of pine logs to the top of a cattle car. It smelled terrible, and she heard various crowded longhorn cattle mooing and milling about below her.

As Sedora got ready to leap onto the next cattle car, she saw that the back of it had a small platform with tools. There were shovels and a 10-foot (three-meter) 12-plait natural tan kangaroo hide Australian style bullwhip. Sedora climbed down the cattle car she was on and stepped to the platform of the next one. She grabbed the coiled bullwhip and fastened it to her side with the snapping enclosure of one of her leather utility pouches. She also picked up a shovel. Then Sedora climbed metal ladder rungs and got onto the roof of the cattle car. She tentatively moved forward as the train chugged through shortgrass plains. She could no longer see Thornby. This concerned her.

Sedora moved cautiously with the thought that Thornby could be hiding on any railcar ahead of her. Soon, she approached a car full of crates. They seemed to provide a high number of hiding places. Sedora became hyper vigilant as she jumped onto the car. She carefully moved over the crates and soon smelled tobacco and unbathed human. Thornby was close. Suddenly, she saw a hand dart up from behind a crate with a drawn pistol. She instinctively swung the shovel she held like a golf club and batted the gun out of Thornby's hand. It discharged as it fell against a rock next to the train tracks.

Sedora lifted her shovel in an effort to strike Thornby again. He jumped back with surprising speed and avoided the shovel, but he fell onto a wooden crate, breaking it. As he reached backward to pull himself up, he felt a heavy plaster-jacketed dinosaur fossil bone. He instinctively grabbed it and threw it at Sedora. It collided with her shovel and knocked it out of her hands. The shovel flew off to the side and clattered against a telegraph pole.

Thornby clambered up a crate and jumped onto a passenger car ahead of him. Sedora followed. Then Thornby stopped and faced Sedora.

"You've got no weapons!" Thornby called out with his English accent. "And you're a woman!"

Thornby charged at Sedora, and they collided near the center of the passenger car they stood on. Thornby punched at Sedora. She dodged and kicked him in the ribs. He doubled over in pain and rolled into Sedora's ankles as hard he could. Sedora swayed to the side and lost her balance.

Just as Sedora knew she was going to fall, she unsnapped the bullwhip on her belt and launched it out toward a telegraph pole just ahead. The end of the whip cracked as it tore through the air and lashed around the horizontal T attachment at the top of the pole. Sedora fell off the train while holding the handle of the bullwhip with both hands. As the train sped past, she dangled from the end of the whip and swung through the air in a 180-degree arc.

Sedora landed back on the train, smoothly moved her wrist, and the bullwhip came off the telegraph pole. In the meantime, Thornby continued to run on top of passenger cars. Sedora pursued as she coiled her whip. Soon, Sedora arrived on the same passenger car as Thornby just as he was getting ready to leap off it.

"No, you do not," Sedora muttered as she swung her whip at Thornby's legs.

CRACK! The whip broke the sound barrier as it sailed forward. Then it wrapped around Thornby's ankles. Thornby fell forward and held his hands out hard against a railcar door to prevent his head from bashing into it. Passengers in the car gasped as they saw Thornby hanging upside down in front of them. His head was only inches from the car's observation platform. He flailed his arms in panic.

Sedora moved forward and gritted her teeth as she pulled on lengths of whip to keep Thornby suspended. Well-honed biceps bulged under Sedora's blouse as she pulled hard enough to lift Thornby back up onto the railcar she stood on. Soon, Thornby was dragged backward on his belly while his hands scratched the roof of the train car in a vain effort to escape.

"What do you want from me?!" Thornby shouted as he struggled to speak over his left shoulder. As he shouted, the train began to chug over a bridge that spanned the Laramie River.

"I will tell you," Sedora said, "but first we have a stop to make!"

As the train moved over the Laramie River, Sedora unwrapped her whip from Thornby's ankles, threw him into the river, and jumped after him with whip in hand. A pair of mallards quacked and flew off the river in alarm. Thornby swam toward the northern shore. Sedora followed. Soon, both Thornby and Sedora were on the shore, catching their breath near a cluster of willow bushes.

"Sporting as it is, I suppose it would be a waste of time to run from you, miss," Thornby said.

"Affirmative," Sedora coolly said. "Give me the metallic device you had yesterday when you were speaking to the law officers." Despite Thornby being soaked in the river, Sedora knew the time machine parameter settings core he possessed would still be functional as it was extremely durable and weatherproof.

"Oh, yes, the strange debris," Thornby said. "Why do you want it? If I give it to you, will you leave me alone?"

"Give it to me," Sedora said.

"You know, ma'am," Thornby said. "You're not a bad-looking woman. Well, for an American, that is."

"Go on," Sedora said as she stood up and walked toward Thornby who was still panting on the riverbank.

"Well," Thornby said through deep breaths, "I've got a cache of gold hidden near Chimney Rock over in Nebraska. We could share it. You're fetching enough to, well—you could use a new dress."

"I am listening," Sedora said as she neared Thornby.

"Well, as I was saying—" Thornby began to say before his sentence was cut short by Sedora punching him in the face.

"Actually, I was not listening," Sedora said as she flexed the fingers of her right hand and blew on her knuckles.

Sedora sifted through Thornby's pockets and located the metallic tungsten carbide-coated parameter settings core.

"Finally," Sedora muttered.

The physicist used her bullwhip to tie Thornby's hands behind his back and bind his feet together. A few hours later, Caddock rode over to where Sedora rested in the shade of a cottonwood along the river. The horses of both Sedora and Thornby followed behind Caddock and were tethered to his saddle horn.

"Woowwwweee!" Caddock said. "You got Thornby captured all by yourself! Well, that don't surprise me actually. Is he asleep?"

"Yes," Sedora said, "he is unconscious." Sedora flexed her right hand into a fist.

Caddock cleared his throat and said, "I see. You find what you need?"

"I have it," Sedora said.

"Good," Caddock said. "That's good. I'm guessin' you don't need to deal with me anymore now that you've got your gadgetry, but I plan to take Thornby to Laramie, and I don't know how long he'll be asleepin.' There's a ranch only a few miles south of here. I know some of the cowhands there, and I can deputize them and get some help, but you wanna ride along with me until I get there?"

Sedora took a deep breath and narrowed her eyes as she looked like she was trying to make up her mind.

"I will go with you," Sedora said.

"Whew," Caddock said as he wiped sweat from his forehead. "That's good. I feel safer with you around. You're like a lady Lassen Malone. Or, uh, somethin.'" Caddock blushed. "Anyway, thanks, ma'am."

"I appreciate your assistance in tracking this renegade," Sedora said as she gestured toward Thornby.

"Just doin' my job," Caddock said.

Sedora rode with Caddock down to the Lazy Juniper Ranch. On the ride, she made Caddock promise he would never talk about her plasma pistol or the parameter settings core. Sedora wished she still had her mind wiper, but she also suspected that sightings of her plasma pistol in action were simply too unbelievable to be taken seriously in the nineteenth century.

After separating from Caddock, Sedora rode north toward Pine Butte on her way back to the time machine. The ride was uneventful and relaxing. Sedora enjoyed the quiet sounds of nature and marveled at how untouched the landscape looked. She saw mule deer, pronghorn, sage-grouse, and a lone badger. She wondered what drastically different wildlife Adalya may be experiencing in the Jurassic.

As the sun set with citrusy orange bands against a clear sky, Sedora saw the time machine in the distance. It looked undisturbed. She took a deep breath and stared off into the sunset.

Chapter 18: Shoreline Ambush

At noon, Lassen, Durango, Kailani, and Adalya rode east toward an enormous lake. Finding Yonder, Graphite, and Ember after the *Allosaurus/Torvosaurus* battle had gone quickly thanks to Lassen's expert tracking skills and Horizon's sense of smell. To reduce the risk of predator attack, the bounty hunters and scientists had at least temporarily abandoned their plan to sneak up on Traxton's gang from within the forest. They opted to first investigate the lake and refill their canteens. Lassen also thought he would spot Traxton's men in the open long before they became an immediate danger. He would at least spot them at a greater distance in the open than he would detect a predatory dinosaur hiding in the forest.

As the time travelers neared the water, the aquamarine lake's immensity awed Lassen. It looked like an inland sea and stretched several miles north, east, and south. Nearby springs gave much of the lake its brilliant blue color and exceptional clarity. The water color reminded Lassen of manatee-filled spring-fed pools he had seen in Florida. Kailani shot numerous photos and videos with her phone as the explorers approached the lake

Scattered herds of green-brown *Camarasaurus* and green-turquoise *Nanosaurus* roamed foothills just northwest of the lake. Lassen soon heard lake waves lap against a beige sandy beach. Extremely fluffy and grand white cumulonimbus clouds floated high above the lake, and many pterosaurs flew close to its surface. A large storm system built in the east where white clouds melded into a wall of gray. Lassen found the scene gorgeous, ominous, and primordial.

Pterosaur sounds filled the sky, and Lassen heard what sounded like sandhill crane calls. Flocks of long-tailed *Harpactognathus*, smaller *Mesadactylus*, and other pterosaur species employed unique feeding strategies as they flew above the lake. The green-red *Mesadactylus* regularly flew high above the water and dove under the surface before emerging with fish in their beaks or in their foot claws. In contrast, the *Harpactognathus* flew low over the water and occasionally jabbed down to grab fish with their sharp, toothy beaks before swallowing them in midair.

Pterosaurs near the lake also perched in nearby tall sequoias and araucarian conifers to enjoy their meals.

Lassen put his hand over his eyes to shield them from the sun as he got a better look at the beach to the north. He noticed many pterosaurs walking on all fours and jabbing their beaks into the sand to retrieve some sort of small prey. He guessed they were feeding on crustaceans, mollusks, or worms. The strangeness of terrestrial pterosaurs fascinated Lassen. They picked and scooted their way over the sand with their wings folded back.

Lassen also saw a group of juvenile *Diplodocus* swimming across a bay. They created muddy torrents in clear lake water as they pulled themselves along with their front legs while the back halves of their bodies floated. Lassen stared open-mouthed and wide-eyed at the diplodocids' swimming style. He had never seen an animal swim that way.

Soon, the time travelers reached the edge of the lake. Everybody except Durango dismounted their horses and stepped onto a sandy beach. Just north of them, a finger of the western forest extended toward the water.

Durango kept watch on horseback while Adalya stood next to Horizon and reviewed holographic images on her database orientation module. Lassen and Kailani moved toward the lake to refill canteens and Kailani's water bottle. Lassen crouched and glanced at his reflection in the water. He now had some notable five o' clock shadow and appeared extra tired, but the grandeur and fantastic nature of his surroundings kept him energized and alert.

Lassen began unscrewing a cap on a canteen. Suddenly, loud snapping tree branches diverted his attention. A dark green male *Stegosaurus* with a yellow underbelly and bright blue tail spikes lumbered out of the trees several hundred feet to the northwest. It kicked up sand as it strode across the beach at a fast walk with deliberate purpose. Pterosaurs in its path screeched and launched off the beach with air-whipping ruffles of leathery wings.

"Something's after that guy," Lassen said while Kailani lifted her phone and started recording a video of the *Stegosaurus*.

Two male *Allosaurus* burst out of the forest just behind the *Stegosaurus*. The *Allosaurus* were striking in the full sunlight of the afternoon with their blue color, red-tipped tails, emerald green stripes, white underbellies, and red head crests.

"Do they see us?" Lassen asked. "Do they care that we're here?"

"Right now, their focus is that *Stegosaurus*," Kailani said as she looked down at her phone, which was still recording video. "Looks like one of those *Allosaurus* is only a subadult."

The *Stegosaurus* was about 200 feet (61 meters) north of the time travelers. It splashed into lake water. Then it steadied itself to make a stand and face its attackers. Waves lapped into its legs while light reflected off the water onto its red plates that had black starburst patterns. The *Stegosaurus* unleashed deep rumbling raspy hisses in defiance. The *Allosaurus* bounded with wide steps, leaving clear three-toed track impressions in sand. The *Stegosaurus* stood in front of miles of sparkling aquamarine water, flocks of flying pterosaurs, and enormous white clouds.

The two *Allosaurus* cooed to each other and hissed as they moved around the *Stegosaurus*. The larger *Allosaurus* abruptly stopped and let the smaller *Allosaurus* move forward. As the subadult *Allosaurus* approached the *Stegosaurus's* head for a neck bite, the *Stegosaurus* shifted its weight to its back legs and pivoted left. With fluid ease, it rotated its entire body 180 degrees. Instead of a vulnerable herbivore head, the subadult *Allosaurus* now confronted a deadly spiked tail. On the end of the *Stegosaurus's* tail, four bright blue spikes in two parallel pairs extended out nearly laterally.

Massive deltoid muscles in the *Stegosaurus's* front legs enabled it to maneuver its tail and body with speed and precision. Well-developed tail and back thigh muscles rippled beneath skin textured with small rounded polygonal nodules. The *Stegosaurus* on the beach had more strength in its tail than an elephant from modern times would have in one of its back legs. When Lassen first saw *Stegosaurus*, he thought they looked clumsy and strange with their back legs being so much longer than their front legs. He now saw that *Stegosaurus* evolution had honed the dinosaur's anatomy for defense against large carnivores, like *Allosaurus*.

Just after rotating its body, the *Stegosaurus* flexed its tail with a ripple of movement. Tail spike thagomizers slammed into the side of the subadult *Allosaurus's* lower jaw. Blood spilled onto sand. Kailani quickly looked up and down from her phone's camera screen to the actual dinosaur fight as she recorded incredible footage.

The subadult *Allosaurus* recoiled in pain and backed away toward the edge of the trees. It then watched while its larger companion attempted to attack. The older, more experienced *Allosaurus* nimbly jumped back from wildly flailing tail spikes, tentatively lunged forward, and jumped back again. This happened several times over the course of a few seconds.

Stegosaurus was a beaked herbivorous dinosaur. Most beaked herbivorous dinosaurs had a latticework of stiff tendons in their tails, which limited flexibility. In contrast, *Stegosaurus* had evolved a supple, flexible tail with strong terminal vertebrae and no bony tendons. It swiftly and expertly wielded its tail.

"Brilliant," Kailani said while the older *Allosaurus* danced to avoid being lacerated by the *Stegosaurus*. "This confirms what the fossil evidence already indicated. *Stegosaurus* used its thagomizer spikes for defense against *Allosaurus*, and the species definitely interacted."

The older *Allosaurus* was beginning to think it should find a baby *Camarasaurus* to snack on: much easier pickings. Then it smelled something unfamiliar and heard strange sounds. It abruptly backed away from the *Stegosaurus*.

Gunshots lacerated humid prehistoric air. Kailani stopped recording video on her phone and quickly put it back in a vest pocket. Traxton, Branigan, and Holt emerged from the forest about 80 yards (73 meters) to the south and fired their rifles as they rode onto the beach. Yonder reared and bucked while Durango struggled to stay mounted. Graphite and Ember bolted into the forest. Horizon stood still and occasionally flinched as bullets zoomed past.

Suddenly, Avarette and Gantry emerged from the forest just north of the *Allosaurus* and fired their pistols at Lassen. The pair of *Allosaurus* panicked and ran south, and the *Stegosaurus* moved back to the forest. With the *Allosaurus* approaching, Yonder bolted south, and Durango barely stayed in the saddle. He was unwittingly headed straight for Traxton, Branigan, and Holt.

In the meantime, Lassen and Kailani ran south along the water, and Adalya grabbed two bolas from Horizon's saddlebags before sprinting to join the bounty hunter and paleontologist. As Adalya fled, Horizon glanced at Lassen.

"It's okay, buddy!" Lassen shouted. "Go!"

Horizon dashed into the forest.

Traxton Gang members fired wildly as their horses spooked because of gunfire and the approaching *Allosaurus*. Chaos ensued. Some shots were aimed at Lassen. Others were focused on the *Allosaurus*. Avarette and Gantry rode to the edge of the lake on frightened horses that soon galloped south along lapping waves. In the meantime, the *Allosaurus* duo ran southward in the sand and bypassed Lassen, Kailani, and Adalya who were now well within striking range of Gantry and Avarette. As little bursts of bullet-shot sand blew up behind their feet, Lassen and Kailani ran toward a cluster of gnarled sequoia driftwood snags on the shore of the lake.

The Traxton Gang was in disarray. As the horses of Branigan and Holt ran to the south, and a pair of *Allosaurus* approached, Traxton aimed a rifle at Lassen. From where he was, he could easily accidentally shoot Gantry or Avarette, but that did not bother him.

As Traxton focused on Lassen, Adalya caught a glimpse of the outlaw. He was far away, but he seemed familiar. While running, she frantically detached her database orientation module from her belt, pressed several buttons, and pointed it at Traxton. Soon, a hologram of Traxton's face appeared before morphing into an image of Brent Cordon's face taken from Area 54's personnel archives. Below the image, text flashed that said "Match Found." In the hologram, Traxton's scarred and rough-hewn stubble-covered face had morphed into that of a clean-cut, slightly pudgy-cheeked computer technician.

Traxton closed one eye, carefully repositioned the bead on the end of his rifle barrel, and moved his finger over the trigger. Suddenly, his horse reared, and his shot went wild as the *Allosaurus* pair ran by. Traxton's horse backed up, turned around, and galloped south. Traxton cursed as he struggled to control his mount. He was not good with horses. In the nineteenth century, he regularly switched between different stolen horses. As a result, he had little familiarity with or loyalty from any particular horse.

In the meantime, Lassen and Kailani reached a pile of sequoia driftwood snags along the water with Gantry and Avarette in hot pursuit. Kailani's oilskin fedora fell off as she ran. As Adalya sprinted toward the bounty hunter and paleontologist, she accidentally dropped her database orientation module when her left hand brushed against the branch of a weathered sequoia log. Adalya left the device behind, somersaulted in the sand, and gracefully stood up behind the snags where Lassen and Kailani took cover.

Adalya handed Lassen a bola while Avarette and Gantry rode along the edge of the water and closed in fast.

Adalya and Lassen swung bola stones over their heads. Adalya bit her lower lip and released her weapon. It knocked Avarette's pistol out of his hand. Lassen released his bola, and its stones wrapped around Gantry's right hand. The outlaw sputtered inane comments and panicked as bola stones suddenly lashed onto his wrist like a grasping tarantula. He wildly flailed his hand and dropped his pistol.

Both outlaws' guns flew into the lake and quickly sank into sand under lapping waves. Avarette and Gantry tightly held reins while their horses galloped past the time travelers, moved up onto the shore, and headed south toward the rest of the gang.

For a moment, as he sped past Lassen, Avarette considered jumping off his horse to fight the bounty hunter. He had seen Traxton do that once in the past with memorable and painful results. However, Avarette wanted to focus more on controlling his horse, and Traxton was not paying him enough to fight Lassen Malone hand-to-hand.

Suddenly, Adalya heard odd crunching and looked just beyond the driftwood snags to see fragments of her database orientation module crushed into sand as Gantry's horse lifted a hoof off it. Adalya winced.

Lassen breathed a long sigh of relief and said, "We just saw all the Traxton Gang members who came to the Jurassic."

"But we lost the database orientation module," Adalya added.

Just then, a flash of lightning lit up the beach. The first thunder of the day rumbled. For a moment, the time travelers looked up at the sky, wide-eyed and open-mouthed. Rain began to fall above the lake far to the east. Sunlight still covered the western shore where Lassen, Kailani and Adalya stood, though patches of shadow began to drape the land.

Lassen wiped sweat from his forehead and looked to the south. He saw Avarette and Gantry still riding away fast. Not far ahead of them, the *Allosaurus* duo veered west into the forest. Traxton, Branigan, and Holt rode about a half mile (one kilometer) farther south. While Lassen monitored the Traxton Gang, Kailani walked away from the lake and picked up her fedora, which had fallen off during the commotion a few minutes earlier.

As a slight drizzle sprinkled the landscape, Lassen noticed Durango rode in front of Traxton with his hands in the air. Traxton held a rifle at his back. Branigan pulled strips of rawhide from his saddlebag. Lassen winced as he realized Durango was being kidnapped. Soon, Branigan tied Durango's hands behind his back. Lassen sighed while Kailani put on her fedora and returned to where he and Adalya stood.

"We have problems beyond losing the database orientation module," Adalya said.

"Yeah," Lassen added as he patted sand off his vest. "Durango's been captured by Traxton."

"Yes," Adalya said, "but who really captured him?"

"What do you mean?" Lassen asked.

"I do not think that man is Traxton," Adalya said. "I got a look at him during the commotion and cross-referenced his face with imagery in my module. I am confident Traxton is somebody I have met before."

"What?" Lassen replied. "That's im . . . probable. How does that make sense, unless . . ."

"Unless he's from the future," Kailani said.

"Precisely," Adalya added. "He is the saboteur Professor Sedora and I were after when we crash-landed in 1879."

"Helps explain why he's so smart," Lassen said. "And some of the stories about his gadgets must be true."

"Gadgets?" Kailani asked.

"There've been stories," Lassen said, "as long as Traxton's been in the West—about him having special technology. Knives made of light and things like that, but people in my time believe all sorts of strange things."

"After leaving 2756," Adalya said, "Traxton must have arrived months or years before Professor Sedora and myself. His real name is Brent Cordon. He appears to have adopted an outlaw persona similar to that in multimedia stories of the Old American West."

"As far as I know," Lassen said, "Traxton's been in the West since 1876, so he might have arrived three years before you or even earlier. How did you know him?"

"I did not know him well," Adalya said, "but I had met him a few times. He was a maintenance technician for quantum computers in my time. He worked at my facility where we developed time travel technology."

"Computers," Lassen said while narrowing his eyes in thought, "machines that compute data and perform calculations?"

"Correct," Adalya confirmed.

"Interesting," Lassen said. "In my time, the term 'computer' is used for people who compute data."

Adalya said, "Cordon—or Traxton as you know him—he stole one of our time machines and fled my facility after killing security personnel. Professor Sedora and I tried to stop him, but we showed up after he had been in the Old West for some time. I need to capture Cordon and question him. I do not know how much more he may have compromised the research and security at my facility. Of course, that will not mean much if Professor Sedora never comes back for us or cannot find us."

"Can we even find the location signaler now that we don't have the database orientation module?" Kailani asked.

"Yes," Adalya said. "I have the terrain surrounding the location signaler area memorized. I can take us there."

"Good," Lassen said.

"The location signaler," Adalya said, "is located approximately 27 miles northwest of us on the rim of a volcano at the western end of a very low valley. After we move north, we will need to cross through hills to reach the cliffs above the valley. Then we will have to climb down. The valley is bounded by sand dunes to the south and lava rock and mountains to the north. It will not be as lush as this area."

"We'll have an opportunity to explore new ecosystems," Kailani said.

"Not so fast," Lassen remarked. "First, we need to rescue Durango. He'd do the same for me. He *has* done the same for me. Plus, we'll need his rope to have enough to descend the cliffs on the way to the location signaler. You don't have to come with me. Might be safer if you don't. You two could go after the location signaler on your own after we find the horses."

"No, thanks," Kailani said. "We'll be safer together." Kailani subtly smiled at Lassen.

The bounty hunter nodded his head in acknowledgement before saying, "Thank you, Kailani. Your dinosaur knowledge will be extremely valuable. Miss Nell?"

"According to the math," Adalya said, "we will be safer together, though the safety levels will decrease once we are reunited with Durango."

"I'll try to make sure he doesn't rope another *Allosaurus*," Lassen said.

*   *   *

By late afternoon, Lassen, Kailani, and Adalya had recovered Horizon, Graphite, and Ember from the forest. Finding Horizon was easy. Lassen whistled for him, and he ran out of the trees almost immediately. Horizon then led the time travelers to the other horses.

The bounty hunter and scientists walked south near the western shore of the lake. They led their horses by the reins. The lightning storm to the east had drifted west. The sky now drizzled with light rain, though the sun had not completely gone behind clouds. Thunder occasionally rumbled.

As the rain increased, water began to stream over the sandy dirt west of the lake, obscuring the horse tracks of the Traxton Gang.

"We might not be able to follow this trail much longer," Lassen said.

"I agree," Adalya replied. "It is already fading. We should move through the forest and head into the hills. Regardless of the tracks, I also want to keep our heads dry."

"Good idea," Kailani said. "The fluvial systems here are immense, and there could be flash flooding if the rain falls in higher levels."

The time travelers mounted their horses and soon saw a lone *Stegosaurus* emerge from the forest in the distance. It ambled onto the beach and carefully positioned its body, so its plates received optimal levels of warming sunlight that had just started to shine through a temporary break in the clouds.

"Brilliant," Kailani said, smiling. "*Stegosaurus* uses its plates for both cooling *and* warming."

Lassen, Kailani, and Adalya rode toward the forest. As they entered the trees, they moved past a small herd of *Camarasaurus* browsing on conifer needles. Kailani shot several photos of them with her phone.

Rain began to fall harder and pattered loudly against the forest canopy. Pterosaurs curled up on tree branches, sheltering themselves with leathery folded wings. The time travelers occasionally saw small groups of sauropod hatchlings scurry away into the undergrowth. As the afternoon faded to early evening, and the cloud cover thickened, the terrain significantly darkened. The forest became shadowy and foreboding. Strange animal calls echoed through the trees, occasionally loud or barely discernible through falling rain.

Soon, the time travelers rode onto higher ground. As the vegetation thinned, the scenery opened up, and the terrain became less dark as it transitioned from forest to low, rolling largely open hills.

Instead of lush forest, the primary vegetation was tough cycad brush. Conifers looked weak and stunted here compared to the floodplain forests. The soil was thinner and rockier than in the lower elevations. It could not support as many plant species as the floodplains. Exposed pink bedrock protruded throughout the hills. The bedrock was comprised of granite with high levels of potassium feldspar, which gave it its pinkish color.

Occasionally, small herds of *Dryosaurus* scattered as the time travelers approached. The 200-pound (91-kilogram) beaked bipedal herbivores fed on the tough vegetation in the hills. Unlike other herbivorous dinosaurs that swallowed their food whole, the *Dryosaurus* thoroughly chewed their meals. Lassen noticed a few baby *Dryosaurus* that were about the same size as robins. They chirped and squealed as they ran off with their parents.

"Adorable," Kailani said.

"They look helpless," Adalya added.

"Yeah," Lassen remarked wistfully as he stared at a distant plume of volcano gases billowing into a gloomy gray sky.

"You're worried about Durango, aren't you?" Kailani asked.

"Yeah," Lassen said with a sigh. "I've always been able to rescue him before, but I wonder if there will ever be that one time when I can't."

"How did you two become, um, partners?" Adalya asked, raising her eyebrows.

"It was about eight years ago in Mexico," Lassen said. "In 1871, an English aristocrat, Sir Niles of Cambridge, hired me to recover a silver statue of a Mayan god that he claimed had been stolen from his archaeological dig workers near some pyramids. In the jungle, I got ambushed by bandits, but Durango warned me, and we fought them off together. His warning saved my life. He was a complete stranger at the time who happened to be riding on the same trail as me."

"How many bandits were there?" Kailani asked.

"Sheesh," Lassen said, "it was hard to tell—maybe 15 to 22. Durango always says there were 47, but he can be prone to making hyperbolic statements."

"And just the two of you fought them off?" Adalya asked.

"Ummm—sort of," Lassen said. "A dam collapse and a pair of starving jaguars did work to our advantage."

"Incredible," Kailani said.

"We spent the next month treasure hunting, I found out there was a lot more to my job than Niles had told me, and Durango swears we were close to finding a map showing a route to the mythical lost city of El Dorado."

"Tell me more," Kailani said, fascinated.

"I will," Lassen said, "but it's getting dark. We should find some shelter."

Lassen and the scientists approached a set of massive boulders that laid against each other and backed into a dirt slope. They tied their horses to sturdy, scrappy cycad trunks just below overhanging rock. The horses would be mostly sheltered for the night. Lassen, Kailani, and Adalya moved under the sheltering boulders with their saddles, saddlebags, and bedrolls.

Thunder rumbled as the time travelers removed supplies from worn leather saddlebags. Lightning occasionally flashed in the distance, sporadically illuminating the terrain outside the shelter.

Rain loudly pattered. Lassen heard it starting to run downhill in distant temporary streams coursing along recently dry washes. As darkness fell, *Brachiosaurus* honks faintly echoed through the rain from far out on the plains. Lassen also heard occasional pterosaur shrieks.

Adalya worked on igniting dried moss and root twigs with Lassen's magnesium and knife while Lassen and Kailani gathered firewood outside. They focused on dry branches and root pieces protected from the rain under nearby boulders. Several minutes later, Lassen and Kailani returned to the shelter of the boulders, soaking wet. Thousands of little frogs on the plains and in the hills began loudly chirping.

"It's been warm the whole time we've been here," Kailani said, "but I think it's finally starting to feel cool."

"Glad we've got a fire," Lassen said as he looked down at a little crackling campfire and smelled earthy smoke. "Let's get some food going. We don't have a lot of options, but I could rustle up dry biscuits and boil some jerky to make a light soup."

"I'll take whatever's on the menu," Kailani said.

"Sustenance is necessary for survival," Adalya added.

"That's a fact," Lassen remarked. "If you dip the biscuits in the soup, they should at least soften up enough to not break your teeth—well, not most of your teeth, anyway."

Kailani lightly chuckled. Adalya cleared her throat. Lassen got a small tin pot out of his saddlebags. He then selected higher-quality pieces of jerky that had a decent amount of seasoning and lacked pieces of fat or tattered membrane. He placed these pieces in the pot and filled it with water before setting the pot on coals after the fire subsided.

Once the soup was ready, Lassen poured it into three metal cups and handed one each to Kailani and Adalya. While grabbing the cup of soup, Kailani felt a jolt of excitement as part of Lassen's hand slightly brushed against hers. Lassen felt the same thing and slightly raised his eyebrows.

"Durango would like the taste of this," Lassen said as he sipped his soup and dipped a biscuit into it.

"How come?" Kailani said.

"It's food," Lassen said. "He's not very picky with food." Lassen's eyes grew wistful. "I hope he's okay."

"Based on what you have told me," Adalya said, "I believe Cordon will keep him alive as a way to get you."

"Cordon?" Lassen said. "Oh yeah, that was Traxton's name before he went to the 1870s. Probably. Traxton knows how to use hostages. To him, Durango is bait to trap me. But Traxton kills hostages the second he no longer needs them. Once, I saw it, and once, I prevented it. I'll need to be careful."

"No clear plan yet?" Adalya inquired.

"I'll—think of something," Lassen said. "Thank you both for helping me out. We're moving south of the location signaler. I can see how you might want to leave Durango behind and head northwest for a potential rendezvous with the professor."

"You and Durango saved my life," Adalya said. "I owe you both. And Brent Cordon—or Traxton as he now calls himself—must be confronted."

"We're a team," Kailani added.

"Thanks," Lassen said.

"So," Kailani said after taking a sip of soup, "what's the full story with you and Durango first meeting? If I remember right, it involved a silver statue, treasure hunting, and the lost City of El Dorado."

"Well, yeah, and in some ways, not so much," Lassen said. "So, in 1871, I was studying in Boston, and I got a letter saying that . . ."

Lassen, Kailani, and Adalya talked long into the night before drifting off to deep sleep with the soothing background noise of rain patter and tree frog chirps.

CHAPTER 19: RESCUE TREK

Lassen awoke shortly after sunrise and stepped out of the shelter of the boulders for a moment. He returned to find Kailani and Adalya awake but bleary-eyed.

"Looks like the rain stopped, but it's foggy," Lassen said. "Still, it's getting brighter. The fog could burn off soon."

Thick fog draped the area where the time travelers had set up camp in the foothills of the Mesocordilleran High. Frogs continued to chirp but not as loudly as they had during the night. *Brachiosaurus* on the plains honked at each other. A distant pterosaur shrieked. The horses tied nearby softly whinnied.

The bounty hunter and scientists rolled up their bedding blankets and put supplies back in their saddlebags. The air carried the strong scent of fresh rain and wet dirt. Soon, Lassen, Kailani, and Adalya situated supplies on their horses. Lassen and Kailani stood next to each other to the right of Horizon, Graphite, and Ember while Adalya stood to the left of the horses.

"That should be the last of my supplies," Kailani said as she buckled a leather saddlebag flap and turned toward Lassen. "The sun's coming out. Look."

Fog rapidly dissipated as pure yellow light began to fill the plains and foothills. Through fading mist, distant mountains and gas-billowing conical volcanoes became visible along the northern horizon. Beams of sun illuminated fog particles into brilliant shafts of light.

Tendrils of water systems and recently enlarged wetlands and ponds sparkled on the plains to the east. Lassen saw a distant *Brachiosaurus* herd and a closer lone *Apatosaurus* feeding on the plains. A pair of bright green dragonflies flitted past his face. He also heard grunting and rumbling as a large animal moved nearby.

The bounty hunter and scientists soon spotted a male *Camarasaurus* move out of the fog. He walked uphill to the west and was scarred from years of survival. His green-brown skin was pebbly and full of wear, and the blue crest on his head had lost some of its vibrancy. The old dinosaur was about 17 feet (five meters) tall at his shoulders and about 55 feet (17 meters) long.

"A lone *Camarasaurus*," Kailani said as she took a photo of it with her phone. "All the *Camarasaurus* we've seen were in herds. I wonder if this one is a male and was defeated by a younger rival.

He could have been kicked out of a family unit and retreated to the hills."

"Could be," Lassen said. "Might have lost his harem—if sauropods have harems. Hey, look." Lassen pointed to the northeast.

A double rainbow was forming over the *Camarasaurus*, dissipating fog, and beams of sunlight. Kailani took a photo of it and put her phone in a vest pocket. Lassen looked up with wide eyes and an open mouth. At the same time, he felt Kailani's hand reach out to his. Lassen turned toward Kailani and smiled as his heartbeat quickened. Then he intertwined his fingers with Kailani's, and they held hands. Adalya did not see the moment of intimacy because the horses were in the way.

Lassen was struck by how tough Kailani's hand was. He expected delicate softness from an academic. His hands were calloused and toughened from years of outdoor living and bounty hunting, and to this surprise, Kailani's hand was not much different.

While holding hands, Lassen and Kailani looked up to see a pterosaur flock fly over, moving south. The fuzzy, leathery-winged reptiles flew right under the double rainbow. Lassen and Kailani craned their necks backward with their line of sight following the pterosaurs. Then Lassen turned to look at Kailani while squeezing her hand. The morning light lit up her face wonderfully. Her hair shimmered, she smiled with bright teeth, and her brilliant brown eyes twinkled. She was gorgeous and so was the prehistoric landscape behind her.

Kailani stood in front of a backdrop of a vast floodplain filled with shimmering water, conifers, tree ferns, cycads, fern prairies, and sauropod dinosaur herds. While holding Kailani's hand, Lassen's spirits soared. Whatever today had to throw at him, he was ready to tackle with adept vigor. Horizon lowly whinnied, pawed his right hoof, and looked right.

"Quite a colorful natural phenomenon," Adalya said.

Lassen cleared his throat and said, "Yep" as Kailani moved her hand away from his.

"However," Adalya continued, "we should get moving."

"Right," Lassen said. "Durango needs us."

As the double rainbow faded, and the fog disappeared, the bounty hunter and scientists rode south through the hills. While horses clopped over rocky terrain, Lassen noticed that the rain had drawn out various snails that oozed along the rocks. He also occasionally caught glimpses of beetles and spotted a few ant hills.

Like during the previous days, tiny mammals were still a fairly common sight. Lassen saw them quickly scurrying from one place to another—often moving into the shadows under rocks or logs. Dinosaurs clearly dominated the largest amounts of open real estate. At least during the day, the mammals seemed to be subjected to low, dark places.

Suddenly, Graphite stopped and whinnied as a dense cluster of cycad shrubs shook nearby to the right. A little *Schillerosaurus* lizard emerged from the plants and sprinted downhill right in front of the horses. It looked to be about three inches (eight centimeters) long. To Lassen, it resembled a small but colorful western fence lizard from the 1870s. An instant later, an *Ornitholestes* burst out of the vegetation in pursuit of the lizard. The small carnivorous theropod dinosaur stood only about one and a half feet (one half meter) tall at the hip and weighed roughly 25 pounds (11 kilograms). Mottled brown downy feathers on its body and longer feathers along its legs and arms shined in the morning sun.

Graphite and Ember neighed in surprise and reared. Horizon whinnied but remained still.

"Easy, easy," Lassen said as he tried to calm Graphite.

The *Ornitholestes* moved downhill and quickly disappeared into forest. Then a pair of very young *Allosaurus* emerged from nearby cycads, chirping. They ran toward the *Ornitholestes* and were no bigger than the dinosaur they chased. The horses reared again, and Lassen struggled to stay mounted. The young *Allosaurus* had long legs and big eyes.

"Brilliant," Kailani said. "I think the juvenile *Allosaurus* here compete with *Ornitholestes* for the same prey."

The *Allosaurus* soon disappeared into nearby forest, and Lassen heard growling, hissing, and vegetation snapping in their path.

Lassen and the scientists continued riding through the hills and regularly stopped to scan the plains with binoculars for signs of the Traxton Gang. During one stop, Lassen adjusted the focus on his binoculars as he began to speak. "Still no sign of people down there."

"They may be traveling in the forest," Kailani said.

"I've been thinking that, too," Lassen added as he moved his binoculars to the north. "That herd of *Diplodocus* about a quarter mile away has been feeding all morning, but they've just stopped. I wonder why."

A herd of *Diplodocus* fed on ferns near the edge of a river. The enormous dinosaurs slowly swung their necks back and forth as they shredded fern leaves with pencil-like teeth and swallowed them whole. The *Diplodocus* ranged from roughly 60 to 90 feet (18 to 27 meters) in length. They were primarily light turquoise with beige underbellies. They also had yellow lateral stripes on their topsides with bright yellow dermal spines. They carried extremely long whip-like, finely-tapered tails.

"I see them," Kailani said, looking through her binoculars. "The adults are swiveling their heads in all directions."

"We will not get very far if we stop to look at dinosaurs all the time," Adalya said.

"True," Lassen replied, "but those *Diplodocus* look nervous. That could mean people are nearby."

"I'm not seeing any so far," Kailani said, still looking through binoculars. "Wait, I see movement at the edge of the trees near the herd."

"I see it, too," Lassen said.

"*Allosaurus fragilis*," Kailani said. "There are two of them. I think they're preparing for an ambush."

"Those sauropods are gigantic," Lassen said. "I'm not sure how well that will work out."

"It does not seem like a practical strategy for food acquisition," Adalya added.

"True," Kailani said. "Theropods likely mostly only eat adult sauropods when they are already dead. They might try to attack a sick or weak adult, but I think they would mainly attack younger, smaller animals. Still one of the larger adults appears to have significant scarring. I wonder if—" Kailani stopped speaking as the scene on the plains transformed into a frenzy of action.

Suddenly, the *Allosaurus* rushed the *Diplodocus*. Several of the herbivores ran in fear. Mud splattered and oozed as massive sauropod feet slammed into the ground. A male and female *Allosaurus* pursued the sauropods. The male had ruby red crests on the top of his head, just in front of his eyes. The female was slightly smaller and had pale blue crests.

One large *Diplodocus* was caught off-guard as a 1,500-pound (680-kilogram) female *Allosaurus* latched onto it. The *Allosaurus* opened her jaws wide, gripped sauropod flesh with powerful six-inch (two and a half-centimeter) claws, and raked most of her teeth against her prey.

As the *Diplodocus* victim retreated, the attacking female *Allosaurus* tore a piece of flesh off its hindquarters. A chunk of *Diplodocus* meat dripped warm blood as it hung from the *Allosaurus's* jaws. The female *Allosaurus* moved her head up and swallowed the meat.

In the meantime, the male *Allosaurus* rushed after the fleeing *Diplodocus*—snapping with voracious frustration. Dark brown silty mud splattered up from the sauropods' feet, and a gob hit the *Allosaurus* in the eye. The male *Allosaurus* abruptly stopped, steadied himself, and rubbed his fingers against his face in an effort to remove the mud. The *Diplodocus* herd continued to move out of harm's way. The male *Allosaurus* panted heavily as he rubbed his face.

An individual *Allosaurus* did not have the size and power needed to regularly dispatch the adult sauropods of the Morrison Basin. Some paleontologists thought *Allosaurus* relied on pack hunting or ambush tactics to take down large or elusive prey.

"Wow," Lassen said with wide eyes as he readjusted his tan hat.

"Not a full meal," Adalya said, "but I calculate those calories will keep that animal going long enough to hunt something else."

Lassen scanned the scene with binoculars while Kailani used her phone to shoot photos of the distant *Allosaurus* and fleeing *Diplodocus*. The panting *Allosaurus* slowly walked back toward its companion.

"Those *Allosaurus* look like they're spent," Lassen said. He moved his binoculars toward the *Diplodocus* herd. "That injured *Diplodocus* looks like it will make it. It's keeping up with its friends. Huh, *that's* interesting."

"What?" Kailani asked.

"As you mentioned," Lassen said, "the *Diplodocus* have scarring. Actually, several of them appear to be heavily scarred near their back legs. I wonder if they regularly survive *Allosaurus* attacks."

"They may be commonly attacked," Kailani said. "This reminds me of a possible feeding strategy I once read about called flesh grazing."

"How does that work?" Lassen asked.

Kailani said, "It could be that some *Allosaurus* plan on only getting a bite of a large sauropod during an attack. The sauropod could end up surviving and provide the possibility for more bites in the future. Those *Allosaurus* are about 1,500 to 2,000 pounds. *Diplodocus* could weigh up to 30,000 pounds. Some *Brachiosaurus* may weigh nearly 100,000 pounds. Animals of that size could sustain occasional theropod attacks. I think two or three bites from a sauropod could feed an *Allosaurus* for a day."

"Intriguing," Lassen said.

"I read *Allosaurus* might mainly hunt slower herbivores," Kailani said, "like *Stegosaurus* and *Camptosaurus*, but based on what we've seen, it appears to be a versatile generalist when it comes to feeding."

"Makes sense and helps explain why they're so common," Lassen said. "I wonder if *Allosaurus's* role in this environment is similar to coyotes in modern times."

"Great analogy," Kailani said. "By the twenty-first century, coyotes are widespread and will eat just about anything."

*   *   *

Three miles (five kilometers) to the south, Tardell Traxton, Shanahan Branigan, Arvo Avarette, Hobart Holt, Jed Gantry, and Durango Mesquite sat in their saddles in the shade of a large araucarian conifer. They were at the edge of forest that separated the foothills of the Mesocordilleran High from the plains. Durango sat on Yonder with his hands tied behind his back. He grimaced as he looked up. His face was in pain, but he smiled to himself as he noticed a *Harpactognathus* nest with chirping babies high in the branches above. His five o' clock shadow was particularly noticeable, and his face was dirty and beaten with a black eye.

"Shouldn't take long for me to check out me horse's hoof," Branigan said. "Might just be a wee pebble." The large Irishman dismounted to tend to his horse.

Branigan and Traxton's horses stood in the front of the group. Gantry and Durango were in the back. Gantry was assigned to guard Durango for the day.

"Lucky Traxton only took one wallop to your face," Gantry said.

"Yeah, I feel real fortunate," Durango said, rolling his eyes.

"Hey," Gantry said. "If Branigan didn't remind him that we needed you alive and healthyish to get Lassen Malone, we might not be having this conversation."

"Speaking of healthyish," Durango said, "could I have another drink of water?"

"Yeah," Gantry reluctantly said as he untied Durango's hands and passed him his canteen. The canteen was metal and reasonably new with only slight battering and no rusting. Gantry drew his gun and kept a close eye on Durango as he drank. Durango considered trying to escape while his hands were free but figured that would result in another beating or worse. His best bet was to wait for Lassen to rescue him.

Avarette moved his horse toward Durango and said, "Stop hoggin' all the shade, Mesquite. It's gettin' scorchin' out here."

Yonder whinnied as Avarette's horse pushed him out of the way.

"It's okay, boy," Durango said as Yonder stepped out of the shade into bright sunlight. Durango noticed he had an open view of the hills to the west. He looked left and right as he drank from the canteen while subtly shifting it at different angles. Late morning light glinted off the canteen in a series of flashes. *Lassen, old buddy, don't let me down*, Durango thought as he composed a Morse code message.

*   *   *

Just after witnessing a pair of *Allosaurus* attack a *Diplodocus* herd, Lassen, Kailani, and Adalya continued riding south. Then something caught Lassen's eye.

"Hey," Lassen said. "I think there's flashing to the southeast."

"I am not seeing it," Adalya said.

"It's just beyond the trees—several miles ahead of us," Lassen said. You can *barely* make it out."

"Maybe *you* can barely detect it," Kailani said, "but I can't see it either. Is it light reflecting off water in an unusual way?"

"Maybe," Lassen replied. He raised his binoculars to get a better look. "Wait, no. It's Morse code. Durango's alive, and he's sending us a message."

"Morse code," Adalya said. "How primitive but still clever."

"He says he's okay," Lassen said, "but short on time. Trap. Traxton plans to set a trap. Well, we'd figured that. He also says he'd escape, but his hands are tied." Lassen readjusted his binoculars and saw Gantry grab Durango's canteen and start tying rawhide around his wrists. "Well, that's the literal truth. Looks like they're using rawhide."

*   *   *

"So, what are you going to do to me?" Durango asked. "Tie me to stakes out in the plains and yell for Lassen to come get me?"

"Might be somethin' like that," Gantry said. "Course, Traxton don't always tell me his plans." As Durango and Gantry spoke, a lone frog croaked from a nearby puddle.

"Traxton seems to be sure your friend is coming for you, Mesquite," Avarette said. "And those women might be with him, too. Traxton won't say much about them, but we need at least one of them alive to get back to our time."

"As much as I would like to think Lassen might help me," Durango said, "I wouldn't be surprised if he's talking science poetry to those women right now instead of tracking us."

"Me horse is fine now," Branigan said.

"Good," Traxton said. "We'll ride to the spot I mentioned and then prepare."

"Prepare for what, boss?" Avarette asked.

"The end of Lassen Malone," Traxton proclaimed, "and Durango Mesquite."

*   *   *

"There were other horses down there with Durango," Lassen said. "It looked like everybody was together at the edge of the trees. We should start moving down into the forest and sneak up on them before they set their trap."

279

"That seems like a logical idea," Adalya said, "but there are a lot of large boulders below us."

"Let's walk the horses through," Lassen said.

Soon, the bounty hunter and scientists emerged on the east side of the boulder field. They were in an area they had not had a good look at earlier. The terrain was generally level but gradually sloped downward to the east and was still well above the floodplains. Here, the stunted vegetation of the hills began to transition to forest edge. As a result, some large trees were nearby, including conifers and ginkgoes.

"There's a nice hidden little meadow over here," Lassen said as he, Kailani, and Adalya walked around a cluster of boulders, holding their horses by the reins.

"I do not think it is hidden to them," Adalya added as she pointed at a small herd of herbivorous dinosaurs that walked on four legs as they emerged from the forest while selectively browsing on short plants. The dinosaurs were about 70 yards (64 meters) directly in front of the time travelers.

"We haven't seen that species before," Lassen said. "They're armored."

"Oh, brilliant," Kailani said as she started taking photos with her phone. "Fantastic. I hoped we would see ankylosaurids. Those look like they could be *Mymoorapelta* or *Gargoyleosaurus*."

The dinosaurs were *Mymoorapelta*. The herd contained six animals. Each weighed approximately 1,100 pounds (500 kilograms) and was about 10 feet (three meters) long. They had bumpy, mottled reddish-brown bony armored skin on their backs. Light green sharply-pointed triangular armor plates protruded laterally from their sides, and their underbellies were light orange.

Kailani said, "*Mymoorapelta* and *Gargoyleosaurus* are related to *Ankylosaurus* and are members of the ankylosaur group. Unlike *Ankylosaurus*, *Mymoorapelta* and *Gargoyleosaurus* are polacanthid ankylosaurs and lack a tail club."

The tails of the *Mymoorapelta* tapered to fine points. Each dinosaur also had a small head. Oval keratin-coated bony plates covered the top front half of each *Mymoorapelta*. A more contiguous solid piece of armor covered the top back half of each herbivore.

Some *Mymoorapelta* emerging from the forest peacefully browsed on cycad shrubs, but one large individual began aggressively grunting. It had red inflamed veins in the whites of its eyes.

Lassen winced and said, "One of those dinosaurs seems irrationally angry, which means it's probably a male. Its body language reminds me of competing elk bulls during the breeding season. Let's slowly back away. Anything could set this guy off."

As Lassen backed up, he put one hand on the lasso tied to Graphite's saddle. Then Lassen stepped on a branch, causing loud snapping. The agitated male *Mymoorapelta* turned his head toward the bounty hunter and scientists. The armored dinosaur uttered a deep, low boom. It saw the time travelers as unfamiliar, bizarre intruders. Then the *Mymoorapelta* bolted toward them.

Instinctively, Lassen tightened his grip on the coiled lasso tied to Graphite just before Graphite and Ember ran downhill to the northeast. Lassen was left holding a lasso held together with torn leather strips while his heart rapidly pounded, and adrenaline set in. Kailani breathed heavily as she broke into a cold sweat. Adalya's typical demeanor of detached aloofness began to break as she released a long anxious exhalation.

"Let's get out of here," Lassen said as he backed up.

"It will have to be on foot for some of us," Adalya said as she furrowed her brow and rapidly moved her head left and right with tense alertness.

"Miss Nakai, get on Horizon and go," Lassen said. "We'll catch up with you."

"Are you sure?" Kailani said as she shoved her phone back in a vest pocket with a trembling hand while her stomach fluttered with anxiety.

"Yes," Adalya said. "Mister Malone and I can handle ourselves. Data indicate that you are most vulnerable because of your uneventful twenty-first century academic lifestyle."

"Alright," Kailani said, rolling her eyes. "Be careful."

Horizon lightly tapped Kailani's shoulder with his muzzle. She jumped in the saddle and rode into the meadow to the north. "Yah!" Kailani shouted as Horizon galloped through ferns.

Lassen and Adalya fled back toward the jumble of boulders from which they had recently emerged. Then an enormous male *Mymoorapelta*—separate from the nearby herd—lumbered out of the rocks. It had distinctive scarring across its face. It saw the angry male *Mymoorapelta* charging Lassen and Adalya and detected nearby female *Mymoorapelta* at the edge of the trees. Prospective mates. Competition. Territorial infringement. Time for aggression.

The newly appeared scarred male *Mymoorapelta* rushed toward the *Mymoorapelta* running behind Lassen and Adalya. The eyes of the bounty hunter and physicist widened as they realized they were now between two hulking, charging armored dinosaurs. The time travelers quickly changed direction and moved south. The *Mymoorapelta* moved at a brisk gallop and closed distance fast.

Lassen tripped on a small rock. As Durango had once told him: "Lassen, buddy, you're good at just about anything, but somehow, you *always* trip."

As he fell onto rocky ground, Lassen grunted in pain but still managed to keep a grip on the lasso from Graphite's saddle.

At the sound of Lassen's agony, the two charging male *Mymoorapelta* slowed and suddenly stopped. Adalya turned around, grabbed Lassen's hand, and pulled as he sprang upright while wincing.

"Thanks," Lassen said through heavy breathing as he continued to run.

The bounty hunter and physicist glanced back at the *Mymoorapelta*. From a distance of approximately 30 yards (27 meters), the charging *Mymoorapelta* made eye contact with Lassen and Adalya. Like bucking broncos let out of the gate at a rodeo, the two male *Mymoorapelta* galloped after the time travelers.

"Why are they so mad?!" Adalya asked.

"Probably males," Lassen said. "Probably also have brains about the size of walnuts based on stuff Kailani was telling us the other night."

The two *Mymoorapelta* gained distance on Lassen and Adalya and were soon only about 20 yards (18 meters) behind the time travelers. Lassen closed his eyes in pain as he ran as hard as he could. Then he opened his eyes and stopped as he felt his chest collide with something powerful and sudden: Adalya's arm.

"Whoa!" Lassen said, looking down with wide eyes.

The edge of conglomerate ground Lassen stood on crumbled into rushing river water 100 feet (30 meters) below at the bottom of a gorge that ran east-west through the hills and was about 25 feet (eight meters) wide. Isolated tall trees lined the gorge's north and south rims. Water surged with foaming rapids at its bottom.

Eutretauranosuchus crocodylomorphs milled about in the calmers parts of the river near shore.

Hungry little pterosaurs squawked from nests along the gorge's cliff faces. Adults were present on only a few nests. Most were off hunting on the shores of the nearby huge lake the time travelers had visited during the previous day. High boulders blocked any escape Lassen and Adalya might have to the left or right.

"What now?" Adalya asked through heavy breaths.

"I have an idea," Lassen said as he uncoiled the lasso in his hands. "That ravine's only what, 30 feet across? And some of the tree branches on the other side are even closer."

"That is too far to jump," Adalya said.

"Maybe so," Lassen replied, "but that tree growing along the opposite side has some sturdy branches." As Lassen spoke, he started swinging a lasso loop above his head. Lassen then mightily threw the lasso loop. It caught around a strong branch. Lassen pulled the loop tight.

"You go, throw the rope back to me, and I'll be right behind you," Lassen said. "Go! Now!"

"That is a reckless move," Adalya said, "but the math adds up! I think!"

"Of course it does," Lassen said as he handed Adalya the end of the rope.

Adalya gripped the rope hard, backed up, got a running start, and launched off the edge of the gorge. She gracefully swung over empty space separating the two sides of the gorge. Far below, hungry *Eutretauranosuchus* looked up and splashed in the water.

The rope held tight, and Adalya grunted as she landed hard on the ground beyond the opposite side of the gorge. Still gripping the rope, she quickly coiled a portion of the lasso, and threw it toward Lassen.

Lassen reached out far with his right hand while dirt on the edge of the gorge crumbled at his feet. Unfortunately, he could not quite grab any of the coils of rope that separated as they sailed toward him. Then he felt hot *Mymoorapelta* breath on the back of his neck, and he leapt into the air. As Lassen sprung off the rim of the cliff, loose dirt disintegrated under his feet.

While Lassen flailed over the gorge, everything seemed to happen in slow motion, and his senses became hyper alert. He saw

Adalya looking concerned on the opposite side of the gorge. The rope moved away from him. Lassen could swear a few *Eutretauranosuchus* below were almost smiling as they snapped their jaws upward. Ugly little fuzzy, leathery baby pterosaurs screeched in their nests, and a few of their parents flew away in panic.

As Lassen reached out with all his might, he glanced over his shoulder. A *Mymoorapelta* had just fallen off the cliff along with a large chunk of the clifftop's loose soil. The dinosaur's rival was farther behind and had managed to stop before a hormone-fueled frenzy led to its literal downfall. The falling *Mymoorapelta* unleashed an otherworldly gurgling hiss.

Then Lassen looked forward. His hands touched rope, he gripped hard, and events seemed to snap back to regular speed. The rope stretched tightly. The *Mymoorapelta* behind Lassen began to spin as it fell. Lassen heard ripping leather. One of the *Mymoorapelta's* sharply pointed green side plates tore a gash in his brown leather vest, which billowed behind him as he swung. The *Mymoorapelta* tumbled downward, booming in alarm.

Lassen sailed across the gorge while tightly gripping rope. Just as Lassen cleared the southern edge of the gorge where Adalya stood, he heard a loud snap. The branch holding his rope broke off. Lassen landed on the ground and let go of the rope upon impact. The rope shot away down the gorge, pulled by a heavy piece of branch.

Adalya held an arm out for Lassen, and he gripped it to pull himself up. Lassen and Adalya then heard an epic slapping splash as the falling *Mymoorapelta* landed in water at the bottom of the ravine. Unfortunately for the flummoxed dinosaur, it landed on its back, which left its vulnerable unarmored orange underbelly exposed to *Eutretauranosuchus*. Whitewater rapids soon foamed red.

On the southern side of the gorge, Lassen and Adalya sat on a weathered conifer log and caught their breath.

"Durango and I have been in some close scrapes," Lassen said, "but there was nothing quite like that."

"My quantum physics career was largely sedentary," Adalya said. "That was *not* sedentary."

"Nope," Lassen added. "We need to reunite with Miss Nakai and find the horses."

"That will pose a challenge," Adalya said, "as they are all on the other side of a river and gorge."

"Kailani will probably come back to look for us," Lassen said. "Let's wait here for a bit."

CHAPTER 20: SOLO SAFARI

Just after the Mymoorapelta encounter began, Graphite and Ember had fled to the north. Kailani followed far enough to see them stop to drink from a pond. Then she turned around to investigate what had happened to Lassen and Adalya. Kailani found a bellowing male *Mymoorapelta* slowly lumbering out of a clearing between boulders to the south. It seemed bigger than the *Mymoorapelta* that had chased Lassen and Adalya, and it had unique scarring on its face. As the *Mymoorapelta* bypassed Kailani and headed toward the other *Mymoorapelta* at the edge of nearby trees, Kailani scanned the boulders with her binoculars, searching for Lassen and Adalya.

After the male *Mymoorapelta* was farther away, Kailani called out. "Lassen! Miss Nell! Can you hear me?"

Kailani got no response, though she caused a *Hesperornithoides* to run away in fear. The paleontologist briefly shook her head in wonder as she saw the small feathered theropod flee. She then looked down and saw where ferns had been disrupted from Lassen, Kailani, and apparently two *Mymoorapelta*. She counted the tracks again to be sure.

As Horizon slowly strode forward, Kailani heard the distant sound of rushing water far below. Soon, she was surprised to find a huge gorge, and she saw Lassen and Adalya's tracks end at the very edge of the gorge.

Horizon proceeded extra cautiously and stopped before reaching the edge of the cliff. Kailani heard scores of squawking juvenile pterosaurs as the sound of rapids at the bottom of the gorge became louder. She also faintly heard something else. Was it human voices?

Kailani stood taller in her stirrups and shielded her eyes from the sun as she looked out over the edge of the cliff. Then she smiled as she saw Lassen and Adalya on the other side of the gorge. They waved and shouted. Kailani waved back but could not clearly hear what they were saying because of wind and rapids at the bottom of the gorge.

Lassen extended his right palm and sharply shoved it forward. Kailani had Horizon back up a bit. She looked over the edge of the cliff to see that soil had freshly eroded. Roots were sticking out of dirt that was still moist. She recognized that the cliff edge was unstable and unsafe, and Lassen was warning her about that.

Lassen pointed at Adalya and himself and pointed downhill to the east. He then held his hands in front of him like he was riding a horse and pointed downhill. Then he pointed at Kailani. Kailani nodded her head affirmatively, pointed to the north where the horses had gone, made a horse-riding gesture with her hands, pointed downhill, and then made a thumbs-up gesture. Lassen returned the thumbs-up. Adalya looked on with the fascination of an anthropologist observing a troop of chimpanzees. Kailani turned Horizon around and rode north.

"Do you think she knew what you were signaling?" Adalya asked.

"Yeah," Lassen said. "She'll find the horses and meet us somewhere downhill."

"These cliffs should level out by the time the river reaches the plains," Adalya said. There may be shallows there where we can cross."

"Right," Lassen said, "we can stick close to the river, cross where it's safe, and find Miss Nakai."

*   *   *

Soon, Kailani rode north along the far western edge of the fern meadow where the *Mymoorapelta* fed. Most of the armored dinosaurs peacefully grazed, but the big scarred male bellowed at the edge of the herd. Kailani observed the *Mymoorapelta* with binoculars for a moment before continuing on.

The paleontologist followed the tracks of Graphite and Ember and saw them grazing near a pond at the edge of boulders far to the northwest. As she rode along the edge of the rocks, a faint crunching noise to the left caught her attention.

Kailani looked left and saw a little terrestrial crocodylomorph chewing on a beetle while it stood on a pinkish boulder. As she took a photo of it with her phone, her first thought was that it could be *Fruitachampsa*, but its body structure was different, and it seemed too small. Then she correctly guessed that it was *Hoplosuchus*. The rusty orange-dark green reptile was about nine inches (20 centimeters) long and weighed about 26 grams (0.9 ounces). *Hoplosuchus* lacked the prominent upper and lower canines that the housecat-sized *Fruitachampsa* had. Kailani thought the small crocodylomorph looked kind of cute, though she did not think the beetle being chewed apart would share that thought.

Kailani looked up to see two pterosaurs swoop over before perching on nearby conifers. They were colorful and members of a species she had not seen before. Soon, Kailani reached the horses, which were unhappily chewing on prehistoric vegetation. They had both grown reasonably comfortable with Kailani but were most comfortable with Horizon. Kailani tied the horses to Horizon's saddle and cautiously rode downhill toward forest to the east.

Kailani considered continuing to ride Ember. The chestnut Arabian horse was beautiful and had been her mount for most of the journey, but she was already on Horizon, and Lassen's horse clearly had a better personality. He was much easier to control than the other horses—and smarter. Actually, Kailani suspected Horizon was smarter than some of her male classmates from high school. After seeing Lassen repeatedly converse with Horizon over the last couple of days, Kailani also suspected the horse could understand at least some English.

Kailani soon led the horses into the forest to the east. She paused as a pair of *Apatosaurus* hatchlings ran past in pursuit of dragonflies. One hatchling leapt high and nabbed a metallic red dragonfly in its little teeth. The dragonfly's exoskeleton crunched as the baby sauropod tumbled to the ground and did a somersault. As it regained its footing, it quickly looked back and swallowed the dragonfly's body while the insect's wings drifted to the ground. The little sauropod then saw Kailani and the horses and ran into a patch of *Equisetum* with its companion.

Kailani smiled widely. She knew a *Ceratosaurus* or *Allosaurus* could be lurking somewhere in nearby shadows, but she was still loving the experience of wandering in the Jurassic alone. Being alone made her feel more comfortable, and some of her natural anxiety caused by being around people dissipated. She was learning and exploring in beautiful nature, and it was wonderful—at least for the moment.

Several miles downhill, the forest faded into plains, and the hills began to level out. Kailani soon rode between a series of clear ponds and numerous streams. She steered the horses to a pond and dismounted as they got a drink. As she walked toward the water, several small reptiles on a rock at the edge of the pond splashed into the water in alarm. Some *Docodons* swimming near the opposite shore also dove underwater. Kailani leaned over the water to get a better look.

As concentric ripples on the surface of the pond cleared, Kailani saw semiaquatic reptiles swimming underwater. Her first thought was that they could be baby *Amphicotylus*. As she looked closer, she realized she was seeing something else, but it was hard to tell exactly what they were. She guessed the reptiles underwater were choristoderes (also known as champosaurs).

In fact, what Kailani saw were choristoderes and were a genus known as *Cteniogenys*. The *Cteniogenys* ranged from about one to two feet (30 to 60 centimeters) in length. They had long slender skulls and looked like crocodylomorphs, even though they were only distantly related to modern crocodilians.

Choristoderes lived during the Mesozoic Era and into the Paleocene Epoch of the Cenozoic Era, which occurred after the time of the dinosaurs. The Paleocene occurred over roughly the first 10 million years after non-avian dinosaurs went extinct 66 million years before modern times. Kailani stared in fascination as a little *Cteniogenys* darted its head out of the pond and snatched a water strider insect that was skimming across the water's surface on long legs.

After the horses finished their drink, Kailani continued riding downhill. She soon saw open terrain to the east and could finally see that the gorge was nearly gone, and the river was flowing over land that was almost flat. However, the river's edges were still thickly forested.

Kailani rode into a clearing that looked like it had been roughly mowed by a few different kinds of mowers. Actually, it had recently been eaten down by diplodocid sauropods. Some of the vegetation was extra short, and there were fresh green sprouts from new growth. Numerous bipedal herbivorous *Nanosaurus* selectively fed on new growth. A herd of larger *Dryosaurus* also fed in the area. Kailani paused to take photos and record videos with her phone.

Then Ember and Graphite whinnied in alarm as a pair of extra small bipedal dinosaurs ran away from their hooves. The dinosaurs were mottled brown-green and had blue striped tails.

"Easy," Kailani gently said to the horses as she peered down at the fleeing dinosaurs and got blurry photos of them as they ran. She was not sure what they were and initially guessed they were baby *Nanosaurus*. She squinted to get a closer look. Upon seeing a pair of disproportionately large lower canines protruding up from one of the tiny dinosaur's lower jaws, she identified the dinosaurs as *Fruitadens*. Each *Fruitadens* weighed only about one and a half pounds (0.75 kilograms).

Fruitadens was one of the smallest dinosaurs in the world in the late Jurassic. Kailani remembered that paleontologists thought *Fruitadens* may have fed on both plants and insects. Then one of the *Fruitadens* hopped up and snatched a bright blue dragonfly as it fled.

Kailani smiled and shook her head in wonder. In modern times, celebrity dinosaurs of the Morrison Basin—*Brachiosaurus* or *Stegosaurus* for example—seemed to get all the attention, but as she had seen throughout the day, many animals in the Morrison Basin were small.

Kailani rode toward a stand of sequoias with thick undergrowth. She saw various small mammals scurry about as she rode through the trees, including *Fruitafossor* and *Priacodon*. Then she saw light ahead as the stand of trees thinned at the edge of the plains. She also felt vibrations resonate up through the ground from something enormous. She soon rode out of the trees, smiled, and burst into tears.

"Whoa, whoa," Kailani said as she stopped the horses and started to breathe harder.

Kailani saw two species of robust diplodocids feeding side by side in small herds. The closest animals were only about 50 feet (15 meters) away and did not seem concerned by her presence. The air was clear, the early afternoon lighting was sunny and bright, and a few scattered clouds and a pterosaur flock nicely framed the scene.

To the left, Kailani saw the same massive thick-necked diplodocids she had seen the day she arrived in the Jurassic, but to the right, she saw similar-looking dinosaurs that had different coloration and were slightly less bulky. They also had necks that were more slender and generally held lower.

It then became clear to Kailani that this was it. It finally happened. She was seeing *Apatosaurus* (on the left) and *Brontosaurus* (on the right) side by side. Both species were diplodocids and part of the apatosaur group. The adults in the herds were also about 70 to 80 feet (21 to 24 meters) long and weighed approximately 40,000 pounds (18,144 kilograms). The *Apatosaurus* were light sky blue with red lateral striping and bright red dermal spines running along their necks, backs, and tails. In contrast, the *Brontosaurus* were forest green with black lateral stripes and black dermal spines. Each herd appeared to have one large adult male. While the large male *Apatosaurus* had metallic dark blue on the underside of his neck, the bottom of the *Brontosaurus* male's neck was a shiny metallic emerald green. Both the *Apatosaurus* and *Brontosaurus* males had saggy, folded neck skin.

Kailani sniffled as emotion set in even stronger. This was her thesis paper brought to life in the most incredible way possible. A lone *Stegosaurus* ambled past the *Brontosaurus* herd while a pair of *Mesadactylus* flew over. The scene looked like it was straight from a children's dinosaur book, but it was real. Kailani laughed to herself with joy as she cried uncontrollably. Then she took out her phone and shot dozens of photos and recorded videos.

Although the two different diplodocid species were making similar bellowing calls, the calls of the *Apatosaurus* were higher-pitched. Kailani realized that the difference in calls was probably due to the fact that *Apatosaurus* had a lighter skull than *Brontosaurus* because of larger skull openings in front of its eyes.

"Brilliant!" Kailani said as she wiped tears from her eyes and rubbed her nose with her sleeve. "Brilliant. Brilliant. Brilliant. The thunder lizard is back."

Kailani put her phone away, sighed with satisfaction, pulled a notebook out of a saddlebag, and furiously took notes for a long time. Despite wanting to stay even longer, she knew she should get moving, and she more closely examined the terrain beyond the apatosaurs. The land finally appeared level, and the vegetation along the river was thinner. She could now ride next to the river, but she would need to find a safe place to cross. Kailani nudged Horizon with her left foot, and she and the horses moved southeast. As she rode away, Kailani looked over her shoulder and wistfully stared at the *Brontosaurus* herd.

When Kailani reached the river, she saw that it had become very wide and placid. It was also clear and shallow and looked like an elongated lake. Little islands were scattered across this part of the river, and dense forest lined the river's southern shores. If everything was going according to plan, Lassen and Adalya should be somewhere in or near that forest.

Kailani looked down and saw fresh huge diplodocid footprints in silty soil. They were the biggest diplodocid tracks she had seen on the entire journey. She thought they were too big to be from an apatosaur or *Diplodocus*. The prints came from the plains to the east, went into the river, and seemed to be headed in the direction Kailani needed to go. As she looked more closely at the trajectory of the footprints and photographed them with her phone, she saw numerous torn-down trees and flattened vegetation way off in the distance on the other side of the river.

Kailani crossed the river with the horses and kept on the lookout for crocodylomorphs. She moved through an area filled with muddy splotches in the water where huge diplodocids had recently moved through. The water was no deeper than the horses' knees, which made threats easier to spot. The recent movement of huge dinosaurs had also scared away some aquatic predators.

CHAPTER 21: CHAOS ON THE RANGE

Lassen and Adalya emerged from the forest in early afternoon. Where they walked, there was no longer a gorge. In fact, the river just to the north of them looked like it widened into a lake on level ground.

"The temperature is much higher on the plains than it was in the shade of the forest," Adalya said.

"Yeah," Lassen added, wiping sweat from his forehead, "but some trees line the river. We can walk in their shade for a while."

"The fact that the river appears to have turned into a lake will complicate things," Adalya said.

"It will delay meeting up with Kailani," Lassen said, "unless she's brave enough or crazy enough to cross this wide spot in the river."

"Crossing here may actually be logical," Adalya said. "My terrain readouts showed that this wide spot in the river is fairly shallow."

After walking in the trees for about a half hour, Lassen and Adalya came upon an area of trampled vegetation where some major trees had been torn down.

"What happened here?" Lassen said. "A windstorm?"

"I do not think so," Adalya said as she pointed at huge footprints in front of them.

"A dinosaur herd plowed right through here," Lassen said. "I wonder if they crossed the river looking for new grazing grounds. Some of these trees just happened to be in the way. What do you think?"

"Could be that way," Adalya said. "I am not a paleontologist or biologist."

"I wish Miss Nakai were here," Lassen said. "She'd know all about this."

"Do you need a ride?" Kailani said as she emerged from behind a fallen log riding Horizon with Ember and Graphite trailing behind.

"Kailani!" Lassen shouted.

"Miss Nakai," Adalya said, more subdued.

"You made it," Lassen said. "Are you okay? Are the horses alright? What'd you see?"

"We're all fine," Kailani said, "and I saw quite a lot. Even *Brontosaurus*."

"Brontos," Lassen said. "Intriguing. What do you think went through here?"

As Kailani dismounted Horizon, she said, "A group of very large diplodocids. Their prints are larger than those made by apatosaurs, and they crossed the river to get here. Might have been after new grazing lands."

"That's just what I was thinking," Lassen said, smiling.

While holding their horses by the reins, the time travelers walked through part of an open fern prairie and then stepped into the shade of groves of ginkgoes, tree ferns, sequoias, and araucarian conifers that bordered the river. Lassen took off his hat, scratched his sweaty hair, and put his hat back on.

"There's something up ahead," Lassen said.

Then the bounty hunter and scientists saw a male *Supersaurus* rise from resting on its belly about 60 feet (18 meters) in front of them. The *Supersaurus* somewhat resembled *Barosaurus* and *Apatosaurus*, but it was longer and larger overall. It was also adorned with different colors. The *Supersaurus* was primarily light purple with green lateral stripes, bright green dermal spines, and a light yellow underbelly. The underside of its neck was bright metallic yellow, and its neck was full of saggy folds, like the other diplodocid species in the area.

As the dinosaur stood up, it stretched its neck. Then it swayed its finely-tapered whip-like tail. The sauropod weighed about 80,000 pounds (36,287 kilograms). As the *Supersaurus's* neck swayed toward the time travelers, they crouched down behind the enormous horizontal trunk of a recently fallen sequoia.

"Let's stay low," Lassen said.

The bounty hunter and scientists quickly tied their horses to strong branches sticking up from the log that concealed them. The horses were largely hidden from sight behind thick stands of cycads. Graphite and Ember whinnied with anxiety but were becoming more accustomed to seeing dinosaurs and were not inclined to instinctively gallop away. Two more *Supersaurus* came into view.

"What are they?" Lassen asked.

"*Supersaurus*," Kailani said with a beaming smile as she retrieved her phone from a vest pocket and began shooting photos and videos. "The biggest diplodocid of the Morrison."

Lassen watched intently as two *Supersaurus* ambled into the open from behind a grove of sequoias. They were females, a bit smaller than the male, and lacked bright yellow coloration under their necks. The male *Supersaurus* was approximately 137 feet (42 meters) long, making it about 47 feet (14 meters) longer than the famous and very long *Diplodocus*.

"If size estimates from 2026 are correct," Kailani said, "that *Supersaurus* is considerably longer than the blue whale, which only grows to be about 100 feet long."

"Son of a catamount," Durango said. "Even bigger than the biggest whale."

"Well, not exactly," Kailani said. "That dinosaur is longer, sure, but blue whales weigh much more, up to 400,000 pounds. By comparison, *Supersaurus* may only weigh about 70,000 to 90,000 pounds."

"Whoa," Lassen said. "How come the blue whale weighs so much more?"

"Living in the water limits the constraints of gravity for whales," Kailani said, "and makes it more feasible to be enormous with heavier body parts."

"Oh," Lassen remarked, "so if there's water to help carry whales along, they can have much denser bones and so forth?"

"Exactly," Kailani said. "Also, although enormous, sauropods have hollow bones and air sacs that keep them lighter than they would be otherwise and make a terrestrial lifestyle more feasible."

Suddenly, a brown-orange *Camptosaurus* emerged from a cluster of tree ferns and ran past the *Supersaurus* group. Claw mark gashes were on the bipedal herbivore's left thigh, which oozed blood.

"*Camptosaurus*," Kailani muttered as she recorded video with her phone. "It's been attacked."

The male *Supersaurus* stood upright to feed on high ginkgo tree leaves. His front legs dangled in the air, and his eyes scanned terrain from over 50 feet (15 meters) above the ground.

Lassen heard something behind him and to the left. The nearby vegetation rustled heavily. Suddenly, a male and female *Torvosaurus* emerged from nearby trees. The horses became especially agitated and started to whinny.

With a mouthful of leaves, the rearing male *Supersaurus* turned his head to see the *Torvosaurus* pair. The huge sauropod unleashed a call of agitation. Saliva-covered leaves tumbled down from his mouth. The two female *Supersaurus* bellowed. Then the rearing *Supersaurus* let his front legs fall to the ground. Lassen expected to feel the earth rumble, but he did not. The huge dinosaur's feet were too well-cushioned to shake the ground.

The male *Torvosaurus* was larger and more colorful than the female. It looked much like the *Torvosaurus* that had battled a group of *Allosaurus* the day before. It had a greenish head with hints of red and purple, a largely turquoise body with white lateral striping, and a chestnut brown chest with white speckling. The female *Torvosaurus* was light brown with dark brown lateral stripes and a plain beige underbelly. The male *Torvosaurus* was nearly 35 feet (11 meters) long and weighed over 4,000 pounds (1,800 kilograms).

The female *Torvosaurus* turned around and immediately ran away at the sight of a massive *Supersaurus* trio. This was the smart thing to do and a normal reaction. Facing down a healthy, alert full-sized sauropod was not logical for any Jurassic predator. The other *Torvosaurus* stood its ground.

"A suicidal male, I bet," Kailani said. "This must be the breeding season, and he's full of hormones, but his partner ran away, so what's the point in showing off?"

The male *Supersaurus* quickly pivoted around and lashed his long, supple whip-like tail toward the *Torvosaurus*. The sauropod wielded a 60-foot (18-meter) tail as if it were a bullwhip. The end of the *Supersaurus's* tail contained small bony rods in its core, and the entire tail included approximately 80 vertebrae. The narrow end of the dinosaur's tail rapidly arced through the air and made a whooshing sound like a whip being swung just before cracking. Lassen did not hear a crack, but the high speed of the tail made him wonder if it was possible for some sauropod dinosaurs to crack their tails like whips.

Dust and leaves rose up, and mammals scurried down into burrows where the *Supersaurus's* tail moved. The *Torvosaurus* snarled and snapped at the male *Supersaurus*. It looked up at a towering long-necked dinosaur with a deep blue afternoon sky behind it. The *Supersaurus* flexed his tail again, powering it with automobile-sized hip muscles. *WHOOSH!* The tail sliced through air just before connecting with the *Torvosaurus's* leg. A bizarre otherworldly shriek/growl/rumble emanated from the injured *Torvosaurus* as he fell to the ground.

In the process, the *Supersaurus* skinned his tail, and bits of blood oozed up from new abrasions. However, it took 30 seconds for the sauropod to feel the pain because of the enormous distance between the injury and the dinosaur's brain.

The hurt *Torvosaurus* barely managed to stand and then shuffled into the trees along the river with great effort. The theropod limped away in pain with blood trickling down his leg.

"Diplodocids definitely used their tails as defensive weapons," Kailani said as she finished recording video and put her phone back in her vest pocket. "Brilliant."

"Intriguing," Lassen added, "but we should keep a low profile and continue moving. Durango needs us, and Traxton could be setting a trap right now."

*   *   *

Durango and the Traxton Gang rode toward a clearing at the edge of the foothills. Massive piles of pink granite boulders bordered the clearing's eastern edges.

"Up ahead is the spot," Traxton said.

"What about those noises we heard a few minutes ago?" Branigan asked. "Malone and the women may have already run into trouble. Those sounded like gunshots."

"Boss," Avarette said, "if a deathnellosuarus got them, this whole ambush setup could be for nothing."

"I don't know what caused those sounds," Traxton said. "Maybe it was a volcano or distant thunder, but when I saw Lassen, he didn't appear to be armed. The women could be, but plasma pistols don't sound like Colt forty-fives."

Durango rode behind Traxton with his hands tied behind his back and his horse tied to Traxton's saddle. Traxton had taken over primary guard duties from Gantry. Durango squinted against hot afternoon sun as he rotated his head in all directions, hoping Lassen and the scientists would show up soon. He noticed the vegetation in the area was particularly lush and attracted many herbivorous dinosaurs.

A mixed herd of *Supersaurus* and *Diplodocus* fed at the base of the hills just above the Traxton Gang. Two small groups of *Camarasaurus* fed in stands of conifers on either side of the diplodocid herd. *Iguanodon*-like *Camptosaurus* fed on the fringes of the sauropod herds, and herds of bipedal *Dryosaurus* chewed on plants throughout the area. Little herds of *Nanosaurus* also hopped throughout the hills, eating plants and insects.

Durango was intrigued to see a small herd of *Mymoorapelta* feeding higher up in the hills. He had not seen those dinosaurs before. He also noticed several *Stegosaurus* feeding between the herds of other dinosaurs. *Mesadactylus* and *Harpactognathus* pterosaurs flapped their wings above the herds. The Jurassic menagerie reminded Durango of the first time he and his time-traveling companions spotted dinosaurs from up on a cliff two days earlier. Had it only been two days? It felt longer than that.

*　　*　　*

One and half miles (two and half kilometers) to the north, Lassen, Kailani, and Adalya rode their horses near trees at the very edge of the plains.

"Ah ha," Lassen said, pointing at dirt to the left. "Horse tracks. Traxton and Durango must have been through here this morning. Looks like their route goes south for at least a mile or so."

"How can you see that far?" Adalya asked.

"It's a gift," Lassen said. "Let's re-enter the forest just far enough to be concealed while keeping an eye on the plains and Traxton's tracks. And let's keep a brisk pace but be quiet."

Kailani and Adalya silently nodded their understanding. Many of the dead leaves and needles on the ground were wet from the previous day's rain, so it was easy to move quietly. The bounty hunter and scientists rode for a little over a mile (one and half kilometers) and stopped.

"The forest opens up just ahead," Lassen whispered as he pulled out his binoculars and scanned the terrain to the south. "There's a big clearing that goes south until it hits boulders and continues west uphill. Looks like a lot of dinosaurs up there."

"The dirt's darker here and up in the hills," Kailani said, peering through her binoculars. "There could be a lot of volcanic ash in this area, which makes the soil more productive for plants and helps attract more herbivorous dinosaurs."

As Lassen looked through binoculars, he said, "I see them."

"How many?" Adalya asked.

"I see Durango and all five gang members who made it to the Jurassic," Lassen said. "Traxton's in the lead, and some mean hombres are riding next to him. There's a gambler named Avarette, a criminal called Branigan, and Hobart Holt: a disgruntled former miner. Looks like the rustler Jed Gantry is in the back. Durango's horse is tied to Traxton's saddle. He's keeping him close."

"How far away are they?" Adalya asked.

"About 200 yards," Lassen said, "and they're in the open. "Looks like they're stopping to talk. They're exchanging weapons. They could be setting up an ambush."

"We cannot sneak up on horseback," Adalya whispered. "It is too open."

"You willing to crawl?" Lassen asked.

*   *   *

Several minutes later, Lassen, Kailani, and Adalya crept through wet ferns on their hands and knees. They moved through a wide fern meadow bordered by hills to the west and jumbles of boulders to the east. They carried bolas coiled around their shoulders. Lassen was surprised at just how much lived low to the ground. He saw snails, beetles, ants, termites, tiny *Ennebatrachus* and *Rhadinosteus* frogs, six-inch (15-centimeter) long *Iridotriton* salamanders, occasional crayfish, and two colorful *Uluops* turtles. The time travelers also spooked more than a few strange-looking tiny mammals. Lassen saw one of them, a *Fruitafossor*, vigorously dig into a termite mound as it licked up termites with satisfaction.

Suddenly, the time travelers turned to the left as they heard hissing, fern rustling, and the shrieking of a small mammal. Lassen lifted his head just high enough to see a *Hesperornithoides* pin a *Docodon* to the ground with a sickle-shaped claw on its foot as the tiny mammal flailed its limbs in a vain effort to return to its burrow. Bits of dirt and dried ferns drifted into the air as the *Hesperornithoides* tore into its prey.

Lassen winced, and he and the scientists continued crawling forward. They stopped when they detected they were at an effective bola-throwing distance from Traxton's men. Lassen winked. Kailani and Adalya nodded.

Meanwhile, Traxton had just finished explaining his plan to his men. They began to separate, and they all had their guns drawn. Gantry and Avarette held rifles. Holt and Branigan carried pistols. Traxton held a powerful rifle and moved straight south, leading Durango's horse.

Durango remained mounted with his hands tied behind his back. Avarette and Branigan rode southwest toward the hills. Gantry rode southeast toward nearby boulders. Traxton had ensured that Gantry would be isolated and in the most vulnerable position.

After riding off on his own, Gantry instantly got bored and started singing. Traxton did not bother to quiet him. He thought the singing would help draw Lassen into the trap.

"He was an old *Salad Bull*," Gantry sang. "Saaaallllllaaaddd Buulllllll. He could eat salad until he got full. He got no pardon when ate up the garden. That old Salad Bull. When the rancher tried to stop him, Salad Bull knocked over a pole and shoved the rancher in a hole. That darn rascally old Salad Bull! Moo! Moooo! Moooooooooo! Salad Bull got in a poker game with a foal—"

Gantry's song was cut off mid-sentence. He gasped while a set of bola stones knocked the rifle from his hands and discharged it. The rifle shot was loud and sudden. It went wild and sliced the leather connecting Durango's horse to Traxton's saddle. At the same time, a set of bola stones zoomed for Traxton's hands. Traxton already had his finger on his trigger, and he inadvertently fired a high shot as bola stones collided with his knuckles.

Traxton sneered with frustration as his rifle fell toward ferns. In the meantime, the bullet from his gun shot up above the nearby hills and tore through the leathery wings of three *Mesadactylus* flying in close formation. All three pterosaurs plummeted to the ground, landing near a mother *Stegosaurus* and her juvenile offspring. The *Stegosaurus* panicked and grunted in distress. They then moved downhill in alarm. The *Stegosaurus* panicked nearby *Mymoorapelta*, which ran downhill. The *Stegosaurus* and *Mymoorapelta* then frightened the *Supersaurus*, *Diplodocus*, and *Camptosaurus* herds farther downhill. The *Dryosaurus* and *Nanosaurus* also became distressed.

In the meantime, four nearby *Allosaurus fragilis* (two males and two females) raised their heads as their prey abruptly burst into action. These *Allosaurus* regularly resided in the forest at the edge of the fertile slope that hosted many herbivore herds. Late Jurassic afternoons in the Morrison Basin were often hot and lazy with little activity. The four *Allosaurus* liked to lay around and watch the herbivore herds for any unusual circumstances that could help them get food. The carnivorous dinosaurs cooed to each other and lightly hissed. Then they snorted and trotted downhill into the forest.

As the herbivorous dinosaurs on the slope to the west began to stampede, Traxton turned toward Durango and snarled, "Malone!"

As Traxton yelled, Durango ducked to avoid a punch to the face from the outlaw leader's fist. Then the bounty hunter spurred Yonder to the north away from Traxton. Traxton reached down for his holstered pistol.

"Mesquite's getting away!" Traxton shouted. "Get him! NOW!"

Durango rode as low on his mount as he could as bullets zipped past him. Controlling his horse was difficult as his hands were still tied behind his back. Branigan, Avarette, and Traxton furiously opened fire. The gunshots further alarmed the dinosaurs in the hills. Soon, a large group of galloping dinosaurs tore downhill toward the location of the Traxton Gang. *Dryosaurus* and *Nanosaurus* took the lead and lined the fringes of the mixed dinosaur herd. *Camptosaurus* ran on two legs in the middle of the action. *Supersaurus*, *Diplodocus*, *Camarasaurus*, *Stegosaurus*, and *Mymoorapelta* brought up the rear.

Gantry's horse bucked in a panic, and the cowboy-turned-outlaw fell to the ground. "Whillakers o' jillakers!" he proclaimed as he tumbled into ferns.

Gantry stood up in confusion, trying to orient himself to the sudden flurry of action. He saw a colossal dinosaur stampede quickly tear downhill. Traxton, Avarette, and Branigan pursued Durango on horseback. Durango rode low and steered Yonder in a dizzying, inconsistent zig-zag pattern. Then Gantry saw three people suddenly appear from under the ferns. As Gantry's horse galloped by, Lassen leapt, landed on its saddle, and held a hand out.

"Get on, Kailani!" Lassen shouted. Kailani hesitated and glanced at Adalya.

"Miss Nakai, get on!" Adalya said. "I can take care of myself!"

Kailani quickly grabbed onto Lassen's hand, and he pulled her up behind him. The paleontologist held her arms around Lassen's waist as their new mount rushed north. She was thrilled and frightened. Lassen was focused and in his element.

Lassen and Kailani followed the Traxton Gang members who chased Durango. Adalya sprinted through the ferns toward the boulders to the east. As she ran, she turned her head to the south and saw mixed herds of dinosaurs moving toward her at a rapid pace with a cloud of dust behind them.

"Hey!" Gantry shouted as he turned around to see a torrent of dinosaurs getting closer. "Wait for me!"

Gantry sprinted north. As he rushed past Adalya, he turned his head in interest and muttered, "Who is her?"

The dinosaur stampede approached Gantry and Adalya as it began to veer northwest to avoid the high boulders to the east.

Durango breathed hard as gunshots tore holes in his hat. His body coursed with adrenaline. Yonder suddenly stopped and reared in alarm as four *Allosaurus* sprang out of nearby forest to the west. Durango contorted wildly to stay in his saddle.

The outlaws' horses behind Yonder and Durango reared and turned around to flee the *Allosaurus*. However, the horses faced a dinosaur stampede moving in their direction, which paralyzed them with indecision. The outlaws stopped shooting, so they could focus more on controlling their horses. The horse Lassen rode—which used to belong to Gantry—panicked and reared as it saw the frightened horses and an *Allosaurus* group not far ahead.

"Easy, easy," Lassen said.

Traxton noticed Lassen and Kailani on Gantry's horse. Then he quickly turned his head, wondering where Adalya was. He immediately fired his pistol at Lassen. It ripped a hole in Lassen's hat brim and launched the bounty hunter's hat off his head. As the hat sailed away, Kailani leaned left and barely caught it with her left hand. She placed the hat on Lassen's head, kissed him on the cheek, and said, "Keep your head on, and stay sharp!" Lassen grinned.

In the meantime, Adalya somersaulted out of the path of a trio of running *Camptosaurus*. She then clambered onto pinkish potassium feldspar boulders as *Camptosaurus*, *Dryosaurus*, and *Nanosaurus* swept past with a lone *Stegosaurus* fast-walking just behind them.

Lassen and Kailani ducked to avoid a gunshot. Then Kailani glanced back. She saw a fantastic menagerie of dinosaurs gallop toward them. She also saw Gantry looking panic-stricken as he tried to dodge out of the way of *Dryosaurus* and *Nanosaurus*. The stampede had reached him. Then it reached Lassen and Kailani.

The commotion of an enormous dinosaur stampede was enough to motivate Lassen and Kailani's horse to move forward to the north, despite the incoming *Allosaurus*. Traxton, Avarette, Branigan, and Holt continued to fire at Lassen, but their horses were going berserk as they ran with and through dinosaurs. Their shots were poorly aimed and only served to further frighten the dinosaurs. Traxton finally holstered his pistol as a *Dryosaurus* brushed past his left leg. He then focused all his efforts on controlling his horse and retreating out of the chaos.

The time travelers were swept up in an epic dinosaur stampede. Grunts, booms, hisses, growls, squeals, shrieks, and all manner of dinosaur noise filled the air along with the sound of pounding reptilian feet and ferns being smashed. To the southeast, Adalya jumped from boulder to boulder as she moved north, attempting to keep up and monitor what was happening.

With his hands still tied behind his back, Durango tightly pressed his legs against Yonder and shifted in strange, contorted ways in an effort to stay mounted and avoid danger. Lassen veered his horse left to avoid being punctured by *Stegosaurus* thagomizers. Then he and Kailani moved right to evade a dangerously flailing whip-like *Supersaurus* tail. Little *Nanosaurus* scurried right past the hooves of Lassen and Kailani's horse. The bounty hunter and paleontologist could also smell the breath of *Camptosaurus* that ran on two legs right next to them. It was not pleasant.

"Lassen!" Kailani shouted, "is this like being in a cattle stampede in the Wild West?!"

"No!" Lassen shouted back over the noise of the stampede. "More like a bison stampede!"

As the time travelers tried to survive the stampede, the four *Allosaurus* entered the melee. Stampedes tended to result in injured or disoriented dinosaurs, which meant easier food for carnivores. The humans mixed with the dinosaurs were a curiosity to the *Allosaurus* but also a cause of confusion and annoyance. From atop a boulder to the east, Adalya shielded her eyes from the sun as she saw the *Allosaurus* join the fray.

In the middle of the action, Avarette blinked hard to try to get dust out of his eyes. Upon opening his eyes, he saw a *Diplodocus* plod by to his right. There was also something huge and purple to his left. Suddenly, Avarette felt like he had been bludgeoned in the stomach as a flexible *Supersaurus* tail slammed against his torso and batted him off his horse. Avarette sailed through the air with a shocked, open-mouthed expression. He had closed his eyes in pain when the *Supersaurus* tail hit his stomach. He then held out his hands to cushion his impact on what he thought would be ferns.

When Avarette opened his eyes, he saw an *Allosaurus's* gaping open jaws. There were rows of curved, serrated teeth with sharp points. Teeth were not uniform in length because *Allosaurus* and other theropods of the Mesozoic regularly shed or broke their teeth and regrew new ones. A few short, white newly grown teeth were mixed with much longer, more yellowed older teeth. The *Allosaurus's* breath smelled repulsive. Its ruby red head crests brightly reflected sunlight. Via a snag-and-chomp maneuver, Avarette's outlaw career permanently ended with a crunch.

Branigan wove his horse around the legs of a giant *Supersaurus*. He frantically scanned his surroundings and did not see Traxton, but he saw Traxton's horse running toward the forest without its saddle. He also saw Avarette's horse running east onto the plains. Branigan saw no sign of Avarette until a bloodied, torn joker playing card flew through the air.

Red-brown leathery fuzz suddenly obscured Branigan's vision as his face slammed into the path of a *Harpactognathus* pterosaur. The pterosaur whapped hard into his face with its wings wrapping around his head. Branigan violently grabbed the pterosaur and struggled to pull it off his face as the frightened animal clawed its feet into his shirt collar. With a mighty tug that ripped part of his shirt collar, Branigan removed the *Harpactognathus*. The pterosaur flew skyward, out of harm's way. Once the pterosaur no longer obscured Branigan's vision, the first thing he saw was an *Allosaurus* waiting for him. Branigan drew his pistol and fired repeatedly.

Lassen and Kailani turned their heads around as they heard a quick succession of gunshots and yells of fury. Lassen thought he heard Branigan, but he was not sure. As a shadow descended over Lassen and Kailani, Lassen lowered his head and shouted, "Duck!"

A *Supersaurus* swept directly over Lassen and Kailani as their horse kept moving forward. With his head low on his horse's neck, Lassen got a close look at the *Supersaurus* as it moved over. Its light yellow underbelly skin was bumpy, rough, and granular. As the *Supersaurus* finished sweeping over, Lassen maneuvered his horse left to avoid the sauropod's dangerously twirling tail. Then Lassen and Kailani leaned right to avoid a startled *Archaeopteryx* that had just been flushed out of ferns.

Gantry tumbled through a medley of dinosaurs. He somersaulted away from *Stegosaurus*, rolled away from *Mymoorapelta*, spooked up colorful *Hesperornithoides*, and ran from *Camptosaurus* when he could manage standing. Finally, the stampede passed. Breathing hard, Gantry watched as the dinosaurs dispersed and spread out onto the plains to the east.

Lassen and Kailani were out of the stampede as quickly as they had been swept into it. The swarm of dinosaurs had moved around and past them. The chaos probably did not last more than a minute, but it had felt much longer.

Still on a horse with Kailani, Lassen glanced east to see the stampeding dinosaurs slow and separate. He also saw Adalya standing tall on a boulder. He waved at her, and she waved back before jumping down and jogging toward Lassen and Kailani.

The bounty hunter and paleontologist got off their horse and surveyed their surroundings. Lassen looked north to see Durango still riding Yonder who had finally slowed to a walk. Lassen then looked south and saw four *Allosaurus* about 100 yards (91 meters) away. Three *Allosaurus* fed with their heads down. Lassen winced as he saw an *Allosaurus* lift its head in an effort to swallow a horse leg.

Then Lassen saw a female *Allosaurus* intently peer into the ferns and slowly walk forward. Suddenly, Holt leapt up from the ferns right in front of the carnivore and broke into a run. The pursuit was brief. Soon, Lassen knew for sure that he would never have to face Holt again. In his final moments, Holt was grateful to at least be in the open, immersed in wide open spaces.

"There goes one outlaw—and at least one horse," Kailani seriously said while looking through binoculars. "Do you think there are any survivors?"

"I'm not sure," Lassen said.

"There was a lot going on," Kailani added, "and we were close to the forest some of the time. Some outlaws might have survived and are just out of sight."

Lassen turned to the north and said, "Durango's up ahead. We should try to catch up with him after Miss Nell rejoins us."

Soon, Adalya caught up with Lassen and Kailani.

"You okay?" Lassen asked.

"I am functioning within established parameters," Adalya said.

"Good," Lassen said. "What'd you see? Did Traxton or any of his men survive?"

"There was a lot of dust in the way," Adalya said. "I did not always know what was transpiring. The man with the mustache got consumed by an *Allosaurus*, and his horse fled into the forest."

"Arvo Avarette," Lassen muttered. "One gamble too many. Anybody else get taken out of commission?"

"Yes," Adalya said. "The one in the gray jacket was successfully stalked while I made my way over here."

"Yeah," Lassen seriously said. "I saw that. Hobart Holt is no more. What about Traxton, Branigan, and Gantry?"

"I briefly saw Brent Cordon—Traxton in your time—in the commotion," Adalya said, "but I do not know what happened to him. Which one is Gantry, and which one is Branigan?"

"Branigan is the big fellow with the beard," Lassen said. "Gantry is skinny and nervous and wears a long coat."

"I saw Gantry on foot," Adalya said. "He was talking to himself and did not seem very capable."

"Don't be too quick to judge," Lassen said. "Gantry can be slippery and get out of most any situation."

"Branigan was there on a horse," Adalya said, "and he was near an *Allosaurus*, but a sauropod obstructed my view, and after it ran past, I did not see him anymore."

"If anybody survived," Kailani said, "they must be crawling on the ground, or they made it into the forest."

"Right," Lassen said. "I can't see anybody from here."

The closest *Allosaurus* lifted its head and sniffed the air toward Lassen, Kailani, and Adalya.

"The wind shifted, and that *Allosaurus* just smelled us," Kailani said. "We need to go."

"Yep," Lassen said as he turned around and walked to the north, leading Gantry's horse by the reins. The time travelers walked to a clearing in the forest to the northwest where they had tied Horizon, Graphite, and Ember. Adalya mounted Horizon. Kailani slipped onto Ember. Lassen once again got on Graphite and tied Gantry's horse to Graphite's saddle. The bounty hunter and scientists then rode north to reunite with Durango.

*　　　*　　　*

"You old son of a catamount!" Durango said as Lassen, Kailani, and Adalya rode up to him. "It's about time you showed up! What happened to you?!"

"More like what happened to *you*?" Lassen said as he pulled out his knife and cut the rawhide binding Durango's wrists. "No offense, but you look terrible. Did Traxton do that?"

"Yeah," Durango said while rubbing his fingers over sore wrists and wincing. "He mentioned something about us stopping his Denver Mint robbery and punched me square in the eye."

"Looked like he was setting up an ambush for us," Lassen said.

"Yep," Durango replied, "but he was too slow. Based on some quick look-sees to the south, I'm guessing at least one or two of the Traxton Gang got chawed by the Jurassic."

"That's a fact," Lassen said. "Holt and Avarette are out. You see any sign of Branigan, Gantry, or Traxton?"

"No," Durango said, "I was ahead of everybody and didn't look back until I was far away."

"I suppose they were trampled or escaped if they were not eaten," Adalya said.

"Possible," Lassen said, "but I'd like to go back there and check it out myself. The tracks could tell us what happened."

"They could," Durango said, "but if one of the *Allosaurus* eats you, that won't matter much."

"We are already far to the north," Adalya said, "and it could be too dangerous to return. Is it safer to return to the stampede site at great *certain* risk for the possibility of *maybe* confirming the survival or death of Traxton and his men—*or* should we immediately proceed with our original mission to find the location signaler?"

"That's a good question," Durango said.

"What if we go back," Lassen said, "one of us gets killed by an *Allosaurus*, and we confirm nothing?"

"Or what if all of us get killed," Durango said. "Forget it. I'm not goin' back."

"Still," Lassen said, "if the outlaws are alive, they could ambush us."

"And if they are, we could still get killed by dinosaurs," Kailani said.

"How about this?" Adalya said. "We focus on finding the location signaler as quickly as possible. If Professor Sedora finds us, the outlaw threat will be greatly minimized as we will be able to use the technology in the time machine to quickly track anybody down—assuming it gets repaired. In the meantime, we can take turns with guard duty at night and proceed with caution like we did before."

"Sounds like a plan," Lassen said. "Let's veer northwest beyond that next grove of trees and start riding into the hills. How much farther until we descend into the low valley with the volcano and the signaler?"

"Approximately 32 kilometers or 20 miles," Adalya replied. "We should plan on camping in the mountains."

Chapter 22: Descent to Desolation

After over a day of trekking through the mountains, Lassen, Kailani, Adalya, and Durango finally arrived at a rim overlooking a low valley. When viewed from below, they stood sky-lined against the blue of a sunny morning with the sun at their backs. They looked like an iconic group of ragtag heroes.

Lassen's pants and vest were torn. Everybody was dusty with scuffed clothes. Durango's black eye looked slightly better, but his face had seen better days. Kailani and Adalya's lustrous dark hair billowed in a slight breeze. Lassen squinted with serious concern as he readjusted the brim of his tan hat. Kailani shielded her eyes from the sun with one hand while she looked down at the valley. Adalya stood confidently with her hands on her hips. Durango yawned as he stretched his arms over his head.

Adalya believed her location signaler could be found on the rim of a volcano across the valley. At least it was there a few days ago according to her database orientation module. Thanks to Gantry's horse crushing her module during a shoreline ambush, Adalya had to lead the search for the location signaler based on memories of holographic terrain images. If the time travelers found the location signaler, Sedora could find both where and when they were. Of course, that was if the professor managed to make it to the Jurassic.

The last day and a half was uneventful. By now, the time travelers could breathe somewhat easier as their bodies had acclimated to the late Jurassic's higher carbon dioxide levels. Dinosaur sightings were occasional, and pterosaurs were a constant presence overhead.

Kailani was excited to find several small and mid-sized dinosaur species in the mountains that were completely unknown to her. She believed this was because there was a strong preservation bias in the floodplain environment. The plains were more conducive to producing fossils because they had a lot of sediment and water action that enabled quick burial and fossilization of animal remains. In contrast, in the mountains, there was not as much water or sediment. Many of the dinosaur remains in mountains were also likely to be crushed by erosion of rocks, whereas others would also simply decompose in place and never be covered with a fossilization agent, like dirt, mud, or sand.

Despite seeing new dinosaur species, Kailani noticed that the ecological diversity and animal density were lower in the mountains than where forest and foothills met floodplains. Before entering the mountains, the time travelers were in a special environmental transition zone—an ecotone—with varied plant species, high ecological diversity, and many habitats, including plains, foothills, wetlands, and forests.

Below the time travelers, a valley of desolation unfolded to the west. To Lassen, it looked like Death Valley, California but with lots of dried-up dead plants and not quite as harsh. Lassen thought back to when he tracked Dortero Guerrero across California's Mojave Desert.

A dense concentration of sand dunes lined the southern edges of the valley. Salt flats stretched across its western reaches. A large volcano and lava beds stood at the far western end of the valley. Light gray gases billowed from the volcano, drifting high above intricate webs of cracked hardpan soil crust that coated most of the valley floor. The hardpan soil indicated the recent presence of more water.

A few parts of the valley sparkled with water and greenery, but it was nothing like the floodplains to the east. A dried-up riverbed bisected the valley and terminated at a muddy area with small amounts of shallow water. The muddy area transitioned into salt flats.

The valley below was normally somewhat dry part of the year, but it was now especially dry because of geologic forces. Crustal uplift and volcano formation had gradually obstructed all access to or from the valley, except for a narrow canyon cut by a river. When water levels were low or moderate, dinosaurs could stroll along the river's banks and enter or exit the valley, but a massive landslide had recently dammed the river, creating a boulder-lined lake just outside the valley, which made entering and leaving difficult and deprived the valley of water. Instead of water overflowing into the valley, much of it instead soaked into the mountains or drained into side channels. Lassen furrowed his brow as he glanced at the lake to the north and began to piece together the valley's hydrological situation. Only a trickle of water made it into the valley, and by this time of year, it evaporated before it reached the muddy lands and salt flats at the foot of the volcano.

Lassen pulled his binoculars out of Horizon's saddlebags. He scanned the valley and said, "There's a sauropod herd down there. Look like diplodocids. What kind do you think they are, Miss Nakai?"

"I see them," Kailani said while looking through her binoculars. "They're *Barosaurus*. Like the dead one we saw up close in the forest. They look malnourished. Also seems like they're digging for water."

Kailani readjusted her binoculars and saw several *Barosaurus* gash their thumb claws into the ground of a dry riverbed, causing muddy water to ooze up. The *Barosaurus* were diplodocids—like *Apatosaurus*, *Brontosaurus*, *Diplodocus*, and *Supersaurus*—and their build largely resembled those species. However, *Barosaurus* necks were particularly long relative to the rest of their bodies.

"Must be a low water table," Lassen said.

Far from its peers digging for water, a lone *Barosaurus* stood on its hind legs and struggled to tear off meager dried needles from a tall dying araucarian conifer. Its thumb spikes scraped through bark as it steadied itself against a weak tree trunk. Its mouth reached high from a neck that was approximately 30 feet (nine meters) long.

This was the time travelers' first opportunity to see *Barosaurus* alive. The *Barosaurus* stood out against the beige sandy background with their rusty red skin, green underbellies, black lateral stripes, and black dermal spines on the tops of their backs.

Lassen saw giant sauropod skeletons protruding out of sand on the valley floor. Huge dinosaur bones were bleached white by the sun. Small dust devils drifted across the valley, which was littered with scattered boulders. Jagged black basalt lava flows stood near the volcano, and Lassen guessed they were from magma that had very recently cooled, turned black, and become a slop of sharp rock jumbles. Piles of shining black obsidian also rested at the foot of the volcano. The geologic features reminded Lassen of volcanic terrain he had traversed in the Medicine Lake Highlands when he tracked Red Duvarney in northeastern California near Mount Shasta.

Kailani lowered her binoculars and used her phone to take photos of the landscape below. Lassen used his binoculars to examine the rim of the volcano at the western end of the valley. Its top slopes were barren and covered in cinders and black ash. However, light brown dried ferns covered most of the volcano's slopes. In the area, ferns were often the first plant species to sprout after landscape-devastating events. The top of the volcano contained the remnants of tall, old, beaten, and partially charred araucarian conifers. *Harpactognathus* pterosaurs circled over the trees. Lassen was surprised at just how many *Harpactognathus* were in the valley.

"That's no Garden of Eden," Durango said as he stared down at the valley.

"No," Lassen replied. "More like some kind of hell."

"I reckon it's gonna be a devil gettin' down there," Durango added, "and then up there." Durango pointed at the volcano.

"I estimate that within several hours," Adalya said, "we should be able to descend these steep slopes with only moderate risk of falling."

"That's real comforting," Durango said.

"You sure we're positioned above the best location for climbing down?" Lassen asked.

"Affirmative," Adalya said. "This area provides a suitable amount of outcrops for gaining traction and tying rope. Plus, the unique folded geology makes the slopes below us not quite sheer cliffs."

"Great . . ." Durango muttered. "Anybody here have experience rock climbing?"

"I don't," Kailani said, "but people in my time do it for recreation."

"What?" Durango said. "Why? They dangle off cliffs for fun—when they don't have to?"

"Well, yeah," Kailani said. "I've never tried it, but some of my friends do it."

"Could be exciting," Lassen said, "in a time without bounty hunting in Wyoming."

"Yeah, maybe," Durango said.

The bounty hunters and scientists gathered key supplies and loaded full canteens and sauropod eggshells filled with water. They also got out all the rope they had, tied pieces together, and figured out how to make the best use out of it. Luckily, there was a lasso on Gantry's horse, which made up for the lasso lost when Lassen and Kailani swung across a gorge to escape a pair of *Mymoorapelta*.

"Be sure to be cautious with the eggs," Kailani said.

"Yeah," Lassen replied. "We're going to need that water. We'll have to leave the horses behind."

"Dangerous for the equines," Adalya said, "but if Professor Sedora finds us, we may be able to bring the horses back to the future."

Soon, the time travelers had taken the saddles off their horses and draped full saddlebags over their shoulders. It was now time for Lassen and Durango to say goodbye to their trusty mounts.

"I'll see you again, pal," Lassen said as he patted Horizon on the neck.

"Yonder," Durango said. "Buddy, I know you don't want to leave me, but you've gotta go." Yonder neighed and licked Durango's cheek.

"Aww gee," Durango said while wiping horse saliva off his facial stubble. "Uh, thanks for that, but you can't come with us this time. I'll be back for you."

"Horizon," Lassen said, "keep an eye on these horses. And stick to the ridgetops where you can spot predators. It's time."

Lassen pointed to the east and nodded. Horizon whinnied in acknowledgement, turned around, and trotted east. He vigorously neighed, and the other horses followed him.

For an excruciating three and a half hours, the time travelers descended the cliffs, using all the rope they could spare. There were some close calls. In one instance, Lassen was saved by a rope that stretched tight. The descent into desolation was sweaty, dirty, and tiring. Finally, by mid-afternoon, the time travelers reached the valley floor.

The bounty hunters and scientists walked west in the hot sun. They journeyed over former wetland bottoms covered in a scattering of fish, turtle, and *Docodon* skeletons along with little petrified frogs that lay on their backs with their legs stiffly sticking out. Because the *Docodons* were mammals, their skeletons clearly stood out and had distinctive skulls and jaw bones.

The time travelers occasionally stepped on desiccated, sun-bleached crayfish and clam shrimp exoskeletons as well as the empty shells of snails and freshwater clams. Husks of dry lungfish carcasses also dotted the terrain. Animal remnants smashed into sand with a crunch as they were stepped on. A slight breeze swept dusty sand up from the time travelers' feet with each step.

Every once in a while, Kailani picked up a dried animal or piece of animal and closely examined it. She also quickly wrote in her notebook as she walked and used her phone to take many quick photos of animal remains.

Lassen spotted a few pterosaur skeletons, but they were rare. He was struck by their unusual appearance. Pterosaurs could look large and imposing with their wings covering a fair amount of surface area. For example, millions of years later, by the late Cretaceous, a pterosaur called *Quetzalcoatlus* would have a wingspan of approximately 30 feet (nine meters) and stand as tall as a giraffe.

However, despite pterosaurs' sometimes intimidating appearance, their skeletons were delicate with fragile, thin hollow bones. This made them unlikely to fossilize and be discovered by paleontologists millions of years later.

Pterosaurs also had tiny fingers ending in claws that looked like little hands attached to the fronts of their wings. These fingers were short, flexible, and evolved for grasping.

"Intriguing," Lassen said as Kailani picked up a pterosaur wing bone with tatters of dried skin dangling from it. "Most of that wing bone is just a super long finger. Isn't it?"

"Yes, it is," Kailani said. "The main support bone for each of a pterosaur's wing membranes is a very long finger that happens to be the last digit of what looks like a small hand. For pterosaurs, one finger on each hand evolved to be disproportionately long, enabling the development of wings."

"Very intriguing," Lassen said. "Birds' wings aren't structured the same way."

"That's right," Kailani said as she handed the wing bone to Lassen. "They're not. Flight evolved in multiple ways in different vertebrate species. Birds evolved finger bones that were fused and reduced to form wings. Bats evolved multiple elongated finger bones to form wings. And, as you can see here, pterosaurs radically elongated one finger bone."

"Huh," Lassen said. "So, it's not like flight evolved in one species and then was shared by all flying descendants."

"Evolution doesn't always work that way," Kailani said. "The variations in skeletal morphology that enable flight in pterosaurs, birds, and bats are an example of convergent evolution, which occurs when similar features evolve for the same purpose in species that are not closely related."

"Interesting," Lassen said. "That helps explain why whales look like fish, even though they're mammals. Both whales and fish needed to adapt to the water."

"Exactly," Kailani said, smiling. "Modern dolphins and Mesozoic marine reptiles called ichthyosaurs also have similar body structures but are very different animals, and that's another example of convergent evolution."

Lassen glanced up to see a *Mesadactylus* fly over with its red-green wing membranes picking up air currents. Durango heavily yawned and was not listening to Lassen and Kailani. Adalya focused on navigating and walked in the lead.

"We should find the location signaler soon," Adalya said, "but I estimate we will not reach it today. Therefore, we should seek shade and travel at night and tomorrow morning when it is cooler."

"You're right," Lassen said, "I guess we've been a little impatient. It's just so nice to finally be able to walk after climbing down those cliffs." Lassen gestured with a thumb back toward towering cliffs to the east.

"There aren't many trees here," Durango said.

"No," Kailani added. "I think we'll have to make our own shade. Let's head toward that sauropod rib cage to the south."

Soon, the bounty hunters and scientists reached an old *Barosaurus* rib cage that stuck approximately 10 feet (three meters) up from the ground. Kailani took a photo of it as they approached. Its bottom portions were anchored in sand, and its spinal column was on top. Dried cartilage still held some of the bones together. The sauropod had died while lying on its belly. A scattering of bones lay under the rib cage, disturbed from their original positions by weathering, flooding, and scavengers. The time travelers propped scapulae and leg bones over portions of the rib cage to create shade. Lassen also draped his damaged vest over the ribs.

The bounty hunters and scientists settled into the shade, which grew as the sun gradually dipped lower to the west. The sand was soft and comfortable. Adalya sat cross-legged. Durango laid on his back, using his saddlebags as a pillow. Lassen and Kailani stood on their knees and closely examined surrounding rib cage bones.

"This sand is kind of nice," Durango said. "Some people might think it's rough and coarse and irritating, but I like it."

"Yeah," Lassen said, "but it can get everywhere."

Lassen picked up his binoculars and positioned them between rib bones to scan a distant malnourished *Barosaurus* herd to the north. The mighty dinosaurs' ribs protruded through saggy, folded skin, and their vertebrae were especially prominent. "There's not much to eat," Lassen said, "but those dinosaurs are scraping off old conifer needles and seem to be swallowing them whole."

"That's the same way *Diplodocus* and *Brachiosaurus* feed," Kailani said.

"Yeah, I don't think they chew their food," Lassen added.

Durango yawned as he sensed the conversation would once more turn overly scientific. In some ways, he missed the small talk of the Traxton Gang. They were not very nice hombres, but at least he could usually understand what they were saying—and he learned of a showgirl performance in Reno, Nevada he planned to see if he ever made it back to his own time. Durango pulled his hat brim over his eyes, ready for a nap.

A lone *Archaeopteryx* suddenly perched on the rib cage sheltering the time travelers and then erupted in flight when it noticed the humans. Durango lifted his hat and looked up upon hearing wing flaps. "Quiet down," Durango muttered.

"You know," Lassen said as he examined the bones around him, "this skeleton looks familiar. These dinosaurs are distant in time from humans, but their skeletons actually aren't that different from ours."

"That's true," Kailani said.

"What are you talking about?" Durango asked as he lifted his hat up from his eyes, abandoning his efforts to nap. "These long-necks look *way* different than people."

Kailani said, "We're more related to dinosaurs than you might think. Humans, the dinosaurs, and any other animals with a backbone and four sturdy limbs—as opposed to fins—are tetrapods. Mammals, reptiles, birds, and amphibians are tetrapods, and tetrapods evolved from fish. If you think back far enough, humans and dinosaurs are basically modified fish. All tetrapods essentially have the same bones, which are homologous to those found in the ancestral species from which they evolved. However, over time, for different species, some bones changed size or shape, fused together, gradually disappeared, or became much less prominent."

"Intriguing," Lassen said. "This ties into the discussion we had earlier today about flight and convergent evolution.

"Whaaaat?" Durango said as he narrowed his mouth and moved his face to the right with a quizzical expression. "Also, I thought only plants had limbs."

"In addition to describing plant branch components," Kailani said, "'limbs' is a scientific term for arms or legs."

Adalya quietly listened off to the side as she tried to rest. Lassen used both hands to clear sand away from a huge bone and lifted it up before saying, "Durango, this is one of the front leg bones of this sauropod. It's a humerus, and it's homologous to a bone found in humans."

"Doesn't look very funny to me," Durango said, "and how is it homologuz?"

"No, 'humerus' is the technical term for it," Lassen said. "An upper arm bone in humans is also called the humerus." Lassen nodded with his chin at the upper part of his left arm. "This sauropod and I basically have the same bones, but in this dinosaur, the humerus is much larger. This dinosaur humerus is homologous to the human humerus because it has a similar shape and the same location in the skeleton."

Durango looked up and touched a *Barosaurus* rib with a thumb and forefinger as he said, "And people and dinosaurs both have ribs. This rib bone could be homologous to one of my rib bones?"

"Exactly," Lassen said. "And dinosaurs and people both have craniums, scapulae, vertebrae, clavicles, and so on."

"All true," Kailani added. "In fact, in my time, some medical professors of human anatomy are also paleontologists. Once you know human skeletons, you can apply your expertise to various tetrapod species. The similarities between tetrapods can be striking." She brushed sand off bones in front of her. "Here's another good example. These are toe bones of this animal, and if you count the tips of them and the thumb spike, you can see that this dinosaur has five digits on one of its front feet."

"It has math on its hands?" Durango asked.

"No," Lassen said, "in this case, 'digits' is just a scientific term for fingers and toes."

Durango nodded with uncertainty.

"We also have five digits," Kailani said as she flexed her right hand's fingers. "Interestingly, some tetrapods used to have more than five digits—some even had as many as seven or eight—but after the Devonian Period, tetrapods only had five digits and continued to only have five or fewer digits. Even animals with flippers—like seals and whales—have skeletons with five or fewer digits inside their flippers."

"Wait," Lassen said, "when was the Devonian Period?"

"It lasted from about 420 to 360 million years before modern times," Kailani said. "It spanned about 60 million years and was about 200 million years before when we are now."

"What do you think limited the number of tetrapod toes and fingers after the Devonian Period?" Lassen asked.

"A mass extinction event," Kailani said. "By the twenty-first century, we had become aware of at least five major prehistoric mass extinction events. A mass extinction happens when levels of global extinction are substantially higher than normal in a geologically short period of time. During mass extinctions, huge numbers of species completely die off. Presumably, the only tetrapod species that survived the Devonian extinction had genetics that limited them to five or fewer digits."

"Fascinating." Lassen said. "And their offspring would then inherit that limitation. How does the fossil record reveal mass extinctions happened?"

"They can be revealed in rock layers," Kailani said, "that sometimes show abrupt absences of certain species' fossils. For example, in modern times, there's a boundary of rock that separates the Cretaceous Period from the subsequent Paleogene Period. Dinosaur fossils are found below and right up to this boundary, but no non-avian dinosaur fossils have ever been found above this boundary. In a geological time context, it's as if dinosaurs suddenly disappeared."

Lassen asked more about the Devonian Period and what caused the Devonian mass extinction. Kailani mentioned that the Devonian was called the "Age of Fishes" but also featured the evolution of the first terrestrial tetrapods, including *Tiktaalik*, which was basically a fish that could walk on land and do pushups.

Even Lassen had trouble understanding Kailani's explanation of the Devonian extinction, which was complicated and not entirely worked out by early twenty-first century scientists. Kailani covered a variety of potential contributing factors, including the origin of Earth's first forests, ocean chemistry changes, marine oxygen deficiencies, major volcanic eruptions, and dramatic temperature decreases and glaciation possibly caused by new forests and algal blooms locking up carbon dioxide.

After Kailani's discussion of the Devonian Period, Durango yawned and stretched his arms while saying, "I wonder what did this fellow in." Durango moved his hands over a series of tooth marks on the *Barosaurus* rib cage next to him. "Something with big teeth settled this critter's hash." Most of the ribs were heavily scarred with a multitude of ragged tooth marks.

"Could be *Allosaurus*," Lassen said. "They've proven to be more common than we'd like. Still, based on the size of this skeleton, I'm guessing theropods scavenged the carcass after the dinosaur died. A theropod would have to be much bigger than a *Torvosaurus* or *Allosaurus* to take down an adult sauropod."

"Whoa, wait," Durango said, turning to Kailani. "Remember when you were talking about all the big carnivore dinosaurs for this time? Wasn't there one bigger than *Torvosaurus*?"

Kailani sighed with discomfort. "Yes," she said. "*Allosaurus anax*. Think of the other *Allosaurus* we saw but bigger. *Allosaurus anax* could be about 40 feet long and up to 10,000 pounds."

Durango whistled, impressed.

"That species could be a problem," Adalya said. "Hopefully, we will not encounter one."

"Aside from those *Barosaurus*," Lassen said, "there's no other large prey here. I doubt any *Allosaurus anax* are around."

The time travelers spent the rest of the day under their *Barosaurus* rib cage shelter. They took turns keeping watch as they had done throughout their Jurassic journey. The day was hot and uneventful. After the sun went down, and the temperature cooled, the time travelers walked west under the glow of the moon and a sparkling spatter of unfamiliar stars.

CHAPTER 23: ASCENT TO INFERNO

Shortly after sunrise, the bounty hunters and scientists neared the valley's muddy remnant wetlands. They were now only about seven miles (11 kilometers) from the foot of the volcano. The area was noisy with a cacophony of squawking pterosaurs. To the north, scores of pterosaurs ran about and hopped on the ground with ease as they moved over mud in search of prey. Lassen was surprised at just how agile the flying reptiles were on the ground as they moved with partially folded wings. *Harpactognathus* and *Mesadactylus* regularly dipped their beaks down into mud to pull out small aquatic wildlife.

With the wetlands drying up, animals—like fish, frogs, crayfish, snails, and salamanders—were stranded, especially concentrated, and easy pickings. For this reason, many pterosaurs had chosen to nest in the valley.

The time travelers trod hardpan ground fractured with intricate networks of cracked, dried mud. Random jumbles of boulders dotted the landscape.

"This area looks like it's starting to get its own extinction," Durango said. "Miss Nakai, if I recollect rightly, a few days ago, you said a big space rock would kill off the dinosaurs and be the cause of their final extinction. What will happen after it hits? Will it look like this?"

"It will look much worse," Kailani said. "Scientists have not always agreed on the exact details, but regardless, it will be bad for the dinosaurs and for much of life on Earth. The collision of an asteroid will have the force of approximately 100 million megatons of TNT exploding in the same spot."

"TNT is an abbreviation for 'trinitrotoluene,'" Adalya said. "There are one million tons in a megaton."

Kailani added, "The collision point will get super-hot as the asteroid plows 20 miles into the Earth, turning rock in its way into liquid and gas as it pulverizes its collision zone and itself."

"That's all supposed to happen far away from here," Durango said. "Right?"

"Kind of," Kailani said, "but not so far on a global scale. Here in Utah, we have a bit of distance separating us. In 1990, irrefutable evidence for the impact will be found in the form of the Chicxulub impact crater along eastern Mexico's Yucatán peninsula — actually not far from where Lassen said you both got lost in Mayan pyramids a few years ago."

"Now there's a story," Durango said.

"When the asteroid hits," Kailani said, "rock vapor—basically steam made of rock—will jump into and beyond the atmosphere from the impact site. It will then re-condense into small droplets of glass—tektites—that will rain down on the Earth, pulled by gravity. These droplets of glass will heat up the Earth and look like an amazing meteor shower as they come down and brighten the landscape. They will create a worldwide infrared heat pulse that will go on for hours, drastically raising the planet's temperature. Massive firestorms will ravage the planet, and dinosaurs and much of life on Earth will broil and burn."

"A fiery blood bath," Lassen muttered under his breath.

"Ultimate barbecue," Durango said.

"And that's just the beginning," Kailani said. "Regardless of how much death happens immediately or within hours, remaining dinosaurs would still starve to death as a debris cloud blocks the sun and causes most plants to die. The herbivores would starve without the plants, and carnivores would starve without the herbivores. Whatever dinosaurs survived the initial impact and tektite heat effects would die from ecosystem collapse. And not just dinosaurs will die. Prehistoric marine reptiles, like mosasaurs and plesiosaurs, will go extinct as well as the pterosaurs."

"Good riddance to those lizard bats," Durango muttered. "They've caused us enough trouble."

"Why do scientists think the Chicxulub impact is the one that causes the dinosaurs' extinction?" Lassen asked.

"Iridium stratigraphy," Kailani said.

"Fascinating," Adalya muttered. "I was not aware that people in your time knew about iridium."

"We've known about it since 1803," Lassen said.

"Stratigraphy," Kailani said, "ties into how rock layers—also known as strata—correspond to different geologic time periods. As I mentioned earlier, there's a certain rock boundary found around the world below which non-avian dinosaurs exist in the fossil record and above which there are none. During modern times, the rock in this boundary is about 66 million years old and marks the end of the Cretaceous Period. The age of this rock layer and the Chicxulub impact crater match each other."

"What about iridium?" Durango asked. "What's that?"

"It's a rare metal," Kailani said. "On Earth, it's much rarer than gold. Disproportionately high levels of iridium will be found in end-Cretaceous boundary rock. In fact, there will be about 30 times more iridium in that boundary than average levels elsewhere on the planet."

"Why so much?" Lassen wondered.

"Because iridium is found in high concentrations in meteorites," Kailani said

"Wait," Durango said. "I thought you said an asteroid hit. What's a meteorite?"

"Good question," Kailani said. "Iridium is found in high concentrations in both asteroids and meteorites, but once the Chicxculub asteroid hits, it will be a meteorite."

"It becomes something else?" Durango said.

"Not exactly," Kailani said. "The terminology can get confusing. When an impactor rock is in outer space, it's called an asteroid, but after it lands on the Earth, it's called a meteorite. Also, when an asteroid or comet is burning up while entering Earth's atmosphere, it's called a meteor."

"Oh, like a shooting star," Lassen said.

"Right," Kailani added. "Shooting stars are meteors and not actually stars. So, an asteroid, meteor, and meteorite can all be the same object at different stages on its way to Earth. When that asteroid impacts, it will unleash incredible quantities of its own airborne debris that will fall to Earth, distributing iridium and meteorite materials around the world, creating the high iridium concentrations in the end-Cretaceous boundary layer."

As Kailani spoke, Lassen observed a little *Hesperornithoides* scamper across hardpan mud and tear into a dried lungfish with its snout. The chicken-sized bird-like dinosaur was gaunt and had dirty feathers.

"So, the dinosaurs will die out, but the birds and mammals will survive," Lassen said.

"Correct," Kailani replied, "but technically, birds are a type of dinosaur, so it's more accurate to say that the non-avian dinosaurs will go extinct. Still, very few birds will survive the extinction."

"Which ones will make it?" Lassen asked.

"About five species," Kailani said. "The survivors are all toothless ground-dwelling birds similar to modern-day ducks and chickens. In the twenty-first century, scientists will know this because of fossil studies and analysis of living bird genetics."

"So, a few toothless bird species will survive," Lassen said, "and turtles, frogs, crocodylomorphs, and various insects will survive. And obviously mammals will survive because well, here we are. The first night here, I saw a dinosaur eat a mammal, and it made me think our species would never have a chance to evolve if the dinosaurs never went extinct."

Kailani explained that mammals were basically held back by dinosaurs in the Mesozoic Era, but after the end-Cretaceous extinction, mammals went from being mostly small, likely nocturnal ground dwellers to major ecosystem players that were much larger and filled roles once occupied by dinosaurs. She emphasized that this happened quickly from a geological context in that all major modern mammal groups would evolve within the first 10 million years after the Cretaceous. This is fast when one considers that mammals had already been around for about 170 million years by the end of the Cretaceous.

Lassen asked why mammals dominated the planet after the dinosaurs instead of surviving reptiles, like lizards, crocodylomorphs, snakes, or turtles. He thought cold-blooded reptiles would have an advantage in a devastated landscape because of their lower metabolic needs. Kailani explained that because of fungi (mold, mushrooms, etc.), mammal dominance may have been more complicated than merely filling vacant ecological niches. She said that fungi would have been prevalent after the asteroid impact because of huge amounts of organic decay. She also explained how mammals are more resistant to fungal infections because of their higher internal body temperatures, which surpass the temperature at which fungi can survive. With this in mind, Lassen realized that cold-blooded animals—like reptiles and amphibians—would be especially vulnerable to fungal infections because of colder temperatures caused by asteroid impact debris clouds and forest fire smoke blocking the sun.

Kailani ended her explanation of the fungi factor by stating, "If not for increased vulnerability to fungi, remaining reptiles may have diversified into animals very similar to previous non-avian dinosaurs, and the Earth might have continued to be ruled by reptiles."

"Intriguing," Lassen said. "A more normal state for the planet than modern times is to have dinosaurs ruling the world. Humans are brand new by comparison."

"If the end-Cretaceous extinction doesn't happen," Kailani said, "dinosaurs may still dominate the planet by the nineteenth and twenty-first centuries, which reminds me of something." Kailani pulled her phone from a vest pocket, turned it on, and opened an e-book. "Take a look at this."

Kailani held up her phone, so Lassen and Durango could see the image on it. Adalya also turned her head and glanced back. She kept to herself that she had actually seen similar beings in the twenty-eighth century when she went on an interstellar vacation.

"Absurd," Adalya said to mask what she was actually thinking.

"Son of a catamount." Durango said. "Spooky. What kind of monster is that? A lizard devil?"

"Intriguing," Lassen said. "What is that?"

"A dinosauroid," Kailani said. "This picture shows a detailed model that a paleontologist and taxidermist developed in 1982. This shows what one paleontologist thought an intelligent Cretaceous dinosaur, *Stenonychosaurus*, would have looked like if non-avian dinosaurs never went extinct, and dinosaurs continued to evolve for 66 million years. *Stenonychosaurus* used to be called *Troodon*."

The picture Kailani showed featured a realistic life-size model of a reptilian humanoid biped. Its skin was smooth and green with shades of yellow on its abdomen and neck. It also had three fingers on each hand, but one was an opposable thumb. Its eyes were large, forward-facing, protruding, and yellow with black slit pupils.

"It looks real," Lassen said.

"It's not," Kailani said. "It's just a model, and this was a thought experiment that happened to be very human-centric in its outlook. If dinosaurs continued to dominate the planet and became super intelligent, maybe some could develop technology and human-like societies but there's no compelling reason they would end up with a human body shape. They could have feathers and still look very much like theropod dinosaurs. Actually, that future is still possible as many birds remain in the twenty-first century, and new research is showing that they can be remarkably intelligent to the point of understanding language and solving complicated puzzles. New Caledonian crows even know how to make tools."

"Most intriguing," Lassen said. "When humans die out, dinosaurs may retake the planet. But wait a minute—modern birds have lost some of the key attributes of theropod dinosaurs. For example, they don't have teeth."

"True," Kailani said, "but old genetics don't just completely go away when species evolve. In many cases, genetics for traits of ancestors are still present but simply dormant."

"Oh, interesting," Lassen said. "So, it's like they are instructions on the shelf that haven't been used."

"Exactly," Kailani said. "In fact, in my time, there's been ongoing research attempting to genetically modify chicken embryos to produce an animal more like a dinosaur: a *Chickenosaurus*."

"How has that turned out?" Lassen asked.

"The results have been insightful," Kailani said. "Researchers managed to modify chicken genetics to create an alligator-like snout on a chicken embryo. A gene has also been activated that creates teeth in chickens. And, efforts have been underway to deactivate the gene that fuses embryonic chicken finger bones into wings. If the wing bones are kept separate—which they already are at a certain embryonic stage—they're more like dinosaur claws. Lengthening the chicken tail into something more like that of a theropod dinosaur tail has posed some of the main challenges, and as far as I know, *Chickenosaurus* researchers had not accomplished that by 2026. Interestingly, though, chicken embryos actually have fairly long dinosaur-like tails, but some sort of gene expression causes the tail to resorb into the rest of the embryo. As a result, fully developed chickens end up with a pygostyle, which is basically a rudimentary nub of a tail. So, the key to getting a dinosaur-like tail in a bird would be to specifically identify and stop whatever genetic processes cause tail resorption."

"Incredible," Lassen said, "so some hidden instructions for expressing traits reminiscent of dinosaurs are still in birds."

"Yes," Kailani said, "but that's not just the case for birds. Even humans can have ancestral traits be expressed from genetics that are normally inactive. For example, it's rare, but every once in a while, humans are born with tails. Some of these tails can even move and contract."

"Egggh," Durango said as he crinkled his face in disgust.

"Hmmm," Lassen said, "it's like monkey genetics coming back."

"That's right," Kailani said.

"Most intriguing," Adalya said. What she did not reveal was how far genetic engineering had come by her time. Lengthening a tail in a bird was nothing compared to what would be possible by 2756.

Soon, the bounty hunters and scientists neared a large pile of rocks about 50 yards (46 meters) ahead of them.

"We can find shade in those rocks and rest," Adalya said as she pointed at a cluster of boulders surrounded by sand.

"Good," Durango said as he wiped sweat from his forehead, "it's gettin' hot, and I don't want to go extinct anytime soon."

Lassen readjusted his hat and squinted to get a better look at the boulders ahead. They were very large, but he saw four shapes next to the boulders and was not sure what they were. They seemed to somewhat blend into the landscape but were oddly elongated, unlike the boulders. Then he noticed spots on orange.

"We've got a problem, friends," Lassen said as he and Kailani stopped walking.

"I see them," Adalya seriously stated while she also stopped.

"See what?" Durango asked.

Suddenly, four *Ceratosaurus* stood up, opened their eyes, and shook sand off their bodies. These *Ceratosaurus* were skinny and hungry, and their nostrils quivered as they smelled mammals. They stood in front of a largely decayed *Barosaurus* carcass, which had blended in with the nearby boulders and was mostly covered in wind-driven sand. The *Ceratosaurus* were unnaturally concentrated because of the lack of food in the valley.

"Those are *Ceratosaurus*," Kailani whispered before she deeply inhaled and broke into a cold sweat. "Their horns are a dead giveaway."

From an earlier sighting, Lassen remembered the horns— one on the top of the snout and one above each eye—but also recognized the dinosaurs' orange-yellow coloration, whitish underbellies, and leopard-like spots.

"I have a bad feeling about this," Lassen said as he bit his lower lip and tensely flexed his right hand.

Durango's eyes nervously shifted left to right. Adalya whispered numbers to herself as she ran through a series of prediction-based math calculations.

Two male *Ceratosaurus* with bright green horns tilted their blue heads up, angrily sniffing. Two less vibrant females with brown horns leaned forward and emitted raspy hissing. The malnourished dinosaurs' skin looked like it was shrink-wrapped as their eyes zeroed in on the humans. The *Ceratosaurus* were under their potential maximum weight of approximately 2,000 pounds (900 kilograms) but still had plenty of energy as their sinewy legs broke into a sprint.

The time travelers turned around and ran. The *Ceratosaurus* pursued and kicked up dramatic bursts of sand in their wake. Unlike some other dinosaurs, the *Ceratosaurus* had fused metatarsal bones in their feet. Their three pelvis bones were also fused into a solid mass. These skeletal characteristics enabled *Ceratosaurus* to better withstand the physical stresses caused by running. *Ceratosaurus* also possessed a tail that was deeper and more massive than other theropods. This tail structure enhanced its maneuverability and stability while moving at fast speeds.

Durango immediately dropped his saddlebags and took the lead. Lassen and Kailani also dropped their saddlebags, which were heavy as they carried sauropod eggs filled with water. As Adalya ran, she maintained her composure, unsnapped one of her saddlebags, pulled out a bola, and then dropped the saddlebags.

Lassen breathed hard. His chest burned. He turned around to see the four *Ceratosaurus* close in fast. The largest member of the group ran in front and was a skinny male. He snarled as he made eye contact with Lassen. Soon, the *Ceratosaurus* were only about 40 feet (12 meters) behind the time travelers.

"This day just keeps gettin' better!" Durango shouted.

Lassen had a bantering quip at the tip of his tongue when he tripped. He cursed as a weathered branch slammed him into sand, face-first. The lead *Ceratosaurus* veered left away from its companions to pursue Lassen. Meanwhile, the other three theropods continued chasing Kailani, Adalya, and Durango.

Lassen got up and ran in a new direction, but his eyes stung and watered as he rubbed them to remove sand and dust. He now traveled toward wetlands, which were not far ahead of him. He saw what looked like lots of logs densely packed in very shallow water, but his vision was blurry from the sand in his eyes. If he could get across the water by jumping from log to log, the *Ceratosaurus* at his back might get stuck in the muck or back off.

Adalya rapidly performed complex geometry calculations in her head as she ran. Then she stopped and swung bola stones with ferocious momentum. Adalya tossed the stones toward the feet of the closest *Ceratosaurus*, which was a male. The bola's ropes tightly wrapped around the *Ceratosaurus's* legs. The *Ceratosaurus* groaned in frustration as his legs tangled, and he tripped. His arms were too short to stop his fall. Compared to *Allosaurus*, *Ceratosaurus* had relatively slender arms and a weak grip.

Adalya gritted her teeth and winced as she heard the mighty hobbled carnivore's neck snap on a rock as he hit the ground. The theropod's companions viciously pounced on him. Adalya ran toward Kailani and Durango.

"Miss Nakai!" Adalya shouted. Kailani paused to look back and saw Adalya and the feeding *Ceratosaurus*. As Adalya caught up with her, she continued to run.

"Mister Mesquite!" Adalya yelled. Durango continued running. "Mister Mesquite!" Adalya shouted again. No response. "Durango!"

"Huh!" Durango exclaimed, glancing over his shoulder while still running. "What?! Son of a catamount! How'd that happen?!" Durango saw Kailani and Adalya rush toward him. Behind them, two *Ceratosaurus* voraciously tore hunks of flesh off their companion.

"I will fill you in!" Adalya said as she and Kailani ran toward Durango. "But we need to get out of here and find Lassen!"

"No need," Durango said as he shielded his eyes from the sun with one hand and pointed with the other. "I see him to the north!"

Kailani and Adalya stopped and spotted Lassen. Kailani looked horrified. Adalya was stone-faced. Durango looked entertained.

"He's movin' *fast*!" Durango said. "I've never seen Lassen run that fast *ever*!"

Lassen never had, and he knew it all too well. Hot *Ceratosaurus* breath moved the tiny hairs on the back of Lassen's neck. The adventurous bounty hunter jumped across the edge of shallow water and landed on a log—or so he thought. The log moved and whipped a neck around to snap gaping jaws at Lassen's feet. What Lassen thought was a log was actually the back of a partially submerged *Amphicotylus* crocodylomorph.

Lassen leapt off the *Amphicotylus* and landed on the back of another, which reacted with similar toothy snappishness. Soon, Lassen found himself jumping from the back of one angry *Amphicotylus* to another. As the valley dried up, various *Amphicotylus* that would normally be scattered throughout streams and ponds had relocated to the only remaining water. They were now concentrated in one large expanse of shallow water along with scores of turtles and many pterosaurs. Alarmed pterosaurs squawked and flew as Lassen woke up partially submerged *Amphicotylus*, dodged jaws and claws, and miraculously managed to *barely* maintain his balance.

The hungry snarling *Ceratosaurus* just behind Lassen provided ample movement motivation. The *Ceratosaurus* quickly splashed into the water behind the bounty hunter. *Amphicotylus* reacted with automatic snapping, but the dinosaur was able to get past them. Most of the crocodylomorphs were only about seven feet (two meters) long and 250 pounds (113 kilograms), whereas the *Ceratosaurus* was pushing 800 pounds (363 kilograms) and 20 feet (six meters) in length. The *Ceratosaurus's* feet crushed in portions of *Amphicotylus* that were too slow to move out of the way.

Lassen leapt off an *Amphicotylus* and landed on the back of another that was now wide awake and unhappy. The *Amphicotylus* was enormous and appeared to be 350 pounds (160 kilograms) and 12 feet (four meters) long. It snapped its jaws back toward Lassen. Lassen backed up, so he now stood on the crocodylomorph's tail, which suddenly and forcefully flexed, disrupting Lassen's balance. Lassen instinctively launched backward and high into the air. Somehow, without trying, he did a backflip for the first time in his life. It was amazing, and he doubted he would ever be able to repeat it. Lassen flew backward, and his entire body briefly went upside down as he sailed into his flip.

Lassen's senses became hyper alert, and actions appeared to occur in slow motion from his perspective. Lassen got an upside-down view of the *Ceratosaurus* opening its jaws extremely wide. He saw the grooves of the bright green keratin on its horns, and he got a close look at dirty teeth of varying lengths. The *Ceratosaurus* was only a few feet behind him. He was headed toward its mouth. A startled *Mesadactylus* flew by to his right. Little turtles burrowed for cover in nearby mud. Two bright blue dragonflies zipped past Lassen's nose.

Then a pair of *Amphicotylus* simultaneously burst out of the water and piled onto the *Ceratosaurus*. One clamped onto its tail. Another tore into a leg. Two crocodylomorphs biting at once were too much for the great beast. The *Ceratosaurus* closed its mouth as *Amphicotylus* pulled its entire body down. Soon, its head splashed into the mud, chin-first.

The front of Lassen's body then swung forward as he sailed back into an upright position. He ended his flip by gracefully landing feet-first on the head of the *Ceratosaurus* while facing the direction from which he had just come. The dinosaur grunted in pain.

With its belly in the water, its arms flailing at its sides, and its legs immobilized, the *Ceratosaurus* struggled to lift its head and open its mouth. Lassen jumped off the *Ceratosaurus*, landed on the back of an *Amphicotylus*, and made his way toward a jumble of boulders at the edge of the wetlands. After a minute of frantic hopping, jaw evasion, and balance testing, Lassen launched into a somersault off an *Amphicotylus* back and landed on soft, dry sand.

While breathing hard, Lassen turned around and saw the fate of the *Ceratosaurus* that had pursued him. It was now about 60 feet (18 meters) away, partially submerged, and buried by *Amphicotylus*. The crocodylomorphs tore the dinosaur apart, though one of them broke a tooth on the dinosaur's tough osteoderm ridges. Muddy brown water ran red, and the *Ceratosaurus's* tail flopped high in the air as the dinosaur drowned.

Lassen winced and staggered forward, ensuring he was a healthy distance from crocodylomorph-infested waters. Then he collapsed with exhaustion near a pile of rocks and several weathered conifer logs. Lassen struggled to catch his breath as he laid back against a log and closed his eyes to block hot sunlight.

Lassen's eyes suddenly bulged open with surprise as a fist plowed into his stomach. He looked up to see Shanahan Branigan standing above him. The big outlaw's beard was unruly and flecked with gray. His eyes were bloodshot and wild. His clothes were dirty and tattered. The loops on his gunbelt contained only two bullets, and he appeared to be disarmed. Claw-induced slashes spread across the chest of his blood-stained shirt.

"Mister Malone!" Branigan yelled. "You do-goodin' scum!"

As Branigan's foot moved toward Lassen's head for a decisive kick, Lassen grabbed it and twisted with all his might. Branigan fell to the ground, and Lassen punched him in the face. The impact of the hit sounded like a baseball bat hitting a pile of old leather jackets. Lassen pulled his hand back and flexed it in pain. Branigan had a *hard* jaw.

Lassen brought his right foot up for a kick, but Branigan blocked it with his arm. Lassen jumped to the top of a nearby log. Branigan jumped after him. As they kicked and swung fists, Lassen did his best to dodge, weave, and not get hit. He found himself continually backing up while Branigan drove the fight. Pterosaurs above squawked and gradually circled lower, curious about the commotion.

"How'd you make it from the stampede to here?!" Lassen asked as he ducked to avoid one of Branigan's fists.

"Wouldn't you like to know!" Branigan said, sneering.

"Yeah," Lassen said with a grunt as he smoothly kicked Branigan in the ribs. "I would! That's why I asked!" Lassen was surprised his wild kick actually worked. Branigan gripped his side in pain and moved back on the log on which he and Lassen stood. Years earlier, the log had fallen on top of a boulder. It sloped downward with Lassen on a lower portion than Branigan.

"Is Traxton alive?!" Lassen forcefully asked, backing up. If Branigan was going to tell him valuable information, Lassen thought he should probably take a brief break from trying to punch him in the face.

"Well, you see," Branigan said while reaching into his boot, "the thing with that is—"

Branigan cut off his own sentence by pulling a derringer pistol from his boot. As Branigan pulled up the gun, Lassen's mouth and eyes widened in horror and shock as he stared just beyond Branigan. The big outlaw smiled menacingly and began to move his finger over the trigger of his derringer. Suddenly, wide jaws opened and snapped shut over Branigan's middle. His shot went wild. Lassen ducked as the bullet ricocheted between surrounding boulders with distinctive pinging.

A giant *Allosaurus anax* crunched its mouth onto Branigan. To Lassen, the 40-foot (12-meter) long theropod looked like a large *Allosaurus fragilis*. However, instead of being aquamarine blue with green stripes, it was dark red with intricate diamond-like black patterning that reminded Lassen of rattlesnake skin. It also had a bright blue dewlap hanging from its lower jaw. The *Allosaurus anax* dropped Branigan to the ground and lowered its mouth to start eating. Lassen did not know where the dinosaur came from. It seemed to materialize out of nowhere, and he guessed it was sleeping on its belly behind nearby boulders.

Lassen jumped off his log and scrambled away through boulders as he heard Branigan's yells of anguish mixed with the sounds of the *Allosaurus anax* feeding. Then, suddenly, Lassen only heard grunting and hissing mixed with crunching. The bounty hunter leapt off a boulder and hit dry ground at a run.

In the open, Lassen caught his breath and looked around. No carnivores in sight, except for two distant feeding *Ceratosaurus*. He saw Kailani, Adalya, and Durango wave at him from across the wetlands. Kailani was looking through binoculars. Lassen gestured with his arm to the right to indicate that his companions should walk around the water to meet him.

Twenty minutes later, Kailani, Adalya, and Durango caught up with Lassen at an isolated boulder where Lassen rested in the shade. Durango and the scientists had recovered the dropped saddlebags on their way to Lassen. Only one water-carrying egg had broken, and Lassen drank heavily from another.

"Son—of—a—*catamount!*" Durango said, drawing out his words with dramatic pauses. "That's the best show I ever saw!"

"I'm glad you're okay," Kailani said as she hugged Lassen and buried her face in his shoulder.

Durango raised his eyebrows. *Somethin' happened while I was gone*, he thought. *Lassen won't tell me details, but I know somethin' happened.*

"It is good that you are intact," Adalya said.

"Yeah, I'm alright," Lassen said as Kailani pulled away from her hug. "Just a bit bruised, out of breath, and mildly traumatized. No big deal. I'm definitely doing better than Branigan."

"We saw what happened from a distance," Adalya said. "Do you know if Cordon—or Traxton as you would call him—is still alive?"

"No," Lassen said, "I don't know Traxton's status, but I asked Branigan. His response was to try to shoot me, but being eaten to death sort of stopped that."

"I'll say," Durango added. "Son of a catamount. Glad you made it, pal."

"So am I," Lassen said. Then he looked far to the east. "Looks like those *Ceratosaurus* are busy eating—on another *Ceratosaurus*. How'd you manage that?"

"Through a bola," Adalya said.

"You're good with those," Lassen replied.

"It is all in the math," Adalya said.

"No need to pull a trigger when you've got trigonometry," Lassen said.

"Precisely," Adalya replied.

Kailani chuckled. Then she looked north through her binoculars. She saw the *Allosaurus anax* feeding behind rocks. She only occasionally saw its head bob into view a bit, but she had a good look at its tail, which stuck into the air while its head was down. She was thankful that she could not see Branigan's body get torn apart by theropod jaws and claws, but she was grateful to catch a glimpse of a rare Jurassic carnivore that had very minimal fossil evidence by 2026.

"That's the biggest theropod we've seen on the entire journey," Kailani said. "That must be an *Allosaurus anax*."

"Mouth cuts like an ax," Durango said. "Makes sense."

Lassen drank deeply once again, and water dripped off his chin and onto the front of his shirt. Then a massive shadow draped the landscape as the sun went behind fluffy white cumulonimbus clouds.

"Looks like a storm's moving in," Lassen said. "With all the commotion, I didn't notice the clouds building."

"If the sun stays behind the clouds," Adalya said, "we can continue our journey without the heat being too severe."

"Yeah," Lassen replied. "If we're lucky, we can reach the rim of that volcano before sunset."

CHAPTER 24: JURASSIC DUSK

As morning turned to afternoon, the bounty hunters and scientists walked over dirty salt flats and neared the foot of the volcano towering above the west end of the valley. They all carried their saddlebags, and Durango also carried his lasso over his shoulder. Salt crunched under the time travelers' feet as they stepped on the dry crust of a playa lakebed. Several months earlier, a heavy rain filled the lake, but its water quickly evaporated, leaving behind salt and other minerals. Over the years, repeated filling and evaporation of the lake left a salty crust with an elaborate network of cracks.

Soon, the time travelers hiked up the volcano. Cloud cover alleviated the sun's searing heat, but the afternoon was still warm and muggy. Lassen wiped sweat from his forehead as he turned around to glance at the valley below. He saw feeding *Ceratosaurus* as mere specks in the distance. Storm clouds continued ominously building. A small herd of *Barosaurus* dug for water far to the north while a pair of dust devils lazily danced across the sandy southern end of the valley.

Lassen, Kailani, and Adalya handled the trek well. Adalya was in the lead with Lassen close behind. Durango plodded and panted behind everybody else but was often joined by Kailani who stopped to take photos of the valley.

Several hours later, by early evening, the time travelers reached the rim of the volcano. They stood on black and red ash and cinders. Large rocky outcrops and tall dead conifer trees lined the rim of the volcano. Many *Harpactognathus* pterosaurs flitted near the conifers, tending their nests, which were nestled between tree branches.

Through heavy breaths, Durango asked, "Are we finally there?"

"Yes," Adalya said. "The last time I checked, the signaler was very close to this location, and it had been immobile for some time."

"I hope it still hasn't moved," Lassen added as he brought binoculars to his eyes and scanned the terrain, searching for a silver cube with a blinking green light that he hoped would merely be lying on the ground. As he scanned the pterosaur nests high in the trees, he bit his lower lip. "Good news and bad news," Lassen said.

"What, pal?" Durango asked.

"Well," Lassen said, "I found the location signaler, but it's about 30 feet up in a dead tree—and it's not alone." Lassen pointed at a nest in a nearby conifer that contained three eggs and two squawking *Harpactognathus* hatchlings.

"It's in a rhamphorynchoid pterosaur nest," Kailani said. "Retrieval will not be easy."

"Oh, I see it blinking in that nest," Durango said. "That's what we're after. Good luck climbing up to get it."

"We've all had plenty of climbing lately," Lassen said, feeling weary. He quickly picked a dried fern frond, stripped off its leaves, and broke it into four pieces. "Short stick climbs," he said, extending the four pieces to his companions. Soon, Lassen chuckled and sighed as he held up the shortest fern stem piece. "Time to climb," he said.

Minutes later, Lassen climbed high up a weathered old conifer. Bark had long since fallen off its branches, and notable quantities of dried pterosaur droppings coated the upper reaches of the tree. Lassen gripped dry gnarled wood as he slowly made his way up, cautiously watching where he placed his hands.

Lassen looked to the west. Gases wafted from the ominous dark mouth of the huge volcano. Low hills and mountains stretched as far as the eye could see to the west, and Lassen wondered if he could see into what would become Nevada. Looking down, Lassen swayed, feeling disoriented. If he fell to the west, he would travel hundreds (if not thousands) of feet into a mysterious gas-filled void. Luckily, the volcano's gases drifted west, which ensured Lassen had clean air and good visibility to the east

Lassen glanced east. He had a fantastic view of the large desolate valley he had just crossed. Dark, thick clouds hung in the air, and Lassen questioned the intelligence of climbing a very tall tree on a very tall landform with a potential lightning storm nearby. Still, he had not yet heard thunder.

Lassen peered upward up as he climbed. The two *Harpactognathus* hatchlings were very loud and distressed by their approaching visitor.

Much of the afternoon had been cloudy, but as Lassen reached the level of the pterosaur nest, the sun suddenly burst through a tear in the clouds to the west. Lassen squinted his eyes against bright sunlight streaming through volcanic gases in dramatic shafts. The light's rich early evening hues covered Lassen and the surrounding landscape in reddish tones.

The sun illuminated the dramatic desert terrain. Far to the east, distant rain fell as blue-gray wisps in front of a slate gray sky over the mountains of the Mesocordilleran High. The rain, clouds, and mountains formed a breathtaking backdrop for a distant herd of *Barosaurus*. In Lassen's frame of view, the foreground was well-lit in front of a dark, water-streaked background, which made for a striking contrast. Rays of sunlight took shape in airborne water particles. Lassen noticed tiny lightning flashes above the far-off plains. Despite the brief sunlit respite, he knew a storm was growing and rapidly approaching.

Lassen turned his attention to the pterosaur nest. It was constructed of an intricate, roughly circular medley of dried ferns, *Equisetum*, and conifer branches and needles. Lassen strained as he reached his right arm toward the location signaler on one side of the nest. He then felt smooth metal, grabbed the signaler, and quickly pulled his hand back just as a little *Harpactognathus* tried to peck his thumb. The hatchling barely missed and ended up pecking a twig in half.

"I got it!" Lassen called down to his companions.

Kailani and Adalya responded with appreciation, and Durango clapped. Lassen winced as he heard what sounded like abrupt violent thunder. All the adult pterosaurs in the surrounding trees suddenly flew away. Distant gentle thunder then rumbled. *That first sound wasn't thunder*, Lassen thought. He muttered, "I have a bad feeling about this . . ."

Lassen looked down to see a faint but growing red-orange glow deep in the depths of the volcano under him. His eyes grew wide, he pocketed the location signaler in his vest, and he began to hastily climb down.

The sun dipped behind the clouds, rapidly darkening the landscape. Light raindrops began to patter on Lassen's hat. More violent rumbling sounded from the volcano, vibrating the ground. As the volcano's glow grew, adult pterosaurs in the nearby dead conifers flew away in fear. Soon, the volcano's red-orange glow intensified and spread over the nearby terrain and Lassen while the bounty hunter quickly let go of branches and grabbed others. Lightning flashed closer, and thunder pounded. Lassen quickened his pace. Soon, he snapped branches as he recklessly descended.

In a matter of minutes, Lassen landed feet-first on ash and cinders next to a rock outcrop near the tree. He struggled to maintain his balance as the ground shook underneath his feet.

"It appears as if this volcano is erupting!" Adalya shouted over the sound of pouring rain, thunder, and primordial deep Earth rumbling.

Lassen steadied his hat as strong storm winds suddenly whooshed past and increased in intensity. Shouting over the wind, Lassen said, "I've got the location signaler right here!" He reached a hand into his pocket and pulled out the small metallic cube with a blinking green light.

Suddenly, two dark figures emerged from behind the rock outcrop next to Lassen, and the bounty hunter found himself tackled into ash and cinders. The location signaler tumbled out of his hand and landed near the rim of the volcano.

"Malone!" Tardell Traxton contemptuously proclaimed.

"Traxton!" Lassen called back.

"Gantry's here, too!" Gantry yelled from a few feet away as he stepped toward Lassen and Traxton.

Traxton was battered and bloodied. His shirt was torn with claw marks similar to those Lassen saw on Branigan. His face was unshaven and dirty. Gantry was also worse for wear and disheveled, and his duster jacket was gone.

Traxton's crazed eyes shifted about as he lifted a fist to pound Lassen. Lassen awkwardly but forcefully twisted sideways to narrowly avoid a skull-crunching punch.

"Get him, boss!" Gantry yelled. "Knock him over like you're an old salad bull!"

"I thought I'd wait for you to get the signaler for me!" Traxton said.

"How'd you know we'd be here?!" Lassen replied.

Durango, Kailani, and Adalya rushed forward to restrain Traxton, but stopped dead in their tracks as the volcano violently rumbled and blasted a series of glowing masses of molten rock into the air. These masses of rock were technically known as volcanic bombs and shot upward with trails of steam and gases spewing behind them like contrails from twentieth century fighter jets.

A massive volcanic spindle bomb landed between the location of Lassen and Traxton and where Kailani, Adalya, and Durango stood. It glowed with intense heat in its interior, and fractured black crusts of older, cooled lava covered its outer layer. Durango and the scientists quickly backed away from the steaming chunk of ejected volcanic debris, twisting and turning to avoid other volcanic bombs and glowing embers. Gantry fell onto the unsteady ground and tumbled and somersaulted his way out of the path of volcanic debris.

Lassen wished he could dodge away from the geologic dangers at will, but he was occupied fighting a twenty-eighth century quantum computer technician-turned-1870s outlaw-turned Jurassic survivalist. For now, luck kept Lassen from being struck by volcanic debris.

As Lassen dodged punches and made some tentative strikes, he tried to keep an eye on the location signaler. It rested precariously close to the edge of the volcano's rim. It was only inches from a nearly vertical drop of hundreds of feet. Rain continued to pound. Thunder clapped. Blue, yellow, and pink bolts of dazzling lightning occasionally lit up Lassen's surroundings.

Lassen and Traxton punched at each other along the rim of the volcano. Lassen sparred with determination but felt overwhelmed and fatigued. Although Traxton was a normal-sized person, he fought with intense personal ferocity.

Lassen and Traxton moved past the bases of the old weathered conifers that had hosted flocks of pterosaurs only a few minutes earlier. Lassen backed into a tree and quickly moved behind it to avoid burning volcanic rock fragments known as tephra. As Lassen moved around the tree's trunk, he grabbed onto a branch above him for leverage. To his surprise, it snapped off. It was about three feet (one meter) long with a sharp pointed tip.

Lassen swung the branch toward Traxton. The outlaw leader ducked and snapped off his own branch, blocking Lassen's advances. As the Old West icons dueled, Lassen maneuvered Traxton toward the location signaler.

Lassen and Traxton's battle resembled a raggedy pirate sword fight happening on a remote Pacific island. From the east, they looked like silhouettes backlit by the orange-red glow of the stirring volcano. Their sticks cracked hard with dense dead wood as they blocked blow after blow. Lassen's vest billowed behind him as he rushed forward. Rain fell hard, fiery debris pelted the ground, lightning fluoresced, and thunder rumbled. Where rain hit molten rock fragments, it sizzled into steam. Forces of good and evil fought above a volcanic crater resembling a mythic hellscape.

Lassen breathed hard through the rain. He smelled newly wet ground and unpleasant volcanic gases. Suddenly, a glowing piece of tephra struck Traxton's hand. The outlaw shouted in pain and dropped his stick. Lassen immediately kicked Traxton in the chest, knocking him back near the rim of the volcano. The bounty hunter then skillfully swung his stick around and pointed its sharp tip directly at Traxton's throat.

"It's over, Traxton!" Lassen shouted. "I'm done chasing you!" As Lassen spoke, his eyes veered to the right. The location signaler was still intact, but it was very close to the edge of the volcano.

Traxton's head hung over the rim of the volcano, and his hat fell off. As it tumbled, it quickly burst into flames and continued its descent as a pile of ashes.

"Sorry about that," Lassen said with casual sincerity, smirking as he panted. "I've always kind of liked that hat." As Lassen pressed a boot into Traxton's chest, Durango, Kailani, and Adalya made their way around large glowing volcanic bombs to rejoin their companion.

"Kick him into the fire, Lassen!" Durango shouted.

"You know I can't do that, Durango!" Lassen yelled. "If I throw him in there, I'm no better than he is!"

With blindingly fast reflexes that resembled his gunplay moves, Lassen twirled his stick around, so he held its pointed end while its wider, heavier end was near Traxton's head. Lassen flicked his wrist and knocked Traxton unconscious with the blunt force of his branch.

Lassen rushed toward the location signaler. The volcano rumbled, and the ground violently shook, uprooting huge dead conifers, which fell into the volcano's crater. The dry dead trees disintegrated beautifully and devastatingly as they crackled into flames and ash. The ashes and dirt under the location signaler began to crumble as the volcano's rim eroded and widened.

Lassen ran forward as fast as he could. Then he launched into a desperate jump and pulled his hat off in midair. His elbows burned with pain as he landed chest-first on the rim of the volcano. The location signaler tumbled toward fiery oblivion. Lassen swept his hat leftward with a frantic arc of movement. Barely, just barely, did the location signaler make contact with the upside-down brim of Lassen's hat. It bounced off the brim and into the hat's crown.

"Got it," Lassen said, relieved and panting. He pulled his hat back and put it on with the location signaler still inside. He winced as he stood up with bloody and scraped elbows and torn sleeves.

"Lassen!" Kailani shouted, her heart pounding. "Are you alright?!"

"Son of a catamount!" Durango added. "That was close!"

"Too close!" Lassen said as he tipped his hat in triumph. "But I got it! Come on!" Lassen grabbed Traxton under his shoulders. "Help me get him out of here!"

As the bounty hunters and scientists pulled Traxton's body away from the edge of the crater, the volcanic debris ejections intensified.

"Lassen!" Adalya shouted. "We have to go faster! The math is not on our side."

"Let's find shelter!" Lassen said.

"The eruption will only get worse!" Adalya added over the sound of thunder. "We cannot stay here and live. Even if we avoid the debris, we will suffocate on the gases, and the wind is starting to change direction. Based on my calculations, we cannot leave the area fast enough!"

"What are we gonna do?!" Durango asked.

"We need to speed up our exit," Kailani said.

Lassen bit his lower lip. "The ground's getting muddy. Maybe we could turn a log into a sled, but how would we maintain sustainable velocity?"

"If there was a way to reduce the friction . . ." Adalya said, arching her eyebrows in deep thought.

"A time machine!" Durango yelled as he pointed at an object descending toward them from the sky. Bright yellow light from a single high beam bathed the time travelers.

"Professor!" Adalya said as her face lit up with a rare smile.

"Your boss?" Lassen asked as he dodged a volcanic bomb. "Sedora?"

"That is correct!" Adalya said. "I knew she would come back!"

The time machine moved quickly and nimbly swerved to avoid colliding with volcanic debris as it descended. Some smaller pieces of debris sizzled into dust as they collided with an energy shield surrounding the vehicle. Then a volcanic bomb violently struck the time machine and shorted out the energy shield as the debris vaporized. Bits of volcanic ejecta left scorch marks on the time vehicle's outer armor. The time machine briefly skidded across the ground near the time travelers as it almost crashed.

On the other side of the machine, Gantry rolled into hard metal, looked up, and grabbed onto a metal handhold just before the time machine floated back into the air. The angle of uplift flung Gantry completely onto the machine's side, and he held on tight to another handhold. As the time machine rose, Gantry hung on hard with both hands and was out of sight of the other time travelers. The time machine approached the bounty hunters and scientists but rose to avoid debris. Then the time travelers heard Sedora's voice through a speaker system.

"A ladder will descend! Climb on, and move with high acceleration!"

As the ladder lowered, Lassen said, "Okay, Kailani and Miss Nell, you should go first, and then—hey!"

As soon as the ladder was in reach, Durango climbed up as fast as he could. "Stop talking, Lassen!" Durango said as he ascended, "and start climbing!"

The ladder consisted of metal rungs about one foot (31 centimeters) wide that were secured to flexible cables.

"Go!" Lassen shouted to Kailani and Adalya. "Go!"

Adalya jumped onto the ladder and climbed up. Kailani followed close behind. As Durango and the scientists ascended, the time machine veered suddenly to avoid a volcanic bomb. The time travelers struggled to stay on the ladder as it flailed and dangled, but they soon made it to safety.

Inside a well-lit metallic room in the time machine, Kailani and Adalya breathed heavily on the floor. They were soaking wet from the rain and sweaty. Nearby, Durango coughed in exhaustion. Sedora spoke over a speaker system. "We have to go now! My sensors show a new and more powerful phase of the eruption is about to begin."

"NO!" Kailani proclaimed with defiant intensity and watery eyes. "We're not leaving without Lassen!"

"I'd be a son of a catamount if we did!" Durango added as he moved back down the ladder with his lasso over his shoulder. Durango climbed fast and quickly threw a lasso loop. It landed at

Lassen's feet. As the volcano rumbled with renewed ferocity, Lassen wrapped the lasso under Traxton's shoulders. Meanwhile, Durango tied the other end of the rope to the ladder. Then he climbed back up.

"Sorry about your friend," Sedora said, "but we are leaving NOW!"

The time machine quickly moved upward and lifted the rope and Traxton. Lassen ran, jumped, and barely caught the rope above Traxton, careful to ensure his feet did not bang into Traxton's head. Lassen climbed higher as the rope pulled tight while the vehicle rose.

The volcano belched a violent profusion of incinerating ashes, glassy debris, gobs of lava, and steam. As the time machine soared to the east, Lassen and Traxton dangled below it, barely out of the way of accelerating violent debris. Lassen struggled to stay on the rope and climb. He quickly glanced over his shoulder and saw lightning begin to flash within the volcano's ash plume. Although a thunderstorm from the plains had moved into the area, the volcano was now making its own lightning. Lassen's eyes grew wide. He had traveled the world but was not familiar with volcanic lightning, which results when densely packed ejecta particles collide with each other, cause friction, and become electrically charged.

The ladder began to rise. The strength and frequency of volcanic lightning intensified. Enormous jagged blue and yellow bolts of electricity bathed Lassen and Traxton in light. Lassen blinked hard to try to clear his vision and saw numerous black spots.

Inside the time machine, Durango, Kailani, and Adalya pulled on the ladder and rope with all their might. Below, Lassen winced as little gobs of lava singed his vest and burned tiny holes in his hat. At last, he reached the ladder. He climbed quickly and pulled himself through a hatch into the time machine just before a volcanic bomb sailed through his former position.

Lassen then helped Adalya and Durango pull up Traxton who was still unconscious. Soon, Traxton was safely inside the time machine. Adalya quickly bound his hands behind his back with the same snap bracelet-like restraints Sedora had used on Blaze. Adalya, Kailani, and the bounty hunters then moved to the cockpit to join Sedora who was intent on piloting.

"Oh, my," Sedora said as she glanced over her shoulder. "Adalya, you look . . . like you just came out of the trenches of World War Four. Who are your friends?"

"Durango Mesquite, ma'am," Durango said while pointing at himself. "You probably read about me in your third-grade history class."

"Um, no," Sedora said.

"I'm Lassen Malone, ma'am," Lassen said. "I'm grateful you came by when you did."

"Oh, I know who *you* are," Sedora said with a sly smile. "I am surprised you are real, though. You made quite an impression on people in Medicine Bow in 1879."

"Kailani Nakai," Kailani said. "Paleontologist from 2026. I was late to the party."

"I wondered who you were," Sedora said. "A paleontologist. What an extraordinary coincidence but who better to guide Doctor Nell through this Jurassic frontier?"

As the time travelers spoke, the time machine flew east. Lassen tried to catch his breath and orient himself to sterile clean metallic surroundings that starkly contrasted with the prehistoric wilderness he had experienced for the last several days. In a series of view screens and windows in the cockpit chamber, he could see what was happening outside.

A massive volcanic ash cloud spewed out of the volcano, and spectacular bursts of volcanic lightning crackled and flashed in the ash plume, which glowed orange in its interior. The area where the time travelers had stood was now covered in debris. If they had stayed just a few seconds longer, they would have suffocated or burned to death.

As the time travelers moved east, the rainstorm died down with some of the clouds clearing. The sun had just set. Swirls and dapples of clouds and volcanic gases to the west began to glow as part of brilliant pink-red sunset formations. Pterosaurs flew past the sunset as black silhouettes. The *Barosaurus* herd in the desolate valley stared up at the volcano.

Lassen noticed that the volcano had apparently triggered an earthquake because the rockslide debris dam on the northeastern end of the valley suddenly shook apart, and jets of water shot through it. The debris dam had blocked a large river's entrance into the desolate valley, but the dam was now rupturing and collapsing.

Soon, the temporary lake behind it quickly drained. Huge waves and torrents of water flowed into the parched valley.

As Lassen saw water rush into the valley, he felt comfort in knowing some of its formerly verdant qualities would return. The *Barosaurus* herd might make it, and some dusty ground would return to fern prairies and wetlands. Lassen pondered the fact that he had just nearly died—not once but a lot of times. He had nearly met his demise, he had spared the life of an adversary, and now, he was witnessing the revitalization of a desolate valley in the prehistoric past. Lassen thought of the purpose of the universe, the meaning of life, and what was important. Then he thought of Kailani and smiled at her. Kailani smiled back.

Lassen spoke as the time machine moved east over the mountains, leaving the desolate valley behind. "Is there any way we can bring our horses back? They should be somewhere up ahead in these hills."

"I think so," Sedora said, "but you will need to tell me where to find them. This vehicle's sensors are substantially damaged. By the way, why were you on the rim of an erupting volcano?"

"Long story," Lassen responded. "A pterosaur took the location signaler. We only had it for about 30 seconds before you showed up."

"You are lucky you found the signaler when you did," Sedora said. "I had just arrived in the Jurassic right before you found it. It took me five tries to get here. You would not believe some of the things I have seen. There are scratch marks on this vehicle's port side from Macedonian sarissa spears and mastodon tusks."

Soon, in the last faint glows of dusk, the time machine hovered three feet (one meter) above the top of a fern-covered hill. Lassen stood outside and whistled. Horizon immediately galloped toward him. The other nearby horses had run away from the time machine in fear when it first approached. "Round them up, Horizon," Lassen said. "They trust you. Bring them close. We're going home."

Horizon neighed and nodded in understanding. Soon, Horizon had herded Yonder, Graphite, Ember, and Gantry's horse to the time machine, and they stood nearby. In the cockpit, Sedora flicked several switches. The horses and time machine disappeared into shimmering iridescent light particles.

In what seemed an instant, the time machine suddenly stopped. "That seemed fast," Sedora said. "Too fast, but I think we might be back in 1879." She groaned. "The chrono display is out again."

"Can't see much out the windows," Lassen said. "It's nighttime. Based on what you said earlier, we're supposed to be in 1879 about a week after we originally left. Right?"

"Correct," Sedora said. "I wanted to arrive late enough to prevent us from interfering with my other self's attempts to get back to rescue you and not so early that you and Durango would run into yourselves, but it is supposed to be daytime."

"I can go outside and take a look," Lassen said.

"I'll go with you," Kailani added.

Lassen and Kailani stepped down a small ramp. Lassen turned his head at the sound of faint rustling on the other side of the time machine. Unbeknownst to Lassen and Kailani, Gantry had tumbled off the portside hull and laid in a grassy meadow, trying to catch his breath. The horses whinnied in confusion.

Lassen and Kailani stood on top of a grassy hill, dotted with ferns, flowers, and pine trees. They saw a river below them that flowed east toward what appeared to be a distant ocean but was actually the Western Interior Seaway, which covered much of central North America during the late Cretaceous Period. Kailani saw a distant lone *Triceratops* graze in the light of a full moon. The dinosaur was a four-legged beaked herbivore with a head frill, two large horns just above its eyes, and a shorter horn above its snout. It weighed about 18,000 pounds (8,165 kilograms) and was about 26 feet (8 meters) long.

"A dinosaur," Lassen said. "We may be in Wyoming, but it's not 1879."

"*Triceratops*," Kailani said under her breath while she smiled at the wonder of seeing a new species. "We must be in an area that will be preserved in the Hell Creek or Lance Formations." Kailani turned toward the exit ramp of the time machine and yelled, "We're in the late Cretaceous Period, probably about 66 million years before when we should be!"

"Acknowledged!" Adalya shouted back.

Inside the time machine, Durango stood behind Adalya and Sedora who worked a control panel. "More dinosaurs," he muttered. "I'm not even going outside."

"Sixty-six million," Adalya said. "Yes, that is a crucial number. "After executing a diagnostic refresh, the chrono display now says a parameter setting for our return was off by 66,038,000 years, 3 months, 19 hours, 42 minutes, and 11.87 seconds."

"Then we can recalibrate," Sedora said. "Parameters were off when I tried to reach you in the Jurassic. I thought the error pattern had become consistent and predictable, and I had adjusted accordingly, but it is still erratic."

Adalya shouted down the exit ramp, "We have identified the problem! It will take at least four minutes and 20 seconds for the geo-temporal calculations to run for a new time and destination! Be back here in under four minutes."

"Understood!" Lassen called back.

Lassen and Kailani were directly across from a point bar in a river that snaked along more level ground below the hill they stood on. The point bar was an expanding loop of the river with a beach of gravel and sand that had accumulated from years of erosion. Beyond the gravel and sand, the river's banks were lined with araucarian conifers, pine trees, gingkoes, and fig trees. A lone *Thescolosaurus* darted out of the trees to drink from the river. It was a bipedal herbivore that had a similar build to *Dryosaurus*, was about half as tall as a human, and weighed approximately 200 pounds (91 kilograms). Sap oozed out of nearby tree trunks that were not far from a pair of *Quetzalcoatlus* pterosaur eggs that were buried in sand by their mother. Inside the eggs' soft leathery shells, embryonic young were nearly fully developed. Bizarre-looking six-foot (two-meter) long paddlefish patrolled the river, using their two-foot (half-meter) elongated snouts to detect the electrical activity of their prey. Sturgeon also swam in the river. Lassen glanced down and saw bark beetles and ants crawling on the grass near his feet. Thanks to bright moonlight, he also saw nearby small mammals scurry into their burrows.

"*Triceratops* was one of the last non-avian dinosaurs to exist," Kailani said as she and Lassen gazed at the herbivore.

"Hey," Lassen said as he pointed down at the riverbank. "There's a dead one down there."

A *Triceratops* carcass was sprawled on the riverbank near the water. A feathered theropod quickly scurried out of the trees and began to feed on the dead *Triceratops*.

"A dromaeosaur!" Kailani said as she quickly pointed at the quick feathered figure.

Lassen was struck by the nimble dexterity and deadliness of the 18-foot (six-meter)-long carnivore. As it moved toward the *Triceratops*, it had kept disproportionately large nine-inch (23-centimeter) sickle claws on each foot held above the ground. Then it used them to pierce hard old dinosaur hide while steadying itself to eat. Lassen thought back to an earlier conversation with Kailani about the lethality of dromaeosaurs. As he watched the dromaeosaur, he realized that Jurassic theropods, like *Allosaurus* and *Torvosaurus*, were fairly tame opponents compared to a large dromaeosaur or a group of them. Just seeing the dromaeosaur sent a cold shiver down his spine. The carnivorous theropod was covered in well-developed pennaceous feathers, and it looked elegant and intimidating in them, like an eagle or hawk. The feathers coming off its arms and tail were longer and more ornate than the other feathers, and its snout was featherless.

"That dromaeosaur may be a *Dakotaraptor* or a super-sized *Acheroraptor*," Kailani said. "*Dakotaraptor's* taxonomic validity was in question in my time, but we did have evidence of a large dromaeosaur from the Hell Creek Formation. The Cretaceous Period—this is amazing. It's longer than the Jurassic, spanning almost 80 million years compared to the Jurassic's 56 million years."

Abruptly, an enormous *Tyrannosaurus rex* emerged from the trees near the river and walked toward the water. As it moved, it left clear three-toed tracks in the sand. Lifting its snout, it sniffed. The nearby dromaeosaur stopped eating and quickly turned toward the *Tyrannosaurus*. The two predators made eye contact. The dromaeosaur immediately fled into the trees and lost a feather as it zipped away. The *Tyrannosaurus* lumbered toward the *Triceratops* carcass while a distant *Edmontosaurus* herd honked, and nearby frogs chirped.

"*Tyrannosaurus rex!*" Kailani exclaimed. She knew this was the king of the dinosaurs, a cultural icon, and a paleontological superstar. "Brilliant," Kailani whispered as she stared at the *Tyrannosaurus* with mesmerized awe.

"Looks fat but dangerous," Lassen said.

Kailani thought the *Tyrannosaurus* was especially heavily built but also remembered that a lot of artistic re-creations in her time showed *Tyrannosaurus* as too skinny and did not accurately convey how bulky it actually was.

"Fantastic," Kailani said. "Dinosaurs are still diverse and successful, even though we moved forward about 84 million years beyond the late Jurassic."

"That's a long run," Lassen said.

"Humanity is closer in time to *Tyrannosaurus* than *Tyrannosaurus* is to the late Jurassic," Kailani said.

What looked like a huge meteor suddenly streaked through the horizon to the southeast, leaving a brief trail of orange light. Gantry saw it, and out of pure instinct, he jumped back on the time machine and held on tight. A brief flash of blinding light shot into the sky from the southeastern horizon.

"Whoa!" Lassen said. "What was that?"

"A shooting star," Kailani muttered as she furrowed her brow in deep thought, "but it didn't fade away while it was still in the sky. It's like it stayed intact after it entered the atmosphere. Uh-oh." Kailani turned toward the exit ramp of the time machine and yelled, "What just went through the sky to the southeast?! See if you can get a scan of the Gulf of Mexico!"

"Okay!" Adalya exclaimed. "Why?!"

"Just check!" Kailani shouted back. She instinctively grabbed Lassen by the hand, and they ran up the ramp back into the time machine. Meanwhile, outside, Gantry closed his eyes and bit his lower lip as he hysterically muttered nonsense to himself in an effort to achieve mental comfort. "Bacon Cat knows where it's at," Gantry said with a pitiful sigh. "Ham Dog jumped over a log. Salad Bull got too full . . ."

Soon, Lassen and Kailani joined the other time travelers in the cockpit.

"Scanning the Gulf of Mexico," Sedora said as she intently looked at a holographic display. "An enormous extraterrestrial object just impacted the Earth at the Yucatán Peninsula."

"Impact from outer space?" Durango asked, raising his eyebrows in concern. "*The* impact? The one that does in the dinosaurs?"

"Affirmative," Kailani said.

"Son of a catamount!" Durango proclaimed.

"Then we're at the very bleeding edge of the end of the Cretaceous Period," Lassen added.

"We don't have much time," Kailani said before wincing. "We need to leave NOW!"

Without looking up from her controls, Adalya calmly remarked, "I recall your earlier description of the fiery death that will soon be inflicted on the Earth, and I comprehend the gravity of the situation."

Next to Kailani, Sedora bit her lower lip with anxiety.

"How far away are we from where the asteroid hit?" Kailani asked.

Adalya swiped through holographic displays, and a glowing blue map materialized with a blinking dot.

"We have more adjustments to make," Adalya said. "We are not in Utah or Wyoming. We somehow ended up in what will become North Dakota, so we are approximately 2,000 miles away from the impact site."

"I will adjust for the current location," Sedora said. "If the temporal transporter operates as intended, we will leave soon. The scanners show tremendous land deformation. At the impact site, more than three trillion tons of rock were just shot into space."

"The asteroid destroyed itself upon impact," Kailani said. "Just like evidence in the future will show."

The entire time machine violently shook.

"What was that?" Durango asked.

"Earthquake," Lassen said.

"Yes," Kailani said. "And there will be others."

In the cockpit, Sedora and Adalya frantically flipped switches, input commands, and adjusted levers. Lassen, Kailani, and Durango anxiously stared out the windows. The nearby river water began to behave erratically with sloshing and jiggling.

The dinosaurs near the river noticed the bizarre water behavior and felt seismic shockwaves but tried to continue with life as they knew it. The *Tyrannosaurus* crushed bone as it chewed on a piece of *Triceratops* carcass. Farther down the shore, a *Thescolosaurus* nibbled *Equisetum* and watched a turtle enter the water.

"How soon can we leave?" Kailani asked.

"It should be a matter of seconds," Adalya said. "We need to wait for the calculations to finish."

The sky began to glow with billions of pinpricks of light.

"What are those?" Durango asked. "It gonna rain fire?"

"The tektites," Lassen seriously said under this breath.

"Yes," Kailani solemnly said. "It has begun."

"The energy shield is no longer active," Adalya said. "That will limit our protection."

"And the horses have no protection," Lassen said.

Sedora swiftly pulled back a lever, and the time machine and the horses near it dematerialized in iridescent flourishes of colorful particles while the sky lit up with fiery rain.

Immediately after the time travelers' departure, molten gobs of impact debris glass tektites pelted western North Dakota and much of the planet. The tektites were formed by rock vapor that had jumped into and beyond the atmosphere and was now falling back down through it. Friction superheated the tektites as they hurtled toward Earth. Huge numbers of paddlefish immediately died in place as tektite glass landed on them and shot through their gills. Death was so instantaneous that many of them stayed in their upright swimming positions shortly after they died. Shockwaves undulated through the nearby river as earthquakes shook the land. On the bank of the river, a small mammal scampered into its sideways burrow and got as in as far as it could.

Six minutes after impact, a seiche wave over 33 feet (10 meters) wide undulated westward up the river from the nearby Western Interior Seaway. This was not a tsunami caused by water directly displaced by the space rock's impact in the ocean off the coast of Mexico. Rather, this was a surge of water displaced by the worldwide magnitude 11 earthquake caused by the impact. The seiche wave abruptly buried a variety of fish, plants, dinosaurs, and other species in layers of sediment. Four minutes later, another seiche wave rolled over the river point bar area where the time travelers had just been. Three minutes passed. Another seiche wave arrived. Meanwhile, a hell rain of tektites steamed as they tore through water.

Each seiche wave surge of Western Interior Seaway water helped coat the freshwater river in seawater and sediments and also carried marine life with it. Sharks, ammonites, marine sawfish, sea turtles, and mosasaur marine reptiles were swept along in saltwater and flung down into the river and its vicinity. The extremely rapid surge of marine water and sediment quickly killed animals while burying them, which would later ensure excellent preservation and fossilization. In this part of North Dakota at this time, life was killed in place and instantaneously preserved instead of experiencing the more common fate of decay, scavenging, and weathering.

The asteroid that hit the ocean at Mexico's Yucatán Peninsula was approximately seven miles (11 kilometers) wide and created an 18-mile (29-kilometer) deep crater as it ploughed into land at a speed of approximately 45,000 miles (72,421 kilometers) per hour. The rebound of the Earth from the impact site briefly created a peak higher than Mount Everest. The energy released exceeded the impact of a billion nuclear bombs the size of the atomic bomb dropped on Hiroshima in 1945. An enormous plume of molten impact debris, comprised of asteroid remnants and terrestrial materials, shot into the air from the impact site, soared into outer space, fanned out, and fell back to the Earth.

The falling debris included tektites with high levels of iridium from the asteroid, which had obliterated itself and gouged the planet upon collision. Some of the debris that fell back to the Earth was hotter than the surface of the Sun and started enormous fires. However, not all debris quickly returned to the ground. Some shot out halfway to the Moon before falling to Earth, and some went farther and began to orbit the Sun as well as planets and moons. Impact debris may have even landed on Mars, two of Jupiter's moons, and one of Saturn's moons, possibly planting organic molecules from Earth on those planetary bodies.

Large tsunamis ravaged the Gulf of Mexico, and winds greater than 600 miles (966 kilometers) per hour occurred close to the impact site. Nearby dinosaurs were destroyed by the initial collision blast, whereas those in North Dakota were left undisturbed for a few minutes because they were farther away.

The destruction of rock at the impact site also unleashed vast amounts of toxic gases, including carbon dioxide, carbon monoxide, methane, and sulfur compounds. The particular location of the impact amplified the devastation because of its chemical composition. For example, aerosolized sulfates unleashed by the impact reflected solar energy and helped contribute to global cooling.

As impact debris fell, the superheated tektites heated up the surrounding air to temperatures exceeding 500 degrees Fahrenheit (260 degrees Celsius). Temperature increase was very rapid. Animals and plants caught on fire on a global scale, massive forest fires raged, and life on Earth was catastrophically transformed within only two hours. Animals living underground—like burrowing mammals for instance—had a better chance of survival, but dark times were ahead.

After a huge amount of terrestrial life broiled to death within hours, dust, soot, and chemical compounds from the debris and fires blocked the sun, enveloping the planet in semi-darkness for about 10 years. As a result, the equivalent of a nuclear winter decreased global temperature. Early twenty-first century scientists believed the temperature decreased by at least 77 degrees Fahrenheit (25 degrees Celsius). However, massive volcanism—in a part of India known as the Deccan Traps—released global warming gases into the atmosphere after the asteroid impact and helped prevent global cooling from being even worse. The volcanic activity at the Deccan Traps was so substantial that some scientists had even proposed it as an alternative cause of the end-Cretaceous extinction.

Photosynthesis greatly diminished, most plants died, and wide-scale ecosystem collapse occurred. Any non-avian dinosaurs that survived the initial tektite hell rain, fires, and air broiling died from food shortages within weeks to months.

The oceans were also devastated. Obstruction of sunlight caused the death of most plankton, which are microorganisms that depend on photosynthesis and form the foundation of marine food webs. The depletion of plankton led to the starvation of most marine animals, including fierce marine reptiles, like mosasaurs and plesiosaurs. The spiral-shelled cephalopods known as ammonites—resembling squids with shells—also went extinct.

Approximately 75% of the Earth's species went extinct at the end of the Cretaceous because of the asteroid impact. Upon the arrival of the Chicxulub asteroid, the Mesozoic Era ended, and the Paleogene Period began. From this point forward, dinosaurs would only rule the world as birds that had evolved from theropods. The surviving birds would eventually evolve immense diversity, global distributions, and command of the land, water, and sky. However, non-avian dinosaurs, pterosaurs, and the large marine reptiles of the Mesozoic were gone forever. Amazing beasts that would never again walk the Earth included the awe-inspiring long-necked sauropods, the armored stegosaurs and ankylosaurs—ceratopsians, like *Triceratops*—and ornithopods, like *Camptosaurus* and *Dryosaurus*.

CHAPTER 25: FAREWELL, TIME

In the shortgrass prairie plains west of Medicine Bow, Wyoming, a prairie dog sniffed the air. It wriggled its nose with curiosity and shifted its eyes in confusion before darting into its burrow. Suddenly, a spinning mass of glittering multi-colored particles materialized above the prairie dog's burrow. The swirling light looked like the results of a rainbow going through a blender. The light took the shape of a hovering metallic vehicle and horses.

Inside the time machine, Sedora and Adalya sighed with relief. Lassen took off his hat and ran a hand through his swooping bangs. Kailani let out a deep breath. Durango stretched his hands, which had been balled into white knuckle fists. Outside, Gantry tumbled off the time machine and rolled into a streamside willow thicket. He promptly fell asleep, exhausted.

"Did we make it?" Lassen asked, "Did we get back to 1879?"

"We made it," Sedora said with satisfaction. "It is 10:29 A.M. on Saturday, June 14, 1879. Our coordinates are 41.94692 degrees north, 106.3962 degrees west, which puts us approximately 16 kilometers—or 10 miles—west of Medicine Bow, Wyoming."

Though the time machine had been erratic, Sedora had confidence in its readings because they had always been accurate throughout her recent misadventures through time—at least they were when the readings actually appeared. She might not have always been when or where she wanted to go, but evidence always indicated she was when and where the machine said she was.

"That's only two whoops and a holler away," Durango said.

"What now?" Adalya asked.

"I want to check on the horses," Lassen said. "Then we need to figure out what to do with Traxton."

"I will handle that," Sedora confidently said, nodding.

Lassen, Durango, and Kailani stepped outside the time machine into the pleasantly warm air of early summer in Wyoming. Lassen noticed the horses were fine and vigorously cropping up grass. He took a deep breath as he patted Horizon on the neck.

"Smells like home, boy," Lassen said. "With less carbon dioxide in the air, I feel like I can breathe normally."

"And I smell sagebrush again," Durango said.

Kailani inhaled deeply. "Doesn't seem all that different from 2026. At least not out here on the range."

"Wildlife's less dangerous than the Jurassic," Durango said as he glanced at a distant prairie dog that poked its head out of a burrow.

"Already starting to seem boring," Lassen said. He glanced up as a red-tailed hawk called and flew over. He instantly flashed back to images of bloody-toothed *Allosaurus*, serenely grazing sauropod herds, and silhouettes of pterosaurs flying past the sunset. His mind snapped back to the present as Durango spoke.

"*Boring*?" Durango said with disapproval. "Boring means not almost dying all the time. I could go for some of that these days."

"Yeah, I guess so," Lassen said with reluctance. "And we still have birds to keep things interesting."

"That's right," Durango said. "They're the dinosaurs' great-great-great-great-and-more-greats grand chicks or something."

"I'll never be able to approach my work the same way again," Kailani said. "I now know so much for a fact. The speculation of paleontology seems almost meaningless."

"It's not," Lassen said. "We were only in two time periods of the Mesozoic. There's always more to be found in four billion years' worth of rocks."

"I guess so," Kailani said, "but why bother when I know people will be able to just go back in time and see for themselves."

"Because the world needs the inspiration and knowledge of paleontology," Sedora said as she walked down the time machine's access ramp. "Without the continued pursuit of paleontology and other sciences, future generations will not be able to develop time travel in the first place. Plus, for hundreds of years, nobody will be even close to developing time travel. Paleontology will be relevant for centuries beyond your time and will provide crucial insights into the future as well as the past. For example, in the twenty-second century, a team of paleontologists will be responsible for preventing the extinction of humanity because of their findings about the past—and do not ask for specifics. I already said too much."

"But what about my notes and photos and videos?" Kailani asked. "Should I keep all that a secret from people in my time?"

"That is up to you," Sedora said. She did not mention that she considered wiping Kailani's memory but no longer had the technology to do so. "I did calculations and ran computer models on the outcomes of you sharing your Jurassic experience in the twenty-first century. If you widely share the story of your journey, you are unlikely to be believed by many, and your life will become more difficult. Your photos and videos will also be dismissed as optical trickery done with computer software."

"That might be so," Kailani said. "More and more, people in my time are not believing basic facts, even if they're on video right in front of them."

"Your career could be ruined," Sedora said, "especially because you are not a tenured professor yet."

"What about us?" Durango said. "What happens if we talk about what we saw?"

"Ran the models on that, too," Sedora said. "You would be taken straight to a mental institution."

"Figures," Lassen added. "There's a lot that people in this time aren't ready for. We can keep a secret."

"We are going to leave soon," Adalya called from the entrance of the time machine.

"We'll be right there," Lassen said as he looked up at a red-tailed hawk.

Soon, the time travelers sat at a small metallic table in the time machine. Sedora pressed a cylindrical device against Lassen's bloodied elbows and sprayed treatment mist onto them.

"Thanks," Lassen said, surprised by how quickly it worked. He watched the abrasions on his elbows quickly fade away as new skin healed over them.

"Just part of a standard twenty-eighth century first-aid kit," Sedora said. "It is my intention to return Brent Cordon—nineteenth century alias Tardell Traxton—to the year 2756 where he belongs. He committed sabotage in my time, and we have reason to believe he is a spy working for a hostile government or megacorporation."

"Take him," Lassen said. "If he's in the future, he won't be trying to kill us here. Plus, he should be unconscious for a while if your scanner was accurate."

"But Lassen," Durango said, "what about the bounty? Getting that doesn't just make sense. It makes dollars and lots of *cents*."

"Forget the bounty," Lassen said. "We're assisting with global justice on a massive temporal scale."

Durango let out a frustrated sigh.

"So, that's that, huh?" Lassen said. "You'll drop off Kailani in 2026 and take Traxton back to 2756?"

"That is the plan," Sedora said.

*　　*　　*

Soon, Lassen and Kailani stood on the plains, saying goodbye. A gentle breeze whipped green grass into undulating patterns, and meadowlarks sang. Sedora and Adalya inspected the exterior of the time machine while Durango cinched saddles and tended to the horses.

Lassen and Kailani stood face-to-face, holding hands and staring into each other's eyes. Their dirty hands were dried and calloused from rock climbing and various Jurassic escapades, but that did not bother them. At the moment, all they cared about was each other. The wind glamorously blew strands of Kailani's hair behind her. Lassen smiled softly.

"I don't know if I'll see you again in the future," Kailani said.

"Or the past," Lassen added, "but I'm seeing you right now, and I like that."

Lassen released Kailani's hands, casually tipped up the brim of his hat, and pulled her in for a kiss. Kailani stood up and leaned in tenderly but assertively. Lassen and Kailani kissed long and passionately. Lassen thought of Kailani smiling on horseback in the fern prairies of the Jurassic with *Diplodocus* herds behind her. He thought of her talking at length about dinosaur phylogeny and ecology. And he thought of them holding hands under a double rainbow during a glorious Jurassic dawn.

Durango turned around after adjusting one of Yonder's saddlebags and saw Lassen and Kailani kissing. He started to mutter jealously. "Always Lassen this, Lassen that. Getting the girls and the key to the city and the smarter horse . . ."

Kailani finally pulled back from their kiss. "You're the *best*, sweetheart," Lassen said.

"Ditto," Kailani whispered, smiling.

Kailani then pulled in Lassen close to her face and used the selfie mode on her phone to take a photo of both of them. She briefly reviewed the resulting photo and thought they looked like a cute couple—who had just wandered out of a homeless camp and were ready to beg for money.

Adalya tossed a small object to Kailani and said, "Spray some in your mouth. You do not know what nineteenth century pathogens you may have just ingested."

Kailani caught a small metal canister and read its label out loud, which stated: "Exotic Pathogen Remover – Now with Peppermint." Kailani sprayed misting into her mouth and said, "You really can taste the peppermint." She held the canister out to Lassen and said, "You want to try this?"

"Sure," Lassen said as he grabbed the canister and sprayed it in his mouth. "Zingy."

Lassen tossed the canister back to Adalya. Then he said, "Thanks. You'd make a good bounty hunter, you know."

"No, thanks," Adalya said.

"Too dangerous?" Lassen asked.

"No," Adalya said. "Too boring. Not enough math."

"Suit yourself," Lassen said. Lassen turned back to Kailani and placed his hands on her shoulders. "Safe journeys through time and space, Kailani."

"You too, Lassen," Kailani replied with watery eyes. "I'll never forget you."

"It's okay, sweetheart," Lassen said as he briefly caressed her chin. "It's okay. I'm glad we got to spend any time together at all."

Kailani turned around and headed back to the time machine. Sedora and Adalya were waiting at the bottom of the access ramp. Sedora and Adalya briefly waved at Lassen and Durango and entered the vehicle. Kailani stopped at the entrance to the vehicle and turned toward Lassen. The bounty hunter held up his hand in a somber heartfelt wave. Kailani waved back and tried to form a happy smile, but it turned bittersweet. Then she entered the time machine, and the door closed.

*   *   *

At high noon, Lassen and Durango rode into Medicine Bow. Citizens came out to stare. The bounty hunters looked like they had been through hell. Lassen's vest and shirt were torn and stained with blood and dirt. His hat contained a bullet hole and tiny holes from burning volcanic embers. Lassen and Durango rode Horizon and Yonder while leading Graphite, Ember, and Gantry's horse. They took all the horses to a livery stable and paid the stable keeper to give them various promised treats. While the horses voraciously demolished oats, molasses, and applesauce, Lassen and Durango walked up the street in the middle of town.

They soon stepped out of the general store with shiny new pistols and gunbelts full of bullets. Lassen smoothly rolled the well-oiled cylinder of his pistol against his left shirt sleeve as he stepped off a boardwalk onto the street.

"Nice and smooth," Lassen said.

Durango smiled in agreement. Lassen and Durango fluidly spun their pistols into their holsters.

"Mister Malone!" two eight-year olds called as they ran toward Lassen and Durango. "Mister Malone!"

It was Lilly and Blake. Lassen and Durango remembered talking to them just before leaving Medicine Bow after their fight with the Traxton Gang. The mangy mutt, Yarfer, limped behind Lilly and Blake. It wore a bandage on its leg that had been injured by Traxton's horse during a jailbreak.

"Well, I'll be," Lassen said. "I feel like it's been 150 million years since I've seen you."

"Only about a week," Lilly said. Both children spoke with animated excitement.

"What happened to you?" Blake asked. "Did you find Traxton? Did you round up his gang?"

"Are they locked up in Cheyenne?" Lilly added.

"They were dealt with," Lassen said.

"Shoot 'em up?!" Blake asked.

"Yeah!" Lilly said. "How many did you get?"

"Hey now," Lassen said. "It wasn't like that. It's a long story."

"What's it about?" Blake asked.

"It's about time," Durango said. "And it's also about time we go to the restaurant to chaw some modern nineteenth century grub."

Lassen saw Athena Pryce step out of the general store with an encyclopedia in her hands. He recalled their brief conversation just prior to the Medicine Bow gunfight. Her brilliant golden hair sparkled in the sun. She smiled and timidly waved at him from across the street. Lassen formed a subtle closed-mouth smile and waved back.

Toby the tabby cat bolted out from under a nearby boardwalk and ran toward Lassen. The large gray striped cat ran quickly, and his legs pounded up and down like little ore-processing stamp mills. Toby immediately rubbed against Lassen's legs while the bounty hunter stood at the edge of the street.

"Toby likes you," Lilly said.

"Hi, little feller," Durango said as he bent down to pet the cat. In response, Toby hissed.

"He don't like you," Blake said.

Suddenly, gunshots sounded, and a group of horses galloped into town. Cowboys fired pistols into the air.

"Old Rancher Nelson must have given his boys the day off!" Blake shouted.

"Now they're filled with the devil's brew and bein' bad!" Lilly added.

"You kids get inside," Lassen said. "Durango and I have got this."

As gun-toting cowboys galloped into town, Toby continued rubbing against Lassen's legs, oblivious to the danger. Lassen cleared his throat and looked down at the cat.

"Get out of here, little buddy," Lassen said.

Toby trilled in response and looked up with big green cat eyes. Lassen pulled a piece of jerky from a vest pocket and tossed it under a nearby boardwalk.

"Go on, get," Lassen said.

Toby dashed after the jerky and launched under the boardwalk to pounce on it.

Durango confidently smirked and nodded. Both bounty hunters drew their guns and stepped into the middle of the street to confront a mob of intoxicated cowboys. Townsfolk ran inside and closed their shutters. Athena looked at Lassen with concern. Lassen slyly winked at her. Vultures circled overhead. Ravens cawed. Sunbeams shot through clouds of dust. Horses whinnied with anxiety. Dramatic thunderheads built on the western horizon.

"Nice to have things back to normal," Durango said.

Lassen nodded, smiling as he cocked back the hammer of his gun. "Normal as it gets for us."

EPILOGUE

At dusk, Gantry stumbled into Medicine Bow. He was delirious and mumbling to himself. As he shuffled into town, people began to stare. A crowd gathered as he approached the boardwalk of the hotel.

"Sauruses, sauruses, where do you roam?" Gantry sang. "Lizard beasties in a far off land wanting to be in the circus with me as their taming hand. Teeth and claws. That's what I saws. Old Avarette gambled and lost when he was chawed off his hoss. Stampede. Stampede. A stampede almost got meed, but I tumbled away. I seed. I seed the sauruses indeed."

Sheriff Gratton and Deputy Caddock walked through the crowd surrounding the spectacle Gantry was creating.

"What's this?" Gratton asked.

"Looks like Jed Gantry," Caddock said. "He's been through some kind of hell, I reckon. Wonder if he tangled with Malone and Mesquite."

The front of Gantry's shirt was torn and bloody. His clothes and body were covered in dust. Little bits of dried ferns and grass were stuck to his shirt, and an entire sleeve was missing. He had a short beard, and the knees of both his pant legs were shredded.

"Malone!" Gantry shouted. "Malone! He was there! He was there! I saw him. He rode through the stampede. He braved the beasts. Volcano! Lava. Eruption! I saw it all! I was there. I saw it, and I'll tell it square. Sauruses. Beware the sauruses! Thems! Thems!"

Gantry dipped his head in a watering trough and drank deeply.

"A *thesaurus*?" Gratton said, furrowing his brow.

"Dinosaurs?" Caddock asked.

"They *were* dinosaurs," Gantry said as he abruptly lifted his head from the watering trough. "Dinosaaarrrrs. Eaters of flesh. Killers of men. They're real. They are real. So real—and I saw them. I was in a place—a different time place. The time was not our time, you see, it was—what did Traxton say it was? The Jurassic. I was in the Jurassic, and I've lived to tell the tale. And what a tale it is. Two-legged lizards with feathers. Elephant lizards with snake heads. Flying pointy-tailed lizard bats."

"He's gone mad," Gratton said, "or he's drunk."

"I don't smell any alcohol," Caddock said, "but I reckon I smell other things." Caddock turned toward Gantry. "That's an interesting story. Curious, though. Earlier today, Lassen Malone and Durango Mesquite said you were taken care of during a battle with Traxton."

"Where are those blood money hunters?" Gantry asked. "They were there. They saw, and they'd believe. They saw. They know. I'm not crazy. They're not, and they know! The dinosaurs! We all saw dinosaurs!"

"Sure you did, Jed," Gratton said. "Sure you did, but you're still wanted, and Caddock and I are taking you in. After handling Nelson's cowboys today, Lassen and Durango went after a bounty in Arizona."

As Gantry deliriously mumbled and sang, Caddock patted him down and handcuffed him. Gratton and Caddock then led Gantry to the jail.

"Excuse me," said a slender man with an authoritative, deep confident voice. As Gratton and Caddock approached the jail with Gantry, the man came into view, stepping under a gas street light.

"I couldn't help but overhear this man's tale," the mysterious stranger said as he scribbled on a notepad with a quill pen. The speaker was about five and a half feet tall and looked to be in his early thirties with a bit of facial stubble. Gratton doubted he weighed more than about 135 pounds (61 kilograms). The stranger dressed in khaki pants, leather work boots, and a well-worn olive green corduroy jacket over a light blue button-up shirt. He also wore a brown felt hat and a leather satchel. He faintly reminded Gratton of Lassen, but the stranger was not as strong, tall, or good-looking as the bounty hunter.

"Who are you?" Gratton asked.

"Trenton Howarth is the name," the man said as he raised a hand in greeting and smiled, a twinkle in his hazel-brown eyes. "I'm a drafter of narratives. A craftsmen with a pen. A teller of true-life adventures."

Gratton grunted. "So, you're a writer. Good for you."

"Howarth?!" Caddock said with recognition. "*The* Trenton Howarth who writes the Lassen Malone dime novels?"

"You bet, son," Howarth said as he put his thumbs on his belt. Howarth wore a simple leather belt and was not armed. "I could sign some books for you if you'd like. You look like a fan."

"Well, gosh—" Caddock started to say.

"If you'll excuse us, Mister Howarth," Gratton said. "Deputy Caddock and I are busy."

"I can take care of Mister Gantry for you if you'd like," Howarth said.

"He's due in the Crowbar Hotel," Gratton said. "Escaped about two weeks ago. Bounty on his head is even higher than it used to be, and his bail is high. Very high."

"I'll take care of it," Howarth said as he pulled a billfold out of an inner pocket of his green corduroy jacket and flashed a wad of cash. "Just tell me when Albany County wants Mister Gantry back for his trial. Marshal Logan Kedrick in Rawlins can vouch for me. I've bailed out his men before, and they *always* go back."

Two hours later—and after Gratton had gotten a telegram from Kedrick—Howarth and Gantry walked through the doors of the hotel restaurant. Gantry had bathed, was clean-shaven, and wore a new suit. Howarth smirked confidently as people stared at them.

As the two men waited for their food, Howarth opened his satchel to remove a notepad and pen. Gantry talked endlessly, and Howarth quickly scribbled notes.

Gantry and Howarth soon feasted their eyes on plates of sizzling steak fajitas. Howarth winked at Sarita Socorro when she brought them their food. She ignored him but glanced down at his notes.

"Egyptian hieroglyphics?" Sarita asked while raising her eyebrows sarcastically.

"No, ma'am," Howarth said. "Just plain old English cursive. I'm a writer."

"I can see that," Sarita said before walking away.

Gantry ate voraciously and talked through bites. Within minutes, he had entirely consumed his food, and he shamelessly licked his plate with a slurp.

"You gonna eat that, Trenton?" Gantry asked as Howarth wrote furiously on a notepad behind his untouched plate of food.

"No, Jed," Howarth said. "Chaw away, pal—and you might as well eat those black beans and rice they gave me off to the side. Right now, feeding my mind matters more."

"Much obliged, Trenton," Gantry said.

"No problem, Jed," Howarth said. "Take your time. I want to check something."

Howarth pulled a publication from his satchel. It was an 1877 issue of the *American Journal of Science*. He flipped through it and marked a page with his finger.

"Jed," Howarth said, "I think those fighting dinosaurs that almost trampled you were *Stegosaurus*."

"Gee," Gantry said. "What a name for a critter. Stegged. So, first thing I did after I got back to my horse was face them down and start cracking my 12-foot bullwhip at them. Tamed them right down."

"This is dinomite material," Howarth said. "Keep going."
"You sure you don't have enough already?" Gantry asked.
"Jed," Howarth said, "I'm just getting started."

FURTHER READING

The following books provide more information on some of the scientific topics in this novel. Many more books, articles, and other information sources exist—and the field of dinosaur paleontology changes rapidly.

Morrison Dinosaurs

Barrett, Paul M. 2017. *Stegosaurus: An Extraordinary Specimen and the Secrets it Reveals*. London: Natural History Museum, London.

DeCourten, Frank. 2013. *Dinosaurs of Utah, 2nd Edition*. Salt Lake City, UT: The University of Utah Press.

Foster, John. 2020. *Jurassic West: The Dinosaurs of the Morrison Formation and Their World, 2nd Edition*. Bloomington, IN: Indiana University Press.

Dinosaurs in General

Benton, Michael J. 2019. *Dinosaurs Rediscovered: The Scientific Revolution in Paleontology*. London: Thames and Hudson.

Brusatte, Steve. 2018. *The Rise and Fall of the Dinosaurs: A New History of a Lost World*. New York, NY: William Morrow - An Imprint of HarperCollins Publishers.

Holtz Jr., Thomas R. 2007. *Dinosaurs: The Most Complete, Up-to-Date Encyclopedia for Dinosaur Lovers of All Ages*. New York, NY: Random House, Inc.

Naish, Darren, and Paul Barrett. 2016. *Dinosaurs: How They Lived and Evolved*. London: Natural History Museum, London.

Sauropods

Hallett, Mark, and Mathew J. Wedel. 2016. *The Sauropod Dinosaurs: Life in the Age of Giants*. Baltimore, MD: Johns Hopkins University Press.

Hell Creek Dinosaurs
Hone, David. 2016. *The Tyrannosaur Chronicles: The Biology of the Tyrant Dinosaurs*. London: Bloomsbury Sigma.

Parker, Tom, Chris Masna, and RJ Palmer. *Saurian: A Field Guide to Hell Creek*. 2019. London: Titan Books.

Witton, Mark P. *King Tyrant: The Natural History of Tyrannosaurus rex*. 2025. Princeton, NJ: Princeton University Press.

Pterosaurs
Witton, Mark P. 2013. *Pterosaurs: Natural History, Evolution, Anatomy*. Princeton, NJ: Princeton University Press.

Extinctions
Black, Riley. 2022. *The Last Days of the Dinosaurs: An Asteroid, Extinction, and the Beginning of Our World*. New York, NY: St. Martin's Press.

Brannen, Peter. 2017. *The Ends of the World: Volcanic Apocalypses, Lethal Oceans, and Our Quest to Understand Earth's Past Mass Extinctions*. New York, NY: Ecco - An Imprint of HarperCollins Publishers.

MacPhee, Ross D. 2018. *End of the Megafauna: The Fate of the World's Hugest, Fiercest, and Strangest Animals*. New York, NY: W.W. Norton and Company.

Cope and Marsh
Jaffe, Mark. 2000. *The Gilded Dinosaur: The Fossil War Between E.D. Cope and O.C. Marsh and the Rise of American Science*. New York, NY: Crown Publishers.

Futurism
Kaku, Michio. 2008. *Physics of the Impossible: A Scientific Exploration into the World of Phasers, Force Fields, Teleportation, and Time Travel*. New York, NY: Anchor Books.

MORRISON DINOSAUR MUSEUMS AND FOSSIL SITES

The following museums prominently feature Morrison Formation dinosaurs and ecology, but the list is not comprehensive. Morrison specimens appear in many museums. Northern Utah has the most exhibits relatively close to each other and near places where this novel's dinosaurs actually lived. For more information on dinosaur museums and to find one near you, visit the link below for a search tool and worldwide map assembled by the *I Know Dino* podcast team: https://iknowdino.com/dinosaur-museums

California
Los Angeles County Natural History Museum
900 Exposition Blvd., Los Angeles, CA, 90007
(213) 763-3466

Raymond M. Alf Museum of Paleontology
1175 Base Line Rd, Claremont, CA 91711
(909) 624-2798

Colorado
Denver Museum of Nature and Science
2001 Colorado Boulevard, Denver, CO 80205
(303) 370-6000

Dinosaur Journey Museum
550 Jurassic Court, Fruita, CO 81521
(970) 242-0971

Morrison Natural History Museum
501 Colorado 8, Morrison, CO 80465
(303) 697-1873

Connecticut
Yale Peabody Museum
170 Whitney Avenue, New Haven, CT 06511
(203) 432-8987

Illinois
Field Museum
1400 S Lake Shore Dr, Chicago, IL 60605
(312) 922-9410

Indiana
The Children's Museum of Indianapolis
3000 North Meridian Street Indianapolis, IN, 46208
(317) 334-4000

Montana
Museum of the Rockies
600 W Kagy Blvd, Bozeman, MT 59717
(406) 994-2251

New York
American Museum of Natural History
200 Central Park West, New York, NY 10024
(212) 769-5100

Ohio
Cleveland Museum of Natural History
1 Wade Oval Dr, Cleveland, OH 44106
(216) 231-4600

Pennsylvania
Carnegie Museum of Natural History
4400 Forbes Avenue, Pittsburgh, PA 15213
(412) 622-3131

Utah
Brigham Young University Museum of Paleontology
1683 North Canyon Road, Provo, UT 84602-3300
(801) 422-3680

Museum of Ancient Life at Thanksgiving Point
2929 North Thanksgiving Way, Lehi, UT 84043
(801) 768-2300

Natural History Museum of Utah
301 Wakara Way, Salt Lake City, UT 84108
(801) 581-6927

Ogden's George S. Eccles Dinosaur Park
1544 East Park Boulevard, Ogden, UT
(801) 393-3466

Utah Field House of Natural History State Park Museum
496 East Main Street, Vernal, UT 84078
(435) 789-3799

Utah State University Eastern Prehistoric Museum
155 East Main Street, Price, Utah 84501
(435) 613-5060

Washington, DC
Smithsonian National Museum of Natural History
10th Street & Constitution Avenue NW, Washington, DC 20560
(202) 633-1000

Wyoming
University of Wyoming Geological Museum
1000 East University Avenue, Laramie, WY 82071
(307) 766-2646

Western Wyoming Community College Natural History Museum
2500 College Drive, Rock Springs, WY 82901
(307) 382-1600

Wyoming Dinosaur Center
110 Carter Ranch Road, Thermopolis, WY 82443
(307) 864-2997

Visit the real Jurassic frontier! The following fossil sites provide opportunities to see Morrison Formation dinosaur fossil bones or tracks in situ, which means you can see them in the natural environment in which they originally fossilized during the late Jurassic. For most sites, latitude/longitude decimal degree coordinates are provided, and these can be input into navigation apps (e.g., Google Maps, Apple Maps, etc.). In some cases, listed location information is for parking areas or trailheads. Research specifics ahead of any visit.

Utah
Copper Ridge Dinosaur Tracks Interpretive Site
Coordinates: 38.830078, -109.763794
(435) 259-2100

Dinosaur National Monument
Quarry Coordinates: 40.438063, -109.307131
(435) 781-7700

Jurassic National Monument
Coordinates: 39.32062, -110.68866
(435) 636-3600

Mill Canyon Dinosaur Trails
Bone Trail Coordinates: 38.712524, -109.73938
Track Site Trail Coordinates: 38.720714, -109.734003
(435) 259-2100

Utah also has many publicly accessible dinosaur track sites from time periods preceding the Morrison Jurassic. For more information on additional sites, visit: https://geology.utah.gov/apps/fossil_guide

Colorado
Dinosaur Ridge Visitor Center and Trail
16831 West Alameda Parkway, Morrison, CO 80465
(303) 697-3466

Purgatoire River/Picketwire Canyonlands Track Site
Coordinates: 37.61682, -103.59808
(877) 444-6777

ABOUT THE AUTHOR

Tristan Howard is a research data specialist with a Master of Science in Geography. He has also worked as a university teaching assistant and environmental planner. Howard grew up on a remote ranch that bordered a shield volcano and wilderness study area. In his teens, he made a wildlife documentary that aired on PBS and was awarded an Honorable Mention for Animal Behavior from the International Wildlife Film Festival. In his free time, Howard enjoys studying paleontology, exploring the wildlands of the American West, viewing wildlife, and making natural history documentaries.

For more information on his projects, visit:
https://www.tristanhowardproductions.altervista.org

www.ingramcontent.com/pod-product-compliance
Lightning Source LLC
Chambersburg PA
CBHW031422240626
47154CB00001B/166